The Microscope was a field one, but of good quality, though using ambient light was enough to make her eyes ache. But she could resolve cellular morphology. For all the good that did her . . . She tilted the slide and looked at the smear of read thereon. In the slides she had taken from the autopsy from the day before, she could see very little that was abnormal. She could talk of toxic insults, hypothesise that the insult seemed to compromise the cerebral vasculature, allowing fluid to be pressed from the blood vessels into the tissues. She could wish for a thin section setup; a high resolution microscope; she could, she thought, with a very thin smile, offer up her very soul in exchange for an electron microscope which might, might, let her resolve an infectious agent, a virus or mycoplasma, or visualise the insult to the membranes.

Absurd, she thought, with her élite training, her élite experience, to leap into space only to be landed back in the middle ages.

Also by Alison Sinclair
in Victor Gollancz/Millennium

BLUEHEART
LEGACIES

CAVALCADE

ALISON SINCLAIR

The right of Alison Sinclair to be identified as the author
of this work has been asserted by her in accordance with
the Copyright, Designs and Patents Act 1988.

This edition published in Great Britain in 1999 by
Millennium
An imprint of Victor Gollancz
Orion House, 5 Upper St Martin's Lane,
London WC2H 9EA

Second Impression 2000

To receive information on the Millennium list, e-mail us at:
smy@orionbooks.co.uk

A CIP catalogue record for this book
is available from the British Library

ISBN 1 85798 564 8

Printed in Great Britain by
Clays Ltd, St Ives plc

ONE

SEED

1 Stan Morgan

Someone said, 'I don't effin' believe it.'

And so, came Morgan's first returning thought, their endeavour was blessed. He drew breath, and the smell of it told him that he was no longer where he had drawn the breath before. There was a strange scent to the air, an aroma almost like spices. The light too had changed, now the light of a tranquil early morning, not the light of spotlights carving open a rainy night.

He had been standing on the spotlit sand, looking out over a black and starless sea. It had been raining on Chesapeake Bay for most of the day and night before they left, raining on people, spotlights and the cameras, mounted and unmanned, which were to record what was to happen for the people who were staying behind. Now he was here.

'Holy God,' said the disbeliever, awed. 'They took us *all*.'

All: he heard a murmur dense with pitches, all languages blended together. The voices rose like voices in a cathedral, hushed and folded in on themselves. His gaze followed the voices upwards and he saw that the nearest wall arched overhead as though in a cathedral, but higher than even the most aspiring of cathedrals. The farthest wall was well over a kilometre away, probably two. The cave – or vault – or chamber – was crudely circular, although the walls bulged and receded in places, shaping shallow headlands and bays. He could not tell whether the walls were stone or metal or some other material, but they were near-white and honeycombed with openings like caves for most of their great height. Light shone from the walls, not dazzling, but giving the sense of a fullness. He looked down, and down, and suddenly saw faces, and more faces, all hues, all ages, both sexes, shadowless in the pervasive illumination. *All*. The aliens had taken them *all*, everyone, it seemed, everyone who had offered themselves in answer to the sparely worded invitation and the simple instructions contained therein. Of every race and colour and walk of life, in every state of preparedness or unpreparedness, bewildered or grinning or wondering. *All*. Simply lifted up and transported . . . here.

'Christ and all his apostles,' he breathed. Nearby, a flaxen-haired woman smiled dazedly at the tone if not the words. She had a very fair, almost porcelain complexion, and pale eyes of either blue or grey. Her parka and black jeans and boots and backpack were all very new. The pet-carrier at her feet was old, marked, the mesh dented, the body covered with the fossil impressions of airline stickers. Something white shifted in it, grumbled, mewed. Near her stood a gaunt, erect and very old woman who leaned on a white cane, and turned an unseeing, alert gaze from side to side. The cane wavered slightly with the palsy in her hands; the fourth and fifth finger of her left hand were gone, with only an ancient, drawn scar at their root. Her coat was a brilliant blue wool. Over her shoulder she carried a battered satchel, and at her feet a tattered carpet bag. Beyond her Morgan saw a plump young man in gold Starfleet costume, complete with badge, which he stood fingering as though expecting an answer; a bearded weekend woodsman in camouflage fatigues and backpack, with rifle; a girl, early teens beneath the makeup, pinning a smaller boy and girl against her, gazing around with stunned, black-daisy eyes. *All.* All the rag tag venturesome vagabonds of the human race. All the crazy people like himself, willing to junk a perfectly good life on Earth for the absolute unknown. He at least had something of an excuse; space was, after all, his profession. In the back of his throat he felt laughter; he did not know what at. He swept his eyes up and over the height of the chamber again, let them return to the stunned and stirring multitude around him. *All.*

'Prof,' the voice from behind said, 'you with us, or Starfleet?'

He turned, to meet the marble-blue, quietly amused eyes of A-team Sergeant A.J. Lowell. Around A.J. and the team's captain, St John Emrys, the other ten men deployed with a casual precision and readiness ill-masked by their civilian dress, edgy and determinedly unawed.

Morgan's employer, NASA, had selected its twelve-strong official deputation from those volunteers with prior spaceflight experience. Insufficient time to prepare others had been their rationale. Ground crew and scientists would fulfil their traditional role, giving support from Earth. More than a few, however, planned an individual acceptance to the aliens' invitation, Morgan among them. He had been in the final stages of wrapping up his affairs when a request from the US army arrived for the services of scientists with expertise in off world habitats and space colonies. So Dr Stan Morgan, aged twenty-six, author of a solid thesis on life support systems for extended voyages, and sundry articles – including a review of all available literature on extraterrestrial life conceived during a drunken graduation party and not intended nearly as seriously as it was received – found himself attached to special forces ODA 202, the thirteenth man of twelve.

At times he wondered how exactly that had happened, particularly when he had the distinct sense that his mission and theirs were not the same. His was an exploration; theirs was a reconnaissance. He was going on a one way journey while, though they had never made it explicit in front of him, they presumed on a triumphant return. But, as he had explained to one of his more outspoken friends, while he did not have the power to dictate to the US Army, the aliens surely did, and Morgan was certain that when the need arose they would. He had grown up in a violent inner city neighbourhood, fitted for victimhood by his mixed breeding and slight build, and rescued by his quirky, lucent intelligence. He knew the ways in which power neutralised power.

He took his first step and looked down, newly aware of softness underfoot. He glanced ahead at the waiting group, then squatted to run a hand over the coarse matting, coloured living green. He was a scientist, he thought with some defiance; this was what he was here to do. The matting had the feel of something not quite living, a little too dry, a little too resilient. Taking his penknife from his pocket, he opened a blade and worked the tip into the weave, feeling its resistance. It tore as he levered it, but not easily. He thought to liken it to a moss or a lichen, though it was likely to be neither. He worked the knife deeper, separating strands. A hand rapped his shoulder and a pair of latex gloves flicked into his vision. He nodded thanks to the team's junior medic, Greg Drover, and delicately cut a square inch from the edge of the mat, and stood up, balancing it on the palm of a gloved hand. The spice smell rose up from the square of green; Morgan caught it. Drover jerked back. 'That better be friendly,' he remarked. 'We probably just inoculated ourselves.' He passed Morgan a specimen bag. 'Captain's waiting,' he added.

He could have been among friends now, Morgan thought, a little wistfully, among friends and fellow NASA mission rejects, people as capable as these, but far more imaginative. People who would stand looking around in wonder for as long as they needed to look. People with whom he could talk, speculate, brainstorm, fantasise, for whom error and absurdity was part of process, part of discovery. People with whom he had already found his place, completed that primitive primate ritual of establishing his status within the tribe. That had hardly begun here, except for the odd verbal cuff; he was still largely outside their notice. He could have been among people whose unspoken language, whose tribal habits, he understood. But he had traded all that for a legitimacy which seemed already tenuous in this huge, motley crowd.

He went with Drover, and received the team's indifferent glances and the captain's cool nod. A.J. looked amused. 'You'd better hope that's not one of our hosts you just served yourself a slice of.'

'Ah shit,' Aquile Raho chipped in. 'A.J.'s been reading that sci fi again.'

Morgan looked at the square of green matter in the zip locked bag. It had never occurred to him. He said, with all the grace he could muster, 'It looks like I should have been reading it too.'

'For the record,' the captain said, 'since my watch has stopped, what time do you make it?'

Morgan's showed 12.00.34, the fluid flow of digits unchanged. He raised his hand, felt his shoulders, which, soaked by the rain of a few minutes ago, were now barely damp. Around him, everyone else had taken on the stillness of a prolonged glance.

'. . . ing stores issue . . .' someone muttered. A.J. gave him a withering glance. 'Minor glitch. Let it go.' Morgan looked at him in mild disbelief and drew breath to ask him if *he* had any idea how they had got here.

'Excuse me,' said a woman's clear voice. Those few who had been unaware of her approach turned as one. The flaxen-haired woman with the pet-carrier stood just outside their group, her wrist cocked to display an overlarge, old fashioned watch, with a mother-of-pearl face and heavy black hands. A starburst crack marred the glass. The time on the watch was two seventeen. 'I don't remember anything of the last two and a quarter hours,' she said. 'Do any of you?'

Morgan felt around him the realignment of attention outwards, without in the least disturbing the tight cohesion of the group. The captain said, 'No, ma'am, I don't.'

'Sophie Hemmingway,' she corrected him/introduced herself, and put out a hand, which he took, shook and released. 'Research neuropathologist, Harvard. We've lost over two hours, I suspect. Or, for all I know, fourteen, twenty-six, or more. I can't remember anything between standing beside Boston Harbour and arriving here.' She looked from one to the other, her expression quizzical.

'I don't remember anything myself, but it was probably only two,' said Morgan, and flicked his fingertips over his shoulder. 'It was pitching rain last night down in Chesapeake, and I'm still damp.' He leaned around A.J. to extend a hand. 'Stan Morgan, NASA.'

'Ah, you're NASA,' she said, with a sudden warm smile, and set down her pet-carrier. The white shape within complained in the skin-prickling tones of a Siamese cat. The nearest man, Greg Drover, crouched for an ostensibly casual look into the depths of the carrier. But he paused to offer a finger to the mesh and the whiskered black nose pressed against it. 'Not what you were expecting,' she remarked.

Nobody, Morgan noted, moved to disavow her of the notion that they were all NASA.

'Not what any of us were expecting,' he said.

'I wonder,' Sophie Hemmingway said, 'if we were unconscious during those two hours, or our memories have simply been suppressed. I wonder why our hosts thought it necessary.'

'They haven't been real forthcoming,' Morgan said drily, and she smiled. Her teeth had that flawless individuality which comes from good, early dental care. Her skin was thin and her smile caught it up in fine creases, but was unblemished aside for the beginning of crows feet at the corners of her eyes. She wore just a trace of make-up, silver-blue shadow above her grey-blue eyes. A cluster of tiny silver leaves hung from a stud in each ear, and on her right hand was a silver signet ring with the initials SJH. There was an air of confidence and privilege about her, an air which Morgan, raised in poverty, and aware of its marks on his teeth, his face, his bearing, had had to learn not to resent. She was in her thirties, maybe six, eight years older than himself. She said, 'True; they haven't indicated much willingness to interact with humanity – one message, and the rest was silence. I wonder what all the cameras they had on us showed.' She lifted her head and looked around, turning a patrician profile. 'Although leaving us entirely to our own devices does seem to be carrying things a little far. But then, I was raised with certain expectations of hospitality,' she said, mildly self-mocking. Looked back at him. 'You say you were waiting at Chesapeake Bay. I wonder –'

From the near distance, a woman screamed.

Sophie started, her head turning. The team tensed, shifting so as to put distance from each other. The screaming broke into sobbing. The nearby crowd swirled, its currents moving towards the sound, fascinated or well intentioned – away, cautious and repelled – or around, caught between conflicting desires. A ripple of sound resolved into an urgent demand for a doctor.

Sophie said, 'I'd better go; I don't know if there's anyone better qualified nearby. Can you mind Melisande for a few minutes?' she gestured down to the cat-carrier.

The team's senior medic exchanged a glance with A.J., then looked to the captain for his nod. Emrys said, 'Take Raho and Travis with you.' The two named detached themselves and followed the blonde woman and Raphael Tejada as they made their way into the gathering crowd.

7

2 Stephen Cooper

Since Fleur's watch was not working, Stephen hunkered down beside her and counted off for Fleur and the red-haired woman who had come out of the crowd to try and raise the dead. As he gave them sixty seconds and sixty seconds again, he was disturbed by the thought of how weirdly sexy it was to watch a pretty woman humping over a man, her feathery red hair straggling into her eyes and her face damp with effort. A sight the old guy underneath her could never appreciate, sprawled on his back with his shirt torn away from his chest, showing its blue scar and flat round lump of pacemaker like an extra tit. Stephen sensed death as surely as he smelled it in the undergrowth of the mountains which were his only home. From behind him, sobs sawed up and down his spine.

'Shut up,' he muttered. Fleur lifted her lips from the old guy's and sent a sideways glance at him out of dark eyes. Understanding what a woman's sobbing did to him. Understanding that he did not know or remember why, only that his whole body urged flight or demanded silence.

Out of the crowd of gawpers emerged four people, a frosty-eyed blonde in stiffly new and very expensive hiking gear, and three men with bulky backpacks that they carried like air. Two hispanics and one white. Though they wore ordinary coats, buttoned, Stephen smelled the metallic scent of force around them: army or law enforcement, or even organised crime. He fought the urge to recoil, to run. Fleur, he knew, would not leave, not until she had fought her fight through to the end.

The blonde said, 'Sophie Hemmingway. I'm a physician.'

The redhead, still pumping, said, 'Arrested immediately after we arrived. He had a two-lead pacemaker implanted three years ago – second degree AV and bundle branch block post MI. CPR initiated within a minute, now estimate four minutes in.'

Fleur said, between breaths, 'Adrienne LaFleurette. Seattle. Parame-dic.'

One of the hispanics knelt, shrugging his kit from his back, 'I've got cardioversion/defibrillation equipment.' Fleur, sensing what Stephen sensed, sent him a sideways look of challenge. 'Raphe Tejada,' he said, by way of answer, establishing his credentials by laying out a compact and very up-to-date piece of hardware. Stephen knew a fence who would have paid extremely well for it, had he ever dared betray Fleur by using what he had learned through her about the value of certain equipment. He watched Tejada warily, now almost certain that he was army – public servants were seldom so well equipped and commercial employees so forthcoming. Tejada slapped leads on the man's bared chest, flicked switches. Lights remained dark, the screen blank. Fleur and the redhead kept puffing and pumping; Tejada cracked a panel, dropped out a battery, popped in a new one. Fleur said to the redhead, 'Pulse check.' The redhead stopped pumping. Fleur's long fingers rested on the man's throat. 'No pulse. Stephen, elapsed time.'

'Five minutes thirty seconds,' he said. Tejada and the others looked at him. Fleur ignored them; he simply looked back, and let them take it as they would. Even before he discovered the woods he had had a freakishly accurate inner clock. Fleur teased him about sensing the angle of the sun or the turning of the Earth; in a playful mood, she would make up the most fanciful explanations, based on her latest reading. Fleur never stopped reading, never stopped learning. She was the only teacher he could tolerate, his foster sister, his friend.

Tejada flicked switches again. Still dark lights, blank screen. His face showed nothing. He said, 'Cardioversion not available.' He snapped open a hard shelled case, showing an array of vials and cartridges like an addict's hope of heaven, shelled a cartridge of its wrappings and snapped it into a syringe. 'Epinephrine,' he said, flatly.

Fleur nodded. Tejada gave the injection.

'You mean,' the woman behind Stephen suddenly blurted, 'you've got all this fancy equipment but none of it *works*.' Stephen turned to give her his best lizard eye, the one that tended to shut up harmless, loud-mouthed respectable people. She was young, trussed in a pink blouse and a skirt two sizes too small, with strain lines in the fabric around breasts and butt. A daughter, maybe. If a trophy wife, she was a sorry case. And anyway, the guy stretched on the matting didn't look like the type. A plain dresser with a simple face, the kind to marry one woman and stay with her for ever, because that was what he had promised to do. The kind of man Stephen did not understand and wanted to despise. Dead now. Even if, in spite of himself, he had not learned from Fleur something of what was possible, he'd know from the tension in Fleur's face, half hidden by curling strands of hair, as she bent, breathing into the dead lungs.

A woman's half whisper said, 'Let him go.'

She came out of the crowd, who, pressing forward, had closed in around her. She was a small woman, her tastefully coloured hair brassy above her grey face, conservatively dressed, overlooked and upstaged. She dropped to her knees beside his head, and pushed Fleur away, holding her away from *her* man's mouth with a gesture which was half protective, half possessive. Fleur kept her fingers beneath his jaw, pushing up, holding open the airway as she had tried to teach Stephen to do. The woman looked down at her hands, a distant storm in her eyes. But she satisfied herself with wiping the traces of Fleur's vermillion lipstick off his mouth, ignoring them all.

Tejada said, 'Are you his wife?'

It took a long moment for her to turn her head, her eyes faintly irritated, as at some presumption. 'I am. Thank you,' she said, dismissively. 'Thank all of you. But keep what you have for people you can help. I've seen this before.' She looked down at his face again, and this time slapped aside Fleur's hands and cradled his head against the last few jolts of the redhead's CPR. Unhappy, the redhead stopped, but left her hands in place.

'*Victoria!* You've got no right,' the young woman said. To Tejada, 'She's just his *second* wife. *I'm* his daughter.' The small woman stared straight ahead, ignoring her utterly.

'I'm sorry, Miss –' she offered him no name, 'we suspect that something aboard this ship may be interfering with electrical or battery powered equipment, including his pacemaker and my resuscitation equipment. Without that, there's very little we can do.'

The daughter screeched, 'Daddy!' and fell upon the body, pulling at it, crying and kicking and hitting out. Stephen was gripped by a sudden, urgent need to get away from the noise, the emotion which charged the atmosphere as if with ozone. He twisted from his crouch and bolted into the crowd, shouldering brutally through it. Outside the crowd, he dropped to his haunches again, breathing hard.

Fleur came after him a while later, looking tired beyond measure, lipstick smeared and wiry black hair disarrayed. They sat side by side looking across the cavern at the dusty green-cloaked floor and the white, shining walls, and at all the people. Presently she took out her comb and make-up case, and began to set right her appearance, combing her hair, wiping off and smoothing on lipstick with a practised hand. He had an impulse to scratch at that polished armour. 'If I don't get away, I'll –'

'Don't,' she said, a little harshly, and after a moment, more quietly. 'It will be all right.'

'I can't breathe here.'

'You couldn't have breathed in jail either,' she said flatly.

10

For a moment he did not speak, disconcerted that she would have said it outright, among all these people. But she was no more careful of his sensitivities than he was of hers. They knew each other too well for that. 'There were the mountains. They wouldn't have found me there.'

She was silent a moment, struggling visibly with sharp words. Struggling, perhaps, not to remind them both that he was the reason she was here. Then she sighed, quietly, letting anger and resentment go, 'Stephen, it's done. All of it.'

All of it. The foster homes – he had no memory of the family home he had been taken from at the age of four – the petty thefts, the spells in juvenile hall, the burglaries ... the woman with dark hair, the woman who had screamed. Until he made her quiet.

He drew a breath that shuddered, but found nothing to say with it. Everything he could say to Fleur, he had said. She knew what he was. She knew what had made him into that. She had been in the foster homes, too. Everything she was now, she was in spite of them. It was the reason she did not condemn him. 'I should have taken my chances in the mountains,' he said, willing her to understand the loss.

'You would have had no chance in the mountains,' she said, patiently, as she had said at regular intervals over the past ten days. 'Once the police had identified you – and it was a miracle they had not already done so – they would have known where you would run. It would have been a manhunt, cops and FBI, and every would-be bounty-hunter. You know that, Stephen. I know that.' She turned her head to look at him. 'That's why we're here.'

He leaned back, 'I don't know what I'd do without you.'

Her mouth pulled sideways in a little, cynical smile, and she did not answer.

3 Sophie Hemmingway

Melisande's carrier in hand once more, Sophie watched the thirteen men move off. Army, she thought ... that explained their reserve, all except the NASA scientist, an obvious misfit, with his slight build, bright eyes, enthusiastic, engaging manner and the NASA mission patch stitched slightly squint on his upper sleeve.

'Army,' said an old woman in a bright blue coat, who was still standing nearby. 'I'd know the sound of them a mile off.' Her accent was crisp and English.

Age had bleached her blue eyes and shrunk her black pupils. Her right eye tracked the movements around her while her left strayed outwards, blind, and with small scars around the orbit and stippling the cheek. Her white hair was lilac rinsed. Her hands, though knob-knuckled with the falling away of flesh, were large and capable, the joints well aligned. There was no taint of dementia about her, no scent of urine, faeces, stale clothing. Sophie envisioned her mother as she might have been, at eighty or more. The old woman thrust out her right hand, the complete one. 'Marian West. Middle name's Amelia.'

They shook, Sophie watching the pale fixed eye and its straying partner. She doubted that even the good eye could distinguish more than light, shadow and movement. 'Lost in the war,' Marian said.

'Pardon?'

'France, 'forty-three. Worked as a chemist for the OSS. Making explosives. Lost the fingers then. The eye was never quite the same afterwards . . . But tell me,' the words seemed to break from her. 'Tell me about this place.'

Sophie did, describing the cavern with its honeycombed walls, the bare floors with their strange green matting, the host of people, starting to thin now as they ventured towards the caves and corridors around the perimeter, or towards a low massif of grey in the centre. The cavern was like a park, but a park envisioned by someone working merely from a description, or a painting. Everything looked slightly artificial. Even the air. Marian worked her hands on her cane as she listened. Melisande, in the carrier, raised her voice in protest.

'Strange place,' Marian concluded. 'Not that I had expectations. You don't have expectations, at my age.'

Sophie smiled, recognising the bait. 'I need to find a place to let Melisande out, somewhere where there are fewer people.'

'Don't manage me, young woman. You think I shouldn't be here.'

Sophie shifted her weight against the carrier. Melisande would not suffer being laid down again, not if freedom did not follow promptly.

'Excuse us,' said a voice. She turned to face two women. One was the small redheaded emergency nurse. The other was chestnut haired, tall and broad shouldered – hulking, even – in her deep blue gypsy skirt and a red bolero. Beyond them, a cluster of women guarded a mound of luggage from the assaults of half a dozen overexcited children.

'We were wondering if you and your mother would like to join us.'

To her yellow sweat shirt was pinned a handcrafted silver badge, an opossum.

'We're not related,' Sophie said, shortly. Busy as she had been in planning her own departure, she had not missed the copious publicity given a group of women planning to leave Earth for a freer life in the stars.

Marian was moving her head from side to side, trying to make out enough to tell what was going on. The redhead said, 'Excuse me,' and took Marian's hand in hers, guiding it to the brooch. It was a move of surprising subtlety and ease. Marian's fingers fumbled over the silver. 'What's this?'

'It's our emblem. It's from a story by James Tiptree Jr. *She,*' a stress on the pronoun, 'likened women to opossums, living in the chinks of civilisation. In that particular story, two women, a mother and a daughter, go off with aliens. That is what we've all done. And we're inviting any women who are travelling without male companions to join us. We're going to build a community here.'

'Never known a mess of women able to build anything,' Marian said, tartly. 'Never able to keep their minds on what's important. Always getting their feelings hurt and going off in a huff.'

The large woman smiled easily. Her voice was deep and warm. 'Then you're even more welcome. You'll challenge us to change your mind and keep us from indulging ourselves. I am Hannah. This is Dove.' The little redhead rolled her eyes. 'Really and truly,' she said.

'Nothing wrong with it,' Marian said. 'Pretty name. Feminine.'

'Thank you,' Dove said. 'But I must say I think you are doing women a disservice. We have been building and keeping together communities for thousands of years. Volunteering, writing letters, arranging celebrations of all kinds –'

Sophie had a sudden, vivid flash of the long table in the summer house at Lister's pond. The memory glowed: the rosewood burnished by the sun, the polished silver glinting, the crystal glasses spreading rainbows across the snow white napkins, all seen in that perfect quiet moment before they all tumbled in. In winter there was Christmas and in high summer, midsummer's eve, as the medievals celebrated it, crowding the festivities because life was so very short. In those years they celebrated two of everything, birthdays and half-birthdays, anniversaries and unanniversaries. Celebrations were magical then. She had not acknowledged a birthday for the past four years. Nobody who knew her well sent her congratulations for the passing of time.

13

'I'm a blind old woman,' Marian said, stubbornly. 'I'd be a burden to you.'

Hannah said, 'How do you know?' Big and slightly awkward under their stares, she regarded Marian with an intent frown. 'None of us knows what we might need here, or who.'

Marian nodded, abruptly. 'My mind's as good as yours. Marian West. Used to be a chemist. Retired years ago.' She put out her hand, making no effort to offer it to either.

Hannah took her hand, somewhat tentatively folding her big, long-fingered hand around the smaller one. Marian firmed her grip; they shook. Dove beamed at both of them.

'And you?' Hannah said, to Sophie.

Sophie shook her head. She could still see in her mind the long rosewood table, laden. She missed the ceremonies, the reclaiming of time. She missed community.

But they were not her community. The community she yearned for was created by silence, by the bone deep understanding of a common destiny writ in the genes. That was the community that had existed around the rosewood table. That – a community which no longer existed – was the community on whose behalf she had come.

She said, 'Thank you, but no. That is not what I'm here for.'

They let her go, saying complacently, 'If you change your mind . . .'

4 Morgan

St John Emrys heard out the senior medic's report with a small, vertical line between his eyebrows. He pulled a handheld location-finder from his own kit, thumbed it on, looked at it, and turned it towards the senior communications sergeant. 'Thoughts?'

Deforest Piett shrugged. 'I'll know better when I take it apart,' he said.

A.J. cocked an eye ceiling-wards. 'Wonder how long the light lasts. Or if it ever goes dark.'

'Shit,' remarked one of the others. 'It'll be like SERE training all over again.'

'You want to keep an eye out for snakes,' said Aquile Raho, with a sideways glance towards Morgan, the civilian.

A.J. gave him a withering look, and then shifted his gaze towards the captain. The captain caught his eye and smiled slightly. He might be prince-in-waiting – under normal circumstances slated for a two year tour on his way to promotion – but A.J. was the kingmaker, a career sergeant with twelve years' age and experience on his superior. They managed the mismatch of hierarchy and experience deftly. The captain, A.J. had allowed in a candid moment, was more trainable than most.

He said now, 'Let's find a place to layover and check our equipment.'

They fell into patrol order, keeping it loose. Morgan was at the centre, with A.J. and medic Raphe Tejada on either side. The yellow yolk inside the shell, in Aquile Raho's phrase. There was a subdued natural antagonism between Morgan and Raho, the junior weapons sergeant. They were of similar background, both from poor, deprived, violent neighbourhoods. Morgan had enough of his Mexican grand-mother's colouring to pass for Hispanic, if it suited him. He could have dated Raho's sister, and been beaten bloody behind the school bleachers for any slur on that sister's honour. They would have had the same dangerous pastimes, the same lawless friends and deadly enemies. But past the age of sixteen their paths would have diverged, until now they were alien to each other.

A.J. scuffed a foot on the green matting. 'What do you make of this?'

'My totally unfounded guess is that this is a support or substrate for other kinds of growth, perhaps analogous to microrrhyzzia on Earth.'

A.J. thought a moment. 'We see a homestead with a porch, and I tell you, I'm off and running like hell.'

'You see a homestead with a porch,' Raphe Tejada said, 'and I got some vitamin H just for you.'

'Aw, hell, don't any of you kids *read*?'

Tejada was of an age with him; he just grinned. To Morgan, 'So can we eat this stuff?'

'I thought you guys were willing to eat anything,' he said, mildly.

'Nah,' A.J. said, 'just in the movies. Seriously, though, Prof, what do you think? Is there anything here we can eat?'

'I think,' Morgan said, and paused to order his thoughts. 'I think it depends entirely on our hosts. Whether their intentions are benign, and they mean us to survive and prosper. Whether they know enough about us not to inadvertently poison us. What this growth – if it is a growth and not somehow manufactured – is supposed to do. If it is responsible for recycling atmosphere, then they should have made it inedible – or unpalatable rather than poisonous. That's assuming they understand enough about people – and don't automatically presume we will understand or respect plant life. For all we know plants could be sacred to them, and this is their idea of a temple.'

A.J. gave him the sceptical eye. 'You think this could be part of a recycling system?'

'Part of it,' Morgan said. 'Based on the biomass here, far from being all of it – unless it is vastly more efficient than the terrestrial plant life it resembles. Maybe it is just here as decoration, to make us feel at home. We have to presume we were the object of some advance study, so we have to assume they know what we eat. We're all here presuming that their invitation was meant in good faith –' A.J.'s face did not change, though Morgan wondered, for a moment, if that were so. There was a qualitative difference between exploration and reconnaissance, and he was aware that there had been briefings which had excluded him. 'Or that the potential gains were worth the risks. I can't see what else we can do except go on. I expect at some point our hosts will make themselves known to us. It may be we're being kept in quarantine.'

'Like rabid dogs,' Tejada said.

'Or that we're being observed to see what we can do with our new environment. To see how we operate in their world, as opposed to ours.'

They approached a honeycombed cliff, looked up and up at the inward curving wall and all the open cave mouths. Water ran in thin streams from some high source and threaded across a narrow border of pale stone into the mat. People were already drinking from it, wetting each others' heads in solemn ritual, or flinging water at each other in an old fashioned water fight. Seeing them watching, a man shouted, 'It's fresh!'

Raphe Tejada shook his head. Morgan thought of the water purifiers they all carried, not that those could support the numbers here.

The wall was a warren of corridors and caves, some shallow and blind ended, some curving out of sight, some two men high, others child sized. A motley gang of teenagers were already exploring the nearest, and exclaiming to each other in excited, unintelligible, north England accents. To a one, they wore dusty black, with silver chains and silver studs marching up earlobes and adorning nostrils. The girls' faces were blanched with make-up, their eyes black-lined, their mouths plump with blood red or black plum. St John Emrys nodded civilly to them as they passed. Fingers and a few scattered obscenities followed them. A girl laughed, shrilly. A.J. muttered, 'Looks like something that belongs in caves. Hangin' upside down.'

In a space between groups, Emrys stopped before a cave. 'This'll do to get us out of sight.' Narrow-mouthed, it bulged into a blind pouch further in. A soft, white light seeped from the walls. Stooping, they entered, but for the four man guard on approach and entryway.

'Let us settle our minds about something,' Emrys said. He pulled out his radio handset, turned it on. There was no sound, not even static. No good-battery light. Around him, hands went to pockets, pulled out handsets, tested them. Nothing. In a ragged choreography they pulled out spare batteries, ejected the non working ones, replaced them. Morgan opened his palmtop computer and thumbed it on. The small screen remained blank. Deforest Piett and his junior dismantled their packs for the field radioset and antennae, and assembled it. Turned it on, nothing.

'Well, we're screwed,' remarked Raho.

'Never mind,' Greg Drover said, looping an arm over his shoulders. 'We still have each other.'

Raho punched him, solidly, in the chest; Drover danced back, hands up in appeasement. A.J. settled them with a look.

'I can't even get a reading on the circuit metre,' Piett said. 'It's not just the batteries – photo-voltaic cells are dead as well.'

'Are they jamming us?'

'I don't think so,' Morgan said.

As they had been speaking, he popped the casing of his palmtop exposing the chipboard. The green circuit board looked fine. The circuitry looked dusty. He brushed a chip with a latex-gloved finger. His fingertip came away coated in thick grey dust.

Someone said, 'What in hell could do that?'

There was a silence. Morgan said, a little helplessly, 'It may be that something natural to this environment breaks down silicon. There are bacteria which will eat just about everything.'

Piett frowned at Morgan. 'So you think some odd bugs which just happened to be floating around got into our equipment, were fruitful and multiplied, and did that in – what, two and a half hours? Is there anything you know that can grow that fast?'

'Your point?' said Emrys, though something in his face suggested he already had a fair idea.

'More likely that we were sprayed with the Prof's bugs than we just picked them up out of the air. There's that two and a bit hours unaccounted for.'

There was a silence.

'Which raises the question,' Piett continued, settling back on his heels, 'what else have we been sprayed with? And why?'

17

'Check weapons,' A.J. said, flatly.

Morgan squatted on his heels and watched as they began the unpacking and stripping of all their weaponry. He had not seen so comprehensive an arsenal since he watched the police raid a crackhouse while he was a young teenager. Himself and three friends, watching from a rooftop through a gap between buildings and tussling over one set of binoculars and his home-made telescope, oblivious to the danger they might have been in.

So then, he thought, a little ruefully, you grew up and found safer pursuits.

If they had indeed been sprayed with chip-eating bugs, and it was not simply environmental contamination, what might that mean? A hostile act? Or a defensive one? Why gut the electronic equipment – even a life-sustaining pacemaker – but leave weaponry seemingly intact? Their unseen hosts were concerned more with human strategy than individual human violence? Or were they thinking to ensure that no word ever got back from the tens of thousands – or more – who had chosen to step into the unknown? He rubbed his forehead trying to remember whether he had seen or heard anything between waiting and arriving. But all he could recall was impatience, nervousness, irritation at the rain and the light shining in their eyes – the light for the unmanned cameras. What, he wondered, had those cameras recorded, if anything? Or had they been opened up again at 12.15, or 12.20, and shown nothing but chips crumbling away. Jesus, he thought suddenly. Suppose they'd turned their bugs loose on Earth?

You're being paranoid, the scientist in him said. Why go through this elaborate ruse of inviting and transporting all these people? A test laboratory, said the paranoid, planning for an invasion. Observing our reactions. The scientist scoffed: too many late night movies.

Coming here was completely crazy.

You've only just figured that out?

A.J. caught his smile. 'Something funny?'

'Just listening to myself argue.'

'You got any ideas?'

'Too many. Maybe it's contamination. Maybe it's hostile. Maybe it's defensive. Maybe it's strategic, to make sure we can't contact Earth and tell anyone back home anything about this ship. Remember they were not interested in giving out freebies. Maybe it's to make us come to terms with this environment, and what it means. There's surely way more to what's around us than meets the eye. For all we know this is some kind of virtual reality.'

'And we ain't here,' Raho remarked. 'This is too weird.'

Somebody began a rejoinder, and the light went out.

There was a brief silence, then a shuffle of feet and equipment, a grunt and a growl as someone jarred someone else. 'Stand easy,' A.J. said. 'Drover, you're nearest the cave mouth. Is it dark out?' A brief exchange between Greg Drover and the sentries. 'Yes.' Time mitigated the darkness to thick, indigo twilight. Morgan could just see, indistinctly, the bulks of men against the cave walls.

'It looks like we could be here for the night,' St John Emrys said. 'Let's get some lanterns lit.'

By the light of the lanterns, deep-set in the cave so neither to impair the sentries' night sight nor to illuminate targets, Morgan packed away his useless computer. His hand encountered a hard case; he drew it out and regarded it ironically, feeling that queasy pressure of laughter in the back of his throat. He had a dozen or so CD-ROMs crammed with images, image reconstruction, spectral analysis and inferometry of the alien ship ... the best of the plethora of images recorded by every Earthside and orbiting telescope that could be brought to bear in the twenty-nine days between the first realisation that there was *something out there* and the alien ship's settling unambiguously into Earth's orbit. What exactly he had been planning to do with them, he could not presently bring to mind. He supposed he had been planning to show off a little, flaunt their vast accumulation of data. He would have deceived no one, not even himself. An accumulation of data was not knowledge, although it might mask the lack of knowledge.

He laid down the case, and searched in his rucksack again, this time drawing out a transparent azure folder. With his thumb he hooked the elastic from two corners, opening it, smelling the faint chemical aroma of the printouts. He laid them side by side, vexed by the way the corners curled, until it occurred to him to weight them down with the coins that still rode in his pocket, carried here by habit. Then he studied them with a freshness of vision that had been unattainable on Earth, when they were merely one instalment of a too slowly unfolding sequence, his perceptions shaped by everything that had come before and everything he expected to come after.

They showed, at roughly one day intervals, the object as it had approached Earth, having been first resolved just inside Mars's orbit, a fast-moving greyish fleck, some twenty-five kilometres in length. An asteroid, they feared for the first twelve or so hours. Perhaps The Big One. But barely had apocalyptic speculation begun when the images of the enlarging object, magnified and smoothed, had shown it as regular,

19

smooth, hollow-centred. And as it converged with Earth, slowing, it had changed shape, the hollow centre filling in, the cylindrical shell of it rounding, until the ship which rode in orbit was ellipsoid, without no visible openings, and in the light of the sun a dark grey with a tarnished tint. The spectral analysis was described by one of its more phlegmatic interpreters as 'challenging', while there were rumours of pistols at dawn featuring two of the more volatile personalities at the European Space Agency. The ship's skin appeared to be a mixture of organic and organometallic compounds, stable at low temperatures, but undergoing slow transition to more stable forms as the ship moved sunwards, and highly absorbing across much of the electromagnetic spectrum. Using the sun as an energy source? Synthetic chemists were even now tackling the problem of re-creation, while protesting that it was tantamount to trying to prepare authentic fifteenth-century oils by gazing at da Vinci's *Last Supper*.

By the time the last of the series had been obtained, on the ship's closest approach to the Hubble telescope, the Internet had been brought to a standstill by the demand for access to the images, the world's major telescopes had seen three weeks of media siege and the networks had experienced a countercoup by scientists who had – through the web – discovered that the lay public could indeed be communicated with. Politicians had made statements, governments had formed alliances and task forces; several had fallen; Nostradamus had been invoked; several big-budget sci fi movies had flopped for want of interest; and xeno-angst had replaced sexual angst as the prime subject of dial-a-doc radio shows. Religious leaders warned about despair and false idols, but Morgan had watched an elderly cardinal capering like a child as he talked about God's infinite capacity to surprise and delight.

For two days the alien spaceship orbited Earth, gliding gracefully through the clutter of satellites, space stations, telescope platforms, while being barraged by every form of communication that human inventiveness could muster. Children with torches flashed painstakingly worked out codes into the night sky. People lit signal fires on hills and open land – with sometimes catastrophic consequences, as in autumnal Australia. Public, private and pirate radio stations broadcast welcoming messages of all tenors, from organisations, individuals and groups, on all channels and in at least nine-tenths of the world's languages. Official appeals to keep the airways clear were disregarded; it was barely possible to secure police and emergency channels. Commercial pilots went on strike, refusing to fly with their communications compromised. International arguments raged about priorities, protocols and regulations. Cartoonists depicted the alien spaceship heading off in search of a quieter neighbourhood, or the little green men's first words being, 'Anyone got Tylenol?', or arriving to serve an interplanetary noise and littering violation on humanity.

Then the aliens replied. The message came in on all the wavelengths humanity had used and in all the languages tendered: specialists argued that it had been the repetition, particularly of the official greetings, that would have given the aliens the Rosetta Stone – a phrase much used – of human language ... and others argued that that was impossible, that one needed a language to *start* with, but what was unarguable was that it was happening. The message, in all its forms and repetitions, was brief. They were representatives of a mixed community of sentient species who had been exploring the galaxy for hundreds of thousands of years. If any human wanted to join them, they would be welcome. They need only be standing within ten metres of the waterline of a body of salt water, at night, in twenty-three days' time.

And thereafter, there was only silence, no answer to the multitudinous requests for expansion, clarification, assurance. The aliens had issued their invitation; they now awaited humanity's response, in the form of those who would offer themselves, on that appointed night.

Morgan pulled out his notebook which he carried always but used rarely. He could not remember when he had handwritten anything of any length or coherence; usually his handwritten notes were a shambles of words and sketches, a thought map unintelligible to anyone but himself. When he had to compose for coherence and not merely for capture he did so at the keyboard. He folded the notebook open at a blank page, trying to find a way to begin. Recalling what he could of the material he had downloaded before leaving, the best of Earth's science. On the beach at Chesapeake, under the lights and cameras. Trying to penetrate that lost two-plus hours. Here, wherever they were, whatever they were in. The ship, they could only presume, in the absence of evidence to the contrary, or suggestions for an alternative. Around him, the team settled to completing its weapons and equipment check, bantering among themselves as though they were back in the team room. They were engaging in a concurrent, impromptu competition as to who could produce the most impressive nonstandard weaponry. Senior Weapons Sergeant Adlai Lecce, appropriately enough, seemed to be the front runner, having so far contributed a crossbow and an aboriginal throwing stick, although in the category of weapons of intimidation Raho's machete would have taken the gold medal. A.J., the captain and Piett were discussing whether at some future date the electronics might be salvaged and, if not, how best to dispose of them. Morgan doubted any of it was salvageable, including his own computer; but he found himself oddly reluctant to part with it for the information that should be on the memory cards. Information, he thought, that was becoming more and more irrelevant with every passing hour. He wondered how far away they might already be from Earth.

Begin at the beginning, he thought. Get the notes down. Decide on the questions. Only when he had defined the questions, mapped out the immense uncertainty, could he start to look for answers.

5 Hathaway Dene

Dear Mom,
   Lt Peta,
   Sir Dave the Dragon Slayer,
   Johnny-o,
and last but never least,
   Joyball,

I am so mad at you and me and all of us for having a big stupid argument just before I had to leave so I didn't have time to write you a letter explaining properly why I was going. What were we arguing about anyway? I've totally forgotten. And now you're going to be thinking it was because of the row that I went even though I tried to tell you it wasn't in my note. I really had been thinking of going with the aliens ever since they asked.

So this is the letter I wanted to write. There are all kinds of ways to send messages across space. You'd know if you listened to Uncle Stan as much as I have. I'll find a way to send this. And all the others I'm going to write. In a spaceship or in an asteroid or in a bottle if I have to. These are the things I want you to know.

Even though I'm leaving I love you all to pieces. I love you more than there are sand grains on the beach. I love you more than there are plankton in the sea. I love you more than there are cells in the brain. I love you more than there are atoms in the *universe*. I love every hair on your heads and every freckle on your noses and every crinkle around your eyes. (Sorry Mom.) One of the things I like about you-know-who (OK Mom, Allen) is the way he smiles when we do the I love you riff. He had such an uptight family. I won't mind if you start cutting him in on the action. Really, truly and with vermicelli. But this isn't about Allen. This is real important, Mom. This isn't about you marrying him. This isn't about life with him being so unbearable that I do anything to get away. I really hate the word opportunity. It's been made cheap, just used to sell stuff and to make us sit up and beg at school. But this is the biggest opportunity ever. I know a lot of people don't believe the aliens would simply offer and who think there has to be a reason for them wanting us – like they want to eat us or lay eggs in us or make us slaves or something else ugly. Aliens are *alien*. Maybe alien enough to make an offer with no strings. (I really hope NASA lets Uncle Stan go. He wants to every bit as much as I do – but if they made him stay don't phone him up and yell at him. He didn't do it. I did.)

OK, so now I have to tell you why. This is the hard part. I know you think your lives are wonderful now and the only thing spoiling them is me. I hope you keep thinking that. (Well, maybe not about me.) I know what it feels to have something you're proud of taken away. So I want you to enjoy the life and the house and the money. I want you even to enjoy *him*. Allen. Even I can see he's not a bad person.

But the big thing is I still don't think we were failures before. I don't think we were a burden on society or low down welfare bums or the kids would grow up to be serial killers and prostitutes. Sure we were exhausted a lot of the time and sure we didn't have enough to eat sometimes and got angry often – but we had *reasons*. Sure the kids were just scraping by in school some months and never had the right stuff to wear or take to school. But that wasn't our fault or yours. You didn't commit a crime by gettting married real young and having five kids. We didn't commit a crime by being poor. We didn't commit a crime by being five of us with just a Mom. Pop didn't commit a crime by dying even if he was a smoker. All those ads and that legal pushing and suddenly his cancer is his fault even though it wasn't a type of cancer that was caused by smoking.

But all of a sudden the life we'd had before was like some great big mistake. If we were good people then we shouldn't have been poor and we couldn't have done some of the things we did or had some of the things that happened to us happen. So it was like we had to pretend it was all a bad dream like one of those TV shows when a whole season suddenly was just a dream. Suddenly I was prematurely independent and taking on the paternal role in the family and my problem with Allen is some kind of transsexual Oedipal thing. How can any aliens I ever meet be weirder than those therapists?? I was just the eldest kid and the biggest and the one who had the aggro. Without me a lot more shit would have gone down. I'm not ashamed of getting strong and staying strong. I don't think I'm damaged. But suddenly he's the stepfather and he and the teachers and the therapists know everything and I know nothing. I've known you for *years* longer than they have. But that doesn't count. Not even with you. You've bought into all that crap about how the life we used to have was bad. You wouldn't let me be the person I was to you.

And about the baby. For the last time I did not get pregnant because I was trying to regain my caretaking role or prove my female identity. I got pregnant because that antibiotic I was on for my septic foot stopped my body from absorbing the birth control pill. OK? The foot was dumb, agreed; I just didn't think it was anything serious. Remember we didn't used to have a doctor we could rush to for every little cut. And you'd think that Doc Zonkout would have thought to *mention it* about the antibiotics. It's not like everyone back there's a virgin until they're eighteen. Ha ha ha.

I'm going to miss you all so much when the baby comes. I've been trying to think how to give her a bit of all of your names without it getting ridiculous. But I guess it may not matter. To the aliens, all our names will be strange. She'll be the first citizen of the galaxy unless there's someone going along already more pregnant than I am and I don't think that's real likely. I mean, I'm six months. At school they looked at me like I'm some kind of crazy pro-lifer for not just going through a nice little 'procedure' before anything showed. They really think it's better to be dead than not to live the perfect life. Mom if you'd thought that when Pop getting sick when you were pregnant with Joy or the time he lost his job while you were pregnant with Dave – those two kids would never have been born. That's all I thought about all the time people were blablablaing about the sensible thing to do and how stressful it was having a kid without a father and the statistics about teenage mothers.

The day I came home after my clinic and threw up for an hour and wouldn't tell you why – this is what happened. They talked about my hitting the boys sometimes and my going for that cop who was such a shit to Peta – you know physically. They said they were concerned about patterns of abuse. They never actually *said* they could take away my baby – they were real careful. But they made sure I got the picture. I just couldn't tell you because *he'd* have told you I was imagining things and I couldn't have stood it. Maybe not in his world it doesn't happen but you and I saw it. Didn't we? I don't want my baby ever to have been where I've been. I don't want ever to feel what you felt the night Peta was brought home raped or I hit the boys because I was so scared they'd turn into killers. I have to think this is going to be a better place.

But since you're staying behind – I'm real sorry but I couldn't even ask because I knew all that would get me was being locked in my room for my own good – since you're staying behind this is what I want to say.

Peta – I want you to go for the Olympics. You've got the fire – don't let anyone tell you you're a no-hoper because you started late. Don't let anyone drag you into spending the rest of your life 'recovering'. It happened – it sucked – but you lived through it. Now get on and do what you have to do. When these TV rays go beaming out into space you'll hear me cheering all the way back on Earth.

Dave – I know you're going to be mad at me for this. You were already half in love with my baby yourself. I've left you that ultrasound photo that looks like squids mating in a snowstorm. You should find a good woman and have ten of them. (Babies I mean not squids). Call one after me (Hathaway, *not* Harriet, or I'll come back and zap you with my raygun). But before you do that you need to get less mad. I don't want you ending up in jail for hitting your wife or killing somebody just because he flips the switch in you. I'd say join the police now I'm safe and far away. They're not whiter than white but you know things that would make you a good cop and might make them better, like why kids like you hate cops. Or put on tights and go be Batman. He may not be real but the wish is. I want you on the side of right. I want you to be a true knight. And I wish you could have believed in the aliens. I'd really have liked you with me.

Johnny – It's OK to love you know who – Allen. Really and truly with vermicelli. Pop wouldn't be mad at you and I'm not mad either. Of all the kids you're the one he likes best. I think you'd make a great doctor if that's what you want to be. But listen, I worry about you sometimes because of the way you need to belong. You don't have to do what everyone else does to be loved. Anyone who tries to take you away from what you want doesn't love you – they're on a power trip. So fix your star and follow it and you'll be OK. You'll be more than OK – you'll be grrrreeat. Just look at Uncle Stan and where he began and where he ended up.

Joy – Little princess. Sometimes the only reason Mom and I kept going was because you needed us between you and the monsters. Now you feel like you've wandered into wonderland. I hope the feeling stays for a long, long time. But please don't turn into one of those rich bitches. I mean it. I think you're going to be an artist, some high powered video producer. You've already got the bossiness for it. Don't get me wrong little sister – I love your bossiness and I hope my baby comes out just like you. Just keep your eyes clear. Don't get dazzled. I'm counting on you being the one to keep me posted. When your movies get beamed out I'll be watching them too.

Mom – Whatever they tell you you don't have to be sorry for anything. You got us through. Everything I give my baby will really come from you. Whatever they say I'm not a danger to her. I'm gonna be one tough momma. Just like my momma.

I love you infinitely and for ever. Have wonderful lives. Mine's going to be just out of this world. Your shooting star,

Hath.

6   Sophie

Sophie had almost reached the wall when the lights went out. She was gazing up at its glistening height, while Melisande twined around her ankles, commenting in her rasping voice on the irregularity of it all.

Darkness was sudden, and all but complete. An eerie twilight remained. Cries, squeals, screams, babbling, mapped out the huge cavern in sound. Sophie set down the cat carrier and crouched to gather in Melisande, hearing feet scuffle on the matting nearby. The cat hissed beneath her hand. A struck match sprayed sparks and lit three staring black-and-white faces briefly. All across the cavern, points of light winked on, for the fleeting life of a match or the longer life of a lighter. Sophie had a moment's fear that the matting might itself prove flammable – but someone nearby had the same thought, without the caution, for a match flame was lowered groundwards – to quench with a hiss and a thread of smoke. Sophie breathed out, glad of Melisande's warmth under her hands. Her heart beat fast, with a primitive fear of the dark, and a rational fear of the unexpected.

Towards the far side of the cavern, someone lit a fire from discarded clothes and papers. As Sophie watched, shadows drifted across it, people converging upon it.

Melisande turned her head up. Her eyes glittered faintly in the twilight, which, like the light, seemed to diffuse out of every part of the wall. Sophie whispered, 'Let's find somewhere to settle, shall we?' The dark-inspired adrenaline was ebbing, and the backpack and carrier seemed heavier than before. She continued as she had intended. The walls were so indistinct that it was feel rather than sight which stopped her, that and the lap-lap-lap of Melisande's tongue as she supped. She should have given Melisande water before they started into the twilight. She cupped her hand against the wall and drank from it, sealing her fate with Melisande's, as seemed only right. The water had the peculiar crystalline flatness of distillate-in-glass. 'Sorry, Mel,' she murmured. Down in the darkness, the white smudge purred contentedly.

She found a dry, unoccupied place and settled wearily, shedding backpack and cat-carrier. She tried to collect the cat and ease her into the carrier, but Melisande balked, yowling until Sophie let her go. 'Just you be careful, dammit,' she whispered as Melisande faded into the twilight like a wraith.

But it was peaceful, here in this alien twilight. She thought of dusk on the pier on Lister's pond. Lights from the cabins across the water. The sound of voices from the porch and open windows behind her. The flickering of fireflies in the thick darkness under the firs. The feel of the cooling air on her bare skin. The kiss of sun-heated water on the soles of her feet. Mosquitoes, whining unseen in the dusk. She never felt the bites that studded her skin all summer.

She wondered now at her ease in time, even in the winters away from Lister's pond when time was marked to others' measures – birthdays expected, school grades worked through, phone calls anticipated. Even she had suffered the exquisite, excruciating boredom of adolescence, of wasting time because it was *her* time to waste. She was old enough to have forgotten her grandfather's death; self-absorbed enough to be untroubled by her aunt's bleak withdrawal, and her uncle's mad, uncomprehending eye. Even when she heard the name, familial Alzheimer's dementia, and heard for the first time the explanation of its inheritance, she summed her chances with all the blithe assurance of youth: if two out of four have it, and there's a fifty per cent chance, that's it – mother shouldn't. She was the youngest daughter's youngest: cherished and protected and spoiled, cradled within the family's golden cocoon. How could any ill fortune attend her?

Melisande flowed out of the twilight, cruising her legs, courting the backpack, crooning her edgy purr. Obedient, Sophie explored the pack by touch, setting aside the useless torch and the packet of matches to be used only in emergencies. She found dish, penknife and food, slit packet with penknife, poured out contents into dish. Melisande groused at the rattle of dried pellets.

'When you carry the backpack, you can be picky,' Sophie told her.

She poured water, Earth water, for the cat, and drank some herself. Then she leaned back on her elbows and thought of the mosquitoes and fireflies, all dead before the summer's end. She remembered how she had sat in the summer's night and secretly numbered all the things she would outlive. If they had time, so too would she. It was the thought of all those brief lives, of insects, of medieval peasants and kings, that comforted and sustained her.

The summer after her mother's diagnosis, while her mother was still too deeply depressed to care about family traditions or family heroism, Sophie herself had polished the silver and set the table, and laid out the cookbooks, and tried to re-create what her mother had created, all those years. That golden place where they would all have time enough.

Ironically it was at her own table that a friend had betrayed her. Rachel, her closest friend among her medical class, whom she herself had introduced to the elder of her two brothers. Rachel, who of all people she thought should understand. Rachel, who at their midsummer feast did what she, Sophie, had chosen not to do, insisted on discussing their genetic fate. She had described the linkage analysis as used to follow the inheritance of genetic defects through family lines; she had proselytised about the benefits to science and to the human community of studying another family with this so common dementia in its inherited form, and she had reared up to declare shiningly that she could not bear children to this man she loved if she must put those children at risk of a disease which would take away their minds in middle age. And so she began the dividing of Sophie's family into the damned and the saved.

Rachel and Sophie's brother had three children now, whom she raised singlehandedly, heroically, while Keith passed in and out of detox. The results of the analysis had cleared him of carrying the mutant gene and, somehow, the prospect of three score years and ten broke him as the prospect of early death never had. Rachel and Sophie had not spoken since the first time Keith had refused to come to their midsummer gathering. Morbid, he called it. Keith's voice, speaking Rachel's words.

She became aware of a whispering, out in the darkness, a soft argument between several voices. One of them rose above the rest, '. . . dead easy. Just watch.' Melisande growled, flattening herself against the grass; Sophie snagged her, felt one-handed for the carrier and bundled the cat in. Her skin tingled with the effort of sensing what she could not see. She was panting slightly, feeling a scream like a physical presence in her throat. Who was there to appeal to, here, in the high dark? She felt for, and found, the opened penknife.

A lighter flicked on, a point in the darkness, nearer than she anticipated. It lit a pale, dark-pointed face, a row of ear studs. 'We're hungry,' the boy announced, brazenly. He cast a glance behind him in the dark and obediently a girl snickered. 'You've got food. We want some.'

'Get away from me.'

The indistinct face moved closer. 'Just give us something, then we'll go away.'

He flicked his fingers beneath her nose.

Without thought, without premeditation, Sophie drove the knife up, catching sleeve and arm. The boy screamed and staggered back; the lighter bounced against Sophie's knee on to the green matting.

'What the *fuck* did you do that for?'

For an instant, she almost laughed, both at him and in incredulity at what she had just done. The laughter turned into a low growl. 'You threatened me.'

His friends huddled around him, holding their feeble lights to his face or to his hand which clutched his sleeve, dark blood trickling between his fingers. She had not done such great damage, her physician's eye told her. The girl burst out, 'We thought it was all some sodding hoax. We don't even want to be here.'

'I'm *bleeding* for you,' said a soft voice from the darkness behind the youths. They jerked around to face it, putting their backs to Sophie. Sophie could see several figures of moving there.

'Sod off,' one of the youths said, but they began to sidle sideways, away from both Sophie and the newcomers.

'Doctor,' said a woman's voice – the paramedic's – 'if you would like to come with us, we can take you where you'll have some company.'

She gathered knife and bowl, spilling food and water in her fumble-handed haste, and pushed them into her backpack. She was trembling. It was the leap of the knife from ground to target, she thought. The way it had happened without thought or planning. She had already been angry, thinking of Rachel and what she had done in the name of her own love, and when a target for that anger had offered itself, she had simply let it leap out, along the point of her knife. She felt ill, appalled at herself.

'What about us?' said the girl, tremulous in the darkness.

A second voice spoke from the group of newcomers, one with a distinctive rasp and Eastern European accent. 'Tonight, you stay outside. Tomorrow, maybe. We shall see.'

'She *cut* him.'

Sophie moved unsteadily to join them, keeping well away from the would-be thieves. She flinched as someone drew closer. 'It's all right,' the woman paramedic said, at her side. 'It's Adrienne LaFleurette. We met . . . earlier. Just follow Stephen. He's got the eyes of a cougar. Safety in numbers may be the rule, at least until things are better organised.'

'In the morning,' said the accented voice.

The darkness was sparsely flecked with single lights and struggling fires. The vast quiet was barely broken by momentary outcries for someone left behind, brief bursts of sobbing, soft conversations and low moans – all borne down into silence by the weight of darkness and strangeness. Far away, several people were singing one of those campfire songs of many, many verses. They sounded drunk. She concentrated on walking and not staggering beneath the burden of her backpack and the shifting, griping weight of Melisande.

When she saw the eerie glow in the dark, she thought it was some illusion of strained eyes. But it was an improvised marker, a cluster of children's fluorescent stickers patched on a staff, making a totem-post which seemed to hover in the air. Someone said, 'Who's that?' and moved, and Stephen said shortly, 'Keep the lantern off. You'll screw up my eyes. I've another stray for you.'

The others lingered by the totem-post, while Stephen guided her over prone bodies. This, she thought, must have been the residue of the crowd drawn by the death; in all likelihood, the dead man lay somewhere nearby. Stephen assured her she would be all right here, and left her to settle herself. Melisande's claws ground and yanked at the mesh. From all around her, people voiced subdued and irritable complaint. Sophie yielded, and released the catch and let Melisande flow away.

Later, she woke Sophie with the nuzzle of a nose and the touch of a paw wet from the waterfalls, pushed at her until the woman uncurled and rolled onto her back, and settled into her usual place on Sophie's chest. Sophie slept again to the gentle kneading of paws.

7 Morgan

He did not know when during the long night he had closed his notebook, slid it from his lap and his jacket from his shoulders, laid himself out on the matting and closed his aching eyes. Most of the team were already asleep, here, or just beyond the mouth of the cave, except for the four on sentry duty. As Aquile Raho put it, a nun in a convent should be so well protected.

Strangely, Morgan dreamed of Earth. He was sitting at a computer terminal in what he knew was his own laboratory, although his surroundings were merely a white mist. A tapered hexagonal tube of vivid blue lines writhed on the screen, winding and coiling like some bizarre serpent. There was text across the bottom, but neither the text nor the buttons were in English, or indeed in any Earthly language he knew to recognise. His fingers sought the keys they knew, and could not find them, not Esc, Delete, Control-C. He looked down, and when he looked down he thought he recognised the keyboard but he no longer knew which keys he wanted. And still the blue lines undulated, the program he had to stop.

Kekulé, you lucky bastard, Morgan thought, waking with the lingering image of that cryptic pattern. He dreams of snakes and comes up with the structure of benzene. I dream of snakes and get . . . 'Shit,' he murmured aloud, aware of a familiar pain behind his right eye. Not unexpected, he assured himself, feeling his way over the coarse lump of his pack to his discarded jacket and extracting the bottle of Imitrex from its inner pocket. He swallowed one capsule, dry, rather than lift his head to rummage for water.

A.J.'s murmur said, 'Prof?'

'Migraine,' Morgan said briefly.

A.J. acknowledged that with an even briefer, wordless murmur. Prior to their leaving, in the midst of eighteen-hour days of planning and briefing, he had found time for a discussion with Morgan about his infrequent but notable migraines, a discussion Morgan had been dreading as a prelude to washing him out. What'll you do if you run out of drug? I guess you'll just have to shoot me, Morgan had said, only half joking. A.J., not joking, had bluntly recommended Morgan take at least a ten years' supply. We might be some time, the team sergeant said, deadpan.

He had – all the team had – an extraordinary facility for compart-mentalisation. Volunteers to a man, committed to going on what might be the longest, strangest long range patrol in history, they seemed to hold side by side in their minds the thought that they would return in triumph, and the thought that they would not return at all. They were all single, but most of them had some female companion and one or two had children – and the plans he had overheard them making encompassed the next year and never – the kid's next birthday party and when the missing were legally dead. Morgan himself had liquidated his life, resigning from his job – defying the instruction to leave his resignation letter undated so that it could be kept on file – selling all his furniture, his car (no loss; only a necromancer or a high

31

school auto fiend would have kept it running through the next winter), giving up his apartment, sending all the clothes that were not to come with him to the Goodwill. His books, music and program CDs he had had shipped to his niece Hathaway, though he had no idea what use she would get from them. The only class in which she distinguished herself was art – his sister said one of her teachers had been rather quizzically flattering about her ferocious commitment to her inner vision – but he had been fanning her contentious passion for space exploration. Self-indulgently and wholly irresponsibly he thought: damn the girl for getting herself pregnant. She should have been here. He enjoyed the thought for a moment, despite the butterfly needle in his eye socket, picturing Hathaway here, asking the infuriatingly elementary, blunt, *obvious* questions which were the vexation of any honest teacher. And which had, on more than one occasion, given him the solution to some technical problem which had bedevilled him. But he had no right to wish a seventeen year old to have come with him on this one-way journey, pregnant or not.

But he had never made arrangements for death, even as he had assumed he was never coming back. That was the difference between himself and the team. Their assumption – trained into them, he supposed – was that for each one of them, not returning meant dying. If they did not make it home, they would have died here, on enemy ground.

A sentry came soundlessly in from outside and exchanged whispers with A.J. – Edward Illes, by the voice. Lacking timepieces they were having to estimate time and, after a brief consultation, Illes began shaking awake the next watch. There was a general stirring and shuffling and someone's toe tapped him in the ribs. Someone else passed a lantern too close to his face and the needle in his eye socket went red hot. He dragged a flap of his jacket over his eyes. Where it brushed his skin, his skin tingled slightly, side effect of the drug.

The darkness and silence were almost unsettling. He'd only heard it so quiet when his lab group at UCLA had gone into the mountains for its annual retreat. And there, the drinking and the talking had left an after impression in his ears so that he could distinctly hear church bells ringing a slow carillon. And even in the mountain chalet timbers had settled, branches had rasped against slates, a pine cone had dropped with a thud on to the roof. Here silence overlaid silence.

He was sleeping when the light came up and woke him, even through his makeshift eyeshade. He winced, by reflex, but all that remained was a dull ache. The Imitrex had worked its usual magic.

Nevertheless, he felt out his prescription sunglasses and slid them on. He sat up, nodded as A.J.'s assessing glance fixed upon him. Senior engineer Kent Hughes rubbed his fingers over a heavily stubbled chin and remarked to A.J., 'Been a long night.' His medical counterpart kidded him about calibrating his chin-hairs to use as a clock. Morgan just eased himself to a cross-legged position and watched them turn out. His adaptability resided in his intelligence, his ability to observe and do likewise. He had no intentions of crossing any invisible lines. By twos, warily, they disappeared from the cave with shaving gear in hand. Morgan found himself escorted by Raphe Tejada and the junior engineer, Boris Djuraskovic. He dearly wished he could have been alone with the straight razor A.J. had lent him. His battery-operated razor had, of course, packed it in. He cut himself twice. Tejada frowned and passed him a tube of antiseptic, of a mix constituted specially for the mission.

By the time he returned, A.J., the captain and the operations sergeant, André Bhakta, had their heads together. Tejada murmured, 'Better get packed quick, Prof. Captain's only got two settings, stop and go. And when he goes, we go.'

As he lifted his jacket, a plastic bag slid from its pocket. He thought for a moment that it was one of his empty ones, but realised the pocket left unzipped was his right pocket, where he had placed last night's samples. When he lifted the bag up he saw that it was not empty. There was a small residue – more smudge than of any bulk – of fine grey dust, like a volcanic ash. He rubbed it between his fingers, through the bag. The night before, matting. Now dust. Common sense – and the recollection of an authoritarian freshman chemistry lab instructor – stopped him from opening and sniffing the powder.

'Problem, Prof?' said A.J., suddenly alert.

'No . . . but . . .' Morgan said, and passed him the bag. 'This is the sample of the matting I collected yesterday.'

A.J. passed it to the captain. It moved in succession through the hands of Bhakta, Tejada, Hughes and Piett, who remarked, 'Looks like what was left of all our chips,' and came back in the end to Morgan without further comment. He was the brain; it was his problem. A.J. straightened up. 'All right, people. Let's move out and see what we can see. Just like we do at home. We'll get the lay of the land, start mapping – anything you think the Prof should see or know about, give him a yell. That's what he's here for.'

Aquile Raho added, *sotto voce*, 'It ain't for his skill with edged weapons, that's for sure.'

8 Hathaway

Dear Mom'n'all,

This is an *a-ma-zing* place. You have to stop right now thinking about gleaming panels and glowing buttons. It's like a garden – all the edges are trimmed and all the leaves have a shiny look to them like they've been polished. All of it I've seen so far is caverns and tunnels. The walls are pale grey like stone when you look at them close, all different crystals and grains, but not cold like stone. Up high they glow. The air is full of glow. The water just runs and runs down the walls like a rain curtain.

It was weird what happened on the beach. I don't remember getting here at all. I got together my stuff and snuck out the sliding door and went straight down the steps to the beach. You guys were all down watching it on TV. I suppose maybe I should be a bit glad of the row because it meant you thought I was just sulking. But I didn't start it deliberately, honest. Sometimes things just get said. Anyway down on the beach it was like waiting for fireworks with all these people standing around. Nobody was talking much. Waiting to be scared or have all the lights come on and people jump up and kill themselves laughing at the big ha-ha-funny joke see how we fooled you. I didn't want to talk to anyone so I looked out to sea and counted down to midnight.

This is where it got strange. I saw something dark over the water, even though I hadn't seen anything coming in to land. People suddenly started screeching and trying to run away like a moment ago they hadn't been shoving and jiggling to see better. Somebody knocked me on to the sand. I was just starting to get up, I remember that. And just like they say in books the next thing I knew I was standing in this place.

(I keep thinking of our footsteps back there on the beach. The way the sun is going to come up on them and fill them full of shadow. The way the sea will wash them away. The way the people who stayed will walk all over them until they're gone. And we won't ever be back to put them there again.)

I haven't seen any aliens yet, just people. There are thousands and thousands of us here. Everyone expected someone to be here to say hello and tell us where to get in line. Instead there was just us wandering around like on the first day of school. Everyone looking everyone else over and wondering if they're worth knowing or just trouble. Some women with little silver animal badges came over all concerned about me being alone and wanting me to join their group which is some kind of women's escape movement. I pasted a big smile on my face and said that my *mother* and my *sisters* were just over there looking around. But they hung around so I waved like I was waving to someone across the cavern and hiked off.

I walked down and across the cavern we started in which has this kind of low bowl shape. There was a tunnel big enough to stand up in which turned out to be a corridor which led to an intersection and eventually to another cavern. On the other side of that cavern there was a little cavern full of short little trees not much bigger than I am. My legs and stomach were feeling crampy and I needed to crap so I snuck into the little trees. This is such a strange place but it's like the aliens are trying to make us feel we belong. I can't believe that the aliens would eat us or lay their eggs in us. They've tried so hard to make this place nice for us even though their ideas of hospitality are strange.

I sat down and finished off my goodbye letter properly. I'd just started this one when the light went out totally. Like that play we went to see about the two bums hanging around. I *know* it was a Classic but it was still two street people hanging around and waiting for this guy who never showed. And that giving birth astride the grave speech was just plain creepy. It was obviously written by a guy because no woman would want to think about babies and graves in one sentence. *I* want to take my baby as far away from graves and death and everything bad as I possibly can. Maybe the aliens saw it too (the play) because the lights just went out crash. I almost thought the moon would plop down on a wire. It got very quiet except for people thrashing around in the trees. Nobody's torches seem to work. They (the people, not the trees – this place is not *that* weird) went away in the end which I was really glad about and I got to go to sleep.

Since I told you the truth about you in the first letter I should tell you the truth about me. I woke some time in the night feeling totally lost. I was lying in the dark on this funny squishy green stuff underneath these weird little trees. And I was thousands of miles up in space and all alone except for the baby. I felt so lonely for that walkup in Skunk Alley with those ripped up pink curtains and that tatty red carpet and that *stink*. I really do think the guy before us had a cougar for a pet. Either that or he was a werewolf. Whatever it was it hadn't been *fixed*. But when I woke up in the night there I could hear Joy's whispery little baby breathing and Dave's deep macho snore and Peta grinding her teeth. I never did get used to having a room of my own. I don't know how long I went on bawling and sort of smothering because I didn't want to make any noise. But eventually I wore out my tear ducts and went back to sleep.

I think it was dark longer than on Earth. When I woke up I just *knew* that it should have been day. I lay there wondering what would happen if it never got light again. I chomped on a couple of granola bars to drown out this breath-held sort of silence of everyone *else* wondering if the lights were ever going to come back on and if someone else would be the first to SCREAM. And then pop! The lights came on and people cheered from in among the little trees.

What I haven't written about is this awesome feeling I had when I saw this place for the first time. I remembered about the explorers – Columbus and Vespucci and Cook and Quadra and my hero Magellan. I can't explain why he's my hero because I know that if we were sitting next to each other on a bus it would be instant hate and loathing. He was a complete fundamentalist and I'm allergic to God-the-Father and all that. But he really believed in his vision. I know it's kind of inconsistent to admire something like that because these people can be real menaces to have around. But there it is. What I started to say is that I was standing looking into one of those caverns and thinking about the guys in those little ships with all those storms and scurvy and mutiny and yellow fever and lashings and maggoty biscuits. I just thought how lucky I was. I'd just blinked and here I was and my body was strong and my spirit was glad and I could really look at what I was seeing. It's hard to put into words. When I've found a place to be I'll get out my paints and start trying to draw what I've been seeing. I might not know what I'm looking for now but I know I'll know it when I find it. It will be the place I want to make my own. I think where I want to be is up in one of the caves in the walls. If you look right at them you can see they're green deep in because there's a sort of green blush. It's not like I don't want to be with people but just that I'm going to be picky. When I find the people I want to be with I'll share my place with them. Until then I'm better off alone.

9 Sophie

Sophie threw an arm across her face in reflex against the light, against dark and frigid winter school mornings, against a careless switch-flick in the on-call room, against prankish brothers. And then remembered. Melisande was butting her head against the knapsack, meowing. Squinting in the sudden light – no different from the fullest light of the 'day' before – she sat up and looked across a dump of stirring bodies, bodies in sleeping bags, under blankets, on blankets, uncovered on the bare green growth. And one, not far away, whom light would never rouse again, the blanket-draped corpse of the man who had died on arrival.

The man's wife, Victoria, was sitting slumped on a suitcase at his head, with her feet tucked well back. She merely lifted her head at the light, and then looked down, nodded slightly, and became still again.

A few people were already standing. The young woman paramedic, Adrienne; her companion, the tawny-haired, tensely handsome man who had kept the count, and later rescued Sophie; a stocky, middle aged man with a weathered, sharp-planed, Slavic face; and a tall, fair-haired man in a white satin shirt, who gestured readily as he spoke. The woman and the second and third man were engrossed in conversation; the tawny man stepped back skittishly as a woman pushed past him, blanket draped around her. His movement, or hers, alerted the stocky man. He looked around, seeing people shuffling needfully from the sprawling group. 'Hey,' he bellowed, in the tones and accent of one of last night's rescuers. 'Piss *away* from the water.' Several of the women flinched; two of the men ignored him. He broke away from the trio, and bore down on them. He redirected them to his chosen area – in a slight dip well away from the walls – and went in a swift scourging circuit of the perimeter, harrying stragglers, whipping the blanket from one squatting woman. She shrieked at him; he screamed back at her. The encampment watched as one, enrapt. She yanked up her jeans as she stood, zipping and buttoning by touch without losing a beat of her invective. A tall woman, she had an inch or so on her opponent, her fair skin scarlet, scalded with embarrassment and fury. 'You've got a fucking *corpse* over there,' she said, flinging out her arm.

'If I did not have to bother with your spoiled habits, I would have seen to that already.'

Several people and groups of people were gathering up their belongings. He turned on them. 'So go! And when you have typhoid and cholera because of your carelessness, do not bleat to me.'

'Arpád,' said the fair man in the satin shirt, 'cool it.' The woman stalked past Arpád, flinging her blanket over her shoulder so he had to deflect it from his face, gathered up her belongings, hissing at the others whom she was travelling with, 'If we were on Earth I'd sue the little bastard.' The women looked sympathetically indignant, one of the two men, neutral, and the other was stifling a grin, poorly. But they gathered up their belongings and straggled after her.

' "The little bastard",' said the man in the white shirt blandly, in a distinctive French accent, 'and having worked with him for seven years

I most readily agree, he is a little bastard,' – Arpád grinned, greatly pleased – 'has for fifteen years been an organiser of refugee and displaced persons camps in Europe and Africa.' He paused, making sure he had their collective attention. 'Now, maybe the aliens are going to show up and escort us to the guest rooms. And maybe they aren't. Maybe these *are* the guest rooms. Any of you ever seen someone with cholera? Ever seen typhoid? Ever had dysentery? Hepatitis? All of them – plus a whole delectable catalogue of others – are fecal-oral transmission. You can guess what that means. All it takes is one carrier. I wouldn't count on the aliens rescuing us from our own carelessness, would you?' A handful more people picked their way out of the camp, refusing to look in his direction. He shrugged and turned his attention back to the rest, dismissing them, and set to organising the building – from camping supplies and sheets – of some modesty screens around the chosen area. Sophie, whose bladder was full but not yet pressingly so, left them to it.

There were still perhaps eighty people in the immediate group, here on the shallow upward slope of the bowl of the cavern. Towards the walls, there were many more, strung out along the edge of the green matting. A number of people were already up and moving, mainly singles and pairs. A kilometre away, perhaps, the floor rose again to a ragged massif of pale 'stone', which, though it looked like the walls, did not radiate light. In the slightly hazy light Sophie might make its silhouette into a castle ruin.

A voice broke her reverie as the white-shirted man came up beside her. 'Sophie, am I right?' He gave her name the French pronunciation. 'I'm Dominic Peltier. You're a physician, I gather.' Seen from close to, he looked older than she had initially thought him, his fair skin aged by sun, the expression lines around eyes and mouth already deepening to grooves, but when he smiled his long face had a certain ravaged attractiveness.

'Yes,' she said. 'But I'd add the caveat that I trained in pathology and have concentrated on research for the past five or six years. If you're looking for a medic, you'd be best to ask around for paramedics, emergency physicians or rural practitioners.'

'Every little helps, and we never know,' he said, and carefully made a note in a burgundy-covered pocket diary.

The camp took shape with surprising speed, water supply at the high end, where the water coursed down the walls and into the green matting, and latrines at the lower end in the hollow. Three side-by-side stalls were already being raised from tent poles and windbreaks, though they listed slightly, the green matting neither deep enough nor strong enough to provide support. People were working with lines and tent pegs and some jocularity to stabilise them, while a short line of others waited. Between the extremes were the bedding and possessions of the night's gathering, in various states of order or strewing. The camp's borders were marked out by three walking sticks set upright in the green matting in a roughly triangular arrangement and decorated with blanched scraps of fluorescent material – the glowing totems of the night before.

She saw Melisande a little way away, nudging and sniffing at a rolled bedroll. She sincerely hoped nobody had either allergies to or an irrational dislike of cats, but as a precaution she lured Melisande back to her with a rattle of pellets into bowl.

A woman picked her way through the bedding to Sophie, an intent expression on her face and a handful of scraps of garish green tartan fluttering in her hand. Sophie shied back as she went to pin one to her sweater, and the woman looked up, startled. 'Oh, sorry,' she said, earnestly. 'Look, you need to wear this. So we know who's allowed in this area.' At Sophie's questioning frown she waved a hand behind her. 'We don't want our belongings looted just because we don't know who's supposed to be in here or not. And it'll help when we get some kind of food distribution set up.' She frowned a little, as though expecting an argument, but when none came she went for Sophie's breast again with ribbon and pin. Sophie let her. 'It's really good,' was her parting comment, as she went in search of another target, 'to have someone who knows how to organise this kind of thing.'

'Sophie!' Dominic hailed her and beckoned her over. He was standing beside the shrouded corpse, along with the tawny-haired man. The paramedic was crouching, her hand on the covers, her face a little pallid despite her training. Sophie started over, but before she reached them the dead man's daughter looked beneath the blanket and shrieked. The noise, thin and arresting, spun out in the still air. People stopped working. The nearest stared; several made sounds of revulsion. Huddled on the ground, the young woman sobbed. The wife, her face drawn, regarded a point on the ground midway between her husband's daughter and her husband's body.

Behind her, Sophie could hear Arpád: 'What are you, *sheep*? Baa, baa, baa. One wanders and all the rest follow after . . .' Dominic murmured, 'Wait a moment.' A man and a woman lifted the sobbing girl and supported her away. 'It's horrible,' she wept. 'Horrible.' The wife raised her head, and panned the onlookers with a cold, disdainful eye, meeting their gazes, one by one. 'What,' she said, sounding hoarse, 'are you looking at?'

They dispersed, except for four of the stronger looking men who were drafted on the spot as sentries. Then Dominic let her turn back the blanket.

The dead man lay in a second shroud, one of pale green fibres, like a fine young growth of the green matting. More like gauze than mould. Sophie looked for a long moment, then scanned the nearby faces, seeing the ribbon-woman standing with gaudy ribbons straggling from her fingers. 'You know where my pack is. Could you bring it to me?' While she waited for her supplies, Sophie peered close, tracking the fine fibres of the shroud down to where they grew into, or out of, the green matting. They branched and intertwined so that she could not tell how long each one might be or whether they were all single strands interwoven, or multiple. Beneath their veil, the man's features were already indistinct, more indistinct than she thought they should be. Was the blurring because, as well as growing up around it, the green fibres were growing into the dead flesh? The messenger returned with her backpack. Sophie rummaged out the instruments and supplies she had assembled – more, she had thought, for show than assuming need – and found a package of sterile gloves. She gloved, put out a hand to touch the shroud, then remembered the man's wife, and looked up, 'May I?' The woman nodded, staring down with steady attention. Sophie brushed lightly and then more firmly at the shroud, trying to spread the fibres with her fingers. Nothing yielded. She opened a packaged scalpel and, with a glance for permission, cut her way into the shroud, to expose the skin of one of the hands that lay on his chest, lightly fuzzed in green.

She leaned forward and delicately with the scalpel tried to peel the fuzz back. She shaved it instead. The fuzz was indeed rooted in the skin – having grown into it, or grown through from beneath and out.

'No . . . more,' Victoria said, putting the words together carefully.

Sophie nodded. She deliberately laid aside the scalpel and, moving her hand to the man's belly, pressed down on it. It felt firm, without the beginnings of gaseous bloat, but under most circumstances it would be too soon for that. She tried to slide her hands beneath him, and took up her scalpel again to let her cut through the base of his shroud, to see if he were bound by one layer, or tethered throughout his underside. She burrowed to several centimetres' depth between grey fabric and matting, but found no end to the fine green thicket. She withdrew the scalpel and said quietly, 'If you'd intended moving him, you should probably rethink. He's well bound down.' She laid the blanket over his face again, and looked around unthinkingly for sharps and biohazard disposal bins. Then, with a rueful smile and great care, she slid the scalpel back into its package and carefully drew off the gloves, keeping them right side out instead of stripping them. There looked to be no replacements.

'What is happening to him?' Victoria asked, in a rusty voice.

'I think,' Sophie said, 'though this is just a guess,' the woman looked vaguely irritated at such evasiveness, 'that his body is being absorbed by the green growth . . . whatever it is.'

The woman blinked slowly. 'He would have appreciated that,' she said. Seeing their shock, she looked briefly surprised. 'Of course,' she said, forgivingly, 'you didn't know him. Ecology was his field.' Grief washed down her face like the water on the walls. She seemed almost taken aback by it. 'I am sorry if it inconveniences your planning, but this is his grave, and so it shall remain. We shall leave him here. And I would quite like to go elsewhere for a short time.'

The paramedic stepped in, took her arm and guided her, or was guided by her, past the sentries. She balked only when she saw herself being directed towards her stepdaughter.

'Some sort of fungus?' the tawny man, Stephen, remarked to her. He had a bright, skittish eye, and a smile which dared her to like him and to try to make him like her. She declined to play. She had delicate antennae for instability.

LaFleurette, returning, picked up the thought. 'I wonder how deep those fibres have penetrated? Or whether they were growing in or out? We've been breathing who knows what particulates and spores for the last twenty-four hours or so. Let's just hope our immune systems'll hold them in check.'

Dominic said, 'I'll thank you kindly not to speculate too audibly on that theme in other people's hearing.'

She gave him a thin smile. 'Of course not.'

'If you're done here,' Dominic said, 'there's something else I'd like you to do.' It was, by his tone, a delicate matter. 'Until we've located a food source we're wanting to establish a central food depot, so we can share and ration our food stocks. I'd like you to go around and speak to everyone, and ask them if they would be willing to contribute to a common store.'

'And if they're not willing,' said LaFleurette, 'what then?'

He measured her. 'I realise this may seem presumptuous to you, but it might be crucial to our survival that we are able to make our food last as long and go as far as we can. And it is also a principle that we intend this community, if it is to be a community, to live by. In answer to your question, if they're not willing, then we shall ask them to move outside our borders.'

LaFleurette shook her head, once. 'I'm sorry,' she said, 'but I'm not going to do that for you. I think it's too early. You're asking for a kind of trust you haven't earned, yet.' She gestured. 'There are people out there who planned and prepared for this. They're the ones you'll be wanting to attract, not the freeloaders who have come expecting to be taken care of.' Her eyes challenged him to take issue with the derogatory term.

Moving black caught Sophie's eye, and she glanced that way without thinking why. A quintet of black-garbed young people, three men and two women, were making their uncertain way into the heart of the camp. One of the boys had a bandaged hand and wrist, and with a shock Sophie recognised the faces she had seen by lighter-flame last night. Their eyes slid by her, unrecognising.

LaFleurette's eyes had followed hers. She said flatly to Dominic, 'Prove you can keep creeps like them in line, and then maybe you'll have the right to ask people for their food.'

The woman with the ribbons accosted them as they moved away. Stephen would not let her pin the ribbon on him but lifted it from her hand, staring her down with a metallic eye. After she had gone, he opened his hand and let it slide to the matting. 'I've got to get out of here,' he said to LaFleurette ignoring Sophie.

The words passed between them like a code. She said, after a moment, 'Be careful.' She watched, steadily, as anger flickered in his face, presently replaced by a twisted smile. 'You want to stay with this bunch?'

'I'll see.'

For a moment their gazes locked, then he shifted his pack – which he had never laid down – and made his way across the strewn ground. She watched him go with lips drawn thin. '. . . my brother's keeper?' she murmured. Then she stooped, plucked up the fallen ribbon and slipped it into her pocket.

'You've known him long,' Sophie said.

'Over half my life,' she said. 'I suppose we should find something to do to make ourselves useful.' She glanced around, shook her head slightly. 'Whatever I imagined, it was not this. So, why's a Harvard-educated physician running away to join the gypsies?'

Sophie gave her a tight smile. 'Haven't you heard? Nobody gets tenure at Harvard.'

LaFleurette smiled more easily. 'You planning on staying with this crew?'

'If,' Sophie said, 'I can find what I need to pursue my research, then I'll stay.'

'And your research?'

'Medical,' Sophie said. 'Neurodegenerative disorders.'

'You're here hoping the aliens will have a cure?'

'Yes,' Sophie said briefly. 'And you?'

'Looking for a different life, I suppose,' LaFleurette said as briefly but her eyes, Sophie noticed, followed Stephen. 'And I suppose because I am my brother's keeper.' She looked back at Sophie. 'Tell me about your work. Maybe I can help.' A twisted smile. 'I wanted to go to med school, once upon a time. No money,' she said without rancour, 'and bad grades, because school was just a place to survive. I didn't even know I could learn until I started night school.'

Sophie studied the striking, guarded face with its carefully applied, intensely coloured cosmetics. LaFleurette was almost certainly of mixed blood, three or four ways, perhaps – black, certainly, native American and/or Mexican, very probably, added to the white donor of those hazel eyes – vulnerable to all people's racism. And for all that, or because of that, a proud woman. 'I've always thought,' Sophie said carefully, 'there was a lot of waste of ability in our system. Back on Earth.'

LaFleurette's smile was wry and forgiving. 'So here's hoping the aliens don't make the same mistake.'

10 Stephen

Bitch, Stephen thought, and broke into a run. His own thoughts appalled him. Like a wolf pack circling in his head. He had never been so aware how love and hate, desire and violence were entangled, as he was now. Bitch. Why wouldn't she come with him?

She *had* come with him, he thought. Left to herself she would have stayed in Seattle, doing the work she was so good at, trying to understand why her love affairs always turned to dust, waiting, enduring and always knowing how much worse things might be – the only kind of contentment she could bring herself to expect. But she had come with him. So why couldn't she come all the way with him? Why insist on staying with those tin-pot dictators and that band of losers? Why couldn't she see how much he needed her, right now? A woman he could trust.

Maybe that was why. She distrusted need, the need which turned into demands – for servicing, for submission. She preferred to meet need within the boundaries of her profession. For fifteen years he had watched her walk away from men who thought 'I need you' was a declaration of love.

But didn't she understand she would be responsible if . . .?

He silenced the thought. She would despise him for it, for the manipulation it was. He could be in the mountains now, he thought. In the North West rainforest, amongst the huge sequoias. He could outlast winter there, outlast winter and manhunts and publicity. He should have gone to the mountains.

His shoulder twinged suddenly, bringing with it a visceral memory of the explosion within, of blood spray and a stinging spatter of fragmented bone. He shuddered, remembering. At twilight a half-drunk hunter had taken him for a deer. He still felt the bullet's impact in his nightmares, and would wake thinking the sweat on his face was blood and waiting for the agony to start. He remembered the round pink face of the man looking down at him, like a flushed moon. Sometimes, after a nightmare, he planned his own hunt. The judge had been lenient. The hunter and his companions had expended the utmost effort to get him to help, applying rudimentary first aid and lugging him three hours down the trail. One had suffered a heart attack immediately afterwards, and stood frail and attenuated on the witness stand. His shamed glances towards Stephen said he understood, understood in a way that only a man who had himself known pain and the fear of death ever could. But the judge decreed that, beyond the original misjudgement, they had done everything they could; he had said, in essence, go forth and sin no more. Stephen had felt no great sense of betrayal; he had lost all faith in the system years before. But he would always cherish the memory of Fleur, in her black courthouse suit, her glossy hair piled on her head, pivoting on one spike heel to spit on the courthouse steps. She despised alcohol users and abusers and all who indulged them.

That was why he had not gone to the mountains. He had been hunted before.

He dropped to his haunches and braced elbows on thighs, balancing the weight of the pack on his back. Pointedly, he called to mind the image of his room in the basement apartment in Seattle, maps on all four walls, doors, ceiling. Maps of Earth as it had been during the great migrations of antiquity, during the great ages of exploration in the thirteenth, fourteenth and fifteenth centuries, as America opened up. Maps of the Moon, Mars and Venus. All these frontiers of history, all these frontiers found and opened by other men. The hope of frontier had always tranquillised him, even in the foster homes. The hope of going somewhere else, quiet, empty, ownerless. He soothed himself on that hope. The voices around him no longer spiked through him, even the screeches of women and children. Fleur he could at this moment forgive. The mountains he could leave behind. He pushed a hand into a side-pouch, seeking his sketchbook. He held in his mind the maps he would make, of this place, of the stars. Held it still as a shield against the intrusions of others, the rage within.

11   Hathaway

This is still the same day and I think I discovered something. Uncle Stan would be real proud of me. I wish I knew whether he'd made it or not because last time I spoke he was worried about being washed out because of his migraines, but I think it was just that he was surrounded by all these superfit military types and his inferiority complex was showing. I guess having seen Dave and Johnny grow up I know what's going on with him. He's not quite gotten away from the old neighbourhood where the guys who ruled were the ones in the gang and the only way to be top the little kids knew was by being big and tough and mean. Even a really smart kid like Uncle Stan who was doing everything he had to to get out. Anyway, if he didn't make it these letters are for him too. What happened was I was sitting down resting – I've kept walking around just seeing what's what and who's who but my ankles were beginning to blimp up – so I was sitting sort of rubbing my fingers on the grey stonestuff and trying to think of how I'd describe the feel. And then I noticed where my fingers were a little ridge grew up. I wasn't sure whether it'd been there before so I moved along a little and tried again and this time I made a little dip. I started experimenting with rubbing hard and rubbing soft and what happens is if you rub hard you make a dip and if you rub lightly you make a ridge and there's a real feel to how hard you press and how quickly you rub. So what I'm doing is sitting against a wall behind the little trees and making a ladder. There's a cave just above me with a kind of green blush like there's greenstuff in it. I want to go up and take a look. The ladder'll be hidden by the little trees at least half way, and light sort of seeps out of everywhere so there won't be any shadows to show the rest of them up.

Mom, remember when you had that job cleaning places when I was little? You'd smuggle me in and threaten me with A Fate Worse Than Death if I so much as left a fingerprint and then you'd sit me down on a newspaper with my paper and crayons like I was a puppy that hadn't been housebroken. And you know something. Even though a little part of me was envious of these people who had what I didn't – especially if there were kids in the place and I got to see all their toys – a lot more of me thought it was everything that I was just there when nobody knew. It was like I was stealing their lives for a while. They'd never know but it would be stored up in my head for all time. I turned into a champion sneaker-in to all kinds of places. Now I'm going to sneak into a cave . . .

And I've done it. (This is the next day.) I finished my ladder in the dark last night – that was some scary – but it went really fast. If you stroke the stonestuff in just the right way it just kind of flows around your fingers. I hauled my stuff up and rolled up in my sleeping bag and zzzzzd until someone threw the light switches. All my fingertips are red and sore and my wrists feel like I've been typing for three days straight. Even my toes hurt. I'm going to just lay around today and think about how I'm going to get up and down later on when my stomach's sticking way out. Even now climbing is not real fun. Maybe I can scoop out some sort of tunnel.

About my cave. It goes quite deep into the wall and is full of these little trees. They're not at all like fir trees or Christmas trees back home though they more or less look it. But they're not even as high as my chest and they're fuzzy like caterpillars all over. Soft but with just a little spikiness. There's greenstuff all over the floor. Water trickles down one side, and I think I can make a kind of piping system. I've picked a spot well away from the water to use for a bathroom. Guess what I forgot to bring – toilet paper. So I'm cutting up and using greenstuff. There's a big smooth wall that I've got my eye on for drawing and painting. I was going to show the aliens how we did art and going to get them to show me how they do art. Remember the downtown mural project I worked on that summer a couple of years ago when I decided I was going to be an urban artist? I never changed my mind no matter how much yakkity-yak I got about *realistic career options*. At school they didn't think I'd a whole lot of talent. The way kids in art class painted all kinds of *droopy* paintings of old homeless people and little starving children and they were all well composed and pretty like they'd seen them on TV. But I didn't paint stuff from TV but stuff I had seen and stuff I had felt. And maybe it was because I just am not old enough to get it right or maybe they're right and I just don't have any talent – but it always comes out looking as though it's been fought over when art is supposed to look easy. Mr Rosen's the only teacher who likes what I do and he says I had no business trying to paint the way I was for about twenty more years. He told me at my age I should be painting all poignant like I'm just discovering how *sad* life is. He said I paint as though I've known life is sad all my life and I've gotten on to painting angry and funny. He said it kind of in fun and kind of like he was warning me. But I don't know about what. Adults have this bizarre attitude to kids like us. It's like we've Lost Our Innocence, and should be pitied. But if our Innocence is so precious how come they do zilch to protect it? I mean, the same people who natter about the Precious Innocence of Childhood vote so that people like Mom can't get enough money together to get us out of Skunk Alley? I mean, what was she supposed to do? (We all know the answer to that. There is something real screwed about a system where the most a woman can ever earn is on her back. Pun intended.)

You know, I'm sitting here thinking that I should have started writing things down like this a long time ago. I guess it's because that dumb family therapist Claris kept trying to *encourage* me that I didn't. For one thing she kept saying how people would *respect my privacy* like this was some big present she was giving me and not something that was mine by right. But I guess she had something. Getting mad on paper makes me feel better not so much because I'm not angry any more but because I know what I'm angry *about*. I've drawn lines about it and found that my anger doesn't fill the world and in fact there are big spaces where I'm not angry at all. I know diaries are supposed to be a girl thing and you would have your nails pulled out one by one before you did anything girly but you should try it, Dave. And lighten up about the boy/girl thing. You're going to miss a lot of fun that way. If I'd believed them about what a girl ought to be I wouldn't be here. So there.

12 Stephen

Light leaped on him, waking him; he started upright, head into fuzzy leaves that tickled like tiny fingers. He shoved them aside, rising. This cavern was smaller than the two he had already mapped, less than a kilometre if the first row of upper caves was at the same fifteen metre height. The fuzz-leaved little trees irritated the hell out of him. They didn't look right; they didn't feel right; they didn't even breathe right – no resin, no pine-scent, no acidic loam and compost.

Yesterday he had traded one of his candles for a protractor and a handwritten list of the common trigonometric functions. He did not miss the candle. It was not that his night vision was exceptional, but that he had learned to extend his senses and not insulate himself from his surroundings with earphones and education. He was growing to prefer the nights, with just enough light and just enough sound to texture the darkness around him. Very few people moved around at night. At night he could almost believe he was alone.

A quiet unease had succeeded the original excitement. They had lighting, warmth and water, but as yet no food. People waited, expectant and fretful as baby birds, to be fed. He despised them. He himself had food enough for fourteen days yet, unrationed, and if he lived lean, twenty-one or more. He reckoned he could last a month or two of outright starvation. Hunger and he were old acquaintances. Water, though, water he had for only a day or so more. He could applaud Arpád's obsession with keeping the water supply uncontaminated, even though he knew he'd go crazy under Arpád's regime. Fleur seemed quite content, wholly involved. Yesterday he had stood watching her bright red sweater from across the cavern as she bustled between groups of people, making her rounds. He was quite sure she was unaware of him; perhaps she had not even thought about him since he left. She seemed to have taken up with the blonde doctor. His thoughts were bitter, and they worried him. In the end, he left the cavern, and extended his explorations. He did not need Fleur, any more than she needed him.

He ate sparingly, and drank well, and peed on a tree, well away from the nearest waterfall. Then he started his circumnavigation of the cavern, counting steps, and pausing at intervals to take sightings of the other side.

He was deep into the cavern, in an area where the little trees pressed up against the dry wall, when he rubbed up against a ledge and saw that someone had worked hand- and foot-holds into the rock. Someone clumsy and not very tall, because the hollows were closer and deeper than he would have needed them. They disappeared over the lip of the lowest cave, but they could have gone higher – he couldn't tell with the light. Still, he thought it worth a look.

His pack not being weighted or balanced for climbing, he shed it, pushing it beneath the shelter of one of the little trees. He would not be long. He breezed up the wall, easy.

The cave was inhabited, he saw that at once. He moved inwards from the lip of the cave, partly for safety, partly that he not attract attention. It was a competent little campsite. A sleeping bag had been laid out on the green matting, untidily, as though left in eagerness. On it was a battered outback hat, complete with corks, and a pair of homemade buckskins with beaded fringes. Beyond that the wall of water had been directed into a quite creditable basin, and on shaped spikes, a bra and two pairs of panties were drying. She wasn't skinny, whoever she was.

He had a sense he was being watched. He turned his head slowly and met the eyes of a girl who had just stuck her round head up from under the matting by the far wall like a gopher out of a hole. Her hair was black, her eyes a dark brown, her brows thick, distinctive and dark. Hispanic ancestry in there someplace. She had a square, almost jowlish face; he understood the shape of it as she heaved herself out of the hole and he saw that the weight was the padding of pregnancy. She was in her late teens, dressed in black jeans and a man's checked shirt in a hideous lime and black check, with hem hanging out and sleeves rolled up saggingly.

She set her feet apart, folded her arms above the solid bulge of her belly and scowled at him. 'What do you want?'

'And top of the morning to you too,' he said, mildly.

'I don't give bugfuck what time it is,' she said, with a tilt to her chin that suggested she was well used to provoking adults.

He went to the edge of the hole and looked down. She had already dropped it more than her own height. He noted that, although the bottommost walls of the tunnel were opaque, the upper walls had already begun to shed their own light, dimmer at the bottom, brighter at the top. 'Fast work.'

She looked down into her hole, then back at him, her face giving nothing away. He had met a dozen girls like her, in the foster homes, girls who gave no ground, passed no slight. He had never understood them. Boys had no choice but to fight. Girls did not have to; why should some invite it?

She said, 'Thank-you-very-much. Goodbye-and-please-don't-call-again.'

He said, unperturbed, 'You've done more here than anyone else I've seen so far. Would you care to show me how it's done?'

'And if I do?'

'Then I go. And if you don't then I go as well.'

She looked at him for another long moment, and then with a grunt slid back into her hole. The light shone up on her skin, showing it shiny, flushed and unevenly blemished. Her eyelashes cast no shadows. He watched her kneel at the base of the hole, both hands on the coarse greyish surface. She swept briskly, two-handed, with a clean, fast rhythm, and the depression deepened seemingly with each sweep. He leaned forward to see whether she had anything in her hands, or whether there was anything, anything at all, that she was doing differently from any of the half a dozen people he had watched at work on the walls. She did not look up at him, but the set of her shoulders was aware and still resentful.

He said, 'That's faster than I've seen anyone else move it.'

She straightened up, hand on belly, and burped loudly at the blank wall. 'They'll get it.'

It might be, he thought, something particular about her, her touch, the secretions on her hands. Or the pressure, or the rhythm of her sweeps . . . They were almost hypnotic. He looked away and caught sight of colour on the far side of the miniature copse, colour which, after only three days of white and grey and green, he already found strange. He got to his feet and went deeper into the cave, and found himself before a wall of drawings. A fan of thick sidewalk chalk lay spilled out of a box at the base of the wall. The drawings were crude, rough as their materials, but they reminded him a little – vaguely – of El Greco, in the attenuated forms and the detailed, languishing hands. That could be none other than Ferdinand Magellan, surely, in his black, with his tense, ascetic face. And that had to be Vespucci, and that the beginning of a reproduction of that immortal photograph of Armstrong on the Moon, the monolithic figure with the round bubble head, barely sketched in. There was more; odd scattered lines, not even recognisable shapes, the artist making notes to herself.

He felt, as before, the prickle of her regard. He said, 'Magellan,' without turning.

'Yeah,' she said, less brusquely.

'I'm exploring,' he said. 'Mapping this ship.'

She blew a strand of hair from her face, a graceless, uncoy huff. 'Then suppose you leave this place off your maps.'

'Suppose I do,' he said, blandly, and pulled his notebook from his pocket, offering the page to her. 'It's rough; it will need to be redrawn.' She came nearer, wary as a wild animal, and stopped near enough to see, far enough to be out of reach. She watched as he knelt to sketch in her cave, depicting it as much shallower than its true depth. He said, 'I thought that that would attract less interest than "Here be dragons".'

After a long, resisting moment, she smiled.

13 Hathaway

Good morning Earth! It's our fourth day up here and your April tenth, I guess, though I might be wrong with the days seeming way longer. I better figure out how to keep track because I'm going to want to know when I'm getting close to D-day. I'm working hard on my tunnel even though sitting all hunched down in a hole gives me *terminal* acid stomach. My pregnancy book says that's normal. It gives me such a laugh, going on about making your partner feel involved (hah! – any time he sees me in the halls his eyes sort of bounce off my stomach and he'd look all sort of *pathetic* like I'd done something to him) and arranging day care and discussing maternity leave with your employer and making sure your other kids don't feel left out. It makes things so complicated. (Though it's way better than that teeny preggy book they gave me at the clinic. That was so dumbed down and *condescending*). But it's all so irrelevant. All the baby needs to do is grow and all I need do is build my cave and draw on my mural and eat and sleep and write these letters. I guess it'll get complicated again because sooner or later I'll have to meet up with people again but I'm not going to rush in.

Well, I guess that's life. Just after I wrote that, I got discovered. It was this guy called Stephen who's mapping all the caves and tunnels (just because he wants to, he says). He was walking around the walls and he came on my handholds and climbed up and found me working away at my tunnel. I wasn't real thrilled. I told him this was my place and anyone who wanted to take it away from me was going to have a problem. I guess I should have realised when he was out surveying alone that he maybe wasn't into being a drone in someone's organisation. He says things downstairs are a bit untidy and they'll get worse if some food doesn't turn up soon. He was interested in what I've been able to do with the shaping and he looked at the mural which I've only just started and liked it. He's got a kind of twitchy secretive face, all very polite and interested but you wonder what's going on inside. He showed me how he was going to draw my cave in on his maps, which is way shallower than it really is with nothing in it that anyone would want to see. He also told me how to bring my tunnel out so nobody could see it unless they were on top of it. I didn't quite know what I was supposed to do then but he wasn't giving off signals like I should get down on my knees and suck so I just thanked him. Maybe I'll see him again. Actually I guess I want to see him again. I'm not a natural loner.

14 Sophie

On the fifth day, Sophie resigned her Camp membership by throwing her tartan ribbon at Dominic's feet.

'It is not enough,' she said, 'that you appropriate my food and ration it out to me, that you lay claim to the equipment and instruments I have brought for my work, that you demand my grandfather's wristwatch as commonhold timepiece, that you expect me to be on call every minute of every hour of every day, to the total exclusion of any work that I might intend. But you do not even have the decency to enforce my wishes about the treatment of my cat, and help me prevent her from being grabbed and fondled by everyone whom it pleases, and now you have the temerity to decree to me that I may not go outside the Camp to look for her now she has had enough of it, because you have decided I am too precious to risk losing.'

They were standing in the shelter of the massif, in a crescent-shaped bay partially screened from the remainder of the cavern by several fused columns of grey 'stone'. It had been taken over by Arpád, Dominic, and the several other men and women who had experience in large-scale administration and crisis management, and who were coming to constitute the encampment's governing committee.

'I realise,' Dominic said, taking a visible grip on his temper, 'we are being been high handed. But we've had good reason. Without food things are going to start breaking down very quickly unless order or fairness are seen to be maintained. If there's a suggestion of privilege or hoarding, we'll be seeing scapegoating and gang action. The difference between these people and the ones usually in refugee camps, Sophie, is that these ones are just so damn well fed and full of energy and full of their rights.' There was anger in his voice now, and she well knew how he was holding himself back from accusing her. 'We've had to pull in our scouting parties because of the situation in some of the other caves – which is why it is not a good idea –'

'You seem to regard people's objections to encroachment on our fundamental rights as mere petulance.' She was almost laughing, but with sheer rage. 'You have no legal justification for what you are doing and precious scant moral justification.'

He seemed to collapse in on himself slightly. 'Sophie, Melisande could already be dead. I do know how people behave when they're hungry, and some of the people in the other caverns have been fasting for several days –'

'My cat?' Sophie said, her voice rising. 'They would *eat my cat*?'

His eyes flickered around them; she let him worry about bystanders and stayed staring at him in appalled anger that anyone civilised could even suggest this, much less *do* it. 'If people are hungry enough, for long enough, they will eat *anything*, animal or human,' Dominic said, and in one hideous image she grasped the shape of his dread.

'My God,' she said, 'have you ever *seen* that?' – a question she rejected the moment it was uttered as naive and effete and which mercifully he did not answer.

'So you understand why we cannot let you leave –'

She brought up her hand, palm out, stopping him. 'I understand,' she said precisely, 'why you are *advising* me against leaving.' She paused, letting him appreciate the distinction. 'And I suggest that you begin to develop something like a formal constitution, so that our rights and obligations to each other may be explicitly understood. Assuming that we do not ultimately degenerate into chaos and cannibalism, for all your good offices.'

She left the ribbon lying where it was, and turned and stalked out of the crescent. She repacked her depleted bag – at least she had managed to keep the cat food – and hefted the cat-carrier. She had known something might have happened to her vagrant cat even before she spoke to Dominic, but the worst she could have imagined was that someone might have shot her for sport or target practice. That someone might *eat* her repelled her far more profoundly than the idea of human cannibalism. Which was not the usual perspective, pointed out the little inner voice she had developed in medical school to warn her when professional fascination was transgressing good taste.

She tacked her way out of the camp. 'A white cat? Have you seen a white Siamese cat?' She refused to discuss where she was going or whether she was leaving or when she was coming back. 'I'm looking for my cat.' Someone thought they had seen a white cat around the massif. Someone else thought they had seen a white cat heading out the major exit tunnel at the far end of the cavern. A third person thought the women separatists might have had a white cat, remarking snidely that it would have to be female for them to keep it. Melisande seemed ubiquitous.

She had just left the massif and surely if Melisande had been nosing around someone would have run after her to tell her. The major tunnel led to a four way intersection, and each one of those tunnels led to more caverns, more tunnels, more people, an overwhelming ramification of possibilities. So she started with the women's cave midway down the side of the cavern.

There was a single woman standing guard over the entrance. She was lanky and moderately tall, with an unbrushed mop of dark hair turning grey. Her earrings were huge fine hoops of purple-plated metal which nearly brushed her bony shoulders. She wore black stirrup pants and running shoes and a purple exercise top with a university emblem. She said, by way of greeting, 'Couldn't say whether you're coming to join us or one of the tartan terrors coming to complain about the markers.' She flipped a bony hand towards the nearest portion of the arc of tartan bedecked boundary poles – a brown tartan this time – which bent sharply inwards to meet the wall on the far side of the cave mouth rather than the near. A shallower arc of empty holes extended from the boundary rim and terminated between the cave mouth and the main exits. 'We're due a right of way, we think,' the woman said. 'Where's your bit of ribbon?' There was Scot in the rasping voice, much diluted.

'I left it behind. And no, I'm not coming to join you. I am looking for my cat. White cat, Siamese. She has a collar –'

'Name of Melisande. Aye, she's here,' she said, a little flatly, and stepped aside so as to admit Sophie.

The tunnel was longer than Sophie anticipated, with a curved floor and too low a ceiling. She straightened up at the other end with gratitude, set down the cat-carrier and unshouldered her knapsack.

At the far end of the small cave, a work-gang of women and children were converting an outcropping of the wall into an impressive system of pools and channels. Half way up the water-curtain, two women hung in climbing harness, bracing their knees against the wall as they sculpted a long, sloping gutter down towards the summit of the outcropping. Another two women perched on the summit, fashioning a groove and a spout, and the rest worked to fashion the stepwise system of shallow pools which would carry the water downwards to ground level. There must have been at least twenty-five of them, helped and hindered by a dozen children. Another dozen or so were busy on the long dry honeycombed wall to her left, working on extruding a ramp up to one of the shallow pockets. White-haired Marian West was one of those. Both groups were being bossed by Hannah, who had a handful of scraps of paper and on her face the intense, muted delight of a visionary.

The children peeled off like a cloud of flies from a discarded hamburger and tore in her direction, a dark-haired, freckle-faced boy at their head. Sophie had experience enough of young cousins to immediately attach the epithet 'devil' to that face. She smiled. Seeing the cat-carrier, he didn't smile back. 'Aw bummer.'

Maybe that was why the lanky woman had spoken so flatly, fearing disappointment to the children. The boy said, 'You oughtn't to take her now, anyway. She's been real sick.'

'Sick?'

The mismatched pair, Hannah and Dove, arrived at a trot. There was an underlay of reserve in their greeting, too, but when she mentioned her errand their faces relaxed and their smiles warmed. At what? That her errand was personal and not representative? Just how much friction had there been between the women's group and the main cavern?

'When Melisande strolled in here a couple of days ago it was as though Christmas had arrived,' Hannah said. 'I have to confess I'm hoping we can come to some kind of arrangement.' Her broad face had the wistful ingenuousness of a huge child.

'I understand she's been ill.'

'Yes,' and a guilty expression crossed Hannah's face. 'But we do have a vet with us and she thinks she's on the mend.'

The women's living area was to the right of the waterfall, a shanty town of ropes slung between points in the walls and posts, and draped with lengths of fabric.

'We agreed everyone would bring wool and fabric,' Dove said. 'The women who sew are outraged at the use we're making of it, but it will survive.'

'It's temporary until we finish our permanent settlement.' Hannah chuckled. 'We haven't been able to agree on what exactly the verb should be. It's more like sculpting than building.'

She needed only the barest encouragement to display the papers in her hands, which were astonishingly detailed blueprints for a three or four level cave-village sculpted from the pocketed wall behind them. The pockets had been deepened, shaped and interconnected within, and the entrances made accessible by ramps, balconies and bridges. It was a far more appealing design than anything that had been mooted in the main camp. 'Hannah was going to go back to school to train as an architect,' Dove offered.

Melisande was lying in a nest of pillows and blankets, attended by a small woman with blonde hair cut in a ragged shag and the weathered complexion of someone who worked outdoors. 'Barrett, our vet.'

'I have to admit I'm more a farm vet than a small animal person,' the vet admitted, 'but she seems to be getting better regardless.'

55

Getting better she might be, but she still looked alarmingly ill. Scenting Sophie, she pushed herself to her feet, and scrambled out of her nest. Sophie dropped to her knees to let her crawl on to her lap, feeling her rattle with her familiar, harsh purr. 'What is wrong with her?'

'We don't know,' Barrett said. 'She ran a very high temperature yesterday and most of last night. As I say I'm not a small animals vet and all I could do was apply general principles. Give her fluids and keep her quiet.' She shook her head and said ruefully, 'I was *very* twitchy because the kids had gotten so involved. I've nothing against small critters themselves. It's the small *owners* who terrify me – all the floods of tears if anything happens to the brutes.'

Melisande squirmed under Sophie's hand and toothed her thumb lightly, a sign that Sophie had caused her insult or discomfort. Barrett said, watching Sophie's hand, 'Yes, there's what looks like a nasty flea bite there on her flank,' Sophie felt the little lump with a cautious pass of her hand, 'but just the one. She seems to find it quite uncomfortable. I don't suppose you brought anything with you in the way of supplies. And food. We've nothing in the way of cat food.'

Sophie gathered Melisande in her arms. 'I've got cat food in my pack,' she said, starting to rise.

'One of us will get –' Dove started, and stopped as she saw Sophie's face change.

That was what had been staring her in the face. She had thought the different atmosphere in here was simply because their leadership was not anticipating crisis and creating tensions. But no. 'We have no *cat* food,' Barrett had said. And though the women might put a brave face on hunger, the children would not.

No wonder her arrival had made them tense, if they had a stockpile of food, while the main encampment was crying crisis and trying to impound all the stores it could access.

She said, testing, 'You're well stocked for food for yourselves, then.'

Dove, Barrett and Hannah looked at each other. 'We should show her,' Barrett said. 'Let her know what to look for.' There was a small pause. 'If they don't find it outside, we'll have to negotiate with them anyway. They'll start to work it out, unless we seal off the door.'

'You've found a food source,' Sophie said.

'You'd better give me Melisande before you go and look at it,' Barrett said with a certain air of challenge – directed at the others. Then to Sophie, 'I'm afraid that it's possible she became ill just after we fed her some of the . . . well, the kids call it gingerbread.'

'What Barrett means,' Hannah said, 'is that we used her as a test subject, deliberately . . . I'm sorry.' Sophie's arms tightened; Melisande purred more loudly. 'It was that, or one of us.'

Sophie swallowed. 'I do understand your reasoning.'

There was a small silence.

'As it turned out,' Dove said, with deliberate cheer, 'the kids had already tried it. When Melisande became so ill we tried to impress upon them that they must not touch it. Mark piped up and insisted it couldn't be the food because he had already eaten it.'

'But it may not agree with Melisande,' Barrett cautioned. 'I'm not sure what you're going to do about feeding her when your own supplies run out. I haven't seen any wildlife whatsoever aboard this ship.'

'Maggie said she saw some kind of flying insect last time she was out moving the boundary posts,' Hannah said.

'That Maggie,' said Barrett, with equal affection and exasperation. 'What does a right of way matter, compared to the rest of it?' To Sophie she said, 'We hope to God there's some out there because there isn't enough here to feed your lot. And I warn you, we won't go down without a fight. We left Earth to get away from being allowed independence only as long as we didn't have something that males felt they were entitled to.'

That bitter determination was shared by all three, and touched something in Sophie that she rarely let come to mind, all the small insults and impositions that came with being female in a male-centred society. She had learned early that if she wanted the rewards of that society there were things she had simply not to notice, or not think about, to be able to live with herself and others.

Hannah said, 'What we mean is that we don't want you to tell anyone what we have. No matter what happens out there.'

'I can't promise that,' Sophie said. She handed over Melisande, who protested with encouraging vigour, and stood up to show Hannah and Dove that she was still willing to follow, if they were still willing to lead.

She had noticed the dark green screen thrown over the very end of one tethering rope and had assumed it was a latrine. But the true latrine, she now saw, was midway towards the door, well away from water and living area. Behind the dark green screen, in the depths of a cleft, a dark amber extrusion stuccoed the wall. Its margins were golden and liquid. Golden syrup, Sophie thought, and indeed there seemed to be a slight syrup smell like the lingering scent from candy making days before. They had made candy at Lister's pond, fudge in the heat of summer, and toffee as the evenings turned cool, and the kitchen had smelled like this for days, fading ever so slowly. She could see finger gouges and knife-slashes where lumps had been levered off, leaving rough cleavage planes.

Dove broke off a handful. 'You're welcome to try some, if you're prepared to excuse my fingers.' She offered it to Hannah, who took it in an entirely matter-of-fact fashion which left Sophie unsure as to whether a point was being made or not. It had the bizarre feel of an afternoon tea, complete with cucumber sandwiches and scones. She took a small quantity from Dove's hand, put it into her mouth, and chewed.

Despite its appearance, it was neither sticky nor overly sweet. The closest analogy she could find for its texture was coconut, but it was softer than that. Dove said, 'Needless to say we haven't the faintest idea whether this will fulfil all our nutritional needs. Maggie – you'll have met her coming in – and Marian West have had their heads together trying to come up with chemical tests. Maggie's a biochemist, Marian was an industrial chemist. They've confirmed the presence of starch, sugar and protein readily enough with bits and pieces from our first aid kit and some chemicals Maggie brought, but vitamins and minerals and all the trace elements, we haven't a clue. We just have to hope that they are included because this is rapidly becoming our only food source. It's not too monotonous as yet, but it would be nice if we could count on some flavourings and variation in texture. You'll notice if you look closely it seems to be secreted or extruded in a liquid form and harden on contact with air. The liquid's quite bitter: obviously we're not supposed to take it until it's finished.'

Sophie swallowed her morsel. Her stomach rumbled for more. 'Thank you,' she said, 'for showing me what to look for. I'm going to leave my backpack and cage here for the time being – there's food in the backpack for Melisande. I'll scout the edge of the cavern. I'll be back to let you know what I find.' She paused. 'I'll let you know if I decide I have to tell them.'

They were not happy, but they let her go.

It was a slow search. Mindful that the extrusion had been in a cleft and would have been hidden from chance discovery even without the screen, she made it her business to peer into every tunnel and behind each outcropping. It could have gone so much faster if she could have had help, but to secure help she would have had to explain herself – and what could she have said without letting it be known that the women had their own supply. Accounting for it if she found it would require creativity enough. Fortunately the majority of the people had moved into the centre to be near the food store, although she found herself so aggressively warned off one side cave that she made a silent resolve that if nothing came of her search she would draw Dominic's attention to this area. They were hiding something.

She was behind the massif and beginning to have a cold sense of failure when she found the first extrusion, a mass of golden brown hidden by a twist of claystone, easily double the size of the one in the women's cave. She broke off a little and nibbled on it; it was the same substance, at least to taste. As Maggie had reportedly said, during the discussion over its use, that form was much more consistent with their environment than neat little foil packages marked 'Ham, eggs and stewed tomato, just add water'. 'And if there were a lottery outlet nearby,' she murmured, 'I'd buy a ticket today.' She noted its location and continued her search. She doubted this one would supply the whole cavern.

But presently she came upon a second and a third, similarly hidden, and could set aside all fears of endangering the women's enclave. Now she merely had to produce a good story to explain why she was looking in all the nooks and crannies and why she was so certain that what she had found was food. She continued her circuit, past a shining waterfall and on to another series of clefts and caverns, her search growing more dilatory, despite herself. She was almost level with the massif on the far side of the womens' camp when she heard voices from behind a nubbly outcropping of rock, stifled voices and snickers. There was a scattering of fresh cigarette stubs still to be absorbed by the matting. She leaned around the outcropping and in the luminous and focused light of the shallow cave saw five black-clad figures, huddled together. They looked up, saw her and went still. One of the girls jammed her mouth full of what was in her hand and closed her lips over her teeth, looking ready to gag on the bulk. 'Aw g'wan,' one of the boys said. 'Is chewing gum a crime?'

At the sound of his voice, her eyes dropped to his hand. She knew what she would see: the bandage, grubby and a little ragged now. He was a surprisingly well-grown and well-favoured youth with studs in his ear, a hoop in his nose, and a James Dean curl to his lip – though if he had heard of James Dean he had probably dismissed him as too *old* and soft to be worth bothering with. A point of tartan ribbon peeked from his pocket.

The girl with him whispered, 'Gareth, it's *her*.'

Sophie said, confidently, 'That's right, it's me. But that's water under the bridge now. I know it's not gum you're eating. That's all right, too. But what I think you should do now is go and tell someone up at the massif about it.'

'Why should we?' one of the other boys said.

'For goodness' sake,' Sophie said to the first girl, who had begun to look white and sweaty, 'spit that out before you are sick.' The girl responded to the brisk school-marmish tone by turning aside and coughing up a large clot of amber-brown matter. 'You should,' Sophie continued, 'because I'm only the first person who is going to find out about it, and I don't mind at all you taking the credit for finding it. As you well know we are desperately in need of a food source.'

'There isn't enough to go around.'

'Not here, maybe, but I've seen three other drifts in this half of the cavern – you can go along and check on that before you decide – and I haven't even searched the other half of the cavern yet.'

'OK,' the boy Gareth said, 'we'll go'n check them out. But this one's ours, right? Finder's fee.'

'It's up to you where you point people. Just point them somewhere, clear?'

'What do you want from doing this?' the third boy said.

She shrugged. 'I've got better things to do than spend hours arguing with the committee about whether or not it's edible.' She paused, and said to the boy, Gareth. 'I owe you an apology. I shouldn't have used that knife.'

He looked at her, eyes narrowed. 'Yeah.' Shrugged. 'Well, I was being an asshole.' Shrugged again.

Sophie let a moment go by, long enough to establish peace without enforcing it. 'By the way,' she added, 'if you want to keep this one to yourselves, I'd be more careful with your cigarette ends.'

Collective gloom descended. 'Those're our last cigs.'

15 Hathaway

Something really cool has happened. My mural has started making its own colours. I was trying to draw Magellan standing on his deck with a sextant when I saw that when I drew a line with the brown chalk this yellow streak appeared under the chalk almost as if the wall had changed colour. So I started drawing lines with my finger and hey presto! The colour you get depends on how hard you press. A little like the claystone where how quickly it shapes depends on how quickly you rub. I can make colours with fingers and hands and paint in great big areas. The colours are very bright with the light shining through and there's every kind of orange green and blue but no red. I just can't press lightly enough. I tried blowing on it but nothing happened. I was going to draw Magellan with a sextant at night but now I'm going to paint him on the deck at sunset, with all the colours in the sea and sky. Neil Armstrong will look a little weird with a glowing blue sky rather than a black one and I don't know how to set the colours back to white once I've changed the wall so I'm leaving his suit until way later, but since the ship has given me its colours I'm going to go with them. I might be able to use chalk dust to darken some of the colours because it's difficult right now to do shapes or shadows. I tried using dead claystone which I'll have to explain about in a moment but the dust would stay for a while and then vanish. I guess it fell off.

About the dead claystone – I worked some lumps off of the wall because I wanted to make it into pottery. But real quickly it all fell apart into little heaps of grey dust. It's the same with the greenstuff on the ground. I cut some of that thinking that I could make a thicker mattress and it all crumbled away. What was really interesting was what happened with the brown goop that one of the walls has started putting out, stuff that looks like maple candy. I haven't tasted it yet though I am getting real tired of granola bars and power bars and vitamins and I'll run out soon. But when I pulled some of the brown goop off the wall and put it on the greenstuff little threads grew up into it and got thicker and thicker until I couldn't decide whether I couldn't see it because it had been wadded up or I couldn't see it because it had been eaten. Anyway a day later the ball was gone and so was the brown candy. But – this is where it gets weirder – I did the same thing putting it on a rock and the rock sprouted the same little threads and balled it up and made it disappear. It just took longer for the little threads to come. I wish I had Uncle Stan here to talk about this stuff. Maybe once my tunnel's made I'll go down and start asking around after him. My acid stomach is getting so bad with being hunched in the hole I'm popping antacid like there was no tomorrow and trying not to think about what to do when I run out. I'm keeping it as small as just fits me and am going to make the entrance low down and kind of long and slanted to keep it looking as shallow and accidental as possible to someone just passing. I can make it bigger as I get bigger. At least with claystone I don't have to worry about getting stuck. I'm looking forward to going up and down. There's some part of me that's lonely lonely lonely since Stephen came by. It's not that I have a thing about him. (Though I have all kinds of weird sexy thoughts that I guess are hormones acting up because they don't seem to be attached to anyone in particular, just sloshing around in me. It's a weird feeling being so *centred* in my own skin. Everything comes back to me and the baby. Only we matter. Everything else is outside my skin and either isn't really important or is a danger. It's a really selfish feeling being pregnant. Even wanting Stephen around or wanting people around is because I think I've a need or a right to have people around me. To *worship* me. My brain tells me that that's crazy – nobody's going to worship me. I'd better not go on about that or you will be thinking I've gone totally crazy, loopy and whacko.)

16 Sophie

The slope beneath the massif made a natural stage, and the hollow in the cavern floor a natural amphitheatre. Dominic, standing in the middle of the slope, called out through cupped hands to the crowd, 'You'll have to come closer. We have no microphones.' But they had no traffic, no piped music and no breeze; his voice carried surprisingly well. Only the rearmost of the gathering had to move in, after a few catcalls of, 'What's he saying?' and 'Can you speak up at the front?'

It was the morning of the seventh day and there was optimism in the air. They were fed, they were warm, they were well-watered and they were ready to be diverted. Sophie would have cheerfully spent the interlude working on what was going to be her pathology/research laboratory, except that Dominic had taken a certain facetious pleasure in pointing out that she herself had challenged them to take steps towards creating a constitution, and she could at least come to observe the process.

On the 'stage', Arpád too looked like he would have liked to be elsewhere. He was crouched and scribbling in pencil on his single sheet of paper, a page already so much scrawled over and erased that it was grey. As far as she could tell, it was the same sheet as he had had with him seven days ago. He muttered as he worked. She watched the hard-planed face with near affection. He believed in order. So did she. It was what had brought her, eventually, to make her peace with him, Dominic and the committee. That and a promise of time to do her work, esoteric as it might seem to them. Though she had to admit to herself, if to no one else, that she could not see what shape her work might take, in such arcane and primitive conditions.

Beside Dominic was a small woman in a navy blue suit, so poised that for a moment Sophie failed to recognise her as the widow of the man who had died on their first day. Sophie thought her in her early sixties, that first day, but she looked ten years younger now, her short hair brushed smooth, points of clear light twinkling in both earlobes. Dominic secured silence for her with a loud whistle and a waving of hands. She only winced a little. Her hands reached unconsciously for an absent lectern, felt empty air, and closed uneasily into each other.

'My name,' she said, 'is Victoria Monserrat. I am a lawyer, specialising in International Law, and I was one of the authors of the legal portion of the Montreal Accord.' She paused, and around Sophie a soft Babel rose as the seven or eight translators within earshot rendered her words to their listeners. Victoria dipped her head a little, listening, Sophie realised, for the ebbing of the sound.

Over the past seven days it had become clear that every ethnic or linguistic group or sect who had attempted communication with the aliens, and therefore received their reply, was represented. The mixing of people in the caverns appeared at first largely capricious. Point of arrival bore no relation to geographical point of departure, leading to such juxtapositions as herself, departing from Boston, Massachusetts, Stan Morgan from Chesapeake Bay, old Marian West from Plymouth, England, and Adrienne LaFleurette and her companion from Seattle, Washington. Arpád and Dominic had been working on an advisory committee on refugees based in London, England; Victoria Monserrat, her dead husband and her estranged stepdaughter had driven to Nova Scotia, Canada. Daily, one or a group of people would pass through, searching for a missing member or members who had been standing a little away on the beach and who had, they hoped, they prayed, been deposited elsewhere in this vast catacomb.

It had taken them a few days to see that there was a pattern, that the common factor was language. All the original occupants of this cavern had been collected from regions where the dominant language of contact was English. Neighbouring caverns were dominated by speakers of English, Japanese, Swedish, Russian, Spanish ... Dominic's scouting parties had reported caves dominated by most of the languages widely spoken on Earth, and some odd mixtures of minorities. Logical, in retrospect, given the nature of the first communications but in a few instances, as with Russian, a common language united old enemies and sectarian fighting had broken out as each group strove to lay exclusive claim to the territory, and expel the others. This gathering was not purely to address matters of individual rights and constitutions.

Victoria unclasped and reclasped her hands. 'I am sure that most of you will have heard of the Montreal Accord, signed by thirty-one nations on the twenty-eighth of March of this year. Many of you will be aware of the purposes of the Accord – to reach an agreement between nations regarding this ship, and nationalist claims thereon, and to extend the provisions of International Law covering Space to include the circumstances in which those of us who decided to come might find ourselves. An exercise much less academic in light of what we have found on our arrival than it might have seemed when we anticipated more alien involvement in our affairs.'

That was putting it delicately, given some of the more vitriolic criticism of the conference. A dozen nations and many more cities had declined to host it, arguing that their resources and facilities were committed for years ahead. Montreal, having suffered a decline in its fortunes with the unremitting uncertainty over separation, seized upon the opportunity.

Victoria continued, 'I have heard it said, and seen it written, that the Montreal Conference was an exercise in absurdity, and in governmental arrogance. After all, what holds us under government now, up here? The bureaucracy, the law-enforcement, the taxes, jails, fines, social penalties – we have left all those behind – and any Accord signed by government leaders of Earth is not binding to us, because we are outwith their jurisdiction and their constituency. It is up to ourselves whether we choose to define ourselves as citizens of any nation of Earth, of Earth itself, or purely of the stars.

'But something rather remarkable – and to me, as one of the authors of the Accord, rather touching – began to happen in the days between the signing and publishing of the Accord and our departure. Individuals who were already determined on going with the ship undertook to set their own names to the Accord, on paper, on the Internet, to the original, in all its full legal wording, or to versions translated into the everyday language of all nations. Even people whose national leaders had not attended, or refused to sign, added their names. In all, some twenty-three thousand people signed. Admittedly,' one corner of her mouth tucked in, 'there were a certain number of Luke Skywalkers and James T. Kirks. But every petition collector knows that Elvis lives and signs petitions.' Muted laughter, and she looked touchingly pleased. 'And since there was so much that is quixotic about this venture already, we have learned to live with mockery. Mockery,' she said, quietly, 'does not invalidate our courage, and our aspirations.'

Near Sophie a dark-haired woman in her late thirties stretched out her legs and sneered. She was model-thin, with a sharply expressive face, papery skin which creased finely with movement, and a wide mobile mouth. As she slung one leg over the other, her leather miniskirt rode up on a long thigh. Idly, she lifted a hand to tug it down, while her eyes strafed any gawkers. On her hand was a heavy silver ring, a skull with green eyes. She rolled her head back to murmur something to the nearest of her several companions, a gaunt man with an array of gold studs in his ear, gold-rimmed spectacles with lenses the size of quarters, and a close-shaven head. He answered her with a surprisingly well-modulated voice, a singer's voice, Sophie thought. And, when her eye caught his, surprisingly gentle eyes, for all he did not smile. Sophie wondered idly how long his supply of razor blades would last. Many of the formerly clean-shaven men in the Camp were already sporting scrubby beards.

'And it seems one of the common aspirations we have is to find harmony with each other – all humanity – and with our alien hosts. An aspiration expressed by those people who signed the Montreal Accord, and who therefore recognised that the Accord was the best expression of a truly international – or maybe super-national – law that we could achieve. And since we find ourselves here – I will not say without welcome, because in the physical comfort of our surroundings we know ourselves well-received – but so far without greeting or instruction, I believe that we should continue the process begun in Montreal, in creating a law and government that express our common aspirations over and above our disparate origins.

'I would therefore like to invite everyone here, and ultimately everyone aboard, to become an individual signatory to the Montreal Accord, so that we have a common framework of law. But more important, I would like to invite everyone here, and everyone aboard, to become involved in the ongoing process of developing a system of government and law based initially on that Accord, but refined by time and our own experience. Those of us who wrote the Accord did so, after all, in extraordinary circumstances, constrained both in time and in information. The document we produced is not the document we could have produced, knowing then what we know now, and it is certainly not the document that we might produce, one, ten, or a hundred days from now. We have the opportunity now – since we find ourselves in quite privileged circumstances, with all our basic bodily needs provided for – to dedicate ourselves, such of us as have a passion for the work, to revising and refining the Accord. It is, I do believe, one of the ways in which we may show humanity at its best, in the eyes of the interplanetary community we aspire to join. Thank you,' she said, and took a step back, with a small, gracious bow.

'Oh god,' said a woman sitting beside the woman with the skull ring – Sophie recognised her as the tall, fair woman Arpád had quarrelled with so memorably on their first morning. 'Let's go, Eilish; it's going to be more of the same old. You know.'

Eilish smiled lazily at her. 'Not yet. I've got something to say when the time's right.'

Someone near the front got to his feet. 'And if we don't want to sign, what then?'

'What is your objection?' Victoria said, in an interested tone.

He folded his arms. 'I didn't say I had one, madam. I was merely asking what would happen if one chose not to sign.'

Arpád rose. 'Here we have Americans and Iranians and Lybians, Shi'ites and Sunnis, Serbs and Croats, Israelis and Arabs, enemies living as neighbours. Here we have myself and other people who work to feed and heal the bodies and souls of the victims of those who demand *independence, liberation, national freedom,* and use noble words to cloak their bloody work. I distrust people who distrust law, and if you wish to live without law, sir, go elsewhere.'

'And who died and made you God?' sang out a woman from elsewhere in the audience half giggling at her own impudence. Eilish snorted. The third woman in her party raised her head listlessly, startling Sophie with a suddenly disclosed likeness. She looked enough like Eilish to be her sister, but where Eilish's hair was a glossy tangle, the woman's hair had been hacked short. Where Eilish wore a boxer jacket, vest and miniskirt, her sister had on a heavy black jacket with overlong sleeves and upturned lapels, over an ankle-length skirt which she had tucked under her folded legs like an envelope, so that neither ankle nor foot showed. Where Eilish sprawled and gazed commandingly around herself, the other woman sat with legs tucked under, hands folded on lap, head bowed.

'God died,' Arpád said, in his rasping, accented voice, 'in the poisoned trenches of France, in the firebombing of Dresden, in the jungles of Malaysia, in the ghettos of Europe and in the streets of Sarajevo.' The shorn-haired woman looked up again, her eyes fixing on him glistening slightly. 'God died day after day after day in the refugee camps of the Sudan. I watched him die, in wizened infants whose eyes were like ageless black stone, in women bled white with childbirth, in twenty-five-year-old men who should have stood like warriors, but whom starvation and old scars bent like dotards. There is no God. There is only man.'

Eilish lounged back on her elbows. 'Good theatre,' she commented, audibly. Her sister dropped her head again. The shaven, studded, gentle-eyed man reached over and brushed her hand with his fingertips, without taking his eyes from Arpád. In profile the absurdly small spectacles perched on a scimitar nose.

'Victoria is a gentle lady; she *invites* you to sign her law. I am not so gentle. I say there will be law. We are all displaced people here, all among strangers, all with old enemies among our new neighbours, all with fears, hopes and uncertainties about whether our way, our customs and morals and religion, will prevail. So many beliefs, so many convictions, so many ways of doing things. All the old questions have come with us. Should women be the peers of men, or the property, or walled away in their own sheltered domain? Is religious practice a private matter, or must it accommodate the standards of the larger community? Can you in good conscience leave unslaked vengeance against the brothers of your brother's murderer? And all the new questions – are men and women still entitled to choose their children's mother or father, or should the medical specialists rule, so as to prevent inbreeding? Do men and women have the right not to become fathers or mothers? Our lives are so public; there are no walls between us; what has become of privacy? We all have opinions on these matters. We all have beliefs. Some of those beliefs may be powerful, even fanatical. And we are no longer insulated by our own subdivisions, our own neighbourhoods. What will affront us will be all around us.

'You have looked to me because I know how to organize sanitation and food and bedding and work. But I know other things. I know what makes chaos and what makes order. So as long as you look to me, I will make law. As long as you look to me, there will be some standard as to what the community will allow and what the community will not allow. Perhaps that Accord of which Victoria is so proud is the law we will have. Perhaps we will make another. I do not demand that that law be mine; I have seen too many different ways of being to believe that mine, or anyone's, is superior. I have no God to lash me on to proselytise or do for the good of your souls. God died in my arms when I was nineteen years old. But there will be law.'

'Hell, Eilish,' the blonde woman said, 'do we have to listen to him ranting?'

'You should sue him for indecent assault,' the fourth woman said. 'We'd soon find out how committed to the law they were.'

Abruptly the shorn-headed woman struggled to her feet against the binding weight of her heavy dress. The blonde woman stood up, catching her arm. With vigour remarkable for her downtrodden appearance, the shorn woman swung on her, catching her an open-handed blow between the breasts, and, as the other fell, bolted. She did not, Sophie noted, hold up her heavy skirts, though they hobbled her. Without prior thought, Sophie found herself on her feet and moving through the crowd.

A small, redheaded figure was moving as well, Dove. When Sophie reached them, the shorn-headed woman was standing with both hands immersed to the wrists in falling spray and her head hanging forward, saying, 'It's all just a *joke* to them,' and Dove was inviting, 'If you want to talk about it.'

The other woman swung on her in a bright spray of water, her hands coming up, fingers half flexed, nails bared, 'No, I don't want to *talk* about it. I want to *forget* about it.' Then she spread her hand over her face, smearing water and tears, 'Sorry, sorry, sorry.'

'No need to be,' said Dove.

'Why isn't there!' the woman said, furiously. 'Shouldn't I be judged by the same standards as everyone else?' She turned away again, and looked up at the shimmering wall. 'A month ago I had no opinions, you know. About sexual harassment, about assault. When the people around me made a joke about it, I laughed. When the people around me got outraged, I got outraged, too. I just did what everybody else did, thought what everyone else thought. And now –' She rubbed her hands on her heavy, paisley skirt, looked down at it with a grimace of disgust, 'And I wasn't even raped.'

'There's no "not even" about assault,' Dove said, firmly. She paused, then pressed gently, 'How long ago did it happen?'

'Three weeks ago,' she said. 'I had a nice life, boyfriend, condo, job . . . and *he* just blew it all apart. I couldn't even go home, couldn't stand my boyfriend touching me. I . . . I know it was impulsive to do this, I knew I was never going to look at anything, never going to trust anyone in the same way again. The old me was dead and I was just going through the motions, dragging around the corpse of myself!'

'Who are the people you're with?' Dove said, low key.

There was a silence, as she struggled, a little resentfully, to climb out of the vortex of her own thoughts. 'My older sister, Eilish,' she said at last. 'And her friends.' She breathed in and out, shakily. 'They're rather radical –' Gave a wan smile of amusement at her own facile judgement.

'She's brilliant; our family's black sheep. I'm the little white lamb,' she said, bitterly. 'The surprise baby.'

'Is there anyone you know here, anyone of your friends?'

She looked startled at that. 'I don't know. I know some of them were talking about going – but everyone on Earth talked about going at some time or the other. And after *it* happened – I know they were trying to be helpful, but I felt like roadkill, and they were like flies buzzing around, attracted by the smell of blood. Isn't that awful?'

'It happens,' Dove said, mildly.

'Oh, I know it happens, but it's awful that I should think it,' she said, in a very young voice. Her inflection flattened, 'Here comes Tara.'

'Rosie, I'm so sorry. That was a thoughtless remark, I didn't mean to upset you –' Her flighty, gushing manner was quite incongruous with her appearance, gawky without being particularly tall and dressed in army surplus fatigues.

'Would you please not call me Rosie. My name is Rosamond.'

'But Eilish –'

'It's not Eilish's name. It's mine.'

'I'm sorry, Rosamond,' Tara said, primly. 'I'm sorry I upset you.'

'There's no need to treat me like I'm made of china. I may crack up from time to time, but I'll paste myself together.' With a poise that to Sophie looked brittle, she said, 'I'd better get back.' She put out a hand. 'Thank you.'

Dove took it, held it briefly. 'If you need me, the group I am with – who are all women – are living in a side cavern about midway down this wall. It's easy to find, since it's the only tunnel which goes to any depth. And most of the time now there's someone on watch outside. My name's Dove. Sophie' – a small gesture – 'is with the main group in this cavern.'

'We . . . are one over,' she gave a small smile, 'out the main corridor, first right.' She bobbed her head and traipsed off, resisting Tara's move to take her arm.

'I think,' Dove said, in a low voice, 'you and I might ask around and see if there is anyone here who has been involved in counselling of victims of assault or trauma.' Sophie nodded, watching her stumble. She had probably been athletic before, long striding, quick moving, with the sunny confidence of a woman who has never known anything but petty vexations. 'She needs to know that people do recover,' she said.

'Yes, and she may need help to reconcile herself with the fact that she left Earth and everything she knew in reaction to it.' Dove rubbed her face with a hand. 'Our aliens plainly don't understand human psychology very well. They should have made it more difficult to be picked up. Or at least allowed a fourteen day cooling off period.'

No sooner had Rosamond sat down, then Eilish stood, tucking her long legs beneath her and rising with the tight grace of the experienced miniskirt wearer. Standing, she shed her boxy jacket, revealing shapely shoulders in a strapless top. Taking her time, aware of her audience, she picked her way to the front, and swung to face the audience, hands on hips. 'I'm Eilish Colby, and I've got an invitation of my own to give you. I didn't sign the Montreal Accord,' she said. 'I never will. I didn't come to rule and be ruled by Earth. In fact, what I am is an anarchist. A pure anarchist, not a bomb-in-the-pocket parody. This seems to me to be the perfect laboratory for a true experiment with freedom, the perfect chance to find out what human beings can actually achieve when they're not being told what to do and how to do it. When you're ready to leave Earth behind, come look us up.' She pointed. 'Out that door, turn right. Only don't leave it too late. There might not be enough room.' She smoothed down the purple skirt, and started to go; and then she stopped as though she had heard her name, and smiled at the gathering, a slightly startled, delighted, luminous smile. Sophie felt her heart skip with surprise and awe, even as the more sophisticated part of her pointed out the precise timing and self-awareness of the expression. Dove's small cynical smile became more marked as Eilish – who had picked her way forward through the throng, looking appealingly faltering and vulnerable – now went by the open alleys with an assured and springy step. She, her sister, and her followers threaded out of the gathering, followed by a handful of others, and watched by still more. The motley group disappeared into the nearest tunnel.

Somebody else got up to speak, objecting to some provision of the Montreal Accord which had to do with sharing knowledge and resources, and wondering whether they interpreted that to mean that the ship should come under a single government. 'I never did pay much attention to political science,' Dove remarked mildly. 'Hannah and Maggie and a couple of others will be tearing it into shreds. Speaking of shreds, what's that coloured rag up there?' She had pointed out the yellow pennant on the highest point of the massif.

'Timekeeping,' Sophie said. 'That means it's between three and six hours after lights up. The Camp has two old analog watches.'

'I remember you were wearing one when we met.' She glanced at Sophie's wrist, then at Sophie's face.

'It's not so bad,' Sophie said. 'The worst should be over, now that we've got a food supply.'

The corner of Dove's mouth tucked in. 'Thank you for being so circumspect about our part in it.' Still, she regarded Sophie with clear, green-blue eyes, waiting. Sophie, well versed in the tactic, smiled slightly. 'I need colleagues,' she said, 'I need to be part of a large, well organised group.'

Dove nodded. 'I can understand that.' She grinned, an elfin expression. 'Remember it's not just because we're covetous of Melisande that we'd recruit you.'

'Melisande chooses her own company,' Sophie said. She gazed out over the gathering. 'It's quieter for her with you.'

'Why'd'you bring her? Most people left their pets behind.'

'I've always taken her everywhere, as much as possible. She's a good travelling companion, and through her I meet people I wouldn't if I were on my own.'

Dove quirked a smile at nothing in particular except the luminous air. 'If anyone had told me a month ago that I'd be riding off to the far reaches on the universe on an alien space ship, I'd . . . I don't know what I'd have said. I could never even get into *Star Trek* . . .' She was quiet a moment. 'Do you know that song they occasionally play over Christmas? I've no idea whose it is, but it's a version of "Silent Night", and running along behind the music are excerpts from a newscast . . .' Sophie murmured, remembering; she had thought it pointed and clever. Dove frowned slightly, pondering the problem of memory, or translating memory into words. 'You've been in Boston E.Rs; you know what they're like. I'm not going to say what you maybe think. It was nothing horrible. A fairly quiet Tuesday night, business as usual, asthmatics, psychotics, the knife-and-gun club. I drove home, six a.m., sun just coming up, trying to find something on the radio that wasn't about alien spaceships. There was some state representative talking about programmes for alleviating social ills, and I had the sudden realisation that it's all . . . symbiotic . . . the violence and the E.Rs, the social dysfunction and the healers. You deal with the horrors by telling yourself you're helping people. But maybe you're not. Maybe you're just enabling the system that causes the suffering. I don't know how to explain it any better. Having that ship up there, in orbit, changed everything.'

Something like a blue spark dropped out of the air and on to Sophie's

71

hand. She felt tiny feet flicker on her skin; then the insect spiralled into the air and flew away across the gathering. Dove said, 'We've seen a few of these in the past day or so, though nobody's had one hold still enough to get a proper look.'

'This is the first I've seen,' Sophie said. 'It's odd, though, that all we've seen native to this place are flying insects. Assuming that they *are* insects as we understand them, because the grass certainly is not grass, and the trees certainly are not trees. The best we've been able to come up with is that it's some kind of fungus, although we haven't been able to find a microscope of sufficient resolution, and the fibres don't stain as living tissue with the limited number of chemical stains I've been able to bring with me . . .' She talked on, drawing the other woman's too keen attention away from what she had left behind and why, until the gathering began to disperse. The members of the women's group who had stayed to attend came trooping over the grass, deep in dispute, Maggie's thickening Scots accent riding over their voices. Hannah guided Marian West with a hand under her elbow. The old woman had the austere composure of the frail, tired and proud – surely that sleeping on the ground, surrounded by strangers, must be exhausting her? – but her head was tilted, alertly, towards the argument. Sophie nodded greeting to them all and went back to work.

17   Stephen

Over seven days, he mapped nine caverns, and saw no end. His first sketchbook was half full, and each successive map he made smaller, from fewer sketches. He was not satisfied with his efforts at mapping the caves' relations to each other – oh, he knew what the linking tunnels connected, but each one curved, and some wound, and all rose and fell in height, and the walls inside were too featureless for sighting and measurement. The map, as he assembled it, looked more medieval than modern. Impressionistic, imprecise. But the making of it gave him great satisfaction.

On the seventh day he met another mapping party, a husband and wife team of professional surveyors. They had retired early and travelled the world for six years, and this seemed but an extension of their travels. When he laid his maps down beside theirs – his looking not only medieval but amateur – they overlapped only by two caverns.

With their instruments they had surveyed an additional thirteen, and had collected word of at least as many beyond that; they estimated that excluding the tunnels the area they had surveyed was at least a hundred square kilometers, probably more, and the population a hundred thousand or up. That last number charmed them as much as it oppressed him; they spoke of meeting and talking to people from all over the world. Every culture – even those whose governments had denied the existence of the aliens, or decried it as a hoax – was represented. Hope of the fabulous, the miraculous, the transcendent, was universal. He and they exchanged measurements and copied each other's maps. He accepted their offer of a spare theodolite, that it might make his mapping more accurate but not that it might speed it – he still wished to pass over every step of the place himself. They parted, having agreed to meet again in five days time. It was an appointment he thought he might keep.

The thirteen caverns they had surveyed formed an irregular arc on two levels around a central area which they had not been able to survey, for the tunnels which led into it were in darkness as far in as they went. They had had torches, but the torches were electric, and they had in the end cached them with other possessions they did not wish to carry. Stephen did not mention the eight long-burning candles or the lantern and oil he had in his pack, but when they had gone he turned not in the direction he had said he was going, but towards the origin of that arc.

As he came into the cavern where they had sited the nearest of the tunnels into darkness he saw that an area of wall had been covered in a speckling of black. Human doing – a group of people near one end were egging on two people, one standing on the other's shoulders, reaching above the dark tidemark to write on the wall. Graffiti on the walls. Jesus H. Christ, the human race. They saw him and beckoned him avidly in, holding out a pen to him. As he came closer, he saw that the graffiti was names, thousands of names. The names and places of origin of everyone who had passed by, spanning thirty feet, and rising twelve. He took the offered pen without thinking and, holding it, let his eyes move back and forth, up and down, over the wall. Such an overwhelming enumeration of humanity, each one claiming his or her own significance. All the unrelenting expectations and hungers and presumptions of people, of society. Everything he had gone to the mountains to avoid, everything he had come with the aliens to escape. He could feel a pressure within his skull, behind his throat. He dropped the pen, heard it click against his boot, turned and ran. He heard a girl's voice behind him cry, 'But don't you want your name on the –'

The entrance of the dark tunnel was a grey smudge in the wall, light spilling into it from outside. He did not like caves, never had. Did not like being closed in. Voices drove him into the dark, around a corner, until they passed. He crouched and lit a candle from his pack, aware of the closeness of the walls, the lack of any escape except onwards. He had never mastered the art of putting aside fear, never learned to ride the adrenalin high. He was always too aware of his own vulnerability.

He shaded the candle with his body and started down the tunnel, breathing shallowly and fast, too aware of his heartbeat, the chill of sweat on his face, the beginnings of a familiar pressure in his bowels. These tunnels were different from the tunnels outside. There was a pattern to their walls, barely discernible in the flickering candlelight, but visible. Seams split, divided, came together and overlaid each other like the strands of a fraying rope. Where the tunnels branched, he took the tunnel in which the seams clustered most thickly. If they were more than decoration, if they were veins or vessels or bundled wires, they would converge towards the trunk or heart or power source.

The tunnel opened suddenly into space. Sides and ceiling all flew away; only the floor remained. He spoke, listened, and then shouted in several pitches hearing faint and muddled echoes. He started along the wall, which was barely curved and so thickly marked as to make a coarse weave. Even the floor was seamed, rough ridges like tree-roots. He stepped over them carefully, though he could have given no reason for his care. Merely a sense that what need not be disturbed should not be disturbed. Animal instinct, and the caution of a man taught young that the powers – human and natural – were capricious.

Presently he reached a blind end in the wall where a broad ramp sloped down the wall to the floor. He set down his candle and by its light filled and lit the lantern. With the lantern held high he could see its long, slow curve rising into the thickening darkness. He left the candle where it was, wedged between two ridges at the base of the ascent, to mark his place. Carrying the lantern, he started to climb.

The gradient was gradual. The walls continued coarse woven, ropy, with that slightly opaque, slightly darkened patterning. The floor was smoother, but for an irregular wedge of ridges every few yards. From the wall he could just see the edge of the ramp. From the edge of the ramp he could look across and down and see the lantern he had left to mark the beginning, a still, unshifting point. There was no sense of draft or air, and yet the atmosphere did not seem stale. He climbed, keeping to the wall, and pausing at intervals to look over, fix and gauge height and distance of that little point of light.

There came a moment when he looked for it and could not see it – finding it blocked by an outcropping of the ramp, a projection towards the cavern's centre. Carefully he picked his way obliquely across the projection, until he found the edge and his light. And then he worked along the edge towards the cavern's unseen centre as the projection rose in a smooth hump. Two or three hundred yards in, a shape appeared in the edge of his light, a huge tusk rising up from the centre of the cave or down from the ceiling. The bridge met with a steep, tight, spiralling ramp wrapping the tusk. He laid down the lamp before him, and, on hands and feet, a four-legged sweating ape, he climbed. He could not help, now, but that his feet and hands would rest on the ridges; he needed their support. Nothing seemed to come of it, and he went on, for what he believed must be a full turn, before he sought the edge of the spiral, and his light. He was forming a picture of this chamber in his mind, a chambered spiral like a whelk shell worn by the sea. He wondered how long he had been down here, creeping in darkness.

Below him and around the curve, suddenly, he saw paired moving lights. He was not so very high up, he realised, now that he had them to judge by. Not high enough up at all, a mere thirty or so metres up, and a quarter of the arc away. It was pure luck that his lantern was propped against a high enough ridge that they could not – *should not* – have seen it. He leaned forward and with a silent breath blew it out. In the intruders' lantern light he glimpsed the long glint of a barrel – and it was all he could do to remain still, not to try squirming away from the last place of his betraying light.

Watching, he became aware that there were more than two, that at the very fringe of the light, he glimpsed figures. They moved as one creature, the four or more of them. There was nothing commonplace about these hunters. They were military, or law-enforcement. One of the two light carriers, a young man, shaven bald, approached his candle, and crouched to study it. The depth of the pit around the wick would tell how long it had been burning. He signalled to the others, the shadows in the dark and the large, silent beast stepped on to the ramp.

One of the half seen ones stumbled, a jerky flicker at the edge of the lamp. No words were exchanged. If he belly-crawled up the steep spiral around the tusk, maybe he could keep it between him and them. His guts knotted, remembering the red spray and the stinging splinters of bone.

At the base of the ramp the light went out.

For a moment he thought someone else had kicked it over or blown it out. But the group on the stairs halted their slow climb, and the lantern carriers laid down their lanterns and moved away. He heard weapons shifting and the muted clicking of catches being released and bolts drawn. Then the two lanterns on the ramp flickered briefly, and went out.

There were a few more sounds, of stumbling, of fumbling, of falling, of a clatter of dropped weapons. He wondered how long it would take for the gas or whatever it was to mount up to his level, and whether he should relight the lamp for the few seconds' warning it would give him. Like the angry voice outside the door or the feet on the stairs – and after only a little thought he chose not to. Much good his instinct towards caution would do him now. Beneath him in the darkness he heard wisps of sound like feathers dragged along bark or fine silk on wooden floors. Indistinct clicks, some like insects' tiny mandibles, and others like claws delicately treading stone. Yet not like either. Not like any sound he had ever heard, even at night, in the forests. The small hairs on the nape of his neck pinched and rose as one. The sweat on his face grew cold. Though he knew better, he strained his eyes staring into the utter darkness, and found himself fighting the irrational conviction that there was *something* close by, something coming up on him, and that the drop before him was less terrible than what was behind him.

Light sparked into being below him, a single, bright point, wavering slightly in the draft of something's withdrawal. His own candle, relit. And by its light he caught a glimpse of something moving away. Only an edge of it, a ragged edge of it, not its colour or shape or true size. The movement was a smooth sway away from the light, and whether it represented a body shifting its bulk, or a single immense extremity being withdrawn, he could not tell. But he knew with utter certainty that it was not human.

His breath in his throat seemed very loud and shrill. It filled the whole cavern. Only by holding it in could he hear the small and alien sounds receding beneath him. He panted in the darkness like a poisoned dog, panted, held his breath, listened, and breathed again. Beneath him, nothing moved. He had the profound sense that nothing breathed.

Some time later, how long he did not know, he found and relit his lantern with trembling hands, and sat staring at it for a little while, staring at it so he need not look around. Then he fastened a nylon rope from his pack to the handle and slowly lowered the lantern over the edge. Belly down, he fed out the rope and watched the lantern burn brightly all the way down to the floor of the cavern. In the pool of light it cast, nothing moved. He let it rest there for several moments, then raised it, smoothly, bringing it back to hand, suffering a moment's dread as he took it in hand and knew himself revealed. Neither voice nor bullet spoke to him. He returned the coiled rope to his pack. Shouldered the pack, lifted the lantern, and started downwards, bent with the cramps in his guts.

There was no one on the floor of the cavern. Neither living nor dead bodies remained, nor lanterns, nor guns. He put lantern down by candle, turned away from it and stood at the light's very boundary, extending all his senses into the darkness. The darkness was electric with menace, but he heard nothing, saw nothing, nothing came out of it at him. He examined the floor where the men should have lain. He could see no obvious damage, nothing to indicate what they might have done to elicit such retribution. He, too, had walked on this floor; he too, had carried light. But he had not stumbled. One of the others had. Here be dragons, indeed.

The ascent was ghastly, even lantern-lit, even more ghastly than the moments in darkness high on the tusk. He picked his way forward, his skin cringing from the thought of touching any of these walls, any of these coarse, ropy ridges. Flicker-frames went through his mind, worn old images of terror and hatred, an outhouse at night, a shed, closets. He could almost feel the coarse textured cloth in his hands as he clawed it away from his face. And laughter. Were they laughing, these monsters in their darkness?

Closed darkness went to open darkness; he fell on hands and knees on the boundary of greystone and matting, his lamp spilling on its side, but blessedly not going out. Night had come while he was down in the cavern. Which night he did not know – he was not sure whether he had been down in the underworld for a few hours, or a few days. He knew he should blow out the light, and allow his eyes to adapt to the thin blue light of the cavern's dark, but his eyes clung to the lantern, and would not let it go. He made his way a little along the walls, and emptied bladder and bowels in long liquid streams, then came back, and this time managed to exchange candle for lantern. He let the lesser light burn for the remainder of the night and, if he slept, he did not know it.

77

18 Morgan

All night they were aware of the candle burning, the candle which marked where a lantern had appeared suddenly, as though carried out of the tunnel into the dark. At first they thought it was St John Emrys and the others, now well overdue from their exploration of the dark area, but the hope had passed quickly; it was but one lantern, and the carrier made no attempt to approach. Some time in the night Morgan woke to a whispered discussion of whether to move now, find out whoever the hell it was had come out when their people hadn't. He was glad, for whoever was out in the darkness, that A.J. had the veto, and used it, for he had seen these men in training and knew how swiftly they made the transition between civility and violence, and how watchful they were over their own. When the lights came up, they were ready, scanning the near distance with bare eyes, the far with binoculars, looking the length of the wall before turning their attention towards the nearest opening, the one where the captain and three teammates had disappeared, and the place where the lantern had so suddenly appeared. Their inspection was swift, the convergence of gazes rapid. In the act of leaning over and snuffing his candle, the tawny-haired man paused; some sense made him look over towards them. His face blanched, but casually, still, he tucked candle into backpack, stood, stretched, and began to stroll obliquely away from them, towards the centre of the cavern and the tunnel which led away from it.

Morgan thought, oh, Jesus, don't provoke them. He felt the same horror he had felt watching a young dealer he knew had defied one of the local suppliers sally towards him down the street, lime green shirt open at the neck and showing dense golden chain, movements loose and brazen, and a clear ring of white between iris and eyelid. Four hours later he had been dead in the litter of a back alley. Morgan's credo had been, then and for ever, Don't provoke them.

Greg Drover murmured, 'Looks guilty as shit, doesn't he?' He had moved into a crouch, fingertips laid lightly on the green matting, a sprinter's pose. A.J. watched the departing man with pale, narrowed eyes, watched him pick up his pace without looking back. 'Drover, Hughes, Illes, go tell him we want to talk to him. Leave your heavy gear; we'll cover. No excessive force. He makes a threatening move, get out of the way.' Drover surged forward, Kent Hughes and Ed Illes on his heels. The tawny-haired man's head whipped around; A.J.'s and Aquile Raho's rifles were up as fast as that simple movement; but the man gave no more than a glance behind and took off, sprinting for the exit at the far side of the cavern. Morgan was aware of scattered watchers, some rising and staring, others seeing the weapons and pressing themselves flat, pulling down companions and children. He held his breath, almost nauseated, not knowing whether he prayed for the man to escape, or be caught before they were out of A.J.'s guardian gaze. Burdened by his pack, the tawny-haired man was losing ground, but very slowly. Raho said, 'Fast fuckhead, isn't he?' A.J. said, 'They'll catch him.' Piett murmured, 'Before that tunnel?' Raho, 'Let's take him down.' A.J., grimly, 'Hold your fire.' The man plunged into the tunnel, Hughes and Illes ten yards behind, passing Drover, the lead man throughout the chase. Raho said, 'Shit.' A.J. said, 'Bet you were the kind of kid who always peeked at his Christmas presents.' His voice was calm and flat.

A moment later, four men appeared from the tunnel mouth. Illes and Drover on either side of the tawny-haired man, Hughes behind him. Drover had the man's backpack slung over his shoulder. The man stumbled a little, hunched over as though in pain, and they pushed him on, with cuffs and thrusts of closed fists. He jerked away from each push but offered no further resistance. As he came closer Morgan saw he had the beginnings of a bruise on his cheekbone, a red puffiness which further skewed a face already blanched and distorted with fear. He looked like a trapped animal. A.J. saw that too; with a gesture to the others to hold position, he lowered his rifle and stood up, frowning. 'I thought I said *ask* him.'

'He didn't want to be asked,' said Illes. Drover added, 'We only hurt him enough.' A mad light kindled in their captive's grey eyes.

Drover chucked a worn leather sheath down before A.J. In it was a bowie knife and a smaller hunting knife. He followed it with a Swiss army knife. 'No fire-arms.'

'I'm A.J. Lowell,' A.J. said. He did not, Morgan noted, otherwise identify himself, nor did he hold out his hand.

The man said nothing, though when he breathed it was with slight shudders.

'Stand easy,' A.J. said, without shifting his eyes from the other man's. Hughes stepped back from his captive; the other men lowered their rifles. 'You were in that dark area yesterday. You came out during the night. We saw your lantern. I want to ask you some questions about what you saw down there. That's all.'

'Not mine,' the man said, hoarsely. 'Not my lantern.' Drover crouched and pointedly upturned the backpack, spilling its meticulously packed contents across the green matting. He plucked open the side pockets, one by one, letting lantern, oil bottles and candles, join the heap. The man flinched towards him; Hughes jerked him back with a hand on his shoulder. Drover held up the bottle, rocked it gently, so they could watch the lowered level of oil flow back and forth.

A.J. said, 'I'd like to know if you saw anyone else down there.'

The man stretched a smile, a baring of teeth. 'Like I said, I wasn't down there, so I don't know.'

Drover turned his attention to the man himself, patting his pockets with hard slaps, unzipping them one by one and rooting out their contents. The man's face blanched with anger. 'Get the fuck off me,' he whispered, and struck hard and fast at Drover, who turned his head only just enough that the blow merely jolted him, and drove a spiked hand into the man's belly. The others stepped back and let him drop. He lay, retching and doubled up on the green matting, unattended as Drover finished the search of his pockets. The notebook he handed to A.J.

A.J. flipped through the notebook, scanning the maps and notes. He crouched to present a page to the tawny man's watering eyes. 'Why are you lying to us?' he said, mildly. 'Why did you run?'

The man pushed himself up on one hand, the other hand held to his stomach, looking past the notebook. 'Why am . . . I lying to . . . you?' he said, gasping and shrill, and shook his head in mock incredulity. 'Why did I *run*? I know all about fuckers like you.'

'And what do you know about us?'

'That you *like* this. And anything . . . I say . . . anything . . . I do . . . just gives you an excuse.'

'No,' A.J. said, with a glance up at Drover and Raho. 'It doesn't. If you'd have done us the courtesy of talking to us willingly, we could have spared you this. But I guess you've run into bad trouble in the past . . . Mr Stephen Cooper . . . and you just don't take chances. I can certainly understand that.' The man was silent a moment. Then he said with bitter resignation, 'Whatever. You will anyway. Nobody'll stop you from doing whatever the hell you want to me.'

'Just remember that,' Aquilles Raho said, and jerked his rifle towards the man. A.J.'s eyes flashed blue, backing him off. Stephen Cooper's face whitened further. 'I've got to shit,' he said.

'Not yet,' A.J. said, with a silencing look at Raho. 'Not until you tell us what happened down there.'

'I told you, I never was down there.'

'I know you were,' A.J. said mildly, 'and you know I know you were. If you hadn't been, you'd say you had. I've had the making and breaking of little shits like you, Mr Cooper. So there isn't anything you can do or say that'll fool me.'

'And if I tell you, you'll let me go,' Cooper mocked, thinly. 'What a crock.'

'What would we do with you? Take you along with us? I'm not interested in you, Mr Cooper. You're just a rat. But rats get places and see things, and I'm interested in where you were last night and what you saw. That's all.'

'Fuck off.'

A.J. regarded the heap of provisions thoughtfully. 'You've got good gear, well packed. You know what you're about. A lantern, candles, food . . . no, I don't want any of it. When I let you go, I'll let you go with everything you came with.'

Crouching, he laid the candles side by side, then the lantern, and contemplated them. 'Six candles, only one burned. One lantern, two bottles of oil, one opened, and one –' he held up the one and rocked the oil gently back and forth. 'We've been here, what, seven nights? If you'd burned lanterns and candles every night, you'd be down to casting from dregs. And you'd keep the stubs for casting. So I don't think you're afraid of the dark, Mr Cooper. But last night, you burned your candle all night.' He gestured towards it, and let them all appreciate his reasoning. 'You don't look too good. You don't smell too good, either, Mr Cooper. I've been with men who've been scared shitless; I know how they look and smell.' He stood up. 'I think something scared you last night. Something that made you burn a candle all night and smell,' he sniffed, 'the way you smell right now.' His voice was quietly mesmerising, his eyes level with Cooper's. Morgan felt its effects; even Cooper was quieter. The other men of the team were still tense, still wary, but without the jagged threat of violence. 'You're right about us, Stephen. We're dangerous men, to the wrong people – or things. We're trained for situations like these, the darkness, the unexpected. We're not interested in you. We're interested in what's down there. Think about it. Whatever scared you so bad is still down there. Whatever it is, who knows if it's going to stay down there for ever? Or think about the next guy who goes down there.

Maybe it'll be kids, playing hide and seek.' He paused. 'Tell us, Stephen. Tell us so we can take care of it.'

'I don't know what the fuck it was,' Stephen said, blinking. The blinking was more reflex than tearing. Nobody moved; Morgan was well aware that A.J. would have blistered a strip off anyone who did. Nothing, Morgan thought, had unnerved him so much about the team as this. The violence, he understood, even as he shrank from it. But this was as though A.J. had simply reached in through Cooper's ears and taken a grip on his brainstem or – as Raho would have said – balls. 'I just saw it for a moment.' He breathed out with a shudder. 'It wasn't human.'

Quietly, not for a moment loosing his hold on captive or audience, A.J. led Cooper through his recitation. It had elements of horror story, and elements of confession. At the end, without censure or apology, they watched him gather up his strewn belongings, take back his candles, lamps and notebooks, A.J. having taken a quick tracing of his most recent map. The team sergeant thanked him for his information, and he nodded as though there had been nothing out of the ordinary in their conversation. Then they let him go.

'Gas,' said André Bhakta.

'You believe him, Sarge?' said Raho, shifting lightly in his crouch, keeping limber, ready to spring.

'Would you lie to this man?' Adlai Lecce remarked.

There was a small silence. 'So,' said Raho. 'We've got gas masks. We've got oxygen tanks. We can go in there. Like you promised Mr Cooper.' He lipped the words slightly. A.J. considered him, his eyes pale as marble. 'What do you say, Prof?'

'Did they have gas masks with them?' Morgan said, eliciting grudging looks which were agreement enough in themselves. 'How long does it take to put them on?'

A.J. glanced up at Kent Hughes, standing. 'Hughes. Candle just went out.'

Hughes flipped the flap on an outside pocket of the bulging pack at his feet, hooked out the mask with its small air cylinder, placed eyepieces, nosepiece, cinched the straps tightly and put his hand on the cylinder's valve. He had not inhaled cavern air after the warning. He blinked at them all through twin discs of glass. A.J. gestured for him to unmask, and he did, breathing deeply.

'We're making the assumption that the gas affected the lantern before it affected them,' Morgan thought aloud. 'If that were not so, if they were already under the influence before the lantern went out, then they might not have been thinking clearly enough to react, or have been able to react fast enough.'

'Under the influence, huh,' muttered Raho, shuffling.

A.J. gave him a narrow-eyed look; he settled into immobility, his face blank. 'You saw Cooper's maps. He says there are six entrances into that place. Piett, Raho, Hughes, you work left; Boris, Illes, you work right. Bag me one each. Talk to people. Find out if anyone else went down there, and whether they came out. One hour. Get me something useful.' Satisfied that they were going, he turned a blue-marble eye on Morgan.

Morgan admitted to himself that Raho's departure was restful. 'The fact that the candle was snuffed as opposed to continuing to burn or even igniting the gas suggests that the gas was inert. The fact that the candle was snuffed first and then the men were overcome suggests that the gas is heavier than air. And the fact that the candle was *snuffed* suggests that a sufficient concentration was required to create an anoxic environment. Which suggests carbon dioxide, nitrogen or one of the heavier noble gases. Possibly it was some kind of oxygen-uptake by the floor and the walls, but in the absence of some kind of exhaust or stirring mechanism that would have been diffusion-limited, and it is hard to believe that the oxygen depletion proceeded so fast your men did not have time to realise what was happening and get their masks in place. Possibly it was something we've not discovered yet, but the chemical elements are standard throughout the universe and so the chemical laws will be too. I'm also inclined to trust that sensible starship engineers would use something inert, not someone that would place the whole crew at risk. Or possibly it's not gas at all. But the *lantern* was snuffed, so it can't be something that was uniquely directed against human consciousness or even the human organism.'

'That's a lot of suggests and possiblys, Dr Morgan,' A.J. said mildly.

'Man has a dim future in military intelligence,' André Bhakta agreed.

'If one of these guys was your brother,' A.J. said, 'and I ordered him to go in, how nervous would you be?'

'You don't know my brother,' Morgan said, which witticism passed unappreciated. He said, after a moment, 'I'd be very nervous. There are so many unknowns. But if it is simply gas, then you have the equipment. Closed breathing apparatus should be protection against it. Where I would worry is . . . if the aliens do not want us in there, and we have protection against the gas, what are they liable to do next?'

'Seems kind of odd,' Bhakta remarked, 'that they leave the doors wide open.'

'Or they don't want us going down there and putting footprints on the furniture,' Greg Drover said. 'Cooper said one of our guys tripped just before the candle was snuffed. Bet it was Metzner. Biggest feet in the army.'

'He could have tripped because he was already affected,' A.J. said. 'Prof, what do you think is in this cavern?'

'The obvious,' Morgan said, 'is some kind of control room. Which is a place the aliens would not want us in unless we know what we're doing. Alternatively, it is the area occupied by the aliens themselves – but that still begs the question why they would leave the door open.'

'They want to catch some of us for experiments or something.'

'Been watching too much sci fi, Cattleman,' Bhakta said, in his gravelly voice.

'We'll leave alien psychology to the Prof here,' A.J. said.

Morgan sighed. 'How about you wait until after I've met one?'

A.J. smiled drily and waved an open hand towards the dark mouth of the descent. 'Be my guest.'

Morgan met his eyes. 'Let me have one of your gas masks, and I will. Scientific curiosity,' he said, biting down on the words.

If there was a flicker of appreciation in A.J.'s eyes, it was fleeting. 'Sorry, Prof. I'm going to have to ask you to stay up top, at least the first time round. Strategic necessity.'

'You could hold your breath,' Greg Drover suggested, without malice. 'Hey, Sarge, what about the miner's canary? When the Prof falls off his perch . . .'

Morgan said, with a bite in his voice, 'When we get back, remind me to vote for whichever congressman wants to cut military spending.'

Now looking faintly amused, A.J. forestalled a rejoinder and steered them back on to the subject. A hostile examining committee could not have more effectively wrung Morgan dry of knowledge, speculation, fancies and opinions. And at the same time he watched the rapid refinement of a plan from protocols for engagements involving chemical warfare, involving built up areas, involving unknown numbers and armament of enemies. He should have known, seeing how astronauts were trained to follow checksheet and protocol, the distilled wisdom of experience and understanding of the engineering. Given the complexities of modern armament and infrastructure, why should soldiering be different? It was a cultural assumption that the Warrior was a masculine archetype, and an ability to wage war was inborn to men. That might be, but the Warrior in him was still back in the stone age, chucking rocks. He did make one contribution, arguing against the firing of a flare in the dark, unknown chamber.

The trio of Piett, Raho and Hughes returned to report that they had verified the nearest entrance on Stephen's map. Hughes was scowling and scratching at the back of his left hand, muttering dark obscenities at the bug which had bitten him. Drover took charge of him, and Morgan looked on, but at first his questions elicited only a 'What are you, Prof, a fuckin' bug collector?'

Drover said, mildly for him, 'No, Soop –' short for Superman, the inevitable consequence of Hughes first name, Kent – 'he's our fuckin' alien environments specialist.'

The gist of it was: it was a bright blue bug. No, it didn't look like an Earth bug. It had landed on him. It had bitten him. He was ready to tear his fuckin' skin off with the itch. Drover examined the puncture wound under magnification – well versed, Morgan realised, in tropical parasitic insects – pronounced it clear of eggs and foreign bodies, and coated it with antihistamine cream.

Shortly thereafter Boris and Illes returned, reporting another entrance verified. A.J. nodded, and gathered them around. Kent Hughes sat fisting and unfisting his bitten hand; clearly the antihistamine cream was having little effect.

A.J.'s plan involved two men going all the way into the cavern to search it, with others positioned with signal lanterns inside the tunnels. Lanterns would be both light and early warning system. They'd have their masks on, but vented, since their supply of compressed air was limited, but at the first snuffed candle they were to switch over and clear out, explorers, lookouts and all. Bhakta and Illes were appointed to search the cavern. Having seen Bhakta move and Edward Illes run, Morgan could see the sense of that. And, as Raho pointed out, they had the smallest feet in the team. 'Prof,' A.J. said, unexpectedly, 'you up to doing a job for us?' Morgan sat up straighter. 'We've got no radios. We need a runner.' And so he found himself despatched with the half of the team bound for the second tunnel, while Piett stayed as designated runner for the first.

He ran the round trip between the two entrances five times by the time the last man, Illes, emerged from the dark to report he had found no trace of the captain's detachment or the aliens. They had climbed the ramp to its first turn, Stephen's reported position, but as ordered had gone no higher. They could not move out of line of sight of their sentry candles. It was, in Illes words, 'Fuckin' huge down there.' And quite empty.

And by the time he came off his duty as lookout, Kent Hughes was hardly able to stand, shivering, retching, and complaining of the worst headache of his life.

19   Hathaway

Stephen came back. This has to be written real quick because he came back so sick it's scary. He couldn't even make it up my tunnel. He crawled into the opening of it like a sick animal wanting to die and I found him when I went down to work more on making the opening look more like nothing in particular. I don't know how long he was there to start with. He's still there – I couldn't move him. His legs are hanging out of the opening and I'm mad and scared, mad at him, scared for him, scared of being discovered. I don't think he even recognises me. Sometimes when I take him water he doesn't know what to do with it and spills it all over his face. Sometimes he grabs it and drinks it like he wants to drown in it. He smells really bad because I can't clean him up and he's had diarrhoea and peed himself. What'll I do if he dies there?

He didn't die (It's the next day). This morning when the light came up, he was awake. The ship had eaten into his clothes where he'd messed them and when he tried to get up they just tore apart. He was filthy and smelly and his face was sort of blank like he'd run away from himself. He made me think of Peta that night, just sitting huddled up with bits of his clothes torn off and not really noticing what all was showing. His right shoulder was all scarred up like he'd been in a bad accident. He had a bruise on his face and bruises on his arms and one on his stomach – though it didn't look like a bad fight, the kind you ought to go to the emergency room after. He also had some kind of swollen bit on his arm like a bug bite, only he'd cut a cross into it. That looked really gross and made me wonder all over again about him. (Don't ask what I'm wondering. Probably it's just I've watched too many psycho movies.) I brought him down a blanket so he could take the rest of his revolting clothes off and cover himself up. I didn't know how to tell him that I'd seen all kinds of men as bad. But it was like he'd never had anything like that happen to him. Or maybe he had. Anyway I gave him a blanket, and got him to follow me up the tunnel. It was difficult – he was still pretty weak and I'm pretty pregnant. He's over by the water wall washing himself like Peta did. I want to leave him his privacy but I guess I'd better stop him soon. The water's not freezing but it's not hot, either. I don't want him to relapse. I guess I'll go down and get his backpack for him first.

He's gone. I don't mean dead, just gone. When I got up from getting his backpack (I thought I was going to go into labour dragging it up the tunnel. How did such a sick guy haul it so far?) he had crawled out of the bath and was just laying flat on the greenstuff like some big foot had squished him. I used one of my shirts to dry him off because he was shivering and looking terrible and I didn't feel right digging in his big fat backpack. I didn't have any more sexy thoughts, that's for sure. I just dried him off and covered him up. But some time in the dark he got up and got dressed in some of the other stuff from his backpack because he was dressed when the lights came on. I could of sworn I hadn't slept for listening for him getting worse but I guess I did. He looked at me with that look guys get in movies when they wake up beside a one-night-stand and try to think of her name before she guesses he can't. It's supposed to be real ha-ha funny. I guess he didn't remember a whole lot and I didn't have to guess that he wanted to know but didn't want to ask. But I knew I hadn't told him my name so I told him that and said where I'd found him and what had happened to his clothes. I left out some of the graphic details. He said when he started to get sick it came on real quickly. He remembers coming through this cavern but he doesn't remember deciding to come to me or crawling into my tunnel. He looked kind of embarrassed at that. He wouldn't talk about who gave him the bruises – just like you guys – but he said the scars were from being shot when he was out hiking years ago and the bite was from some kind of blue alien bug and he'd cut it open to get any poison out. So no weird self-mutilating rituals – like I should have known better growing up in darkest LA. There's some stuff I really could of known about camping and things up here. But I expected gleaming panels and short little humanoids with big eyes, didn't I? Anyway I offered him chicken noodle soup out of a packet if he had hot water and he took a short fat candle out of his backpack and lit it, and we waited ages in this terminal first-date-ish excruciating silence while it warmed up the water. I had a mug and he had a metal cup so we had lukewarm chicken noodle soup. He told me that people are eating the brown stuff that's coming out of the walls. I'd kind of figured out it was food. Before he took off he sketched a map for me by way of thanks. It shows all the caves near here and all the groups and people who've settled in them. He said he was walking for six days before he got sick and he didn't see anywhere near everything. I think he's hoping that the ship will be too big to walk all over. Now I know who my neighbours are. I'm thinking who to go visit.

TWO

BLIGHT

20 Sophie

The first death occurred on the ninth day, just before lights up. Lying awake on her sleeping-place on the open slope, Sophie heard her name, spoken in a forced whisper. She got soundlessly to her feet and picked her way to the white-flagged corridor between sleeping bodies to meet the whisperer. It was Adrienne LaFleurette.

'Sophie, sorry, but we need you up in the infirmary.' Her hand caught Sophie's arm, to guide or more likely to be guided. She joked about early vitamin A deficiency, but her night-sight was worse than most. Sophie murmured, 'If they want me to look at more specimens, I'm going to have to wait for full light. Can't see a blessed thing under candlelight.'

'It's not that,' she said, and no more.

The interior of the massif was as untidy as the exterior, the barely started resculpting conveying the sense not of reconstruction but of collapse. They entered a corridor whose walls in places were only knee high, a thin webbing between columns of claystone. They passed the infirmary, now the only place allowed to consume the Camp's meagre store of candles and combustibles. As far as anyone could tell, nothing aboard the ship was flammable. The infirmary had a peculiarly purgatorial look, dotted with candle flame, bodies and faces dimly and part lit, and casting heavy shadows. Forms recumbent and upright, the recumbent tossing and shivering, the upright moving carefully, uncertainly in the terrible light. There were more than there had been.

'Thirty cases now,' Adrienne said.

The pathology lab at least had walls higher than eye-level. Sophie insisted upon it, wanting to work undisturbed and without fear of her equipment being picked over by any thoughtless adult or child. Her skin prickled with irritation and primitive territorial response as she realised that the room, her room, was full of people. The remainder of the medical staff were here, as were Arpád, Dominic and several committee members. And then the small hairs raised as she realised what else was present. The long, slab of claystone she had been smoothing and planing to use as a workbench had been cleared, and on it lay the body of a man. The light of the single lantern, placed in a niche in the wall, shone on a livid, dead face.

'Ah, Dr Hemmingway,' said Altman Meyer. 'We are wondering if you

would be so good as to perform an autopsy on this young man for us.'
He peered down at her from his daunting height, a very tall man with a
fine patriarchal beard. A senior thoracic surgeon who had turned to
medical administration when he decided that he had lost his edge,
Meyer would have been the obvious choice for the head of their
medical team – had anyone thought about appointing a head before he
assumed the position more or less by acclimation. He was soft spoken,
mild mannered and the most benign of despots. Most of the junior
staff were terrified of him. As the youngest resident had said, within
Sophie's hearing, 'If he would *shout*, just once, then we would know
the worst he can do. But he *doesn't*. And we *don't*.'

Sophie asked, 'What did he die of?'

Altman Meyer said gently, 'Dr Ellis, why don't you tell Dr Hemmingway
what you know?' The traditional pseudo-invitation to the most
junior amongst them. The young woman swallowed audibly. She was a
second year internist, and had admitted to leaving Earth on impulse
after an affair with a fellow resident had ended humiliatingly. 'If I'd
had to see his smug, *loathsome* face day after day, I'd have done
something violent, I'm sure of it.' But she was a robust, spirited young
woman and although she didn't know it was becoming something of a
favourite with the head – who expressed his favouritism by subjecting
her to constant challenge. She swallowed again and started into the
case history. Male, twenty-seven, formerly in excellent health both by
his report and by report of his wife who had accompanied him.
Children aged four and two. One of the other physicians, a woman in
her late fifties, winced; she had left behind grandchildren that age. He
developed the first symptoms of a 'flu-like illness yesterday. 'What
exactly do you mean by 'flu-like, Dr Ellis?' Sudden onset of fever,
headache, nausea, vomiting – no, no stiff neck. Suffered a series of
grand-mal seizures just before lights down and never regained consciousness afterwards. 'How does this differ from the expected course of
the disease?'

'Dr Meyer,' she said, looking trapped, 'I'm not sure we know enough
about this disease to make judgements about the expected course.'

'Please go on.'

'He developed decorticate posturing about six hours ago, and ceased
spontaneous respiration about two hours ago. We assisted respiration
for an hour thereafter, but both pupils were fixed and dilated, and all
cortical reflexes were absent, and we conferred both between ourselves
and with his wife and decided to discontinue our efforts and he was

declared dead at 12.30 p.m., April 16.' She saw the expressions of doubt and said, 'Allowing for our thirty hour day.'

Sophie nodded thanks to the young woman and shouldered through to stand beside the body. She noticed that they had laid him on a collage of plastic bags and plastic sheeting, to prevent the fibres growing in. Someone had been thinking. She said, 'I can't get started in this light, and I'd like to talk to the next of kin myself. I need to explain what exactly an autopsy entails.' And since she was lacking usual facilities, there were some additional questions she needed to ask about blood borne diseases. Mentally she reviewed the equipment she had to hand. 'I presume you're going to want me to open the cranium? I've got small instruments with me, but I'm going to need something to use as a saw.' She turned away from the body, her foot brushing against the case containing the lab's field microscope – borrowed from an amateur biologist – and a stack of slides and stand ins for slides. Now if she could just have a proper high power microscope, a frozen section apparatus, viral and bacteriological labs and, oh yes, let's not forget electron microscopy. Plus all the technical support she was accustomed to.

'What's the state of our knowledge?' she said, a little wearily.

Little changed from the previous night. They had, the consensus ran, an outbreak of a 'flu-like illness – that useful catchphrase – of still unknown origin. They could still hope that in the morning they would find someone who had already had it, preferably before leaving Earth. Making it familiar, not alien. Someone more callous of personality made a remark about the Andromeda strain which passed unacknowledged. What had changed from the previous night was the knowledge that the illness could be fatal. Whether this was a variant, or something peculiar to this one victim, they did not yet know, could not yet say. Someone muttered, 'I could sure use a coffee,' and a second person yawned, with an audible crack of the jaw. Arpád suffered the ritual with barely restrained impatience. Meyer invited him to advise them, then, of the cause and cure, since he seemed so assured their discussion was to no purpose. A whiff of sulphur hung in the air.

One of the nurses stuck her head over the wall. 'Dr Meyer, Dr Ramachandram ... Could you please come?' And they began to disperse, leaving her alone with the dead.

She started the autopsy at lights up, having spent the previous hour carefully explaining to the dead man's numbed wife what exactly that entailed. She had a vague sinking sense that that was not enough – but lacking refrigeration facilities and needing information she had to proceed. She did her best to be thorough in her briefing, and to have the woman and the man's brother sign and initial her notes and the consent form she had prepared, so that they would not be shocked when they saw the results of her work. She had reassured herself as much as she could that the man did not constitute an infectious risk.

But still she had him moved out of her laboratory and to a presently unused section of the massif, and had Arpád arrange a guard to prevent the curious from peering through the gaps between claystone mounts. There was no smooth slab there, so she must work kneeling.

She took great care laying the plastic. At one point the previous day she had gone to move her foot, and felt it snag before tearing free – and looked down to see a stain on the side of her shoe and sole grown grey and fuzzy. A little longer and she would have had a hole in her shoe. She was competing with a devastatingly efficient salvage system, and would almost have preferred carrion eaters. She would have felt some kinship with vultures, she thought grimly as she laboured, sweating beneath her improvised mask and plastic gown, begging help as she needed to cut through bone. She felt as though she were back in her earliest training, appalled at the rendering of a human body to a hollow shell and heap of glistening organs, and then on to mere darkening meat . . . before she had seen the art and the authority in it, learned the precise and ordered interrogation of the flesh. But this time she was doing the rendering, and rendering it was. For want of proper tools and instruments, half her interrogation would go unasked and the other half would be muddled. Unworthy of her; she was ashamed. But she had to know, she thought, she had to know. Had it only been the others asking her, she might have declined, but she had to know. Still, she felt more like butcher or barbarian priestess than trained pathologist. She had never developed any facility for morgue humour – indeed, for compensatory humour of any kind. She was too close to the dead herself.

When she was done, still plastic-gowned and bloodied, she set the organs out on their plastic beds, and holding the excised brain called the others in. She offered it up; its stigmata would be plain enough to the medically trained and as for the others she said, 'I think I have confirmed what we have suspected. This is a very swollen brain – see how flattened the gyri . . . folds are.' She brushed away the bloody, gelatinous covering of the brain, exposing grey matter. She showed them all the bruised places on the underside of the brain where swelling above had forced portions of brain and brainstem against each other and the base of the skull. The swelling seemed generalised, at least now, but perhaps there had been focal swelling at an earlier stage – the convulsions suggested that. There was no suggestion, in any of the gross specimens, of why the brain had expanded to its own destruction. She surmised a toxic insult of some kind, but she had no way of knowing what. She turned on Arpád with a quite unreasoning bitterness. 'You are going to have to give greater priority to finding me equipment now.'

Arpád looked back at her with a singular blandness. The Hungarian was proving to be a paradox; the starker the situation, the calmer he became. He was vitriolic, choleric and dictatorial in enforcing his precautions, but as true disaster was manifest he became almost serene. Seeing vindication, perhaps. Or confirmation that the world was as malicious as he thought it.

She turned her attention back to the other organs, laid out on their sheets, sectioned neatly; that part of the work she had been able to do to her own satisfaction. They were normal, healthy, young organs from a healthy, young person. The liver was a little yellowed and enlarged, and in places darkened with damage, but that was likely as not agonal. There were signs of change in the kidneys, placed side by side on the plastic. She stood aside while her colleagues scooped up the organs, passing one small set and one large set of gloves down the line from hand to hand. A couple of them, more adept with pen and paper, made detailed sketches. They all had come to appreciate that, lacking any means of preservation, there would be no re-examinations. All the information to be gathered must be gathered now. She eased back, a little impatient for them to be done and gone. She had to take the fresh tissue specimens to the microscope, as soon as possible, though she had managed to formalin-preserve another set, from the small bottle she had brought in her stores. She really had not packed well, she thought; envisioning that anything she brought with her would be redundant, if not a relic, she had packed more for curiosity than function. She was bone tired, physically and emotionally. Forgetting, she leaned her hip against a hump of claystone – and when she moved away, when Arpád gestured to her from the doorway, she felt the tug of snaring threads on a smudge of drying blood.

With Arpád were Stan Morgan and three of his companions from the first day. Stan Morgan looked unsettled and a little revolted at the sight of her bloodied apron; she paused, turned away, shrugged out of it, and laid it inner-side down in the shelter of the hump of claystone, gloves on top. None of the men offered their hands when introduced, the three as members of a US special forces team on reconnaissance, and Stan Morgan as their scientific adviser, from NASA. Morgan quirked her an apologetic smile. He was a slight young man who looked younger than the twenty-five or so years he would have had to be, with a heart-shaped face, black hair, and eyes which were black or very dark brown, and sparkling with intelligence. His front teeth were gold-filled and he had two healed stud holes in one ear. On the shoulder of his beige jacket was the NASA mission patch, the twelve stars representing the official members, and the flowering of outstretched hands, white, black, yellow and red.

The senior of the three soldiers was Team Sergeant A.J. Lowell, a man in early middle age and of unremarkable height who ran to sinew rather than brawn. His eyes were an unsettling marble blue. The medic was Gregory Drover, a wheat-haired young hunk with steady, darker blue eyes. The third was an engineer, Boris Djuraskovic. There was no sign of the medic she had already met, or the young captain. Sick, she thought. Or dead?

'Sergeant Lowell has three men down sick,' Arpád said. 'He came to us because we're the best organised group around, and he thought we'd be the most likely to have some useful information.'

She rubbed palms against jeans, leaving powder smears. 'I wish we did. As you can see, I've just finished an autopsy of our only fatal –'

Arpád was shaking his head, slowly. 'Another one died, just after lights up.'

Sophie nodded acknowledgement. 'The victim was twenty-seven, in excellent physical condition, with no apparent health compromises whatsoever. He developed the first symptoms mid-yesterday, suffered a series of grand-mal seizures just before lights down and never regained consciousness afterwards. He became steadily more unresponsive, developed decorticate posturing, and ceased spontaneous respiration just before lights up. Both pupils were fixed and dilated, and all cortical reflexes were absent. We discontinued resuscitation efforts and pronounced him dead just before lights up. The autopsy confirmed our clinical suspicion of cerebral edema, leading to tentorial herniation and brainstem compression. There's some suggestion of premortem liver and kidney damage, but it's slight. There is no indication in lungs, stomach or intestines of any kind of growth or infestation, no sign of premortem embolus or thrombosis . . . Cause of death appears to have been cerebral edema, query toxic insult, query encephalitis, query unknown.

'At present we have over thirty cases – none predating yesterday –

five of whom are showing the same pattern of deterioration. It is one of these, I presume, who just died.' Arpád nodded. 'The majority of sufferers are young; none has a pre-existing health condition. There is no consistent pattern of contact. There is no common source of food or drink. There is no common point of origin, as far as we know.'

'So you don't know the cause?'

'Our diagnostic equipment,' Sophie said harshly, 'consists of stethoscopes, rulers and reflex hammers. The batteries in otoscopes and electrical instruments disintegrated, of course. Since most of us arrived with references stored on PDA or computer, our knowledge-base consists of what we carry in our heads, and the contents of a number of pocket manuals and paper references. For laboratory equipment, we have assorted field microscopes owned by hobbyists, dissection cases, small quantities of stain, preservatives and some disposables packed by myself and others – more for curiosity value than for use – assorted magnifying glasses and lenses, whatever we have been able to scavenge in the way of plastics and glassware –'

'We might be able to help you there,' Lowell said. 'We're used to being out in the field.'

'We need all the help we can get,' Sophie said. 'No denying that.' She glanced over her shoulder. 'I need to have a word with my assistant about preparing the body for internment, and then I'll be going back to the lab to examine the specimens and try and get the formalin-preserved ones stained and sectioned so I can see something. Could I see you there? We need to put our heads together and find out where this thing is coming from, particularly now.'

'Well, as it happens,' Drover said, 'I've got some ideas on that.'

'Sophie,' Adrienne LaFleurette appeared at her shoulder. 'I've got someone you'd better see.' Her manner conveyed both determination and urgency, and she left Arpád to introduce Drover to the rest of the medical team.

The someone was Stephen Cooper, lurking on the far side of the massif. He was a changed man from the tawny woodsman she had watched prowl away, his face bruised and haggard, his movements at once listless and twitchy. He took in Sophie's approach with a glance and turned his head away, eyes ranging over the landscape. His turning head showed all the fine painted colours of the bruising, two days old at most, shading from black to purple. In his hand he held a crushed tartan ribbon.

He said, 'Watch those sons of bitches,' and jerked a chin towards the massif. Turning, she could just see several more familiar figures loitering outside, half hidden by grey boulders. His eye glanced off hers; he spoke to her but looked at LaFleurette. 'From what Fleur says, I've already had and gotten over your Centauri 'flu.'

'It's possible,' LaFleurette said, 'he's our index case.'

He glanced at her and said to Sophie, 'I got sick a couple of days ago, and just holed up until I got better or fed the rug,' he gestured downwards towards the green matting, making meaning plain. ''Course, I didn't know then that feeding the rug was a possibility. Fleur says people are dying of this. I only wanted to die. But what Fleur also wants me to tell you is that just before I got sick I got bit by one of those pretty little blue bugs.' He held out his hand. Beneath the dense, light brown hair of his forearm was a long crusted weal, crossed with two short, deep incisions, scabbed black. He said, 'I did the snakebite drill. You've spent the time in the woods I have, you respect wildlife. Didn't make a blind bit of difference. About four hours after it bit me I had the headache and the wet and dry heaves.'

The 'insects', Sophie thought. It made a certain superficial sense. She said to LaFleurette, 'Will you look into it? Find out how many people who are ill have been bitten. And how many people who have been bitten have fallen ill?'

She nodded, but did not move. Sophie wondered at that; she had a sense that LaFleurette was not prepared to leave them alone. There was a watchfulness to her – but she sensed no jealousy. There was tension between the other woman and Stephen, but it was not sexual. Stephen glanced her way, and his mouth twisted. He had an expressive face, for a man.

'Would you be prepared,' she said, to Stephen, 'to trap me one of those bugs? Are you up to going out again?'

'Sure thing, your ladyship,' Stephen said, ironically.

'Wait a moment.' She threaded her way into the massif, disregarding would-be walls to take the straightest route to her laboratory. The medical team were still milling around outside, the We-Brought-It-From-Earth versus It-Came-From-Out-There wrangle in full cry. She heard someone discoursing on insect-borne diseases. Somebody else said, 'Sophie!' She looked around the wall. 'If it's bugs, I just heard. I'm putting people on it,' and kept going before she could be drawn in. In the laboratory she rummaged in the horde of odd pill bottles, used up cosmetic jars and mismatched sample vials, pulled out several glass vials and carried them back to Stephen and Adrienne. As she handed them over, a blue spark dropped suddenly from the air on to her skin; she flicked it off, with reflex revulsion. Stephen and LaFleurette watched with narrowed eyes; only when it flew off did they breathe again, look at each other, smile identical thin smiles. LaFleurette cuffed Stephen lightly on the arm. 'Come on, let's go catch us a bug.'

21 Hathaway

I went down to visit the women on Stephen's map. They're still in the cavern we landed in but they've got themselves a good place (not as nice as mine!) in a small cavern off the main one, with just one long tunnel. They're all camped at the far end and they're building what looks like a really impressive washing and bathing area and a sort of multistorey cliff house out of the caverns and holes. I'd have stayed longer to help but there was this bossyboots nursey-type who started trying to take me over. She wanted to measure my stomach so *she* could tell *me* when my baby was due. Like *I* couldn't count. Next she'd be wanting to know about my *living situation* and my *preparedness for motherhood*. I came up here to get away from people telling me what was best for me and then making me into a problem when I didn't agree with them. Fortunately – well for me at least and maybe for her because I was ready to give her a faceful – one of the other women came back from outside sick like Stephen was and kept her busy.

I did get to talk to this incredibly old woman with an amazing English accent like Masterpiece Theatre. She was more or less blind with one eye sort of going off in its own direction. Her hair is this surreal whiter-than-white like it had been washed in whiteners. I like that way and away better on an old person than fake-young dyed hair all around a wizened up old face. Her face has lines to spare but it isn't wizened or saggy. Actually she has this great Katharine Hepburn bone structure with her skin kind of *pitched* over it like a tent. Her hands are all blotched and leathered and scrawny like they've been buried in a peat bog for thousands of years. She was wearing a woolly and proper skirt and sweater in old lady lavender and sneakers so junky no kid would be seen dead in them at school. She has an old-fashioned teacherly way of speaking that makes you sit up straight with a kind of racial memory of all the schoolkids since the caves. But we talked about things you never expect to talk about with old ladies like about illegitimate babies and abortions. She knew a girl who gave herself an abortion because she was pregnant by a German soldier back in World War II. She's seen a lot of life. I guess it takes as much guts for an old lady to come along as it does for a kid.

After I'd seen the woman sick at the women's camp it was like on my way back every camp I passed had someone sick in it. I got a lot of complicated hard looks from a distance. Most times hard looks from a distance are simple. Guys decide whether you're worth hitting on or not and girls decide whether you're competition or not. Having a pumpkin stuck up under your shirt generally makes things real simple. But this time people looked at me like I could have been a lot of other things beside a good lay. I started thinking of those grotesque stories they made us read in English where people start putting all the evil on to one person and then killing them to make the evil go away. I hated those stories. Obviously I got back here fine but I'm not going downstairs again for a while. I don't want to catch what's going around. Being that sick wouldn't be good for the baby. I'm going to stay put up here and work on my mural. I'm getting really good at bringing out the colours and I'm working on using the wall colour as a base and then putting on paint over top. That lets me put shadows in or change the colour from a quick walk through the rainbow. Mr Rosen's theoretical stuff about lights and pigments is starting to mean something. So you can tell him it maybe took a while but it stuck. I had a lot of fun figuring out how to overlay the paint because the stroking of the brush or my fingers would change the colour underneath. I can make a spray-tube from a straw cut almost in half and bent over. The only trouble is I don't have ink and the paint has to be watered a lot to get it sprayable so I have to spray a *lot* of layers to get the colours I want, and ever since I got pregnant, way before the baby got big enough to crowd anything, I've had no puff. So I get to watch little black spots with bright white edges while I'm doing it. But with a lot of blowing and panting (sort of like preparation for labour) Neil Armstrong will get his black moon sky. I am real pleased with Magellan. The sky behind him just glows. I wish I'd thought about bringing my polaroid after all and hadn't got so into leaving everything about Laguna Beach behind so I could send you pictures. You'll have to make do with a drawing.

22 Sophie

Through the broken and tumble down walls drifted the tune of the twenty-third psalm, sung by voices not quite in unison, dragging and stumbling over each other. Another committal to their burial yard. Sophie sighed and laid down the microscope, rubbing her eyes.

The microscope was a field one, but of good quality, though using ambient light was enough to make her eyes ache. But she could resolve cellular morphology. For all the good that did her . . . She tilted the slide and looked at the smear of red thereon. In the slides she had taken from the autopsy from the day before, she could see very little that was abnormal. She could talk of toxic insults, hypothesise that the insult seemed to compromise the cerebral vasculature, allowing fluid to be pressed from the blood vessels into the tissues. She could wish for a thin section setup, a high resolution microscope; she could, she thought, with a very thin smile, offer up her very soul in exchange for an electron microscope which might, might, let her resolve an infectious agent, a virus or mycoplasma, or visualise the insult to the membranes.

Absurd, she thought, with her elite training, her elite experience, to leap into space only to be landed back in the middle ages.

She slid from the stool, a stalagmite with a flattened cap, and stretched out aching shoulders. Rolled her head, listening to the crepitus in her neck. The psalm meandered to a close. A man's voice began the eulogy. That would be the eighth death since the outbreak began. That the majority of people, like Stephen, recovered was not as comforting as it should have been. It must be nearly nightfall; she squinted against the brightness overhead, but could not see the coloured pennant from where she was. In all probability it would be dark blue, and presently the warning drum would sound and dark return, leaving them in the infernal light of a few candles.

'Sophie!' Stan Morgan, swinging a leg over an unfinished wall, made her start. He thrust a stoppered glass vial at her. In it, a fleck of brilliant blue beat upon the walls like a maddened fire spark. 'They caught one.'

She slid the vial into the microscope, and leaned forward, seeing blue flickering in and out of focus as the captive jiggered. She pinned the vial in place with her finger and eased back. Stephen and Adrienne had come in through the door, Adrienne looking desperately tired, eyes hidden behind a pair of hiker's sunglasses. Stephen gave her a savage look, which she did not try to interpret. 'Thanks,' she said, and he bared his teeth.

Abruptly, the little mote ceased its mad darting and slipped into the gutter of the vial. She leaned forward slowly, so as not to startle it into new frenzy, shifting the vial only slightly to bring it into view. And thus she was almost too slow to see it at all. For when she found it, it was already crumbling, dull blue and losing definition, ash falling away from it. In the time she took to draw breath it was gone, and in its place was a tiny smudge of pale grey. She said softly, 'My God.'

Stephen Cooper said, 'What?' Morgan stepped forwards. She leaned aside so that he could bend down to see. He glanced into the eyepiece, squinted, and then lifted the vial. The little smudge of ash quivered, dispersed and vanished.

Morgan's expression was intent, deeply absorbed. Sophie felt a paradoxical nausea at so clean and traceless a decay. Morgan said, 'So now we know why we haven't seen any dead ones around.' Sophie repressed a shudder at the thought of the fine, invisible dust coating skin, tongues, being breathed and eaten. She said, 'I didn't move fast enough to get a good look at the shape of it. It had a body, but I could not make out mandibles or legs or any kind of stinger. Whatever happened, happened very fast.' She half closed her eyes, trying to visualise the insect as she had first seen it. She had a sense that some insight was waiting just beyond the horizon of her understanding. Stone which could be moulded and extruded, but would crumble away when separated from the whole. Trees which dropped no needles, a ground cover which, when plucked, turned to dust within minutes. An insect which went from frenzied animation to dissolution within seconds. All the same. She felt her thoughts bunch and resist at the stretch of it. Stone, plant and insect, the same, not merely in elemental composition, but molecularly, structurally, perhaps even functionally, the same. She sat, gripping the edge of the stool, anchoring herself as the world tilted sideways beneath her. She could see, as with a strong, slanted light, the long shadows of all the assumptions and presumptions of her specialist training, the separation of plant from animal, of animate from inanimate.

'The question is,' Morgan said, 'whether it's organic, or mineral, or a product of nanotechnology, or something we haven't got round to imagining.' He met her blank stare and something in it halted him. He looked past the raised vial, questioningly. 'It's all the same,' he said, in a tone which apologised for pointing out the obvious.

For a moment she hated him, for his supple mind and his diffidence. It was as though he mocked her with his respect, with his presumption that she was his peer. But for her the understanding that stone, plant and insect were all the same had seemed a long reach of imagination, while he had tripped over it in an instant and danced on to consider what that sameness might be.

Damn him, she thought, damn him. I am out of my depth here; if I find what I have come for, I might not know it.

Morgan said, 'Sophie, we're all out of our depth here.' The realisation she had spoken the first part of her thought – if not, mercifully, the second – made her flush. 'Yes,' she said, 'but some of us were at least thinking about the prospect of going into space, if not about the fixtures and fittings.'

He slid on to the stalagmite at her side. 'We've been assuming, you know, that the fixtures and fittings were here to make us feel at home. That might have been why they are the shape they are, but their function is quite different. The green matting on the floor does the job of sucking up waste, presumably for recycling. And the trees – have you noticed how they've grown? – could be involved in gas exchange. They're not photosynthesising, but they're cleaning up the gases – catalysis, maybe.'

'And the bugs?' she said, flatly.

He seemed not to hear her. 'But the claystone's the most interesting of all. It's not like anything on earth. It's not familiar, and yet people have taken to it as though it's nothing unusual, shaping it into all kinds of things, but what's the purpose of it? If you make the assumption that this substance or machine or whatever it is could be anything it needs to be, then the forms it takes have a reason behind them. We need something to sop up our waste from the ground and the air, we need something to sit on and to lie on, we need food, water, shelter. And maybe because of the nature of this substance or machine then the shelter has to come in the form of caves rather than rocks or bricks – but we're used to moving rocks and bricks around, so why this? There's an inconsistency here. What I don't think we've been seeing is that we are in a very smart environment. And it's *acting* on us, modifying us. It started acting on us from the very beginning – the hours, or maybe days, or who knows how long we actually lost? – the fact that none of our electronic equipment works, the way those periods of darkness make us quiescent, the precise tactile stimuli we have to give to mould the claystone. We've been assuming that because no little green men have come among us and said "Welcome Earthlings" that we've been left to manage as best we can. But it's likely there's a purpose to everything around us, and it's not just our environment. I think we're being trained by our interaction with it.'

'Trained for what?' she said, curious in spite of herself.

'I'd like to think we're being trained to communicate with or interact with the ship. Of course it's also entirely possible that we're simply rats in a maze, undergoing stimulus-response training,' he grimaced at the thought. 'Maybe this is some kind of entrance exam. Given the diversity of species they claim to have recruited they must have refined some way of selecting and training crews. Wonder what they do with the washouts?'

'I trust,' Sophie said, 'we never find out.'

Morgan gave her a wide, dark eyed look, and she realised that the question was more rhetorical than not, that he feared he knew what they might be doing with the washouts.

Adrienne LaFleurette cleared her throat. She had slid down the claystone wall, to squat with her back against it, her vivid red anorak bunched up to frame her face. Stephen stood over her protectively. 'Some things I don't think I need to hear,' she said, huskily. 'We were right about the bugs.' She hitched a hip to drag her notebook from a back pocket. 'Every single person who's sick was bitten. The people who aren't sick, haven't been bit.' She flipped the pages of the notebook at Sophie, balancing forearm on thigh with the notebook trailing from her fingers. 'C'mere. I haven't got it in me to get up.' Sophie went to her and took the notebook, noticing how LaFleurette's fingers trembled slightly as she gave it up. Beneath the concealing shades her mouth was tight. She dropped her hand – and Sophie, in the act of stepping back, stopped. On LaFleurette's left wrist, masked by the dusky skin and until then covered by her red cuff, was a raised welt. LaFleurette followed her gaze down, and said, 'Yeah.'

'How long ago?' Sophie said, crouching before her.

LaFleurette leaned her head back against the wall. 'Three, four hours. It wasn't the one we brought in, though we tried for that one. Must have fallen apart. I was kidding Ste about missing the catch. Sorry, Ste.'

She understood now Stephen's suppressed anger, unfair as it was. With her fingertips she eased the cuff back to expose the welt, which was easily three centimetres in breadth. LaFleurette's skin was hot and damp.

'Whatever they shoot in is irritating as all hell,' LaFleurette said. 'You spend a couple of hours wanting to gnaw your hand off just to be rid of the itch, and then the headache starts and you probably wouldn't notice an amputation unless it were capital.'

'Photophobia?' Sophie said, to her twin miniature reflections.

'Yes.' LaFleurette swallowed. 'Let me see if I can give you a precis. There's a one hundred per cent correlation between bug bites and the Centauri 'flu. I haven't met anyone who hasn't been bitten who has it, and I haven't met anyone who has been bitten who doesn't – could I have some water, please?' Morgan scrambled to bring it. 'Thanks,' she sipped. 'Symptoms, in the majority, headache, myalgias and arthralgias, muscle spasms and swelling in the affected arm, fever, nausea, vomiting – think of influenza A with superimposed black-widow bite, and you'll get the picture.'

'I can't wait,' muttered Morgan.

'Trust me, Professor, you can,' she said. 'Most people recover after one or two days' acute illness, like Stephen, seemingly independent of any intervention. But in the minority there's a progressive downhill course – seizures, coma and death. I've seen eight or nine people who will not make it without a miracle. All of them young, fit and up until now healthy. Which brings me back to the bugs. The people who've been bitten have all been young, fit types, none of the older people, none of the kids, nobody who's got any kind of chronic illness. One of the docs I spoke to a couple of caverns over – older guy, some health problems – said he'd watched one of those bugs walk all over himself and three other people, before it finally bit the fifth, who's a trail guide and hunter, and doesn't look like she's had a day sick in her life. She's damn sick, now, one of the ones we're probably going to lose. So,' her mouth twisted ruefully beneath the protective shades, 'I suppose it's a compliment, but I've had ones I liked better. It's not as though we have the resources to do a damn thing about this sickness, except last it out, and try not to get bit. But I had gloves on – and the thing got in between my cuff and my glove.'

'It's possible it's some kind of self-assembling nanotechnology –'

'Self-assembling nanotechnology, huh?' LaFleurette said, heavily. 'So I'm being assimilated by the Borg, am I? I'm too sick for this man,' she remarked to the claystone walls. Morgan drew breath. LaFleurette held up a hand. 'Prof, I'm sure you two have come up with some really nifty ideas. But we have an epidemic on our hands; we may know the vector, but we know damn little about either the vector or the disease itself, including how wide it's going to spread, how much worse it's going to get, or how to stop it. So I strongly suggest that you apply your combined genius to creating a better mosquito netting, or some kind of bug-repellent, and work out the whys and the wherefores later.'

'If these bugs are self-assembling machinery,' Morgan pointed out, 'mosquito netting will probably not stop them. They'll be able to disassemble as much as they need to to get through.'

'You're such a comfort to a sick woman,' LaFleurette said. She put a hand up to Stephen. 'Ste, give me a hand here.' With surprising gentleness he raised her, and helped her out the door. 'I hope,' he flung back over his shoulder, 'this was worth it.' She said, 'Shh. Ste, it's not their fault.'

Sophie opened LaFleurette's notebook. Her hands felt cold and stiff as she turned pages, not reading, but looking at the other woman's handwriting, black ink, the letters large and square in form. She flipped past notes of the early days of their arrival. The later handwriting hardly changed, though the notes were made in haste, and told of unfolding disaster. Even the final pages, after LaFleurette had been bitten, were readable, though the handwriting was hectic and in places the ink had been smudged by a sweaty hand. The notes were, if anything, more coherent and less cryptic. LaFleurette had no longer been writing solely for herself, but for an audience who might take up this book when she was no longer there to interpret. The knowledge that she might die was a subtext to every complete sentence, every expanded abbreviation.

Morgan looked shaken. He hitched himself up on to the stool and sat staring at his hands, turning his heavy class ring on his finger. 'Sophie,' he said, 'why are they doing this?'

'Why not?' she said, a little angrily. 'They can.'

He looked at her, got up as though to leave, sat down again. He was not certain, she realised, how to react to her. 'They have treated us,' he said carefully, 'exceptionally well up until now. Our environment has been managed to be safe and suitable, and to provide for our needs.'

'You said yourself that this environment was acting upon us. Maybe this is yet another instance of that. A test, to see how we perform. Or a stimulus to make us learn something.'

He looked troubled. She wondered if, like her, he had been indoctrinated with gentle Jesus meek and mild. Coerced into faith in a benign and harmless Power when a truer manifestation would have been the Old Testament God, capricious, arbitrary and inexplicable. Children understood those things; lacking understanding or power, they had no choice. It was only adults who insisted upon a sugar coating.

Morgan said, 'That's a disturbing thought.'

'That they should treat us like we have treated inferior beings for centuries? Yes, that is disturbing.'

'Maybe it is just their ignorance. Maybe they simply do not know enough about us to know that this is going to hurt us.' He sounded uncertain, not about the thought, which was valid enough, but about what it implied.

'Does it really matter at this point, why?' she said. She handed him the notebook. 'Adrienne's right. We don't know enough to think about mechanisms or meanings. We have to first deal with what is happening, and how we stop it.' He wanted to continue the argument, reason perhaps a defence against fear. 'It doesn't matter why,' she said, with finality. He took the notebook, yielding. He leafed through it, and then started to read, his head hunched down and his hands held lightly over his ears, only his right moving to turn pages. She knew she should do something while he read, something to advance their cause or simply pass the time. But she did not know what.

She heard a movement, and looked over at Morgan. He was holding the book between his spread hands, like a butterfly, and spoke as soon as she met his eyes. 'How do the bugs *know* people aren't healthy?' He tapped a page, 'She's got this great long list of what people have who haven't been bitten. NIDDM, LE, ME, CAD, CVD, COPD, ADHD – at least I have to presume these are medical conditions,' he finished, sounding pained. 'Everyone accuses physicists of talking Greek . . .'

Sophie went to his side, looking down at the book. LaFleurette had indeed started listing the conditions of the people who had not been bitten. The data was incomplete, scruffy, having been started in the middle of the survey, as the pattern became clear to her. She slid into a squat, taking the book from his hands, and leafing through it. It wasn't good data, not scrambled together as it was, and yet . . . 'Presumably the bugs could get an idea of people's state of health, if not their specific disease, from their skin – constituents of their sweat, secreted metabolites etc. So you'd get excess urea in uremic states, excess glucose in diabetic states, and so on. If they were to sample capillary blood – which they might be able to do without the host noticing – they'd have electrolyte balance, lipids, cells, blood gases, clotting factors, enzymes, in fact, the whole body chemistry profile. And then if they were to sample DNA they would be able to identify genetic disorders, assuming that they knew enough about us to know what a normal chromosome was.'

'Suppose we could convince them,' Morgan said, slowly, 'that healthy people who haven't had the Centauri 'flu are sick? I mean, somehow change their sweat or their body odour so they *smell* sick. Maybe we should even try to make them sick with something less serious than the 'flu.'

'If it is just smell and skin chemistry –'

'Change clothes,' Morgan interrupted her. 'Healthy people wear the clothes of sick people. Or perfumes. Maybe there are particular perfumes that would repel the bugs. Maybe we should be thinking about bug repellent, not vaccines, as Fleur says. Maybe even insect repellent. Maybe we should try not to smell human. Maybe smell like the ship itself. Suppose we rubbed claystone dust all over ourselves.

What would immersion in water do . . .?' He stopped himself with a visible effort and a shudder, staring at her, willing her approval, contribution . . . 'It may not be good data,' he said, passionately, 'but it's damn smart of her to see the pattern! There has to be a reason for the way the bugs are biting. It'll take hardly any time. I haven't been bitten. You haven't been bitten. We should get hold of clothes from someone who has something wrong with them – clothes that have been worn.' He got up. 'Half the camp – the ones who're still well – exchange clothes. The other half . . . And we'll go out and ask about perfumes, aftershaves, bug repellent – see if there's a pattern. If nothing else we'll confuse the bugs, give us time to work out something better. We don't have time not to do anything. None of us may . . .' He checked himself, and said, 'Oh, damn, I wonder if migraine headaches count. I wonder if that's why they've been avoiding me. Sophie? Do you fit that list? I mean, is there a reason you may not have been bitten?'

For a moment she looked at him, and then she felt a false, wary smile form on her face. 'Just lucky, I guess.'

He nodded, satisfied, and went out.

23   Hathaway

All of a sudden, I've got bugs. I saw them downstairs the day before yesterday but I was so bugged by people I forgot to be bugged by bugs. They're strange bugs like someone made them out of frosted glass stained deep blue to hang on earrings or something. I can't actually be sure whether I've got just one bug or a bunch because I only see one at a time. It finds some skin and crawls on it and then flies off again and disappears. Then another one comes.

But the big news is my picture wall has grown a picture all its own, low down and at the edge like whoever did it was shy! It would be creepy if I thought someone had been up here or maybe I'd been walking in my sleep, but it gets so dark that people just don't move around and any time I'm not properly awake and try to get up I fall over because I don't balance the way I used to. So I think the ship did the picture all by itself. It's a picture of the ship like the pictures the telescopes gave. Only not really like. On the telescope pictures the ship looked like a funny oval moon, all sort of grey and pitted and crescent shaped or squashed oval shaped depending upon where the sun was. On this picture the ship is all there and the light trails off it like seaweed. I'm kind of disappointed to be honest. Special effects are for movies. I want to see for real and I'm sure that the ship doesn't really look like that from outside. One thing though – the sky around it is totally black. Nothing shines through. I rubbed my finger on the black spot but nothing came off. It's a bit like a big round dark freckle.

Later. This picture wall really is the greatest thing. After looking at the new picture I decided I'd do a picture just above it of one of those sailing ships that fly on the solar wind. Uncle Stan thought they were the neatest. (I wonder where he is.) I guess I was thinking that maybe the picture of the ship was the ship or the aliens answering all my paintings so I was trying to show them I understood. Anyway I started sketching really lightly so I could change up the orangy yellow and then I noticed that the first line I sketched was turning black as black. Just the first one. I went to a spare bit of wall and started experimenting but nothing worked and I was just standing scowling at the wall with my arms folded when I remembered touching the big black freckle around the ship's ship. I thought maybe it's like a sort of drag-and-drop display like those fancy computers they have at school. So I went over and touched the freckle again and came back and touched the wall. And hey presto! Black. And there was nothing at all on my finger, not even a smell (though my nose has been so snuffy with being pregnant I'm not the best person to say. But I'm the only person here.) So then I thought it might work the other way and I touched the wall and went and touched the freckle and where my finger hit it went white. So then I went and touched all my colours and dabbed them on to the wall and then I touched the dabs and made more dabs. I went a bit wild for a while doing fingerpainting and handpainting and foot painting. And I know this will sound kinky but I even took my clothes off and did boob and stomach and butt painting. I'm real glad that Stephen or somebody didn't decide to call right then. My baby is going to have so much fun here. All this colour colour colour and no messy fingerpaints for me to yell at her about getting on her clothes.

Only I'd forgotten about the bugs and one landed on my right boob (a nice big fat target of course) and bit me. I swatted it. It felt like a bead and came up stuck to my hand and when I flicked it off it flew away. It's a bird – it's a plane . . . it's Superbug. Anyone bring some Kryptonite along? It's come up in a big, red lump and it itches so bad that I've scratched all around it trying not to scratch *on* it. I've tried putting water on it. I tried putting white paint on it to act as a lotion but it still itches and it's driving me insane. I'm going around with my shirt off and I'll stomp on any bug that shows its buggy little face with my whole 150 pounds. I haven't seen any since that one bit me but still I'm trying to work out how to make a mosquito netting. I don't trust them. Crawling around me like they were harmless and then chomp!! I need a real fine thread and I'd take anything of mine apart if only I knew how to spin one. I wish I'd brought a book on weaving. I guess I thought there'd be replicators or something. I bet Captain Picard never got bit by bugs!

But the ship picture has changed. It's passing by a planet. I recognise the planet from the pictures Uncle Stan used to send me. It's Jupiter with its big red eyespot and it doesn't look any different from the ship. Just duller. Uncle Stan said that they'd done all kinds of image enhancement on the pictures with the distance and darkness and all. And they sometimes changed the light to be like a light on earth so human eyes would see best. I wonder what kind of eyes the ship is expecting. We must be moving some if we've reached Jupiter already and we've only been up here for eleven days. Though it's probably a bit longer. I read about people locked up underground and how they completely lost touch with time outside. I guess maybe that woman was right about having to measure rather than count to know how time was passing for my baby but that still doesn't mean I'm going to ask her. I've started measuring my stomach around with a knotted string and I'm reading the book over carefully so I can find clues about how big I'll get when. It's still all hung up about counting days. Sorry, digression city. Being pregnant makes me totally self centred. Getting back to where I was if Jupiter is where we are at we're boogying right along. Earth spacecraft take years to reach Jupiter though of course they go by some loopy routes to take advantage of slingshot effects and all. But even flying direct a rocket wouldn't be nearly as fast. Maybe the picture wall will show the ship joining the whole fleet later on. If there really is a whole mob of them. Gypsy Green Men. Hell's Aliens. Intergalactic Hobos. I guess people were disappointed that they hadn't come to have serious conferences about human-alien relations and the state of the galaxy. I'm not. Nobody'd ever have let me into these conferences. But hey all you experts. I'm talking to the ship and the ship she is talking back to me.

Pregnancy is such a drag. I'm starting to get a headache and feel really gross. Too much excitement, I guess. So I'll put my shirt back on and go lie down for a while.

I'm sick. I think I've got what Stephen had. My head feels like the world's worst migraine. The light hurts my eyes so bad and I feel sick to my stomach, way worse than I ever did with morning sickness. I'm sorry I was ever sulky when Uncle Stan couldn't do stuff he'd promised to when he had his headaches. I didn't know.

It's dark now, so my writing's bad. Head hurts. Hot. Stephen, with greenstuff growing in. Think about it, throw up again.

Maybe running away wasn't such a hot idea after all.

24 Sophie

On the second day of her illness, Adrienne LaFleurette died. The death was but briefly deferred by the improvisation of a hand-powered respirator. Seven men and women laid hands to the piston, one after another, forcing air into the tube in the young woman's throat. In, out, in, out. Stephen huddled at her head, looking near demented. On the respirator, his fine sense of timing had deserted him, and he had forced the air faster and faster until A.J. Lowell had pulled him away. Lowell had remained until the medical team came to consult, and pronounce on her. Sophie did not. She was too tired even to berate herself for a failure of courage.

In the laboratory, Morgan looked up at her from the microscope from eyes sunk in smudgepits. 'They're going to pronounce her,' she said, before he asked.

'Damn.' Morgan's eyes filled with tears. He half turned away. 'If we'd just realised sooner . . .' He stood a moment, struggling with himself, muttered, ''Scuse,' and left.

She spread out Adrienne's notebook. She had continued it with her own notes. Her own handwriting, her own words, looked feathery and dead as dust. Somehow, she thought, she had dreamed, she had deluded herself that she had left behind death, on Earth. And this, these deaths in this unimagined place, had broken something in her. She watched, as through glass, the discipline of her colleagues, the valiant energy of Morgan and the handful of other scientists who had gathered in the massif – she knew that theirs was the only way to face it, and that the glass was only in her mind, needing only an internal gesture to break it down. And yet she could not make that internal gesture. This, she supposed, was depression. She had been well fortified against depression all her life, titrating out pleasure and energy, self, disciplining her thoughts, her aspirations, her relationships. At all times, control, no risks, no recklessness. And then the aliens' message, risk, recklessness, unimaginable hope. She could have wept at the folly of it all, but within the glass was a vacuum, airless and tearless.

111

A man's voice rose in a wordless, almost bestial howl. She shuddered, as the sound peaked and fell away to silence. It was not repeated. A few minutes later Morgan returned, very pale, looked at her, shook his head.

He was wearing the clothes of a larger, heavier man, white shirt, dark blue trousers belted into the waist and with the ankles rolled up, giving him an almost comic air. They were the clothes of the elderly physician Adrienne had spoken to, who had had bugs land on him but not bite. In the end they had included him in their experiment and he had drawn the black counter for experimental rather than control. Sophie still wore her shirt and black jeans. In her pocket was the black counter she had palmed from the draw; on the bench, beside the microscope, was the white one she had presented, for no better reason than thinking she would contaminate the result less as a member of the control group. But still, it sat there, accusing her scientist's conscience.

Morgan said, 'He won't let her go.' He shook down his cuffs, pushed them up again. 'He won't let her go.'

She thought a moment about going back to the ward – but there were people there, medical staff and their helpers. They had both the expertise and the brawn to deal with Stephen's grief. 'People react in many strange ways to unexpected death. And sometimes the ones who react most violently are not the ones we need to worry about.'

'Right.' He began to roll his cuffs up again, looked up with a brittle determination and said, 'So, how are we doing, otherwise? Still no more bites.'

'No.'

'So it's working.'

'Morgan, there have been *no* bites at all for the past day, not even among the control group.'

'Maybe the aliens have realised they've made a mistake; maybe they're alarmed that some of us are actually dying. I haven't seen a bug around for several hours, have you? Maybe,' he said, tentatively, 'it's over.'

There was a sudden sound of raised voices from the direction of the ward. Through the half finished walls and columns and mounds of slumped claystone they caught glimpses of stirred bodies. Stephen's tawny head appeared in the middle of the group. People moved well aside; it was that that told Sophie what he was carrying, what he was using to push them aside, even before he stepped into full view. She went out to meet him. He stopped, eyes flat on hers, looked down at Adrienne and with a hunch of his shoulder jolted her head so that it lolled forward and not back, her chin on her chest, her damp temple against his chest. His arms hunched around her. 'You can't have her.'

'Stephen,' she said, 'what are you going to do?'

'What the fuck do you care? She's just another carcass to you.'

'That's not true,' Sophie said. 'She was a colleague and was on her way to becoming a friend. I might like to pay my respects as well.'

'Go ahead then. Say you're sorry.'

'I *am* sorry.' She glanced past him, at the people gathered behind. A.J. Lowell in the foreground, arms folded, his pale eyes on Stephen. One of the special forces team – Boris Djuraskovic – had died the day before. 'I am sorry,' she said, a little less emphatically. 'I am sorry that the insight she had, which may have saved other people's lives, came too late to save hers.' He drew a shallow furious breath, and pushed past. Adrienne's trailing hand swung with his movement and slapped her thigh. She could feel the slap long after Stephen was gone. A moment later, one of Lowell's team moved down the aisle after him. The medical staff, uneasy, returned to their work. She and Morgan went back into the laboratory.

Morgan said, 'You don't think it's over, do you?'

'I fail to see,' Sophie said in a still voice, 'why it should be. We have done nothing to stop it.'

'Why does it have to be something we do?' Morgan asked curiously.

'Because if it isn't,' she said, 'we haven't learned anything.' She turned away, towards the microscope, and the tape-labelled slides – made from scored and broken fragments of glass. Of the slides labelled in her handwriting there were none she had not already examined, to the best of her ability.

'Sophie,' Morgan said suddenly. 'Why did you come?'

She lifted her head, turned to look at him. He made a half movement towards self-deprecating dismissal and stopped himself. 'I mean – I came because I'd been thinking about space ever since I was small. I grew up poor, and it sure beat what was around me. I'd have applied for astronaut training if I thought I'd have had the chance. But I loved my work. I ... I can't say I love being here, not with the present circumstances, but everything I've done with my life has been pointing to this moment, this place. Even if I didn't know it was to happen. But you ... you're not like that. You're feeling your way along, you're doing your best, but you're just ... lost. I guess,' he said, and now he did smile in apology, 'I'm wondering why someone like you, bright, privileged – I mean, Harvard – beautiful,' he stumbled slightly over the word, reminding her suddenly of her own younger brother in his prolonged adolescence, 'would leave.'

113

'I had my reasons,' she said, after a moment.

He bit his lip slightly, colouring a little. 'Are you using the microscope?' he said carefully, though she was sure she had moderated her tone. 'I've got some slides I want to check.' He carefully lifted a clipboard with several glass slides, each with a small particle of matter. 'We may not have any bugs, but since it looks like the bugs, the claystone and the matting all break down in the same way, we might be able to get some idea – though the dust is so damn fine . . . I'm also trying to determine if the presence of organic matter – the kind of thing that gets reabsorbed – determines the length of time to breakdown. In other words, whether isolated ship's stuff for want of a better term, breaks down because of lack of nutrients. Assuming,' he bent his head, bracing the microscope on the bench, 'that the organic material is nutrient for the ship's stuff and not merely being recycled for us. I'm not entirely convinced this isn't some kind of nanotechnology . . .' his voice wavered, and she knew he was thinking of Adrienne, 'that maybe doesn't have chemical input at all, but does need to remain in contact with the ship to hold its shape . . . maybe energy or a signal. You know when you isolate a piece of matting until it disintegrates and then put the' – he paused, to scribble some hieroglyphics in his own notebook – 'dust on a smoothed bit of claystone it vanishes in a very short time. Reabsorbed or –' Without warning Morgan jerked back violently. Sophie lunged to catch the microscope as it bounced from his hand on to the bench and before it rolled to its destruction on the floor. Rather to her surprise, and not without a heart stopping fumble, she did. She looked up at him, incredulous – and saw a blue spark wink against his overlarge white shirt, like a spark or a small demon's eye.

They stared at each other a moment. Her mouth was suddenly dry.

'Did it –?'

Silently, he held out his hand. A tiny bead of blood stood on the soft skin at the base of his thumb.

He looked so stricken that she carefully set down the microscope and took his hand in both hers, avoiding the area of the bite. His fingers were cold and hooked convulsively around hers. She said, quietly, 'It'll be all right, Morgan. I'm sure it will.'

He shook his head. 'If the biting starts again – if it starts on people who're already sick –'

'One swallow does not a summer make,' Sophie said. 'Let us wait, shall we?'

'I should have listened to you. I shouldn't have presumed – shouldn't have been complacent.' He looked at his neatly arranged slides and her fingers tightened on his hand, fearing for them. 'Shouldn't have let myself be distracted.'

'Morgan,' she said, mildly, 'you're a scientist, and you well know that we're at a stage in our investigation that we have no idea what the . . . *hell* might be relevant.'

There were advantages to being considered a lady; when one cursed, one had an impact. His hand relaxed slightly.

She said, 'I'd like to take a scraping of the inoculation site.'

'What –?' but he had heard; he kept his wrist held out as she turned away to collect one of her sterile scalpels. He watched her scrape the bead of blood from the skin and deposit it on a slide, and then endured as she worked more blood from the bite. He said, 'If you want to cut, go ahead,' but she shook her head. He grinned with wan bravado. 'Don't tell me. You don't like the sight of blood.'

She turned away from him, to find the best possible light. The slide showed the same familiar smear of tiny, fragile cells, all the more difficult to see, unstained. But if she were going to see anything, she believed, she must see it now, or never. White cells were ghostly, red cells tiny pink points. Platelets she could whistle for. Yet for a moment it seemed she saw something else, like a glitter of chips of glass. Before it faded. A residue, left by the bug. Or an innoculum. She had seen nothing in the blood samples taken from the victims or the tissue samples taken from the autopsy. She reached past Morgan again and took up one of his slides, but the texture of the ash was not the same; it looked coarser. She said, slowly, 'How small might these assemblers of yours be?'

'Theoretically, molecule sized,' he said. His hand twitched, as he aborted a scratch at his bite. It was already reddening and swelling. A good vigorous response. He didn't ask her if she'd seen anything, so she shook her head gently and laid down the slide. 'I'll stain this up,' she said. 'Thank you.'

He closed his hand, rubbed his fingers against the bite. 'I'd better finish looking these over, while I still can,' he said.

25 Hathaway

    story, from somewhere   pregnant woman and tree   she fell
    it snowed   all winter   spring they found skeleton   between its legs,
little cluster of baby bones
    horrible story
light again   still sick
my baby
whoever finds this – don't send this letter back home in the bottle
owls
    blue

                                         flower faces

26 Sophie

Atop the massif, a pennant of dark blue replaced the cyan, marking the
beginning of the last two hours of light, when Sophie left the massif,
alone. She found herself slightly disorientated by the changes in the
human landscape. Although their group had not enlarged its territory
in the past few days the loose association of people had condensed into
one large and several lesser encampments. Corridors radiated from the
massif in a ragged, six or seven pointed star. Each encampment had its
own gingerbread and water supply, and between the encampments,
boundaries had been laid out. Eyes watched her suspiciously as she
walked an internal boundary line towards the women's cave. Her
mouth tugged sideways in an expression which was not a smile. There
were still many who did not believe that the insects were the vectors of
the disease, that their better place could be so malicious or flawed.

As she climbed up the final slope, she could see the graveyard to the
right and below the massif in the lowest section of the cavern. She
could see the long, low mounds, some completely green and flattening,
some round and full, a couple still showing the faint colour of skin or
clothing. Very little decomposition occurred before absorption. There
was not even much disagreeable smell. Some day soon she would
investigate that. Figures moved between the dead. For some the process
of dissolution into the mats had a macabre fascination. Others – like
the A-team members – stood guard over their dead against the curious
and necrophiliac.

The tunnel leading into the women's encampment was curtained with silver survival film, worked into the claystone of the tunnel roof. A double layer, she found as she shouldered under the first. A voice from within responded to the rattle, 'Who's that?'

'Sophie.'

A hand appeared beneath the second film and lobbed an unravelling bundle of clothing towards her. 'Please get changed,' the voice said. 'Then you can come through.'

Awkwardly, stooping in the tunnel, she changed into a shirt and jeans slightly too large for her. She left her clothes, shoes and backpack in the tunnel, tucking only her instruments into her pocket, and crawled through the second film. The young woman on the far side met her with a twisted grin. Her name was Astarte, and on Earth she had been a police officer. 'I know it's crazy, this, but some people just can't be convinced the bugs don't come in on clothing, like fleas.' Her perfume hung heavy in the air of the tunnel, thick in the nose and cloying in the throat. Sophie sneezed, despite herself. 'Godawful, isn't it,' the woman agreed. 'But it seems to be working. We've only had one person down since you sent along your suggestion – Dove, unfortunately. Go on in. I'd take you, but I'm on watch on this end.'

'On watch against whom?'

Astarte gave a little wry flip of her hands, as though that too could be laid to others' foolish fears. But she would not leave her post.

They had almost completed the multilevelled pool complex, ending it in a wide wading pool which overflowed thinly on to the matting. Hannah and several other women were washing out bedding in it. Hannah scooped up her sodden bundles and came to meet her.

'Nothing like having holes eaten in your dirty laundry to make you zealous about washing it,' she greeted Sophie. Her perfume made Sophie's nose itch; she sneezed again. 'Sorry about the stench. But it does seem to be helping.'

Sophie said, getting it over with, 'I had to get away from there. The walls were closing in . . .' She had spilled most of her remaining formalin while racing the darkness. The smell still clung to her hands. 'Several more of our people were bitten today.' Stan Morgan was miserably ill, but not fatally so; the knowledge was hardly a comfort, not now.

'Damn,' said Hannah. 'You've had people die of this, haven't you?'

'Yes. The fatality rate has been about four or five per cent. And if our countermeasures are losing effect –'

Hannah stopped beside an outcropping of rock that the women used for a drying area. 'Now what do I tell everybody?' she said.

Sophie had no answer for that question, as meant. She answered it as asked. 'We are more convinced than ever that the bugs are some kind of extrusion of the ship. We've caught several and the same thing has happened: they fall apart, into a dust that looks very like the dust you get by cutting the matting or isolating a piece of claystone.'

Hannah gave her a small, twisted smile; she had, after all, asked for hope, not further argument for the malignity of their environment.

'We have discussed making some kind of vaccine from serum from people who have had the disease and survived, but without any means of virus-testing . . . the risk was unacceptable.'

Hannah slapped sodden cloth on to the claystone beside her, ignoring the water that seeped from it, staining her skirt. She gathered it up, twisted a wad of material, wrung the water out of it with a force that made the tendons stand out on her hands and her neck. She shook out the sodden bedding with whiplike snaps of her arms. Water sprayed, brightly.

Sophie said, 'How many of your people have had it?'

Hannah unfurled the bedding over the claystone. 'Twenty women out of forty-one. Four kids out of eleven.'

Sophie said very quietly, 'You've been lucky, you know, not to have lost anyone.'

Hannah did not answer. Sophie neither pressed for acknowledgement nor tendered an apology.

They found Maggie, Marian and Dove behind the innermost partition, against the wall. Maggie was propped up on a heap of backpacks and carrier bags, scrawling in a notebook. She let her pen fall and flipped the notebook closed the moment she saw them. Marian was sitting upright in her alert stillness, stroking Melisande. The old woman turned her face towards them; the cat lifted her head and purred more forcefully, but did not move, sprawled in languid comfort and utter content. Dove opened her eyes to slits and closed them again. Her heart-shaped face was drawn and pale. Sophie went to her but she only said, eyes closed, 'I'm all right. Go away and let me sleep.'

Hannah crouched down by Maggie's bunk and spoke in a low murmur. 'Sophie says the bugs are starting to bite again out in the main cavern.'

From behind the screen a child's voice said fretfully, 'But *why* can't I go out and play. *I'm* not sick.'

'And I don't want you getting sick, so sit quietly and read your book.'

Maggie said brusquely, 'Well, are we surprised?'

'Maggie,' Hannah said, 'do keep your voice down.' She beckoned Sophie close.

'Well, are you?' the lanky woman said, more quietly. 'Look, you know this came from the ship . . . oh, come, the timing's so suggestive.'

'Of what?' Sophie said.

'Some kind of selection process.' She had hazel-green eyes, which glittered with weakness and outrage. 'Or to reduce the numbers.'

'I would have thought it would have been more . . . humane,' with a wry smile at her own choice of words, 'if they'd selected beforehand.'

'Then they miscalculated. They assumed the ship could support a larger number. It's a closed system. Even with recycling, there is a lag between absorption of nutrients and their being made available through the gingerbread. There's a pool of nutrients outwith our collective biomass which needs to be established and maintained. If there are any limitations on synthetic activity, the pool has to come from human sources. Human bodies are absorbed the same way any other organic waste is. It's an obvious extension of the mechanism. Damnation woman, you're a scientist,' she said, her voice rising, 'Look at it square.'

Sophie was not aware of having stood up, but she had. 'I see no purpose to thinking of it that way.'

'There's no such thing as a free lunch.'

'Maggie –'

'Hannah!' came the guard woman's voice from outside, urgently. To quickly stifled sounds of indignation, Stephen shouldered through the screens carrying a blanket-wrapped body. For a moment she thought it was Adrienne; there was the same fury on his face. But lain down on hastily assembled padding she was an old seventeen or a young twenty, with a squarish face and childish, bitten nails, ragged black hair, and bare stubbled legs. Beneath an ugly black and green shirt her abdomen was distended with a six or seven month pregnancy. Sophie went to lift her shirt; Hannah stayed her hand, and rose, going to Stephen and guiding him away. The women gathered, whispering, as Sophie unbuttoned the shirt. They hissed at the sight of the multiple weals on the girl's bare arms and breasts. They muttered as she examined the girl; over Dove's foetoscope, she glared them into silence. But the silence became complete as she shifted the bell low. Sophie had the sense of breaths held. The foetus shifted, rippling the skin, and she caught the thready patter of its heart. She heard the woman sigh, having seen the movement. But her mind was already moving forwards – had they a hope of saving the foetus? For surely the girl was lost. She noted the absence of response to pain, the sluggish response of her pupils to light, marking the descent on the fatal course. One of the woman whispered, 'Is she going to be OK?' But they would not know, cloistered here in their cave. They had not seen this, yet.

Hannah, timely as ever, crouched beside her. 'Her name's Hathaway. She's been living up in one of the caves, alone.'

Sophie straightened. From the height of her uterus the girl could be twenty-six, possibly twenty-eight weeks pregnant. They might, *might* save her child by emergency C-section, if it were opportunely done. She needed to get across to the Camp, to consult with the general practitioner who was serving as their gynaecologist. If there were no vertical transmission the baby might have a chance. 'You need to keep her airway clear, keep her breathing, get her temperature down. I want her head elevated to reduce the swelling in her brain. I want her rolled a little on her left side. I need a board of some kind.' Women scuffled for position, bringing water and screens. The girl lay breathing roughly, her face blotched and uneven, but the damp taut skin of her belly almost pearly with youth and newness. They eased her shirt off her, laid her against the backboard rummaged from a rucksack, padded as best they could with blankets, tucked more blankets beneath her legs to hold her from slipping. Her breathing became quieter; she moaned and moved one hand aimlessly in the air as though to ward off the light. And as though in response, darkness dropped upon them. Women scrabbled for candles, and lit them, tainting the air with candle-wax and burning crayon, beeswax and oil. They set candles around the girl like votive lamps around a sacrifice or a bier. Sophie stood up. She had to find someone and hand it over to them. She had to, while she could still make sensible decisions and keep down the need to howl with bottomless despair. She turned, and walked out from behind the screens, turning away from the feeble candles, towards the deeper darkness. Somebody said, 'Where are you going?'

'To consult.'

She walked until fetched up against the silver film. She had an instant's violent destructive impulse to tear it down, to *shred* it into scraps and scatter the scraps in the still air. She held her hands in fists, the nails cutting into the palms. She would not take away even from those deluded women their belief in their immunity. They would know it was illusory soon enough.

She stepped out into the cavern. She felt the wall rise away behind her, heard the soft, soft sound of the running water. She remembered coming out on to the porch of Lister's pond, remembered the feel of the boards beneath her bare feet. By these splinters and roughnesses, by the little splinters of broken glass, her blood would mingle with the blood of her parents, her grandparents. She stooped and unravelled her laces; heel to toe, toe to heel, she worked off her running shoes, and then her socks. She set her bare feet on the matting, coarse and prickly, a little damp, like grass in the hour after sunset. The matting, the trees, the insects, all were part of the same organism, or the same system. They were within the belly of the beast, whether they wanted to acknowledge it or not. She left her shoes lying on the grass, and walked on, pulling off the overlarge shirt and dropping it behind her. The bare skin of her arms was faintly luminous in the candlelight, as a thin dissolving barrier between her and the air.

'Sophie,' Hannah said, behind her, 'what are you doing?'

She turned, looking at the big woman's silhouette, at the faint lineaments of her face. She could not see her expression.

'What is it about you?' Sophie said. 'I know why not me, but what is it about you.'

There was a silence. The line of Hannah's chin was long, as though her mouth had opened before she found words. Don't look like that, she remembered her mother saying to her, you never know what will fly in. Hannah's mouth closed; had she spoken aloud?

'Don't say, "You're upset",' Sophie said clearly. 'Don't say, "Come inside and let's talk about it." I don't want to talk. I want –'

'Will your being bitten make you feel better?' Hannah said. Her tone was an extraordinary accomplishment, neither accusing nor incredulous; quite sane, as though it was a question worth asking.

'Yes,' Sophie said, heard the absurdity, gripped her arms across her chest. 'I know more about this than you. I've read about the plague. Doctors died with everyone else. They were impotent and their efforts at cure were more magic than medicine, and absurd. I don't want to be immune.'

'Most people would,' Hannah said, as though she were making sense.

'Most people are not me!' Sophie said. 'Is this going to go on until only the sick and the halt and the lame are left?' Wordlessly, Hannah held out her discarded sweat shirt. Sophie merely stood looking at her, beyond explanation. From her bare right foot she felt a sudden, vicious sting. In the blurred, dim light she fancied she saw a dark spot twitch a little. Or maybe it was just the jumping of a tendon. She tilted

121

her foot, very aware of the articulating joints, and felt something slide away down the new slope. She stooped, collected wet warmth, smelled blood on her fingers. The bite must have punctured a superficial vein.

All the madness drained out of her. She began to shiver, absurd reaction, far too soon. 'That was stupid,' she said. 'Grossly irresponsible. I am a doctor.'

'Unavoidable, perhaps,' Hannah said. 'If, as you say, we are no longer confusing them.' And then, mildly, 'Are you satisfied now?'

THREE

FLOWERING

27 Hathaway

It's been a while since I wrote last but I'm OK, honest. Stephen found me completely out of it up in my cave and brought me down to the women's camp. I guess I ought be grateful but I wish he'd looked after me himself and not dumped me here. I looked after *him*. And the *jerk* hasn't even been back to find out how I am! Which is not too bad considering they thought I was going to die. Everybody calls it the Centauri 'flu except for a few people who have no sense of humour and think it's too frivolous a name for something which killed people. But actually not so many people died in the end. The woman doctor who's been coming in (she's nice – Chinese American and little and grandmotherly. Her daughter had a baby when she was eighteen so it's not shock-horror how could you do such a thing what about your career what about your baby's security blah blah blah.) Where was I? This doctor said that on Earth it happens that way – bugs (sickness bugs, not insect bugs) get milder as they get passed along. But she frowns a bit when she says it like she's not really so sure that's the explanation but doesn't want to get into it. Maggie – who likes to look a real hard case even though she's just human marshmallow around the little kids – thinks the 'flu is something the ship did to us like an inoculation. Everybody got it in the end and Maggie thinks that only people who were really healthy got it first so the aliens could be sure how strong to make it. Only they made it too strong first time round. That completely freaked some of the women out. But Maggie and Marian talk about it when nobody else is around.

It's not too bad here. I like Hannah who's sort of the leader as much as anyone is. She must be about six foot tall and built like a linebacker and always wears a blouse and skirt. To be honest she looks a little as though she's in drag with her big hands and her big feet and big shoulders. But if that's the way she likes to dress that's her business. She's a music teacher and she's started to teach some of the kids violin. She brought five violins with her. Really. Two ordinary ones, a violin on steroids which she calls a viola, and a couple of kid sized ones. It's amazing to watch her great big hand wrapping ever so carefully around some little kid's teeny little hand to show them the right fingering. I hope my baby wants to learn once she's got past the drool, gum and bash stage.

Even though I like Hannah and some of the others there's something I'm probably not going to tell them. I don't know why. Well, I guess I do. I'm not scared they won't believe me – with all the weird stuff going on I bet they would. And that would make it too real. What it is is that when I was sick I kept seeing these huge creatures like owls with shimmery feathers and faces like flowers. I don't know how long they were around since time got all warped but they put bugs on me, on my arms and on the top of my breasts. Everyone else has only one bug bite but I've got six. Maggie says that the bugs were the carriers of the disease and I'm the only one they know about who got bit so many times. I just remember getting bit once so all the rest I must have got when I was too sick to know what was going on. So were the owls real or was I tripping? Were they trying to kill me? Shouldn't I have been painting on the walls? I've asked in a roundabout sort of way about what else people have been doing but nobody's said anything about painting on the walls. But if I wasn't supposed to be painting why did it give me all its colours? That was like an invitation, I thought. But I'm still scared. If I got that sick again I'd die. Or the baby would die.

But I love my cave. And I'm so curious. About that little painting the ship made and about the aliens I maybe saw. And the more I think about that rather than about maybe dying or maybe losing my baby the more I want to go back to the cave. I guess what I mean is that if I'd wanted to be safe I should have stayed on Earth. But I came and I'm not sorry.

28   Stephen

Every morning when the lights came up, he washed in the cold bright water, dressed and went to the very back of the cave, to Fleur. By the third day he could barely see the blue of the cheap, ruined sleeping bag he had wrapped her in. And by then he was coming to regret his cowardice in doing so, longing for the last sight of a red jacket or a lock of dark, crinkled hair.

He had no idea how much of the day he spent watching by her. For the first time in his life he was unaware of anger or fear. It was as though he had finally found an empty space large enough for him to live. He was surrounded by the ghosts of women: a mother, an all-but sister, and two strangers, one he had murdered, the other he could not save. The girl, too, would be a long mound of green in the communal burial ground. All that remained of her were a small heap of clothes and gear, some photographs, some letters and a mural.

It was not until the third day he thought to look at them. He was not aware of what else he had done in those days besides watch as

Adrienne's shroud thickened. Once darkness fell on him while he was still there and he simply lay down by her side and slept. His dreams were full of butterflies. He avoided thinking of the obvious symbolism; that way lay madness. He sat for a while with his feet hanging over the edge of the cave, looking out over the cavern. If he unfocused his eyes, the little trees, just below, might blur into great trees, Earth trees, far below; the alien light might become a mountain light; the pale shining stone of the far wall the face of Mount Ranier, lit by early sun. But someone hallowed him from down below, and after that he kept out of sight. He remembered, too, crumbling gingerbread between his fingers, and watching the rug creep up and around the fragments, forming pile-balls of green. He did not remember eating.

But eventually that little mound of leavings called to him. The compulsion to explore other people's things had grown on him early. It was something distinct from his thefts. He stole only from strangers, and then only objects which he could sell. From people he knew, he stole intimacy, the knowledge of things they would not tell him. It had nearly cost him Fleur's friendship, the one time she had allowed him to live with her, just after he had been released from hospital, when she had caught him going through her old letters. But he knew, and she knew, he would have done it again.

This girl's possessions were curious. It was as though she lived two lives, and the materially poorer life was the one she prized. The cheap photograph album was carefully stored in a ziploc bag, while the leather writing case lay open on the matting, its lining ink-stained. In her pencil case, disposable biros and crayons rubbed up against a silver plated, black enamelled pen and pencil set. The plain, nameless cotton socks had been washed and laid out to dry. The designer pair were balled up and rank at the bottom of her knapsack.

The photograph album was half full of snapshots wedged into the plastic pages. He studied them with an anthropologist's eye. He knew family photographs to be important to their owners. But to him, they were portraits of alien and inexplicable worlds.

He had not gone unphotographed, of course. Each set of foster parents had taken photographs of him and the rest of their oddball tribe. Usually one or other of the kids would freak out beforehand. Maybe, like him, they hated the fakery of it all, knowing how they looked, a bunch of rejects clumped together to do the human act. Knowing that the pictures themselves would show the lie. Real families, like the girl's, went on together through time. In the first of her photographs a heavy-eyed woman and a thin, sickly man sat in a garden, a child on his lap and two others swinging from their elbows from the arms of their deck chairs. The girl had resembled her mother, he noted, the history of colonialisation written in her dark eyes. Then the woman stood alone, one titch in her arms, and four grouped around her, a protective ranking, all daring the camera, just daring it. The third was a Christmas photograph of the family before an opulent, light-laden tree. The woman was self-conscious in a dark red, quilted dressing gown. The smallest girl posed in a tutu. The other children crouched over their heaped spoils possessively. The girl herself was not in that picture. There were other pictures of the children, alone, or in twos, threes, fours; a newspaper clipping of one of the girls skating, a strained smile of exertion on her face, shaved ice flying from her blades; the printed flap of a birthday card, signed by Mom, Peta, Dave, John and twice, once printed in an adult hand and again in a pre-literate child's big clumsy copy, Joy.

Tucked away in the writing case was a sheaf of handwritten pages. He drew them out and settled cross legged on the matting. Presently, he got up and went to her painting wall, and stood reading with the brilliant sunset colours shining over the paper. She wasn't a polished artist, but there was something undeniably alive about her paintings. The same crudity and vitality enlivened her writings; he read, with a chill, her description of him in his illness. She was entirely too observant. And up here, he realised, one ill-educated, solitary teenager had achieved the most sophisticated communication of them all. He crouched to examine the peripheral image. The ship hung in space, a gift, an exchange. What a joke on all the experts, he thought, just the way she said.

The final page was a scrawl, sweat marked and in one place bile-smeared. He shuddered; his hands clenched, crumpling it, wringing it into a ball. He wrung the words out of it and flung it against the wall. The smell clung to his hands.

What a joke on them all.

He scrambled together all her leavings, thrusting them into the backpack any which way, photo album and writing case, homemade buckskins and outback hat ... As he lifted the hat, something which had been resting in the bowl dropped free with a thin flash of blue. Through his mind went the associations, knife/feather, but though it had the shape of one and the colour of the other, it was more like a scale than either. A blue scale, eight or nine inches long, mediterranean blue at the centre, shading to pale blue with almost a fawn tinge at the edges. The surface was lightly ridged. He had never seen anything like it; his hand moved towards it, stopped – for the translucency suggested a very thin, sharp edge – and then completed the motion, with cold recklessness. Let it cut; he was already bleeding. It surprised him, proving not rigid but slightly flexible, bending with pressure. As it bent, the colours shifted slightly, greening. He brushed a finger along it, feeling the ridges. They rasped, softly, at the touch of a nail.

Blue, she had written. Flower faces. And owls.

He got to his feet, still holding the scale, and went to retrieve the sheet of paper he had flung so violently away. Crouching, scale balanced on his knee, he smoothed it out. The scrawled words were as he had read. He thought of the ragged edged, unsizeable shadows he had glimpsed in the dark of his pit. Had the owls – the blue – the flower faces of her delirium been the aliens themselves? Had they come to . . . to what, to study her? To help her? To gather her up and take her wherever they had taken the men from the pit? Had she, like those men, enquired too deeply to be left unpunished?

His guts clenched, his old weakness. He breathed against the pressure until it abated and then meticulously unpacked the contents of her knapsack and re-examined each in turn. On hands and knees he searched the green matting. He found nothing aside from minute undigested shreds of her sleeping bag – but then he had not thought to take care at the start, and the area was heavily marked with his own footprints. He folded the scale and the letter in the leather binder, and extended his search to the rest of her cave.

He found nothing, no tracks, no more scales, no bent branches or bruised needles, no other entrances or exits. Darkness came before he finished, and he worked his way back to his supplies in the thin, indigo light and lit one of his precious lanterns. He did not sleep.

Two days later, she returned.

He was struggling bitterly with the colours in the wall. It was a wonder and constant reproach to him that she had laid down whole lines of single colour while his orange wavered into yellow and his yellow into green with – he would have sworn, and did, viciously – no shift in pressure. But he had a question for the unknown aliens: why? If he had to learn their language, so be it. The wall mocked his efforts. His knuckles were bruised. So too was the wall, marked purple where he had struck it in his frustration.

She said, from behind him, 'What the fuck are you doing to my wall?'

He turned so fast he overbalanced. The inside of his skull seemed to go white. The back of his eyes bleached. Even the tooth watering green of her check shirt faded to lime. 'Hey,' she said, 'I didn't mean to scare you, but this is my wall.' Sharp, very alive, sloe eyes took in his efforts.

'I thought,' he managed to say, 'you were dying.'

She scowled. 'Sorry to disappoint you.' She looked around, saw her knapsack and the leather case open beside it. 'Did I say you could look in that?' She stalked over, dropped to her knees, snapped the case closed and pulled the knapsack to her. 'You didn't even come to check on me and you just move in here and take over.' Her temper rose higher. 'I'm not dead and this is my place and you, Mister Cooper, are out of here. Now!'

'I thought you were dead,' was all he could find to say.

'You're a doctor? You're some kind of coroner? You thought I was dead?' she mocked. She swung at him with her backpack; he jarred back against the wall, trying to fend it off with his arms. 'You didn't even come to see how I was. You just dumped me on them.'

'I'd seen someone die of what you had.'

That silenced her, temporarily, and he slid aside, smearing colour on the wall, to her sound of disgust, and walked towards the rear of the cave. 'Hey,' she said, slinging her backpack on to her shoulder, 'the exit's that way!' Not quite knowing why, he led her to Fleur's burial mound. It was now quite perceptibly sunken, more so than he recalled the last time. How long since he had last been here – he could not remember. She stared at the long, green mound, and took a step back, her face wrinkling in disgusted realisation. 'Oh, gross. You brought a dead body up to my cave!'

He looked at her with flat, dangerous eyes. 'She was my friend.'

'You are such a weirdo,' she said, fiercely.

He made a reflex, involuntary movement towards her. She did not flinch, but dropped the backpack and brought her hands up, strong fingers hooked.

The fingers that had stroked the bright, perfect oranges, yellows and blues out of the blank wall. The fingers that had made Armstrong, and Magellan, and drawn from the ship its answer. The hands that had written those letters. He did not move. He looked at her; she at him, for a long moment.

'Your friend, huh. I guess I'm sorry.'

She glanced again at the grave, and then looked closer, and dropped to her knees to pull at a shred of fabric, a tuft of down, which protruded from the mound. 'My sleeping bag.' She twisted to look up at him with new betrayal. 'You buried my sleeping bag!'

'There wasn't much left of it.'

With her hands she tore at the mound, shredding thin strips of it back from the buried relic. Bodily, he heaved her to her feet, and she turned on him with nails, knuckles and blunt toed sneakers, throwing her bulky weight against him, stomping and cursing. He held her off with more difficulty than he expected. She was a street fighter born, even six months gone. He pinned her by both wrists and still she tried to kick. 'You bastard. You lousy bastard.' The tendons under the skin were like fine wires, moving as she fisted her hands. They moved together, swaying, in a violent, clumsy dance.

'Let me go,' she gasped at last and, when he did, shuffled over to an outcropping of claystone and lowered herself down on to it, holding her stomach and breathing hard.

'Your bag was pretty putrid. The matting had grown into it.'

She turned her head, swept back her ragged hair and simply stared at him, unblinkingly.

'I didn't want to watch it happen to her,' he said, at last.

Her lips compressed. 'You owe me a sleeping bag, mister.' She jerked a thumb behind her, without turning. 'What happened to hers?'

'I don't know,' he said, 'I guess it's back at the camp.'

'Yeah, well, you owe me.' She heaved herself to her feet. 'I guess I better go and see what else you messed up.' She cast a sideways glance at the wall and she passed it, and gave an audible 'Huh'. After a moment, as she moved out of sight, he followed her.

She unpacked her backpack, checking everything. She scowled again at him as she pulled out her hat, which he had rolled up and stashed, and jammed it pointedly on her head. The brim and bobbing corks half hid her face.

She flipped open the leather case, spilling letters. Her hand went to the crumbled and smoothed-out sheet; she lifted it, glanced it over, wrinkled her nose. 'Gross.' As she lifted the sheets and patted them into order, the scale slid from among them. She froze, staring at it, then her head whipped round, corks thrashing. 'You put this there?'

He dropped to a crouch opposite her. 'I found it inside your hat.' He reached out and snatched the hat. She swiped at it; he held it just out of reach. 'Those corks are bugging the hell out of me.'

She recovered the hat on the second grab. 'Tough titty, Mr Cooper. You're not a teacher and this ain't school.' On went the hat.

He sat back on his heels, folded his arms, and smiled narrowly. 'Hell on wheels, aren't you?'

'Patronising, aren't you?' she retorted.

Curbing his anger, he gestured towards the scale. 'You want to tell me what that might be.'

'Give me one good reason.'

'I'm interested. I don't care that you're living alone up here. I don't care that you're pregnant. I don't care how old or young you are.' He got to his feet and went over to her picture wall, crouched, pointing to the small, low picture of the ship in space, the one she had not painted. 'You're the only person I know of who has done something like that.'

'I didn't do it.'

He stood up. 'You know what I mean.' He made that his last word, folded his arms, and waited.

'Yeah,' she said at last. Her eyes strayed to the scale. 'Well, I had these dreams, see, when I was sick. These – things – they looked sort of like owls, only they had shiny blue feathers . . .' Her voice trailed away. 'Shit,' she said. 'I guess that means they were for real.'

'Could you draw them?'

Plainly, the idea had not yet occurred to her. 'Guess I could.' With a glance of narrow-eyed calculation, 'How about you go get me a new sleeping bag while I draw?'

Wordlessly, he went over to his own campsite, lifted his neatly rolled sleeping bag and set it down beside her, then retreated to his comfortable distance. She looked at it, him.

'I buried yours, so I'll give you mine. I've kept the liner. It's not that it's cold here, or rains a whole lot.' He pointed at her pencil. 'Draw.'

She picked it up. 'OK, but don't sit there gawping.' She jerked her head towards the wall. 'Go paint. You could use the practice.'

He gave her a flat-eyed look, warning her. She returned it. She was better at it than Fleur had ever been. Tougher. There was – had been – a deep down gentleness in Fleur, or maybe an old tender wound, that made her vulnerable. He was glad she was so much younger, a kid really, for all her pregnancy. She was safer that way – he from her, she from him. He watched her almost with affection as she furiously erased some portion of her drawing, scuffing eraser-goobers off her page, and scowled past the corks and her straggling hair at the scale. Presently, he drifted back to the wall, and began, again, trying to trace a line unrippled with colour.

He heard her get to her feet with a stifled grunt of effort. He did not turn, merely continued making a line, grading from pale orange to deep violet with the pressure of his thumb. She came up beside him and thrust a worked-over piece of paper at him.

They did indeed look like owls, with rosetted eyes unsettlingly wide apart in their overlarge heads. The sketch suggested faceting, like a fly's compound eye. Her scowl deepened when he queried it. 'Sort of,' she said, 'I dunno. I was sick, remember.' There was no sign of ears. A multilayered torc of larger scales ringed the neck, and then smaller scales covered breast and arms. One was extending a hand, four-fingered, with perhaps a double-opposable thumb arrangement. The sketches ended at the waist. 'Were they standing?' he asked her. 'Kneeling? You were lying down.'

She frowned, losing something of the scowl in honest effort. 'I dunno.'

'Lie down,' he said peremptorily. She opened her mouth to argue. 'Lie down. It might help you to remember.'

'Maybe I don't want to remember,' she said, but she lay down.

He stood over her. 'Like this?' Dropped to his knees. 'Like this? Close your eyes. Think about it.'

She pushed herself up suddenly, her face disquieted.

'What?'

'I got the weirdest feeling.' He waited. 'Like the reason I don't know what the rest of them looks like isn't that they were sitting down but that I was lifted up.' Her brow furrowed.

'Do you remember them lifting you?'

'Why the hell do you have to know, anyway?'

'I want to talk to them. I want to know why they killed Fleur.'

She opened her mouth to say something snotty and offhand, and a moment later thought better of it. To her credit, it seemed an impulse of true compassion, not just caution. 'I guess I wasn't thinking real hard about what I was trying to say to them.'

He ignored that. 'Only I haven't been getting it.' He gestured to the wall.

'Yeah,' she said, chewing on her lip. 'I can see that.'

There was a silence. She seemed to be brooding on something. 'So I guess,' she said, a little abstractedly, not speaking her thoughts, 'you want me to help you.'

He nodded, glad she had made it so easy.

'So tell me,' she said, 'why should I? I mean, you took me down and dumped me with those women. Then you came up here, took over my cave, took over my stuff – I bet you even read my letters – screwed around with my wall, and you think I should help you? Like, why? I mean, why should I bug them with what you want to know?'

'Suit yourself,' he said, and pushed past her. 'Hey!' she said. He ignored her.

She watched him as he packed, hand on hip. 'Boy oh boy do you ever remind me of my kid brothers,' she remarked. 'You want to talk to them. You haven't got real far on your own. But you're going to go off in a huff rather than do the one thing you got to do.'

'Which is what?' he said, after a moment.

'Say you're sorry.'

She was enjoying herself, a teenager savouring power over an adult. He could appreciate that, at least in part. He settled back on his heels. 'For what? For getting you to medical care. For being mistaken? For not being as good as you are at the wall?' He shrugged, finished his packing, and went to the lip of the tunnel. He felt her watching him.

'Hey, Stephen?' she said, abruptly. 'What were you trying to draw?' He paused, allowing her another sentence, but did not turn his head. 'Like, how were you going to ask them that question?' Her tone was casual.

He slid into the tunnel, shoulder high. Then he pulled his sketch pad from his pocket and flipped it open, and dropped it on to the matting. She strolled over crouched, knees splayed, to look at it; became interested and picked it up. 'Hey. AIDS and the Black Death. Not bad.'

The corner of his mouth tucked in with sour amusement. 'I took the idea from your space exploration pictures.'

'Yeah,' she said, and glanced over to the mural, measuring it with her eye. 'And maybe I'd like to know, too.' She got to her feet, and carried the notebook over to the mural. Reached out, and with her thumb drew a single, shimmering green line in an arc over her head. She turned and looked at him. Wagged the sketchbook in the air, then set it down on the claystone. And began to draw.

Presently, he lifted himself out of the tunnel and went to join her.

29 Hathaway

Hi! I'm back. Yesterday I came up to the cave thinking maybe I would just pick up my stuff. Deep down though I wanted to test myself and find out whether I could live alone again. I found Stephen had moved in. I could really see where the three bears were coming from even though we're supposed to identify (like they say in English class) with that little twit Goldilocks. He'd been through all my stuff and painted on my wall and planted a body in the matting at the back of my cave. Gross huh? The body's a woman called Adrienne LaFleurette. Stephen said she made her name up when she was just a teenager and didn't want to keep the names her family gave her. I hope my name doesn't sound as fakey. Anyway she died of the Centauri 'flu. He didn't want her being dissected – the doctors at the Camp were doing autopsies on people who died. So I guess I understand. I wouldn't have wanted to be dissected either. I haven't completely forgiven him because every so often he shows off things he knows about me from reading my letters which pisses me off. And if he's not in the back of the cave staring at where she was planted (here it's not really buried because all you do is lay someone down and wait while the greenstuff grows up and around them) he's working on this big angry painting with the Black Death and yellow fever and all those things. It's his way of asking why the plague. He's OK at making maps but he has a lot to learn about painting – I mean, if he has any artistic influences it's probably comic books and his hands are all bruised from hitting the wall because it won't do what he wants. He reminds me a lot of Dave. He's got a mad on with the world. Which gets spooky. Even you spooked me some time, Dave, and I knew where your buttons were. But he's never touched me except for when I first came back – and all he did was hold me back from beating on him. But I'm still worried about him hurting the owls if they come or scaring them off so they don't. I guess maybe I'd feel differently if it was somebody I knew well who died (it sounds prissy saying it that way but I can't figure out how well he did know her). He doesn't know about the other bug bites on me. I miss being able to go around naked and I was looking forward to making a big pool to sort of wallow in. The water's kind of cold but I had the idea of drawing hot springs and tropical beaches on the wall above the pool to see if the ship could get it. Maybe when she's (the body) all gone he'll go back to his mapping and I can have my cave to myself and maybe get to see the owls again.

30 Sophie

The fifth day after her illness began Sophie woke with the conviction that it was past time to get back to work. She was in her sleeping bag in its usual place, having been moved from the infirmary two days before, but her view was now bounded by low claystone walls. She scrubbed a hand in her filthy, tangled hair, gripped the nearest wall and raised herself a little higher so that she might see over it. All around her the slope was sectioned with walls of various heights and readiness, raised from beneath the green matting like the excavated ruin of a neolithic village she had seen in Orkney. Her little room-to-be had a door and the beginning of a shelf which might, with time to shape and accustom herself to it, become a bed. The neolithic villagers at least had reeds and grasses to sleep on. From the peak of the massif hung the red pennant that indicated the first three hours of daylight.

She pushed herself up further, until she was kneeling. Now she could see the graveyard. The mounds in it were no more numerous and less full than they had been when she walked out of the camp five days ago. The air was luminous and quite clear of small blue sparks.

'Sophie!'

Stan Morgan came running from the direction of the massif, hurdling walls at some peril to himself and others. He looked hale and young, his black hair uncombed and in need of a cut, and delighted to see her, though the delight turned bashful as he stopped on the other side of her wall. She felt suddenly self-conscious, with her bare legs, her dirty hair, her grubby, smelly shirt. She could smell the miasma of illness and depression about herself. 'Sophie, we were worried about you.'

The slightest invitation, she sensed, and he would have hugged her. She withheld the invitation, feeling awkward and unclean, but let herself be warmed by his smile. 'What's happening?' she said, her voice creaky. 'I know you've been telling me things, but I wasn't taking them in.'

He started to sling a leg over the wall, stopped, looking as though he had committed a solecism. She said, 'Go ahead, come in. Or over ... Did you do these walls?'

'Some of them,' he said, looking pleased. 'I did a bit of bossing to get them ready for you, or as ready as they are.' He dropped down on the wall, bracing elbows on jeaned legs. 'It looks like the outbreak or whatever it was is over. Everybody's had it, from what we can tell from our contacts with the rest of the ship, but in the second wave over the last five or so days nobody died and we haven't seen a bug in the last forty hours.

'What else? We have a much better idea how big the ship is – at least a couple of hundred square kilometres. Somehow it's got a name, too, *Tevake*, some Polynesian seabird. I don't know who thought of that. There are about two or three hundred thousand people on board, which makes our geneticist happy – you won't have met Marcellin yet! He moved over from one of the neighbouring caverns, the one that the anarchists have taken over – you know, that woman Eilish Colby. He's started a royal row about who should have children and how many, with the survivalists lining up on one side saying we should breed and breed and the reproductive rights people on the other side saying it's nobody's business but the individual's.' He whistled softly. 'Victoria's tearing her hair out trying to get them to either listen to the law as it is written or come to some agreement as to what rights and protections they might agree on. And you should just hear Arpád on the subject of Americans and their hysterical puritanism. Me, I hide in the lab. No one wants my genes anyway.'

She smiled, with an effort. He meant to amuse her, expecting her to share his view that there was nothing worth such passion other than science. He had no idea of the resonances such an argument would have to a woman, much less a woman with her genetic background.

What he said next was completely unexpected. 'Listen, before you left – before you went out of the path lab that last time – did you spill something?' His expression willed her to give him the answer he wanted.

'Some formalin,' she said, slowly, thinking back. Remembering sitting watching the spreading liquid, and the sense of utter hopelessness. 'I spilled my stock of formalin. I just left it. I –' But she foundered on the explanation, unable to admit what she had been feeling. Ice-princess Sophie, who never confided, especially despair.

He grinned at her – plainly that was the right answer – and stood up. 'Come on! There is something you have got to see!'

'Morgan,' she said, firmly. 'Give me time to wash and get dressed, would you?'

'What – oh, yes.'

Their laboratory area showed signs of energetic application. Another bench had been moulded from the wall, with a second pair of stalagmite stools. The walls were no longer more gesture than substance; they reached chest level in most places. They had been honeycombed with shallow recesses, although most of their equipment was still spread over the benches and the floor. 'I figured you'd want a say in where things went,' Morgan explained himself. Where she had been working last, in the first bench, had been completely cleared, and in the middle of the clearing was a shallow well, filled to the brim with clear liquid. Morgan stopped beside it, with a gloating expression. 'Smell!'

She bent and, wafting a little of the vapour towards her, sniffed it. 'Formalin.'

Morgan reached over and lifted a bottle from the back of the clear area. She recognised it as the one she had spilled, the label smeared. He showed it her with all the panache of a headwaiter displaying the label of a fine wine. It was full. He set it down, and picked up a second bottle, a larger one, and flaunted its label. Formalin, neatly printed in what she took to be his hand. It, too, was full.

'You found another source,' she said. 'Thank you.'

A pained expression crossed his mobile face. 'Would I be as excited,' he said, a little plaintively, 'if I had simply found a cache in someone's luggage? Sophie, this comes from the ship itself.' He paused. 'When I first got back in here it was dripping off the bench on to the floor. I had no idea what had started it, but there was your bottle, so I figured somebody had had a spill – I didn't think it was you because it looked like it had only just happened. So I started mopping up, and then realised that it was welling up out of the bench. I felt like the Sorcerer's Apprentice. I eventually sopped it up completely, and kept mopping until it stopped flowing, and then I poured a little on the bench and started it flowing all over again. And then I got smart and hollowed a well, and sopped up the edges until it took the hint. Which sounds straightforward but it took me the best part of two days. But I've got it so now it only produces when the level falls. If I were to dip some out, the level would rise again.'

'A veritable fount –' she said, a little dryly.

'Of formalin,' he supplied. He folded his hands one over the other, leaning on the bench, contemplating the small, shallow pool of clear liquid. 'What I don't understand – well, one of innumerable things I don't understand – is where it is getting the raw materials from. It seems to me to be ridiculously energy-expensive to try and crack gaseous oxygen and carbon dioxide, though I'm not as up on my catalytic agents as I should be and I suppose it could be some kind of catalytic process. But you can see the surface in the well looks coarser than the surface of the bench itself, and at 50X magnification it *could* be porous, so synthesis could be going on elsewhere and the product piped in here . . . but I'd bet a year of my presently nonexistent pay that if we scooped the whole area out we wouldn't find any pipes – it'd be reshaping all the time.

'I wish to God I knew what kind of signals we had to give, and whether this was a communication or just some kind of reflex, just an automatic tendency to shuffle molecules to copy whatever it's exposed to. Though if there weren't some kind of overriding intelligence or programming we'd be on our way to suffocating as our exhaled carbon dioxide primed production of more –'

She thought how seldom she had seen an adult show such uninhibited delight in thought. When he looked at her, she nodded, inviting him to continue. 'And I don't see any evidence that our air quality is declining. But I'm damned, I really am, if I can see rhyme or reason in this prize puzzle of ours, or theirs . . . or whoever's. I'm beginning to wonder if there isn't some kind of programme running which – like it or not – we have to learn how to interact with to have any chance of controlling our environment, never mind fixing it if anything goes wrong. And I know just how difficult it is to keep a closed environment operating and balanced, even one we've constructed and modelled and know inside out. Having our very survival dependent on a technology we don't understand at all and have to figure out as we go along from phenomenology alone would give me the screaming heebie jeebies if I thought about it too much. And then, something like this ship, with the apparent complexity of its functions, possibly the ability to replicate itself – I mean if it is some kind of nanotechnology, with programmable assemblers capable of synthesis from the molecules up – and it has the programming to build more, and to programme them, and the blueprints to build more of itself – well, I mean where do you draw the line between what's alive and what isn't? Because that's more or less what human beings are, if you leave aside the matters of consciousness, spirit and soul. Self-repairing, self-programming, self-replicating . . . He stared a moment at the little pool, as though at a crystal ball, then abruptly straightened with a slight rueful laugh. 'Eternity in a grain of sand,' he said, with a headshake.

It was quite possible, Sophie thought – a humbling thought after her earlier envy – that she was in the presence of genius. 'So,' she said, after a moment, 'what are you going to do with it?'

'That was what I wanted to talk to you about. I mean, this is another puzzle. Or another gift. Or another invitation. We have to explore it. I think we need to find out whether other parts of the claystone will behave in the same way, what can be synthesised, whether there's some kind of minimum allocation required to prime it – I mean, what tells it to synthesise and not to absorb, since we've seen the phenomenon of absorption from everything from faeces and discarded foodstuffs to our own dead. What tells it to synthesise formalin but not carbon dioxide? Is it area specific? If you were to apply formalin to the walls would you get the same effect, or is there something special about this area, away from the walls, away from the food and water supply? I mean, there are all these questions about the way things behave but none of them, none of them, even approach the fundamental question of the nature of the world. I feel as though I've suddenly been pitched back in time by six hundred years. I might as well be talking in terms of angels and phlogiston –' He threw up his hands, pivoted and said, 'I am so glad you're back. I need someone like you, to be honest, if you're not insulted. I need to be grounded. I fly off on tangents too easily. I've got – I had – a colleague used to do that for me. At one point I thought about marrying her. I suppose that sounds a little odd, put that way – maybe it was just one of those twentysomething biological clock things – the urge to settle down. But I couldn't persuade her. She told me I was out of my mind when I said I was going to accept this invitation.'

'Women aren't interchangeable,' she reproached him mildly, a little sad that it had come to this, so soon.

'I don't mean they are,' he stumbled, and recovered, 'but people, people have traits, and those traits express themselves in certain ways. I mean, look at all of us – yes, there's great variety, in age, occupation, past history – and yet there's a fundamental similarity, an adventure-someness.'

'Or a discontent,' she said. 'Or a fear. Or a carelessness about life. Or boredom. Or ambition. Or an overactive fantasy life. Or a wish to transform their lives. Or a wish to be special, to be famous – there was, after all, a quite gratifying amount of attention given those who made public their desire to come. Or, quite simply, scepticism, disbelief, the desire to prove it was all a confidence trick. I don't see any similarity.'

'Which one are you?' he said, curiously.

She shrugged, letting irritation show on her face. 'I'd rather try and make some progress towards interpreting this invitation than play the "getting to know you" game. Who knows when our next crisis will overtake us?'

He looked quite crestfallen. 'Was I that obvious?'

'Yes,' she said. 'You were. I was bracing myself for the "we're going to be on this ship together for the rest of our lives" speech. Or the "you're a beautiful woman" speech. Or, God forbid, the "we'll have to have kids with someone and I'd like it to be you" speech.'

He went scarlet, making her regret her bluntness. She was usually much defter than this. Bravely he said, 'I won't try any of these if you'll spare me the "I hope we'll be friends" speech.'

'I do know better than that,' she said in a still voice. 'Trust me.'

He looked at her oddly, but said nothing, and they turned their attention to the bench.

But in the middle of smoothing an array of shallow wells, he said, 'But what about the family you left behind?'

She sighed. He said, not looking at her, 'Oh, damn.' And turned to face her. 'Sophie, this isn't a coded asking about a boyfriend or a girlfriend or anything like that. I was close to my family and I miss them, and not talking about them it's as though they don't exist any more. Maybe I should have come out and said I wanted to talk about mine rather than asking you about yours – but will you listen to me talk about mine? Please. You don't have to ask questions; you don't have to show polite interest, just lend me your ears . . . please.'

She gave him a look of mock resignation. 'Photographs and all,' she said, mildly. He nodded, abashed, but to his credit the photographs did not come out until he had sketched out the family tree – seven siblings, himself the second youngest; an even dozen aunts and uncles, starting with four blood relations and compounding with first, second and in one case third marriages; an ever-expanding company of nieces and nephews and cousins of various degrees; a family scattered to the four winds, and occupying all points of the socioeconomic scale, from the postgraduate scientist and the articling lawyer, to the destitute drug-addict, and the whole spectrum of ethnic identification from the social worker living and working in the Hispanic districts of LA to the fair-skinned housewife and mother whose grandmother was Mary, never Maria. He had a fat cache of snapshots sequestered in his wallet. He laid them down, pointing out faces, talking quickly, fond, excited and a little brittle, trying with talk to outpace feeling. A photograph caught her eye and her attention suddenly became more than polite. It was a poor photograph, technically, the subject caught with the light behind her. Her face was underexposed, but the wilful tilt of it was familiar, and the curve of the cheek was young, and her belly rounded with pregnancy beneath a mustard, red and black plaid shirt.

'That's Harriet,' Morgan said as she lifted it. 'My favourite niece. Sharp as a whip when she wants to be.' His brow creased a little. 'I hope to God they can keep her from messing up her life. She hasn't taken at all well to my sister's remarriage – not so much her stepfather, but the whole social set up. She's been more or less running the family for years – my brother-in-law died of testicular cancer while the kids were young. And suddenly she's been pitched into an environment where young people are financially and psychologically dependent on their parents until they complete their education, often in their mid twenties, but at the same time extremely sophisticated in their tastes and recreations. Her stepfather's quite wealthy; he's high in one of the established computer companies. A good man, but they've butted heads from the start . . . and the latest, as you can see, is that she's pregnant.'

His affection and concern for his young niece was evident. She pretended to smile as he told her about Hath's curiosity about his work and her quick mind, desperately tempted to just let him go on thinking that the girl was safe on Earth. But, if she did not tell him, who knew when and in what circumstances he might discover otherwise? She said, 'Morgan, I know this girl. I've seen her here, on the ship.'

He looked at her in disbelief, and then his face lit with a joy that was almost unbearable to see. 'Hathaway? Here? Where?'

'Morgan, I'm sorry, I have some bad news for you. When I saw her she was . . . showing signs of the fatal form of the illness.' She recalled the twitch of the girl's hand, warding off the light, but told herself that meant nothing, and even if it did, to raise his hopes was cruel. 'I was bitten myself just afterwards and never got a chance to follow up,' and that was a lie, she told herself, shamed. She had never had the courage to follow up. 'I'd asked Emily Linn to go over. We should go and see if we can find her – she'd be able to answer your questions.'

'You asked Emily Linn to go over where?' he said in a small, precise voice.

'In the women's c– Morgan –' He vaulted on to the chest high wall, ran along it, jumped across the corridor. She watched him leaping and scrambling across the half altered massif. Only when he vanished did she think to go after him.

'No,' he was saying – shouting, rather – as she came within earshot, 'I'm trying to find my niece.' Two women were barring the entrance to the women's cave, the wiry-haired, wiry-bodied Maggie, and the cropped blonde vet, Barrett. Maggie was saying, 'She is not *your* anything, and you should get it through your thick head that if she's not with you maybe she doesn't want to be with you –'

Barrett stepped between them, forcing them both back. Maggie folded her arms. Barrett said in a soft, not particularly friendly voice, 'Go and get Hannah and Dove, please, Maggie. You're not helping matters in the least.'

'What am I supposed to help?' Maggie said. 'I know him, even if you don't: he's the lackey for thae sojers over there,' this straight at Morgan, her accent broadening.

'Hannah!' Barrett bellowed over her shoulder, with barnyard lungs. There was a rustle behind her and the big woman came stooping through the tattered silver sheet. Maggie opened her mouth and Barrett said grimly, 'Bag it, Gladys, or I stuff your mouth full of matting and hope you choke. Hannah, this man's looking for his niece.'

'Hathaway,' said Morgan, in a clipped voice. His jaw seemed to lock with emotion or anger. Sophie supplied, 'This is Dr Stan Morgan from NASA. His niece is the young woman brought down four days ago . . .'

'She's gone,' said Maggie.

The dismissiveness of her tone made Sophie stare at her in outright disbelief.

Hannah said swiftly, 'Maggie means she left, yesterday. Alone and under her own steam, as far as I can determine.'

'Oh, aye. I wasn't meaning she was dead,' Maggie said, offhandedly. 'Alive and kicking she was. Bolshie youngster, that one. Likes things her own way. Found some of us a bit meddlesome. So she'll have gone back where that young man found her. Maybe gone back to him. She wouldna say.' Maggie stood with arms folded, unapologetic. 'Now, would you like to go back to your lot and tell them ta but no ta, we don't want to sign their constitution or join their club or party or whatever it is this week.' She kicked at something on the ground, a broken boundary marker. There were several, lying scattered around the entrance. 'And they can quit putting up their wee posts and tell their sentries to mind their own. We'll be making another way in and out, ta very much. We don't need anything from them, and they're no' getting anything frae us.' Without waiting for a rejoinder she ducked underneath the silver sheet, snapping it down behind her.

Barrett said to Sophie, 'Maybe I wouldn't have put it quite like that, but I agree with Maggie. We've been pushed far enough.'

Morgan said, 'Did she give you any idea where she might have gone?'

The women exchanged wry glances, and Hannah said, 'When I realised she was gone I asked around, but no. She hadn't said anything to anyone. Nor did the man who brought her in.'

Sophie nodded. 'Morgan, if she's just been ill she can't have walked far in a day, and somebody must have seen her. If you go back to the main camp and talk to Dominic . . .'

'Yes,' Morgan said, with an effort. 'Thank you.' He focused on the two women's faces, said, 'Thank you for looking after her,' turned and left without a farewell. Half way back to the massif he started to run.

'I . . . tried to prepare him for the likelihood she was dead,' Sophie explained. Paused, 'She's not still with you, is she?'

Hannah's smile was rueful. 'No, Sophie. She did leave. And she did not tell any of us where she was going.'

There was a brief silence.

'Is there anything I can help you with?' Sophie said.

'I'm not sure there is,' Hannah said. She looked tired. 'It's just this damn unremitting pressure to fall in with bigger people's plans. Your lot seem bound and determined that the ideal is that the whole ship toes the same line. They have attractive enough justifications for it – decreasing the potential for conflict, making sure there's freedom of movement, making sure that there's no one segment of the population being oppressed or abused, making sure basic liberties are universally understood. It all seems so Mom and Apple Pie . . . But after a while we started to notice there was something missing. There's no fundamental recognition of the right not to belong. In fact, we're hearing the opposite, that respect of our rights is conditional on joining. And how can we know that sooner or later something we truly cannot live with is going to come down the pike?'

Barrett chuckled, darkly, 'It's like saying "I do" on the promise of a fifty-fifty split in childcare and your work being as important as his. He says, "But don't you believe me?" and you can't very well say, actually no, darling, but by the time you figure you were right you have three kids and no job.'

Hannah said, 'We are afraid that we will have the choice of living within a system which could in time demand our subordination or living outside a system which defines us as outside their rules and open to predation and exploitation.'

'Just like Earth, in fact,' Barrett added.

'I think,' Hannah said, 'what we'd like to see – see, not hear – is less talk about what we're expected to do and how we're expected to behave and more concrete indication of what you – plural – are actually going to do and how you're going to behave. We don't want promises and reassurances. We want to see behaviour that tells us your people appreciate and respect our position, and aren't simply assuming that if you – plural – keep harping at us we'll see sense and tumble into the bosom of the fold.'

'And I'd better warn you,' she continued, 'there's deep, deep distrust among us of the military presence in your camp. We doubt very much that what they're here for is what we're here for, and we are certain that if they stay – and it looks like they are well established – they are going to affect the social and political structure of your camp for the worse.'

'Although,' Barrett said, judiciously, 'there was an intrinsic tendency to overregulation – which,' she said, parenthetically, 'is a far more neutral word than any Maggie would use and maybe more neutral than

I might ordinarily use, even before them – witness the situation when the food began to run short.'

Sophie said, 'It was the food shortage, and the response to that, that started people thinking about the need for a constitution in the first place.'

'I have no objection whatsoever to your setting your house in order,' Hannah said drily. 'But let it be your own house that you set in order first, and let your neighbours mind theirs.'

31   Hathaway

I want to throw up. He's gone but I don't know for how long. We had this no-holds-barred screaming row and he hit me and ran off and I don't know what to do because he says he's going to tell people about the owls. It started when I found him putting the owls into the plague picture like monsters on a horror movie poster. I told him that wasn't fair and they wouldn't come anywhere near him if he was making them into monsters. He yelled that if they didn't come and answer his questions he'd tell everyone about them and they'd hunt them down. I screamed that he had no right because I was the one who'd told him about them and I hadn't told him about them so he could hurt them. And then he said that he'd watched them carry away a bunch of the green beret guys and the rest already knew about them and wouldn't stop until they'd hunted them down. I grabbed on to him which was major stupid – I should of picked up something and hit him on the head with it – and he punched me in the stomach and that was end-of-fight. It was weird because I've been punched way harder and kept fighting but all I thought of about was the baby and I just let go of him and rolled up on the ground. Which was stupid because in a real fight I'd have got kicked to mush. But he didn't do anything else and I heard him scrambling down my tunnel like some kind of big bug.

So I've done a painting it made me cry to do with an owl being shot with a gun. I've done pictures of guns and bullets of all different kinds and bows and arrows and knives and all the dangerous stuff I could think of. I don't know whether it's just the ship that sees the paintings or whether the owls do too. But maybe that will warn them what people could do. I may not know what the owls did to me but even if they're not always the good guys they still don't deserve what Stephen and people with guns would do to them. If Stephen hadn't found that feather.

I AM SUCH A DUMBBELL. He didn't take any *proof* with him. Maybe that won't stop some people believing him but I'm sure the green beret guys wouldn't go off hunting aliens without something else than they've already got. I'll hide all the evidence and tell everyone's he's crazy. He ran away with a corpse and I've got a bruise on my stomach – just a little mark now but I know how to make bruises look real bad. I'd know I'd be in real trouble if anyone else threatened my baby because I'd just turn into liquid jello. So I'll have to go to Hannah and the women. They're not real thrilled about the army guys and they won't let anyone hurt me and my baby. If I hide the feather and all the drawings and the letters that talk about the owls – I guess if I hide some of my letters I'd better hide them all just in case anyone else noses into them and thinks about why some seem to be missing before I get copies faked with all innocent stuff. Oh this is so hard and it doesn't seem fair but it's got to be done. And Mr Stephen Cooper can go – well, you know.

32 Stephen

Everywhere there were people. Everywhere human clamour, human demands, human accusations. He ran until he was winded and then he walked until he could run again, and still there were people, cavern after cavern of them, clustered tight or thinly spread, living in the caves or sprawled across the matting, coming towards him with clutching hands or with pointed gun. He ran and walked and ran again, and in his mind Fleur stood in judgement and let him know he would have to go back.

Oh, yes, he knew she was dead, and any conversation would be exclusively one sided, but he did not need to hear her say anything to know what she would have said once she was through spitting fury at him. She would have said you go back and sort it out. You go back and make sure the girl is all right. She would have said, you don't have me any more. You're going to have to learn how to do this yourself. She would have said, grow up, Stephen. He remembered Fleur pacing in the shabby kitchen of one of the many low-rent, shared apartments he lived in when he had to come back to the city, talking about things she had seen, things that he would never have let anyone else talk to him about, while he tried to ignore the twisting in his belly. That night she'd been talking about a man who had beaten his pregnant lover so badly that when the paramedics arrived she was unconscious in the bathroom with a half-born foetus wedged between her thighs. And why, she cried, was not the true measure of the crime not just the death of someone the law hardly recognised as a person, but the sum of the pain of all the people who saw that death – mother, elder child, paramedics, physicians . . .?

What would she say to him now, she who understood so much?

For her there were certain songs on the radio, songs that had played in the night; an aftershave her stepfather wore; the laundry detergent her mother had used for their bedsheets; phrases spoken in a man's voice; the thrust of a man's hand between her thighs. Suddenly the past gaped like an open grave, at any moment, anywhere. In brilliant sunlight at the funfair; standing in a queue for the bank; in bed for the first time with a new, impatient lover.

For him there were only certain pitches in a woman's voice, and the way a woman's screams burned down his nerves. He did not know why. From the first five years of his life he remembered very little. He never thought he had to.

Until he had killed a woman to stop her screams. Killed her, and doomed himself to slow death in prison; been saved again by Fleur, and brought here, to this place which had killed her. If, he thought, if he had never broken into that apartment; if *she* had never come home. If she had not screamed. If he had not touched her . . . Stumbling, he halted, standing beside a wall with his back to the bright waterfall, feeling the vapour of it dampen head and shoulders, and in some part of him hated all the careless, worthless survivors, those women with their little silver badges and shoddy dreams of Womanland; Arpád and his acolytes; prim, golden Sophie, with her scientific detachment and bloody instruments; most of all that insufferable teenager, Hathaway, whom the aliens had saved. All the living ones, all the ones who still laughed and chattered and squealed in their shrill voices which plucked at his nerves.

He hunched down against the wall, letting the water soak his shoulders, and then shifted and laid his head back against the wall and let the water wet him, head, neck, back, buttocks, uncaring. If anyone came wanting to know if he was 'all right', he thought, he would break their jaw. But nobody did; this cave seemed mostly occupied by Asians; they stared, but at a distance, and whispered in their soft, bubbling voices. He did not understand them. He had never had the chance to learn the languages he wanted to learn, the languages he could have travelled with. 'I'm sorry . . . Stephen . . . Cooper, is it? You joined the school too late to register . . . Yes, I know you moved homes and had no choice but the class is full and I really do think that a European language would improve your job prospects more in the long term, maybe Spanish, there are openings in Spanish . . .' He had struggled at home with library books and shoplifted tapes, had gone, once or twice, down to Chinatown to listen, but slowly he had lost hope of ever learning the language, of ever being able to afford a round-the-world ticket and the visas and the health insurance and everything else, of ever reaching the places where the voices were different and the women spoke softly and only the tropical birds screamed in the night. 'It's Shangri-La, you want,' Fleur said, 'or Lotos Land . . .' and she laughed at him, but sadly, certain there was no such place on Earth. And here these quiet, foreign people looked at him as though he was a large injured dog, something to be feared and avoided. He pushed himself out of the water and, bent over, trying to diminish himself, he felt his way into the nearest tunnel.

There was no one else he would have let howl in his kitchen of the horrors he knew too well. No one else he could have gone to after the woman in the condo. There was no one else who knew the best and the worst of him. There was no one for him in this teeming, clamouring crowd. And without her he was becoming a monster, a shambling, horror movie wreck of a man lurching down the tunnels with his clothes dripping. She should not have left him. She should not have left him.

Who the hell do you think you are? Heathcliff?

That was exactly what she had said in his hearing, over the phone, to an ex-lover who was swearing he could not live without her. He could see her sitting in her red bathrobe, seven fingers slick with the scarlet nail varnish she had been painting on her work-clipped fingernails, holding the phone between two fingers and thumb. And now he thought he had no idea why she had come. He had assumed that it was because of him, but now for the first time he remembered that the day he arrived there had been a stack of neatly addressed envelopes on her desk, far taller than would be needed for the handful of bills she fielded each month. And he remembered that she, not he, had been the one to mention the aliens. And that answering machine had already been unplugged and the incoming mail was dwindling away. As though she had already decided for herself.

He stopped, bewildered. He had no sense that he might have been travelling in a circle, but this intersection was one he knew. Somebody, inspired no doubt by the wall of names, had dubbed the four tunnels Oxford St, Piccadilly Circus, Charing Cross Road and Hyde Park Terrace

148

in fake stencil handwriting. He had come down the second, he knew it
. . . hours and miles ago. Had he travelled so short a distance, fleeing?
But then it seemed he never travelled very far; he always ended up in
the same place.

He heard people behind him, a woman's voice overbearing the rest.
He did not turn to look at them, but stepped around the nearest corner
and pressed himself to the wall, shaking slightly with the chill of wet
clothing. The woman's voice crested over him, heard but not understood, and washed on.

'You.'

The timbre of the whisper made his muscles flinch, as though all the
nerves had been plucked as one. He turned his head and saw her, a thin
woman in truly ghastly drag, her dark brown hair cropped ragged. Her
hands had gone out towards him reaching or warding off. Her lips were
parted, as though her breath came in gasps.

He knew her, though he had never seen her before. He knew her
body only as a silhouette against a hallway light, her eyes only as
shadows pressed deep in her skull, her face only as a motionless profile
against soft carpet. He did not know her skin, though he remembered
the muscles straining beneath it. He had known her hair, the glossy
curling warmth of it, as he drew it across to hide her face. But she had
cut off her hair. He did not know her voice at all, except as a scream.
She did not scream now. She said, 'You.'

He shook his head reflexively, answering the terror in her voice
rather than the words.

She shuddered all over, and he remembered how her body had
bunched and then stretched into its scream. But still she did not
scream. She said, without moving her eyes from him, 'That's the man
who attacked me.'

She was not dead. The thought brought him towards her, starting to
reach out, though he was far too far away to touch. Even if she would
have allowed him to. She started backward, with a gasped, 'Stay away
from me.' And he stopped. Merely to see was enough. To see all of her,
the alien light giving a sheen to her pallor, penetrating the depths of
her eyes, touching up her ragged hair. All these things he had not seen,
in half light and panic. 'Fleur,' he said, aloud, tears coming into his
eyes, 'Fleur, do you see?'

'Be careful,' someone said. 'He's crazy.' It was not her voice, tense,
but beneath the tension excited and even gloating. Behind her a
shadow moved, and when he blinked the shadow became another

woman, watching him, like her, yet not like her, hair still curling and full, legs long, high-booted, bare, eyes full of light and triumph.

And suddenly the world was peopled again. They were no longer alone. Four men were moving around him in a ragged ring. For a moment – a moment in which he nearly lost himself – he did not understand. He half raised a hand, to point towards her, to say, 'But she's still alive.' And then it seemed some psychic wind shifted and he felt the tribal vengefulness of them wash against him. He feinted hard forward, towards her. The woman behind her cried, 'Rosie!' and clutched at her. The men surged inwards, but their thrusts fragmented; only one still came at him, while two thought to get between him and her, and one dithered. He swung away from the man still coming at him and into the man instinct told him was the weakest, driving a fist into his face, so that his clutching arms flew apart, and up to his bloodied nose. Stephen bowed aside from the nearest man's belated grab, and hurled himself forward, ahead of the man still following like a wave, or a train or a falling tree. Desperately, he dodged, jarring knees, hips, and skull, slammed against a corridor wall, spun away from it. The other woman screamed out, 'Seth, get your gun.' And then he was sprinting full out towards the fixed green eye of the forest's entrance, his gut cramping and his wet clothing scraping his skin, feeling the sear of the bullet towards his back. 'Seth!' more distantly, as though she too was running, calling to someone further away, 'Bring your gun. That's the man. That's Rosie's rapist.' And then he was in among the little trees, running and rolling and burrowing deep into their soft concealing heart.

33 Hathaway

You guys are never going to believe this but I've met up with Uncle Stan. I practically wet myself when this army guy stopped me as soon as I walked into this cavern on my way to the women and said, 'Is your name Harriet?' I suppose if I'd thought for a moment I'd have thought that Stephen didn't know me as Harriet – but like I said I practically wet myself that he'd told them everything already and they'd caught me. But it turned out to be Uncle Stan who'd found out from the doctors who'd seen me when I was sick that I was up here. We had this hysterical reunion scene. Uncle Stan kept saying how wonderful it was to have found me and talking about all the amazing things he had discovered about this ship at five hundred words a minute – and in between he wanted to know what exactly I thought I was doing here and how could I be so irresponsible and didn't I realise what a dangerous environment this was for me and my baby? Sort of the kid showing off his new toys to his new playmate and the Heavy Uncle all at once. I couldn't keep up so I just let him hug me and bawl me out and tell me all the great experiments he had planned and that he was going to get me back home where I belonged as soon as possible. Some of his ideas are really crazy like the ship is kind of alive except that everything that looks like it has grown has really been kind of built out of very tiny moving building blocks. He's really excited about this weird thing that happened when Sophie (that's one of the docs) spilled a bottle of chemical and didn't wipe it up right then and the greystuff it was spilled on began making more of it. So they're experimenting like mad to see what else it can replicate. It's funny to watch him with Sophie because she's just the type he goes for and can never get to first base with – you know like the girl he teamed with in undergrad chemistry and that woman he worked with at NASA. It's nice that he likes women who're so good at what they do but a little embarrassing that he doesn't hide it so well. Sophie's this New England ice princess with real blonde hair (the roots would be showing by now) and Grace Kelly looks. She's snooty and maybe kind of insecure even though she comes from Harvard and he can obviously think rings around her but she sits and kind of nitpicks until I could just about scream. But all that happens is that he comes up with even more ideas until even I think he ought to be on lithium or something. He's obviously having

Someone came by and I had to hide the paper I was writing on. This camp is kind of a communistic set up and if they knew I had paper they'd confiscate it for their records and the textbooks people like Sophie and Uncle Stan are supposed to be writing. The guy who runs this camp (which everyone calls Kastély after a Hungarian folktale about a flying castle – Repülo Kastély – not bad) used to work in refugee camp directing. He's got them totally organised with places to pee and places to collect water and places to do laundry and places to collect gingerbread. (That's what the brown edible guk is called. I'm going to work on Uncle Stan to try and replicate some flavourings if anyone's brought some. He can eat the same thing every day the way he lived on won ton soup and fried rice and bananas when he was a student but the rest of us have tastebuds that get bored.) Arpád is kind of a dictator – he's out to take over the whole ship and get it organised his way – but where we're totally in agreement is about what's important to do first. Some people were wanting to get the kids into school saying that we just couldn't lose Earth Kul-chur (I know how it's spelled – I'm being sarky) and he just said no – what was important was to learn about the ship. I practically jumped up and down and cheered when I heard that. A lot of the older kids get to go out on patrols but they won't take me because I'm preggo. The adults are teaching the kids on the fly the way Uncle Stan teaches me but it's all relevant. So that bit of it's OK.

There are a bunch of green beret guys here like Stephen said. They're in with Arpád talking all the time about how to organise and how to do things and they're getting some of the others trained into a sort of fighting/exploring squad. They're really big on mapping and exploring and it was true that some of them went missing in a big dark room nearby and maybe the aliens were involved. One of them also died from the 'flu. So I think they're trying to find out about the missing guys as well as everything else about the ship. Uncle Stan is sort of their adviser on spaceships and any idea he has that makes it past Sophie he then passes to them. So I've kind of been noted as Uncle Stan's niece and I bet they'd be able to pick me out of a crowd of clones in a disco with smoke and weird lighting. But I guess Stephen didn't say anything to anyone after all. I wonder where he is.

It's getting near dark. They have wind-up watches, and hang out coloured flags from the top of this smoothed down castle thing which they use as HQ so everyone can tell the time more or less. It's a dark blue flag which means it's in the last three hours. They're making a city here cutting down into the matting (it seems to be OK as long as you don't cut it off completely) and raising the claystone from underneath and they've given me a little room beside Uncle Stan's though the walls are still a joke and if you want to strip without being seen you have to do it more or less by lying on the ground. Not too many people have moved into the caves in here except the ones with the entrances near the ground. I thought about saying you can live up higher but I'm not ready to tell them about my cave. I've just told Uncle Stan I camped in the little trees. Which was sort of true. You should hear his ideas about the little trees. I'll tell you later – it could go on a bit. He got all parental and made me go visit the women as if I hadn't been going there anyway when I got stopped. He wanted me to tell them thank you for looking after me and show them I was OK. He wanted me to say sorry I'd left but there are limits. I'm my own person. They were pleased to see me and the nursy woman was real relieved that I have a parent figure now. She didn't say anything but then she didn't have to. That's OK. I can handle Uncle Stan. (I really hope that we can make some lamp oil or something that'll burn so we can do things at night.) Anyway, before the light goes out totally Uncle Stan got talking to Marian (Miss West) who turns out to be a chemist. So she's going to

it just went dark Goodnight

34 Sophie

'Times two hundred and sixty-six magnification,' Sophie said. 'From a bead of glass dropped into a hole in a sheet of brass. That's a quarter the magnification of the oil immersion microscopes left on Earth and two and a half times better than our field microscopes here.'

Her motley audience regarded her with expressions ranging from outright scepticism to mild indulgence. There had been a time when she thought pathologists, psychiatrists and epidemiologists in the same room constituted diversity – but then she'd never anticipated standing on an alien spaceship describing Anthony van Leeuwenhoek's pioneering experiments in microscopy not only to physicians of every stripe, but to biophysicists, molecular biologists, one special forces engineer, sundry computer *cognoscenti*, two glass blowers, a silversmith, an optician and a lensmaker, an elderly chemist and a runaway adolescent. Travel is indeed broadening.

'They're not sure how he made his lenses,' she had to admit, 'but there's been some work done on reproducing them, and it looks like they were blown rather than ground, and blown in rather a particular way – the best reproductions came from blowing a bubble in a glass rod and then melting the stub of the rod into a kind of button on the side of the bubble to make an achromatic lens . . . which he then freed by breaking the bubble and mounted on a brass slip with a small hole in it and screws which drove the sample stage in three dimensions –'

'You're talking,' one of the glass blowers said, 'about a lot of trial and error –'

'With supplies and equipment we don't have,' the silversmith finished. Sophie had not yet decided whether they were married or simply long-term cohabitees. They were both in their late thirties, from Lancaster, and had brought with them her brother – the second glass blower – and four children. 'Fed up being stiffed by the Inland Revenue,' had been their offhand explanation for leaving Earth. They had loosely adopted the quintet of displaced youth who had tried to rob Sophie on the first night, as well as Victoria's estranged stepdaughter, and had moved their extended family into one of the caves off the main cabin, prepared to tolerate the cavern's government if not enthuse over it.

'That is so,' Sophie said. 'But that's the situation I'm in, and mine's improving. I started out without, or with a limited supply of the chemicals I need to fix samples – now we've found out how to make some of the basics and I'm starting experiments on staining blood smears and tissue samples.'

'But what's the point?' the silversmith asked. 'We've been through this illness . . . What's the point of looking back? And if you say what about future illnesses – well, what can you do? We're pretty much limited by our environment.'

'But becoming less limited all the time,' Sophie said, wondering a little – and the woman must have appreciated her wondering and said with a half laugh, 'Doctor . . . we're certainly not of the "thou shalt not seek to know what is not given you to know" school. It's just that we doubt you have the least idea of the difficulties involved in even beginning to do what you ask. Your van Lee-whoever had the whole industrial revolution for his technological base. We have' – She spread her hands, showing fingertips greyed with worn-in metal dust – 'just this . . . whatever it is. But Dylan and I have been going daft trying to figure out how to use what we know here, and we're not going to refuse the free run of your factory. We just want you to know it may not work.'

'For one thing,' the second glass blower said, 'you're not going to get a hot enough flame from most of the liquids you've been cooking up here. You've got to be able to melt glass – you've got to get the glass to melt . . .' The optician was opening her mouth when from the pathology lab's door Dominic's voice said, 'Sophie, a word with you, if I may.' His expression was grim. She sighed and said, 'Can I leave you to start hashing out where to begin . . .?' and did, hearing a gratifying rising of voices as she followed Dominic through the massif and out on to the grass. Victoria was there, as was Arpád and the leggy agitator from the nearby cavern known as Erehwon. They had pursued their principles of anarchy and seemed little the worse for it so far, which some of the more committed organisers in Kastély took as something of an affront.

Victoria briskly offered her a photograph. 'Sophie, would you please look at this and tell me if you've seen him recently?' Eilish's lip curled a little at the phrasing, but she merely watched Sophie with sharp eyes.

The photograph was old, the tawny handsomeness unformed and the eyes evasive and secretive, but it was unmistakably a younger Stephen Cooper. Made wary by Victoria's phrasing, she passed it back, saying, 'What's at issue here?'

'I'll tell you what's at issue. That man raped my sister.'

'That was not,' Victoria said stiffly, 'my initial understanding.'

'He might as well have. He could have killed her.'

Victoria leaned back a little to look at her. 'Ms Colby, if you expect our help in locating this man and bringing him to justice, then you are going to have to refrain from . . .'

' "Rabblerousing?" ' she supplied.

'. . . Making exaggerated claims and accusations and using your considerable charisma to manipulate others to join your campaigns of harassment. If your sister wishes to come and make accurate representation of her injuries –'

'Rosie's a wreck!'

Victoria held out the photograph. 'She has my deepest sympathies. Tell her that we are prepared to try Stephen Cooper in a duly constituted court of law, but we are not prepared to aid you in dispensing summary justice.'

Eilish pushed the photograph away. 'Show it to his next victim. If she lives.' She turned and stalked away.

Dominic signalled and two women and a man left off their seemingly idle conversation and moved to flank her. All wore shirts of shades of green, the uniform adopted by the Camp's scouts. Victoria glanced at him with a wry expression, and then sagged, shaking her head, 'What are we going to do about this? We can't even agree on how much contact we want between caverns, never mind on a matter of criminal justice.'

'I tell you this,' Arpád said. 'I will not have that woman or her rabble causing trouble here.'

'Arpád,' said Victoria, sounding pained. 'The Montreal Accord allowed for open access free sharing of whatever we found and learned between people of all nationalities, political alliances –'

'The Montreal Accord is full of very fine words, but those words were written in a tower above the clouds.'

'We are in a –'

Dominic interrupted, 'Given the way Cooper reacted to his companion's death I'd have to agree with Ms Colby's insistence – much as I'd like to call it alarmist – that he could be a danger to others. And since we are probably the largest and best organised group in this region of the ship, I fear it might be incumbent on us to make an effort to find him. We have the resources and, despite a few contentious neighbours, we have generally good relations with everyone we have contacted.'

'Even though I did not practise criminal law I know enough to advise against making any move to arrest him in the absence of a formally laid charge,' Victoria said, firmly. 'Which, I suppose, we'd better be prepared to make, in the event that the woman herself is prepared to come forward.'

'Sophie,' Arpád said, 'you know this man.'

'I have seen him,' she said.

'Last time, when?'

'Last time eight, nine days ago. He was the one who brought Dr Morgan's niece in from wherever she was living.'

'I think,' Arpád said, with a sideways flicker of dark eyes at Victoria, 'we must speak to the niece. The law allows that, yes? You are a lawyer; you will be present.'

'Dr Morgan should probably also be present.'

'Send for him,' said Arpád. 'And for her.'

The girl arrived first, looking truculent and tramplike in her mustard, red and black plaid shirt and battered maternity jeans. The cuff of the shirt was stained red and a faint aroma of vanilla hung around her. She huffed a strand of crow-black hair from across her face and set her heels, looking from one to the other, then said, by way of greeting to Sophie, 'Some of them are still talking over there, only the guys who were saying it couldn't be done are now sure, and all the ones who were real keen are now saying yeah but –' She shrugged and summed up, 'People are weird.'

Victoria said, 'We have a problem we believe you might be able to help us with . . .' Hathaway looked at her impassively, and Victoria handed over the photograph. 'Do you know this man?'

She studied it, looked up, 'Yeah, that's Stephen. Jeez, this is some old photograph. He's just a kid here.' He would, Sophie thought, have been about Hathaway's age.

'We may need to find him. Do you have any idea where he might be now?'

'Uh-uh,' she said, promptly.

Victoria said, in a patient voice, 'Hathaway, it is possible that Stephen may have a criminal charge against him from Earth. This photograph was given me by a woman aboard – who claims that it is the photograph of a man who physically assaulted her sister in the course of a burglary.'

'So where'd she get the photograph?' Hath said. 'From the police? They don't give out these things, trust me. And why's she got it with her? Just in case she ran into the guy? Give me a break. You don't know whether that's the guy who knocked over her sister or the guy who stood her up in eighth grade.'

'Where she got the photograph can be investigated at another time,' the lawyer said, sounding faintly irritated. 'Right now what we need to do is decide what to do about investigating the charge. If Stephen committed a crime, he should answer for it. How, we don't yet know. But it should be to the best of our efforts both fitting and humane and should fulfil the requirement of preventing him from being a danger to himself and others.'

Hathaway folded her arms, setting her feet solidly apart. 'I don't know how as you think I would know. He just dumped me on those women. It wasn't like I was living with him. Or is that what you think, that I was living with him? Like I couldn't make it on my own without some guy.' They looked at her. She scowled. 'That woman sounds like a coward and a whiner. My sister got gang-raped when she was thirteen. If she'd run away, those guys would have got off with it.'

Victoria said, 'Hathaway, that's not really the point.' She paused, then said, thoughtfully, 'Forgive me a personal observation if you will, but I feel you distrust people who sit in judgement over others. Because you are young, you have had no opportunity to help make the law, you have only been subjected to it, or other people's interpretations of it. And some of those will have been based on their own ideas of right and wrong, and unreliable. But there is a law, and there is a need for law.' She paused again, putting no pressure on the silence, just letting a space open.

Dominic said into the silence, 'If the story spreads – and it probably will – he could be in danger from anyone who got it into their heads to dispense summary justice.'

Hathaway returned his gaze steadily. 'I dunno where he is, sorry,' she said. This time, with a transparent sincerity of tone. 'Really, I don't.'

At that moment, Stan Morgan wheeled into the crescent at a run. 'What's going on here?'

'It's OK, Uncle Stan,' Hath said, insouciantly. 'No problem.'

'I heard Stephen Cooper has a charge of attempted murder pending against him. And you were being questioned.'

'They wanted to know if I knew where he was,' Hath said. 'I don't. Dabba dabba dabba Dat's All Folks.'

'Then why were they asking you?'

'Because Stephen Cooper brought her down to us when she was ill,' Victoria said. 'Dr Morgan, please calm down. We are just trying to find this man in case he presents a danger to others.'

'And I don't,' Hath said. 'The end. Can we, like, go now?'

An expression Sophie had never seen – or indeed, never expected to see – formed on Stan Morgan's face. Until now she had perceived little resemblance between man and girl, for all their shared colouring, the coarse black hair, the near black eyes, the olive and terracotta under their skin. Morgan's eyes sparkled with intellectual energy and abundant enthusiasm while, for all the time Sophie had known her, Hath's demeanour had been pure 'wanna make something of it?'. Morgan had that expression now. 'If you're going to ask Hath any more questions,' he said, 'then I think you should see that she has a criminal lawyer present.' She moved in to him, her shoulder overlapping his, expressing solidarity. It was the first time she had seen, beneath the bright young scientist, the boy from the wrong neighbourhood to whom the law was merely the other enemy.

'Before you go, Dr Morgan, would you please tell me where you heard there was a charge of attempted murder involved? That was nowhere mentioned in the message I sent you, and I would like to keep it as quiet as possible for the time being.'

'Then you've already missed your chance. There were six or seven people talking about it just on the other side of the massif.' And he and Hathaway turned and went out.

35 Morgan

Only Marian was there when they got back into the lab, making painstaking notes with a paintbrush and washable blue ink on a smoothed area of claystone, which she had taken to using as a blackboard. The carefully drawn structures and names looked less shaky and somewhat smaller than they had the day before, and there were fewer smudged lines where Marian had dribbled enough ink to prime the synthetic machinery. The chemist waved her three-fingered hand at them and returned back to dabbing blue on the claystone.

Morgan let them both get inside the door, then said very quietly. 'Hath, I've known you all your life. I know you're an honest person –'

'Gee, thanks,' said Hathaway. She patted her stomach. 'He can't make me an honest woman, but at least I'm an honest person.'

'I think,' he said, in the same, quiet voice, 'you do know where Cooper is.'

'Oh, Jeez,' Hath said, throwing up her hands, 'not you, too. Some guy I hardly know lugs me in and dumps me and I'm turned into his main squeeze.'

He looked at her, tougher, more suspicious, and more vulnerable than he had been at her age – or any age. The thought of her alone with a killer terrified him. He said, 'I pulled you out of there because I wanted to protect you, not Stephen Cooper. I didn't believe they had the right to question you, and I certainly wasn't prepared to let them connect you with Cooper – particularly in the public mind. But nor am I prepared to let you shield a man accused of assaulting a woman.'

She shrugged, blankly indifferent. 'I gotta go pee. All this excitement's bad for my bladder.'

'Hath,' he said, 'why? After Peta, why?'

The blankness became inward looking. Perhaps she too was seeing Peta, aggressive, athletic Peta, standing before the apartment door and gathering together all the courage she had in her for the simple task of opening it and walking out into the world. Hath said in a small voice, 'He has a real ugly scar on his shoulder. He said some drunk guy shot him, out in the woods, some guy who said he thought he was a deer.'

'So you know him well enough to have seen his naked shoulders, do you, Hath?' he tried to put some life into the tease.

'Yeah,' she said, after a beat, 'yeah. When he got sick, he came to my place. His clothes were real foul, so the matting ate them off him. Uncle Stan,' she said, suddenly sounding very young, 'he's like Dave. Or Dave could get like him.'

He took her by the shoulders. 'Was he violent towards you?'

She looked down. 'He hit me. Once. Not very hard.'

He gave her a little shake. 'Hath, you know that how hard doesn't matter.'

She looked up, appealing. 'I hit him first. I was trying to stop him –' She checked herself. 'It's easy for you to say I ought to turn him in. You don't know him. You only know that woman's side of it. I bet she's got all kinds of people feeling sorry for her sister and wanting to get the guy who did it to her. And that's not the kind of thing that Arpád and Dominic and Victoria can stop! You know that, Uncle Stan, or you wouldn't be so freaked about me being involved. You wanna turn him over, fine. But you won't get me doing it. Because I know that once I turn him in I won't have any say in what they do to him. But first, you gotta see him. You got to talk to him. You got to *know* something about him. Before you turn him over in cold blood.'

'I have met him, Hath,' Morgan said. 'I was here when his friend died.'

Marian stood up suddenly. 'Is this man armed?'

'He hasn't got a gun,' Hath said, while Morgan looked around him, panicked that he had forgotten to lower his voice sufficiently.

'You are certain of that?'

'He hates guns.' Hath sounded less confident. 'But he's got knives.'

'I do believe your young niece is correct,' Marian said to Morgan. 'Whatever the surface order, the situation is still close to anarchy, and anarchy breeds rough and summary justice. But your uncle is also correct,' to Hathaway. 'If Stephen Cooper represents a danger to others, he must be contained. The decision to turn him over or not must be made, and if you do not want to be the one to make it your uncle and I must,' she said. 'You would certainly be followed if you tried to leave the Camp alone and, if it were up to me, I would have your uncle watched as well. But nobody would expect that you would take an old woman to seek out a desperado.' She scrabbled in the cubby bin which held their collection of plastic bottles, and came up with a handful. 'Wash these well. Give the impression you are going to collect more samples for replication. Observe who watches you; make note of their faces. We shall need to know if we are being followed. Do not let yourself be drawn into talking about, or defending, Stephen.' Hath snatched the bottles out of her hands and was out the door before Morgan could speak.

Marian turned her face towards him, squinting a little, waiting for him to speak. Her divergent gaze was disconcerting, particularly since the blind eye twitched in its socket, straining to align with the other. 'I am', she said quietly, 'a thoroughly wicked old woman, I know.'

'Why?' he said at last.

She slid a hand down to rest beside her on the pleat of her dress. 'I am very old,' she said, 'and like many of the old my most vivid memories are memories of my youth. And some of those vivid memories are of watching summary justice being meted out to collaborators, traitors and informers in the latter days of the war. Quite often a whisper was all that was needed, a whisper and some old grudge or gain foreseen – a land claim, perhaps, or a deflection of suspicion. These are memories from long ago. I do not care to relive them now.'

'No,' Morgan said, 'I am not going to let you go up first.'

Hathaway folded her arms, and puffed at a trailing lock of black hair. The hair, pinned down by her hat, flipped weakly and settled back into place across one eye. The corks swayed gently, casting moving shadows. 'I'm getting to think this was a real dumb idea.'

'I already know this is a real dumb idea.'

'Fine, you go back.'

'You know I cannot let you do this alone,' he said, patiently.

She put hands on hips, spreading the homemade buckskin jacket, its pockets bulging with plastic bottles. 'And you're going to do like what? Throw me over a shoulder and carry me off, kicking and squeaking and beating your back with my little fists. You agreed we should do this.'

'I agreed,' he reminded her of the taxonomy of that agreement, 'to prevent you from going off on your own again. Can you imagine what it was like to hear you were on the ship but might have died, then find out you hadn't died but you'd disappeared . . . again?'

She looked woefully wronged. His uneasy sense of having been waylaid was confirmed by Marian gently clearing her throat. 'Hath,' he said, 'let's do what we came to do.'

'Without me, you won't even know where to go.'

He forbore to point out that this was not his idea in the first place and other futile objections. Merely having – fairly recently – been a teenager left one ill-prepared for the responsibility of one. He watched her upright back as she picked her way on behind the little trees, the bush hat with its peeling corks, the hank of black hair, the fringed buckskins not covering the mustard plaid shirt, and the worn jeans. There was a slight waddle coming into her walk, as it had into her mother's by her seventh or eighth month.

'I'm not up to her,' he murmured to Marian, on his arm. 'I'm praying Cooper has realised Hath knows where he is and has taken off. I feel sorry for him, losing his friend the way he did, but if he did assault that woman, I'm just as glad Hath needn't –' He broke off. 'Listen to me. I sound like her father.'

With her three-fingered hand Marian reached over to pat the arm she held. 'She needs a father, though she'll never admit it. She's but a child herself. I was hardly older when I went to France. I never knew until years later how much my superiors argued about sending me. I was too reckless,' she said, more loudly, so Hath could hear. 'Though it was not my recklessness that almost killed us all, but treachery.' She did not expand – he knew her well enough now to know that there was in her as little resentment of human frailties and venalities as there was indulgence of human follies. 'I spent four months in German hands and was sent to Amiens prison in January nineteen forty-four. I was one of one hundred and twenty prisoners scheduled to be executed. The history books say it was Saturday, the nineteenth of February – I had no idea. The British sent in mosquito fighters and bombed the walls of Amiens. Operation Jericho, it was called.'

'And you got out,' Hathaway said, turning back.

'I got out,' Marian said. 'Others did not. They found their bodies in a mass grave at the end of the war.' Her voice was very quiet; he wondered at her telling them this, not knowing whether the quiet was distance or pain. And she looked at him, as though reading his mind, and said, 'Lest we forget, even here.'

There was a silence, then Hathaway slapped the wall where a lip of claystone curled sideways out over a low hole. Her palm made a sharp, decisive snap. 'This is it,' she said, defiantly, 'you can go up the wall' – she indicated the lowest of a series of hand and footholds – 'or up the hole.' She dropped into a deep squat and shouldered into the hole.

He had a fleeting impulse to take her by the ankles and haul her out, but it was fleeting. She would have fought. He watched the cuffs of her aged jeans and her soft, cheap sneakers scrabble and disappear, thinking how very like her it was to defy him right under his eye. Brazen defiance, he knew many would have seen it, but he knew it as Hathaway's in-yer-face honesty.

He said, 'I must go after her. I'll go up the wall.'

She was standing in the centre of a little cave when he pushed his head over the edge. Alone. She turned and came quickly to him, went down on hands and knees and held out a hand. 'Don't grab the greenstuff, it's not stuck down so good.' He took her hand; she heaved determinedly, and he scrambled up and over, saying, 'Hath, don't strain –'

'I don't want your butt hanging out over the edge,' she said, truculently. 'This is a secret cave, like.'

He raised himself, and looked back out over the cavern of little trees. 'Have to be for oxygen exchange,' he murmured. 'Though why the green –'

'It looks good,' Hath said, walking away. 'You can come in.' She threw over his shoulder, 'He's gone and so's all his stuff. And she's pretty much gone, too.'

He knew then whom she meant, Adrienne LaFleurette, that dark, handsome woman, buried at the back of Hathaway's cave, dissembled, if he were right in his hypotheses, into her component molecules.

She bit her lip. 'It's a bit creepy, but I think he might have been lying on her grave.'

He looked at her closely, and chose not to pursue the subject. 'So this is it?'

'This is it. Take a look around.' She waved her hand casually – with the expression of a child waiting for him to open a well-wrapped present. Colour near the rear of the cave caught his eye, orange, yellow, green and blue. In his peripheral vision he saw her smirk. She went with him saying, 'That one's mine –' pointing out the better drawn of the two, the one with Armstrong, Magellan, and a solar sail-ship sketched in. Lower, there was a reproduction of the images of the alien ship. 'That one's Stephen's –' a cruder, harsher rendering, a jumble of limbs, bodies and heads in the foreground, with masked shapes and flagellants in the background, and behind them a docks, ships and rats. Faint smudges of blue remained above, as though the artist had regretted a joyous blue sky.

'Hath,' he said, in wonderment, 'these are splendid. How –?'

She stepped forward and swept a rainbow arc on the wall with a flattened palm. 'You get different colours depending on how hard you press.'

Fascinated, he reached up, stopped himself just before his fingertips brushed unmarked wall. 'May I?'

'Sure,' she said, pleased. He watched as wavering blue and aquamarine spun itself out behind his fingers. 'You're doing better than Stephen.'

A sound behind them made them both turn. A papery, knob-knuckled hand brandished a cave from the hole like an octogenarian lady of the lake. As one, they moved to raise Marian West the rest of the way. She was winded, but triumphant. 'I thought I'd give it a try,' she announced. 'Oh, my!' The small, watery blue eye caught by the bright colour from the rear of the cave. 'Whatever is that?'

Hath led her eagerly to the wall. Marian asked no permission to lay both hands on the wall, leaning her face so near her skin assumed an almost opalescent cast. 'Oh my!' Marian said again. 'How beautiful. And you needed no paints –'

Hath shook her head, corks bobbing, 'No paints.' With exuberant sweeps of her hands she re-enacted her discovery: the first coloured line appearing beneath her chalks, the realisation that touch alone would generate other colours, 'but no red,' she said. 'I've never been able to get red.'

'Of course not,' Marian West said. 'It's a wonder to me that you have obtained the longer wavelengths; in nature this type of colour is almost entirely restricted to blue.' Hath was caught in open mouthed silence – an expression, Morgan thought, that none of her teachers would ever have been allowed to see, no matter how profound her ignorance.

'Structural colours, my dear, which I think these are, arise from the diffraction of light from a lattice, such that most of the wavelengths interfere with each other and cancel out, leaving a single hue. Do you notice how directional the light is in this one part of the cave, compared to the others?' He had not, but it was true – the light had pooled above the wall. 'The direction of incidence, because it affects the projection of the lattice, affects the colour perceived. In nature most blues and some greens are structural in origin, with a lattice of melanin particles embedded in keratin or chitin – I wonder if this is some kind of liquid matrix, compressed by touch, or whether . . .' She ran spread hands lovingly across bare wall, leaving an arc of green. Morgan became aware that Hath was trying to catch his eye. Marian sensed that. 'I suppose,' she said tartly, 'you resisted the influence of the public education system as strenuously as you have resisted the influence of social services.'

'I don't need social services,' Hathaway said, a squaring off of tone, if not of posture. 'I helped bring up four little kids. I know what babies need. And school physics was way less interesting than the stuff on the NASA Website.' There was a small pause. 'So, can you run that by me again? I didn't get all of it.'

Morgan smiled to himself, and stepped forward. Nothing in Marian's charge was untrue; he knew his niece. He also knew how readily she learned, when she cared to, and that she thought best in pictures. It took only a sketch of lattice and incident and scattered light, using the white wall as drawing-board, for her to grasp the essentials. 'Wow,' she said, looking up at the brightly coloured lines. 'Neat.'

'I wonder,' Marian said, thoughtfully, 'why the ship simply did not reproduce your paints, in the same way it has been reproducing chemicals. Unless it was because the paints are not a true solution, but particulate . . . Curious that, if it has to do with your painting, it has not appeared on the wall of names, or even on my 'blackboard' downstairs. It's almost as though different areas have different functions, and this is . . . what?'

'Uncle Stan,' Hath said, in a suffused voice. Her expression was one of intense, almost breathless expectancy; he felt a spike of alarm – the baby! – and a wash of embarrassed relief that she pointed behind her at the wall before he blurted anything out. '*That* picture isn't mine.'

He had noticed the picture earlier but had not found it remarkable enough to warrant interrupting the flow of conversation. Marian said, 'I presume by your tone you are also implying that it is not Stephen's either.' She knelt stiffly but still gracefully, like an ancient heron, to peer at it.

Hath said, blunt as ever, 'So how much can you see anyway?'

The old woman answered a little brusquely, 'My right eye was damaged in the explosion and has never been right; I lost its sight completely some twenty-five years ago. The other suffered what they call severe macular degeneration. I used not to be able to see anything in the centre of my vision, but it seems it is not quite as bad as it was.'

Kneeling beside her he saw that what he had taken for a reproduction of telescope images of the ship was not in fact that: the textures were quite different from any he had seen – and he had seen them all. They were higher resolution, showing a fine texture of the skin of the ship more like the mottling of a living skin than a hull. Hath said, 'It changes. Before I got sick, I saw Jupiter beside the ship.' She leaned over the adults' shoulders, hands braced on knees. 'It was really showy when it first appeared. Like special effects. I like it better now.'

Maybe an interaction with the solar wind, Morgan thought; and firmly quenched his own notion that this was a true image of the ship. Hath, seeing his expression, scowled. 'You don't believe me that *Tevake* did it all by itself.'

'That isn't – what I don't believe,' Morgan said. 'But Hath, think about the viewpoint. If this is a picture, who is taking it? It's more likely to be artificially generated –'

'Another ship,' Hath said. 'The aliens said there were more ships. Or even if it's alone, surely the ship knows what it looks like. I mean, I could do a self-portrait without looking in the mirror. I know I didn't do it, and there was nobody else here.'

'And think of the distances. Jupiter, in what – eleven, twelve days – that's nearly eight hundred million kilometres at present. Think about the acceleration that would require – it's up in the hundreds of kilometres per second by my reckoning. One gravity is ten *metres* per second. Even if it were possible to achieve such accelerations, we could never survive them. We'd be red smears on the floor at a fraction of that –'

She folded her arms. 'You're standing *here* telling me what's possible and what's not?' He just looked at her, utterly at a loss to realise why this apparent fact had thrown him so offbalance. It was, he supposed, because it was something he understood. The results of equations were inarguable.

Marian was stroking the wall beside the image, shading yellow to apple-green with a feathery touch. 'How very strange,' she said. 'Most everywhere else, touch moulds the wall. But here, it colours it. I wonder if the difference with my blackboard is that I am simply too light. You were drawing, you said.' Raised her head, 'Have you tried drawing anywhere else?'

'Like have I had time?' Hath returned. 'Besides, I didn't know if it would work downstairs.'

'You were', Marian said, 'not unaware of the implications of this, I suspect.'

'Yeah, maybe I was. But maybe I knew it would be like get back to your parenting classes while us real scientists handle it.'

Morgan said, 'Hath, I have never dismissed your ideas, or treated you disrespectfully, and both Marian and I have given you our fullest attention. Remember that it was on your word that we came to find Stephen Cooper.'

She looked down, grubbed the toe of her sneaker in the durable matting. 'Yeah. OK. Sorry. You wouldn't.' Abruptly she pivoted, and went to the far wall, at the edge of the cave. They watched her burrow skilfully into the base of the wall. Marian said, 'That young woman has rather a chip on her shoulder. And won't her parents be worried?'

Morgan sighed. Worried would be an understatement. Frantic and self-accusatory would be more like it. Which Hath would merely interpret as one more slight against her competence.

'Here,' she said, returning with a ragged sheaf of papers in her hands. She pushed them at him, one handed. He caught a glint of blue in her other hand and looked at her questioningly, but she pushed it out of sight behind her back. 'Go on. You can read them. They're meant for Mom and the kids but they wouldn't mind.' She gave Marian a dark glance. 'I left them a letter.'

'And that', Marian said, 'makes everything all right.'

'I bet you didn't go home and tell them you were going to make bombs in a farmhouse with German soldiers all around.'

'I was of age,' Marian said. 'And I did not involve another person in my decision.'

Hath shrugged. 'Kids have been taking the same chances as their moms all through history. At least the air's clean and the food's good, if boring, and there's no bullets or bombs –'

He left them to it. One of Hath's mostly unappreciated virtues was that she did heed people she respected. After a thorough testing, and not without exhausting all the arguments. But he sensed Marian West had the wind for it. With a glance at that age-marked face he wished her long tenure aboard . . . at least until Hathaway was thirty.

They were watching him when he looked up at her from the broken phrases on that one smeared and crumpled page. 'Hey, Uncle Stan,' she answered his expression, 'it's not so bad.' And then dropped to her knees to hug him, awkwardly. 'I wouldn't do it again for a million dollars, but I'm still here.' He put an arm lightly around her shoulders, and felt her settle against his side. 'Go on,' she said. 'This is the bit I really wanted you to read.' He read the page – her recollections, or hallucination, or dream, of the encounter with the aliens. Re-read it, and looked at her. She gasped out her held breath, a puff of warm air across his face. 'For such a brilliant guy you are *such* a slow reader. Are you dyslexic or something?'

Marian said, drily, 'If you think you are in suspense, I invite you to consider my position.'

With Hath breathing in showy gasps beside him, Morgan read aloud Hathaway's description, turned the page, scanned it, and was just about to look up again when a shaft of blue jabbed in front of his nose. 'They left that,' she said, triumphantly. 'Stephen found it,' and to Marian, 'I guess those are more of your structural colours.'

He put down the papers, to free a hand for his hand-held microscope. Low resolution showed a surprisingly even blue, with an overlapping, scaling pattern not unlike an insect's shell. He could just see ghostly threads within the body of it; the pattern suggested veins, whether plant or animal. He found that his hands were trembling slightly and his focus on the leaf fixated and determinedly narrow. Something in him, something that surprised him, resisted thinking of the implications – that this had been shed from an alien being, a creature not of Earth. He had seen the alien transmissions. He had seen the high resolution photographs of the alien spacecraft – this spacecraft, in all likelihood. He had awakened here, in an environment quite unlike any he had ever known. He had listened to Stephen's account of the disappearance of St John Emrys and the others in the haunted dark, had heard his description of the ragged lit edge which might, might, be made up of overlapping tips, like these. And yet – and yet it had taken this, a small thing that he could hold in his hand, to make them real.

'Uncle Stan,' Hath said, uncertainly. He looked into the squarish, slightly jowly face of his niece, seeing her with that same focused attention. Her crow black hair needed washing. Dark hairs flecked the bridge of her nose. Her skin was oily, blemished and uneven. Her shirt sagged as she leaned forward, showing the upper curves of her breasts, and the line of a black bra. Her humanity was like an overpowering scent. She flapped a hand in front of his eyes as his brothers used to do, and he started back, irritated. 'Sorry,' she said, 'but you looked *weird*. Like you were receiving brainwaves, or something.'

'I must do something about expanding your vocabulary.' He passed the feather, or scale, or whatever it was, to Marian. She looked deeply fascinated, but not as profoundly disorientated as he had felt. Hath watched her stroke it with a proprietary air. He said, 'You can wear it in your hat.'

She scowled at him. 'You better keep reading.'

He read on, as Marian called her over to describe the object she could but barely see. Read through Hathaway's ruminations on the aliens, her rediscovery of Stephen, their work on the paintings, and the argument which had led to her leaving. He looked up at the plague painting. His oblique view distorted the colours, but he could still see rainbow smears where she had scrubbed out Stephen's accusatory portrait of the owls. Then he spread out the sketches she had done, and knelt, gazing down at them. His mind was strangely empty. He supposed that any biologist might have been able to have made inferences about the environment, the evolutionary process, that had produced them. He told himself he had seen stranger creatures on Halloween.

Hath shuffled towards him on her knees. 'I didn't know what to do about them. I mean, there are other people like Stephen down there, other people who had friends and family die from the bugs and the sickness. And I know I was out of my head and dreaming, but I had all those bug bites on me and I remember the owls all around me and I maybe remember them putting bugs on me.' She trailed off, briefly. 'I suppose I ought to care about the people who died, I suppose I ought to be mad, but I remember them being gentle. I think I somehow knew they didn't want me to die. I mean, I've no reason to think that, maybe it was just the way they lifted me up. I'm sure they lifted me up, but I didn't feel them lifting me up, so they must have been gentle –'

'It is entirely possible,' supplied Marian, 'that those additional bites did carry some kind of antitoxin, or inoculum, without which you would have died.'

There was such gratitude on Hath's face that he could not bring himself to remind her of St John Emrys and the others, gone into the dark and never seen again. Despite her poses of antagonism and cynicism, she still harboured a childish wish to believe in the goodness of the powers that be. Then she bit her lip. 'Why me?'

'Perhaps it was your youth,' Marian said. 'Perhaps the infant you carry. No one who died of the illness was with child. Perhaps this –' she gestured towards the brilliantly coloured wall. 'As far as I know, this is a unique achievement.'

'Oh, wow,' Hath said. Tilted her face to the ceiling, 'Thanks, guys. Whyever, I really appreciate that.'

He could not help but smile at the whimsy of alien interpreters rendering that in translation. Why not? Perhaps these aliens were neither mysterious nor exalted, but forgetful enough to shed scales where they could be found, and generous enough to prevent a girl and her unborn baby from dying.

'Nevertheless,' said Marian, holding the scale like a quill, 'if the colouring and drawing technique is significant – perhaps as some kind of interface – it would be criminal if Hathaway did not continue with her work, not merely from a scientific standpoint, but from a diplomatic standpoint, for making contact with these creatures –' Morgan offered her the sketches; she waved them away. 'Draw them, my dear. Up there.'

Morgan watched her working with fingers and palms, and strong, assured movements. Everything that had happened had directed them towards discovering how their environment could be manipulated, the shaping of the claystone, its synthetic properties, and Hathaway's walls. 'Oh, my!' said Marian as the picture took shape. 'Bloddeud. Welsh legend,' she explained, 'the woman of flowers.'

Hath paused, 'You mean they've visited Earth before?'

'Of course not,' Marian said, testily. 'I just thought of it, seeing . . .' she paused a little, 'seeing.'

'There,' Hath said, a little later, dropping to her knees beside them. She looked up at the large blue alien; its light gave her face a faint, cold sheen. 'I'm kind of sorry I've only got half of him . . . her, but I never saw the bottom half, that I know of.' She took a deep breath. 'So now what do we do?'

Marian said, 'I would hate to bring harm to such beautiful . . . people.' There was a note of longing in the words that made both of them look at her. She merely turned her head, smiled at them, and returned to gazing up serenely at the alien, her paler skin almost blue.

Hath looked from her face to Morgan's. 'Guess that's decided, then,' she said, and started to gather up the letters. He resisted, not enough to tear the paper, but enough to make her frown at him. 'I'm going to put them back,' she said, as though it should be obvious. 'Where I hid them. Maybe Stephen could still tell, but people won't listen to him, not now. I'll see if I can paint downstairs and, if I can't, we can tell about the painting without having to tell about the owls. And if you're right and it's the painting that matters, then we don't have to, until the owls make it official. Maybe they violated some kind of prime directive helping me, and we shouldn't make a big noise about it.'

'Hath,' Morgan said, 'Stephen obviously did not tell you that he might have seen those aliens before. The team I was with lost four men in an unlit area of the ship. Stephen was the only eyewitness, and his account suggests that they were first overcome by poisonous gas, and then removed – by the aliens.' Hath opened her mouth. 'He didn't see them, not as you saw them, but he described a large shadow with a ragged edge. We had no reason not to believe him – he had obviously been terrified and Sergeant Lowell can be very persuasive.' He felt the chill again at the memory of that interrogation.

Hath said outraged, 'It was them that beat him up!'

'He tried to run,' he said, trying not to sound, or feel, defensive. 'They were a little forceful in stopping him. But A.J. didn't lay a hand on him. He's a very skilled interrogator.'

'He was all bruised!'

'He wasn't badly hurt, and he was the sole witness to the disappearance, possibly deaths, of four men. And he wasn't prepared to tell the truth.'

'Guys beat you up,' Hath said. 'Mom told me about that.'

'Hath,' he began. But there was nothing he could say. He could not begin to describe the difference, the sense that this was physical force contained and applied to a purpose. Not mere bullying. But maybe she had the right of it. There was no difference. Just that someone else had been the victim.

Hath said defiantly. 'I already knew.'

Marian West interjected, 'You said this was an unlit area of the ship.' Her small eyes hooded. 'I would have said that much of the flammable material would have been consumed during the illness in the wards, but –'

'But we're making more,' Hath put in, and for once Marian did not look irritated at the interruption, but simply nodded, and continued the thought. 'Methanol, and lantern oil. We have synthesised both.'

'You'd have thought,' Morgan said, momentarily deflected to follow her thought, 'that if the ship or the owls or whoever didn't want us looking into the dark places, it wouldn't have replicated anything that could be used to make lanterns. After all it quite handily prevented us from maintaining contact with Earth, or relying upon our gadgets.'

'Maybe something's changed.' Hath folded her arms. 'Maybe it wants us to go looking down there. Maybe we'll find those missing guys – oh, come on,' she said, to them both. 'You believed me about Stephen. Can't you believe me about *them*?'

Marian tilted her head slightly, with an odd expression on her aged face. 'You were uncertain yourself, I seem to recall, about the reliability of your judgement and where your responsibility lay. The subject of the original dilemma has relieved us of it by going elsewhere. But that dilemma has been superseded by this one – and I must confess greater uncertainty here. I have eighty-odd years' experience of humanity,' she said, casting an upward glance at the wall. 'But of these . . . people, none.'

'I don't want people hunting them,' Morgan said slowly. 'There's too much danger involved, to them as well as the aliens. Stephen thought that the captain's team touched or knocked something, but it may simply have been that they were carrying arms. But I cannot see failing to warn them about a hazard –'

'Jeez, they already know. Listen, if we tell them anything, and people start thinking the aliens have been disappearing people and sent the bugs, they'll freak. They'll be hunting aliens all over the ship. I never would of told you this if I thought you'd get them killed!'

'A.J. Lowell is the last person to go off half cocked.'

'I don't care how much you admire this guy!' cried Hathaway. 'All it takes is one crazy person.' She scrabbled papers and drawings and feather together, and heaved herself to her feet, standing looking down at them in helpless awareness that whatever she did would be in plain sight of both of them.

After a long moment, Marian said, 'We have merely speculations – which may seem to you like wordweaseling and hairsplitting but is in fact the truth. We have a length of scale, which could have come from anywhere, perhaps even from the wall itself, like the insects, and a description and sketches, but Hathaway is the first to admit that she was desperately ill when she saw, or might have seen, the aliens. Can we justify spreading alarm on the basis of that? I am of a mind to do as Hathaway suggests. Leave her scale and sketches here and do what we can to make sure that nobody is endangered by their ignorance. But hold our peace. For now.'

While Hath went to return her evidence to its hiding place, Morgan helped Marian to her feet, which she suffered with courtesy and an air of largesse. But as he did so, she went slightly off-balance, and something in the pocket of her woollen skirt thumped against his thigh. Something whose weight and feel and cold iron touch he well knew from his youth. She sensed his stiffening, and for a moment was still – weighing answers to unasked questions. Then she tilted her head back and said quietly, 'It's in the way of the young to be trusting, not the old. I shot in competition for forty years.' She paused. 'No one, after all, would expect that of a harmless old lady.' Hath closed her hiding place and clambered awkwardly to her feet, scowling in their direction in a vague, defensive way that dared them to remark upon her clumsiness. Marian tucked his arm in hers. 'I will not tell her,' she said. 'Will you?'

36 Stephen

Quite deliberately, he made his first steps into Hades careless ones. Instead of stepping over the thick, corded ridges on the floor, he let himself stumble, as the unseen soldier had stumbled – just before the lights went out, and the bodies fell and the whispering clicks and scrapes began. He stooped and set down his lantern, and waited for the flame to stifle, ready to draw his final lungful of air and lie down, and wait. If they came too soon, he would have them. He would get his questions answered.

So he stepped, and he stumbled, and he set down the lantern. And waited.

The flame burned steadily.

He struck at the ropy creases with his foot. Kicked harder and harder until chips of them flew off into the darkness.

In the immense, motionless silence, the lantern flickered with the draft of his exertions, steadied and burned on.

He yelled, 'I'm here. Come and get me!'

Nothing whispered. Nothing moved. The flame bunched and squat-ted lower on the wick. His foot lashed out at it, sending it arcing across the darkness, to smash and spill burning oil. A splash by the tip of his boot blazed briefly. His breathing was harsh and small. His guts churned with fear and anger.

'Come and get me!' he screamed.

The darkness disdained him. Gradually the spilled oil burned itself out, the light glinting feebly on the shards of broken glass. Some time after that he lit a candle, and gathered up what he could salvage of the lantern, which was almost cold. 'Cowardly bastards.' He smiled around, with a cold smile. 'I'll be waiting.'

He made his camp on the long ramp, a full turn up, against the wall. From the ruins of the smashed lantern he fashioned a pan and wick arrangement. For the time being he had light. He did not think about what would happen when the light ran out. He would decide then. He might move on, find somewhere where they had never heard of him. Somewhere he could ingratiate himself, persuade people that he could not possibly be what they said he was. He had seen it done, by Jacob, pious church goer, straight A-student, and murderer at the age of thirteen.

But Jacob had made a study of people. He knew that the art was in finding what they needed to believe to protect their understanding of the order of things, and setting himself at its right hand. He neither loved nor feared them. Stephen feared them, and so he made a study of wilderness, and escape. He was no Jacob. He could not make others see him as he wished to be seen; they saw him as they wished to see him, deer, or villain. By the light of a single candle, he shuddered, remembering the hunter's bullet, remembering the closing ring of men, and her eyes. He saw himself ringed again not by four people, but by hundreds, and moaned as his bowel wrung again. On hands and knees, he crept over to his sleeping bag liner and lay stomach down, which made the twisting of his guts more bearable.

Fleur, what would you tell me to do now?

Her shroud had been nearly empty when he left her. In a last urge for connection, he had lain down on her grave mound, and felt the brittle bones shatter under his weight. She was almost, finally, gone. The body which he had stolen – the first thing he had ever stolen to keep – was eroding away. That, more than fear of the girl bringing the hunt, was what drove him from the cave. He did not want to be there when Fleur vanished for ever.

What he needed was a place like Hathaway's, a place nobody knew about. A place nobody went, like this, but with water, gingerbread, light, and a wall like her painting wall, somewhere he need never leave, and nobody need ever come because nobody would know it was there. A map began to form in his mind's eye of a catacomb hollowed out of the walls of the ship. Of himself, living like a gopher or a rabbit in the very walls, removed from people, safe. A precarious safety, true, since at any time tunnelling might break into one of his spaces, but if he had several systems of caves and tunnels, and if they were not connected and he had planned escape routes. He could still come out at night. He could make spyholes, high in the walls, and watch them, so he would be forewarned of breakthroughs, and maybe, just maybe, he could find other people – but his thoughts shuddered away from that, because once one person knew, there was always the risk of torment or treachery. The only person he had ever trusted was Fleur.

You didn't trust me, her voice said. *You only fancy you did now I'm dead, and it'll never be put to the test.*

'Jesus!' he said, pressing his hand to his ear.

No, you're not going mad, she answered the half formed thought. *Poor Stephen.*

'You never called me that in your life.'

I thought it, she said. He rolled away from her voice, curling up around his cramping belly. And she was silent. As his gut gradually settled, he persuaded himself of the difference between remembering and hearing voices. He could not have been hearing her voice; some of these things she would not have said.

As he settled himself on the sleeping bag liner again he suddenly remembered that when he rolled he had had a sense of something tearing away from the side of his head like a very old bandaid, losing the last of its stick. Drew the lamp closer, tilting it carefully so he could bring it as close as possible to the surface without spilling oil. He saw nothing, no stain, no grey fuzz. He felt his face, found it clean, with just a little crust of dried tears and saliva. He shuffled off the sleeping bag liner and lifted it, but it came easily, clean. Just as a precaution, he spread his plastic undersheet.

Even so, the voice came back in his dreams. Somewhere in the middle of a conversation, with her telling him, *you have to*, and he was saying, *no, I don't*. It might have been one of dozens of conversations – she was always the one to tell him what he had to do and he the one to resist. If he could not be right, at least he would yield in his own time.

Stephen, she said now. *Open your eyes.*

Why?

Because I want you to.

He saw blue, blue that shifted like leaves, or water, or neither. The scalefeathers were like leaves, each one an individual facet, but they moved like water, like a single connected surface.

Backwoodsman's instincts kept him still, looking up. She said, softly, *Ahh, good, Stephen. Good.* His eyes shifted, looking for the source of the voice that seemed almost at his shoulder. She said, *You know I'm not here.*

There were four of them. They were smaller than he expected from

Hath's sketches, no more than human size, if oddly proportioned. Head and shoulders overemphasised as though each wore an overlarge cape of animate decorations, and lower bodies sheathed in smaller scalefeathers which rippled only a little. They had broad, trefoil feet, with long hooked nails or stubby claws. He thought, they have the eyes of nocturnals, and the insight let him see them with a woodsman's eye. Like humans, they were outside their natural habitat, but like humans, they carried it with them, in the cast of their bodies. Vision was important to them; the dominant eyes, the absence of apparent ears. Or apparent mouths, he realised, with a sudden shock, a sudden sense of the grotesque. And as though his thought had been read, the two most in front of him leaned forward slightly and, with a sudden parting of scale feathers, a three cornered hole opened in each chest. From them, like a pale worm, rose a stubby, mobile tube. Even in dream he felt the revulsion, and jerked away, his hair snagging. Adrienne said, Stephen, don't be such a child. He pulled further away, pulled himself free, and she was silenced, and it was dark.

Just a nightmare, he told himself.

From the darkness, there was a rasp and a click and silence before he came awake enough to sort dream from reality. His heart was beating hard enough to make him tremble. He listened with all the anguished intensity of his first night out alone in the forest, as a thirteen year old runaway with a threadbare sleeping bag and an airgun between himself and primeval terrors. A terrified little rat of a boy for whom dawn's slow coming had been salvation so prolonged as to be a torment. The starlit black going indigo, and the clear, cloud smudged dark blue. The flecks of white sky towards the west. The first sunlight on the very topmost spires of the sequoias, as far above him as the lake's surface to the long drowned. He saw the slow-seeping gold, drizzling down towards him, picking out the branches needle by needle. He felt the cold, sunk deep in his bones, so intense he thought movement would snap them. His fire had gone out because he had been too frightened of what was out in the darkness to get up and feed it. Which was as well, the older Stephen thought. He knew nothing, then. Nothing about standing in the dreadful day-after devastation of a forest fire, feeling the dull heat of the earth beneath his boots, the sting of the fine blowing ash against bare neck and cheeks. Nothing about watching a veteran firefighter weep without shame over a boy's belt buckle. Nothing about the glow of the sun through the haze of a crowning fire.

And you think you're a coward, Fleur murmured in his ear. She had said that in life, he remembered. He woke shivering, after the heat of his dreams. He had rolled half off the protective plastic, and lay with his head uncomfortably pillowed on a flat area of stone. He cursed himself for giving the girl his sleeping bag and not taking it back when she left. An absurd point of honour, that he prove himself no worse than she already thought him. Woodsman's habits told him he must make himself move, though his impulse was to curl tight, lock all his muscles, endure. He lifted his head gingerly, but nothing pulled. He found his lantern, lit it with cold hands. The dim light splashed upon colour overhead, where none had been before. Above him, stretching out of the light above and on either side, he saw moss-bearded trunks and arching ferns and the white points of berries like pearls. He pulled himself out of the sleeping bag liner, stiffly, still looking up, lifted the lantern, held it as high as he could. High up on the wall, sunlight touched upon the topmost spires. Beyond the sunlight he saw high cloud, still a little gold. He set his hand on the wall and leaned into it, aching with loss, hating the people who had driven him out of his wilderness, and hating himself for letting himself be driven. And afraid. He said, in a whisper, 'What the fuck are you doing to me?' There was no answer.

So are you going to run? said Fleur's voice, startling him so that he jerked his hand away from the wall and swung round. The light sloshed along the walls. There was silence. Rubbing his stinging palm, he settled to his knees and laid down the lamp. So am I going to run? Where to? Back to the caverns, to whatever they planned for him. Like hell. He'd stay here. Next time he'd be ready for them. Next time he wouldn't be taken by surprise. He settled cross-legged on the plastic, looking up at the wall.

Light, he wished.

Light, please.

Nothing happened; he smiled a little, in relief, and leaned back. The heel of his hand slid on to claystone – and he froze. He remembered the pull as he moved his head, the transient sting as he lifted his hand. Almost, he pulled his hand back, but let it rest. His heart rate quickened.

He thought, light.

Light.

And then he closed his eyes and envisioned the wall before him, with the light glowing through, like the light through a stained glass of a cathedral.

And the light came to him.

37 Sophie

Rosamond Colby appeared in the pathology lab some time after lights out. Marian, Hathaway, Morgan and Sophie were playing poker by the light of the newly constructed oil-lamp wall array over the microscope table. The cards were Marian's, of WW II vintage. Perhaps, as Hathaway suggested, she did know every crease in them; certainly she had little difficulty reading her own hand, and the battle for the pot was strictly between Marian and Morgan. Marian had learned in the war ('My poor mother had me bound on a straight course for perdition . . .') and honed her technique in the cutthroat play of a retirement home, while he was pure LA cardshark ('Babyfaced Spic – like taking candy from a baby, that's what they think . . .') who had supplemented his schooling from his winnings. Between them, Hathaway and Sophie had lost enough to draw the attention of the International Monetary Fund. As Morgan observed there was no point in playing high class poker for peanuts.

Rosamond announced herself with a breathed, 'Oh my.' Waiflike with her ragged hair and oversized clothes and her air of innocence newly wounded. 'Oh, how beautiful,' she said, stepping in. 'I knew you had light but –' Above the night workbench they had mounted the bases of five glass bottles in hoops extruded from the claystone, so that the light from the burning oil shimmered through and down. Morgan and Marian exchanged a truce-making glance and then laid their cards on the bench, face down. 'We don't have anything like this in Erehwon,' Rosamond said, drifting up between them. 'They don't believe in making changes to what's around them.' She reached up and traced the underside of the hoop with a finger, light rippling with the flame and catching the four silver filigree rings she wore. 'I'm an interior designer. I could do something with these.' She took a deep breath. 'But that's not what I'm here for. I'm Rosamond Colby. You maybe,' with a glance at Sophie, 'know what happened to me before I left Earth . . . the reason I left Earth. But I . . .'

'You are the young woman whom Stephen Cooper is said to have assaulted,' Marian said.

Rosamond Colby turned to her gratefully. 'Yes,' she said. 'I am. And he did. It wasn't rape. I know . . . my sister has been saying . . . and I've asked her not to . . . she does like to dramatise –'

'So what do you want?' Hathaway put in.

She looked at Hath, stout and antagonistic in her green plaid shirt. 'I . . . I wanted to come without Eilish or any of the others . . . so I could make up my own mind. It's difficult when they're all . . . harrowing at me . . .' Her straying eyes came to rest on Morgan. He cleared his throat, a small, nervous sound, plainly searching for something to say.

'You came here in the dark?' he said.

'Yes,' a small laugh. 'It sounds crazy, doesn't it? I've been utterly terrified, just about paralysed, ever since it happened. And I'm not someone who scares easily. I love horror movies, suspense movies . . .' Hathaway rolled her eyes, eloquent of scorn. 'But in the strangest way seeing him helped. The one thing I've been absolutely dreading has already happened. Nothing else could be as bad. And . . . I didn't remember seeing him properly. I know I gave the police a description, but it was as though that was someone else. Whenever I thought about him I saw this faceless nobody. I could feel him, pushing me down . . . smothering me . . . but I couldn't see his face. And then . . . I saw him. He was just a man.' She glanced from Morgan to Sophie and Marian, appealing for understanding. '. . . Just a man who looked so . . . so stunned and . . . awed and almost relieved . . . to see me, as if I'd been as much a burden on him as he had on me. I could have talked to him. I think I would have, if Eilish and the others . . .'

'So you want to talk to Stephen,' said Hathaway, her voice flatter and harsher than ever in contrast to Rosamond's.

She flinched. 'Oh, I know it sounds foolish and naive . . . On Earth I'd never be given the chance . . . But I just want to know why he did it. Why he did it to me.'

'I am afraid,' said Morgan, with visible unease, 'we do not know where he is. He has not been seen in or around the camp for a number of days.'

'But you knew him,' she said, looking up. 'I heard you knew him –'

'I had met him,' Sophie said. 'He was with this Camp at its inception. Hathaway met him briefly, I believe.' The woman's glance flickered to the girl, and away again. 'But I don't think either Morgan or Marian ever knew him well enough to speak to him.'

She sighed, softly, then straightened up and turned, a silhouette against a wall of flickering light. 'Then I shall just have to wait . . . until they find him.' She waited a moment longer, and then left in a muffle of heavy clothing, her head lowered.

Hathaway scowled after her a moment, and then slid off her stalagmite. 'Betcha she never came alone,' she said, and padded after

Rosamond into the jumbled shadows of the massif. She returned shortly afterwards, looking disgusted. 'She sat down on a rock outside and snuffled away until someone asked her what was wrong, and then she said she wanted to speak to Victoria. So he's taken her off to see Victoria. Bitch,' she said, feelingly.

Marian folded her hands atop her cards, maimed hand over sound one. 'Curious,' she observed. 'I have to confess I cannot be certain whether that was a genuine, if foolish, effort to make peace with herself and with her assailant, or a calculated appeal to our sympathies to elicit information about Mr Cooper's whereabouts. And to what degree there were other influences at work in her shadow.' To Hathaway, 'I suspect your earlier caution might have been justified. We can but hope that by the time he does reappear, the responsible elements in this camp have prevailed. It will happen. Those people who are prone to gallop hither and thither loudly clamouring their cause have little stamina for the long run.' She gathered up her card, dismissing the matter. 'Have at ye once more, Dr Morgan?' she invited.

In the morning, their first visitor was Victoria, looking tired and frustrated. 'Rosamond Colby has decided to lay charges against Stephen Cooper,' she said, by way of greeting. Hath, decanting chemical with her back to the lawyer, mouthed, 'Bitch.' 'She has given us the information we need, and we've started a search for him. What I need – since this is becoming a formal legal proceeding – is for each of you to be prepared to state, on oath and before witnesses, that you do not know where he is.' She paused. 'Hathaway?'

'Sure,' Hath said, without turning. 'Standing on my head, singing the "Star Bangled Spanner" in the nude. Whatever.'

'Do I have to explain the laws governing perjury?' she said patiently.

'I expect Hath's legal counsel will do that,' Morgan said.

She measured the young man with her eyes. 'I have not forgotten your request,' she said mildly. 'This is as much for her protection as anything. There are strong feelings in the Camp. It will be the first trial of our emergent legal system – and unfortunately, since the crime took place on Earth and all the evidence and records are still there, it will depend very much on the arguments.'

'A fact,' Marian said, 'of which the Misses Colby are well aware. We had the younger sister in here last night, expressing a wish to speak to the man.'

'She wants to "understand",' Hathaway said, sarcastically, turning.

Victoria let a few beats elapse before answering. 'That is not at all an unusual response in first-time victims of violent crime. I will ask her counsel to explain to her that she runs a risk of producing either a mistrial or an acquittal if she tries to go outside due process.' She looked around at them. 'There is much more than Stephen Cooper's guilt or innocence here. This will be as much a trial of our community as it is of Stephen Cooper.'

'The greatest miscarriages of justice have come about when justice is tainted by politics, opportunism or prejudice.' Marian observed.

'I understand that,' Victoria said, stiffly. 'I –'

'Victoria –' One of Dominic's runners, a young teenage girl. 'Can you come quick? Sophie, you better come too. You know them, Dominic said.'

'What's the trouble?'

'It's the women. They won't let the scouts in to search.'

They could hear the shouting and the singing as soon as they left the massif's jumble of claystone. There must have been over a dozen green shirted scouts, along with three of the special forces soldiers, Arpád, Dominic, and several other committee members, by the women's entrance tunnel. They were facing forty or so women, most of whom had linked arms in ranks across the entrance. Swaying and shuffling, they sang, 'We shall, we shall not be moved,' the sound an incongruously cheerful counterpoint to Maggie's voice: '. . . let ye pass any more than we'd let one set o' wolves into the field to hunt another. Ye'll just have to take our word for it, the man's not here!' Three other women wove between the lines, pulling at arms and arguing; one or two of the singers broke off for long enough to snap a response, before their neighbours swayed harder against them, yanking back into the rhythm. From all across the cavern, people laid down their tools and set aside their tasks and began to stray over to watch.

Arpád's expression on seeing Victoria and Sophie was one of relief – reasonable women, Sophie thought, cynically. Maggie dismissed them with a glance, though Hannah gave them a surprisingly bitter smile. With them were the two former police officers, Astarte and Lillian, and a solidly built black woman Sophie had not met. The woman was saying, crisply, '. . . neither the legal authority nor reasonable grounds for insisting upon a search of these premises . . .'

A middle aged man answered her, 'An argument based on the claim that this represents private property, invalidated by the Montreal Accord, which specifically disallows all nationalist, corporate or individual possession of any part of this ship.'

Maggie said, accent thickened with ire, 'Well, we didnae sign yer precious Accord, did we? This is our home and yer no' coming in without an invitation, and it'll be a cold day in Hell before ye get one. Did ye really think we'd just stand back like guid wee lassies and let ye come traipsing in whenever pleased ye?'

'No, but we expected you to behave like reasonable people and assist in the apprehension of a dangerous criminal –'

'Stephen Cooper', Victoria said, 'has been charged, but not tried and certainly not convicted, and the law presumes innocent until proven guilty, as you well know, Laurence. He is entitled to due process of law and a fair trial. Victoria Monserrat,' she said, to the black woman. 'International Law.'

'Amanda Sumner,' the woman said, giving Victoria a powerful handshake. 'Public defender's office, Philadelphia. If your Mr Cooper needs an attorney, he's got one. I understand you're responsible for the Montreal Accord. There are some serious omissions in that document, particularly regarding rights of the individual. I suggest you call off your search – not just of this cavern but of all the others – until we get those resolved.' She jerked her chin behind her. 'These women are prepared to offer physical resistance to this unwarranted intrusion into their home.'

One of the dissenters came forward, a prim-looking woman in her thirties. Sophie knew her name was Helen and that she had brought a daughter with her. 'All they want to do,' she told the lawyer, in a chipped-flint voice, 'is satisfy themselves that we're not harbouring a fugitive. For all they know he could be holding our children hostage and making us protect him.'

'Aye, and you've been watching too many of thae trashy Hollywood films,' Maggie put in.

Helen ignored her. 'If an invitation's needed, then I'll do the inviting. I can do that, can't I, as a member of this community?'

'An' undermine the whole principle of the thing,' Maggie said.

'Your principle,' the woman said, her voice stinging. 'Not mine.' She looked at Victoria and Sophie. 'Will you come in?' It was as much order as invitation. 'And if they come in,' this flung at Dominic and the scouts, 'will you accept what they say?'

'There's nothing legal about this,' said the middle aged man.

'Quite so,' Amanda Sumner said. 'What Helen has offered, she offers as a courtesy so you may sleep easy in your beds tonight. It's an offer you may accept or refuse. You're not entitled to anything more.'

'We will accept,' Dominic said, 'Sophie and Victoria's report.'

The search took them the better part of two colours – as they re-emerged, red was just being replaced with cyan. They had no choice but to do a thorough job of it, alone. Certain members of Kastély would be satisfied with nothing less than an examination of every man-sized cranny in the women's cave, and certain women begrudged even their admission. In the end it had been Sophie who did much of the searching, while Victoria stayed down on the cave floor to ensure that no fugitive slipped from a yet-to-be-searched into an already searched pocket behind their backs; a ridiculous precaution, to their minds, but they were aware they were not doing this to satisfy themselves. Victoria spoke with the women at some length, while Sophie had a chance to examine their progress on their cave-dwelling – Bedrock, it had been dubbed – so neither felt their hours had been completely wasted. But they were both heartily tired of suspicion and intransigence, and Sophie was glad that she could in the end retreat to her lab, while Victoria went, in poor temper, to face the deputation from Erehwon that had arrived, seeking their missing member.

38   Stephen

Having come at call, the light would not abate, though he laid his hands on the claystone and wished, envisioning darkness in all its forms, it did not abate. You don't like the dark, Fleur murmured, and he said aloud, 'I like to sleep. This is like a fu- a holding cell in here.'

No it's not, Fleur said, laughing.

And no, it was not. It was a place which stopped obscenities on the tongue, a place of pure wonder, which made him again the boy discovering the cathedral in the trees. The light was softer than out in the main cavern, with a yellowed tint, as though shining through thickening cloud or shell worn almost translucent. It bled from all surfaces, all forms, filling the immense space. That, too, was shell-like, a huge single-chambered nautilus with parallel spiral ledges up outer wall and inner core, linked by bridges like the one he had ventured across in the dark. The chamber tapered with height until inner and outer ledges fused into the root of the inner core, some five hundred metres up. That inner core was suspended rather than supported, its rounded nadir twenty metres off the floor, just below the level of the first cross-bridge. Although roughly spindle shaped, it broadened and slimmed, unevenly, and the bridges, he noticed, came off its widest portions. All the surfaces were corded and ridged, in some places, as on the inner core, finely, in others, as on the floor, coarsely, in a mixture of smooth folds and rough knotted cables, not unlike tree roots, he told himself at first, seeking familiarity in the strangeness. And then, some time during the first day he had ceased to need something to find it familiar. It simply was, as the forest had simply been, some fifteen years ago.

So the first day he began to explore his new domain, taking the long ascent up the tightening spiral wind, to where, crouching, a great height above, he could step from outer wind to inner and descend via the core. He grew familiar and rather than stepping over the corded roots would step from one to the next, like the boy on tree roots. With his head brushing the ceiling and his feet dangling over the long drop he took his notebook and made his first fumbling attempts at putting what he had seen into words, the way the girl Hathaway had. He envied her her audience. His was only himself, and a dead woman he talked to in his sleep. His unpractised handwriting was clumsy, the writing of the tenth grade dropout he was. He did not know how to make words from the wonders around him.

He rested his head back, and let his eyes unfocus. Fleur's voice said, clear as if she were standing behind him, *Don't drop your notebook, Stephen*, and he jerked his head up – feeling the slight sticky tug and the tearing of a few hairs at their follicles. He twisted to look at the claystone ridge where his head had rested, and saw the collapsing grey fuzz shrinking back on to the claystone, and meshed with it a few strands of dark hair. He started so violently that the notebook jumped from his hand and fell, bouncing on the inner spiral and sliding down it, and snagging on one of the cords eight or nine metres below. He suffered a momentary impulse to hurl himself after it, to escape the ship's tendrils fleetingly in a short flight through empty air, and to escape his awareness of them for ever in his fatal landing. And mocked himself, shivering, the instant after. He did not have the guts. He huddled on the ledge, waiting for the ship to reach through his clothing, or down from the space over his head and take him to itself. But it did not. Fleur, who was not Fleur, did not speak again.

In the glimpse he had taken over the edge he had seen the patch of brilliant green. He had scarcely been able to look at the mural at first, so true was it to the image in his mind that he could not pretend that some probe had been sent down or some television broadcast intercepted. It was no one else's image of Earth but his, surely taken from his mind. That made him feel ill, violated, as violated as when he had confided his hopes for his adult life to his social worker as she drove him between placements – far from the office and her notes, feeling for the first time she listened to him as a person, not a case – and the next visit he saw among those notes a sheet detailing everything he had told her. He had not confided in any of them, again.

But she had diminished his confidences, painted them unrealistic, unattainable, escapist. He was merely another antisocial juvenile delinquent. The ship, he thought now, the ship had not done that. He stalked carefully around the thought. If the ship had this picture, it could have had everything in his mind. Yet of all the images, of all the experiences, it had taken the most beautiful, and transformed it into something even more beautiful.

He left his notebook lying where it was. He felt still too shaky to venture across to recover it. He drew his cuffs over his hands so that he need not touch the claystone, and crawled a turn downwards until the ledge was wide enough that he could be sure of walking without falling. Then he stood, and made his way down the winding spirals to the picture, and sat crosslegged in front of it, looking up, as he had looked at the trees the first day, cold, hungry, purged of terror . . . and most important free of the fear that there would never be a place for him.

He had been such a fool, he thought, to leave there, to go to the city, to try and live in city ways. He did not blame himself, still could not blame himself, for the ends he went to to try and escape the city. That was their doing; they, the decent people, had made the city what it was. His was only in leaving the only place he belonged.

He would not err that way again, he thought, and slowly, taking most of the courage he possessed and all the time looking up at the ship's love letter, he laid his hand flat on the claystone beside his thigh.

You're not Fleur. Are you an alien? Or are you the Ship?

There was a pause. *This will take time.*

I've got time.

39 Sophie

'Hey, Hannah. Hi kitty-cat.'

Morning, red pennant. Sophie was in the synthetic lab, decanting freshly synthesised stain from its well. At Hathaway's greeting she looked up to see Hannah in the doorway, Melisande flowing from her arms like poured cream. The cat ignored Hathaway's outstretched sneaker, batted at the tuft of Marian's shoelace, sniffed at Morgan's trouser cuffs and lifted her pointed face to Sophie with a 'where *were* you?' plaint. Sophie tripped her way towards the water basin in that erratic pas de deux of cat owner and soliciting cat. 'I've got to wash my hands before I touch you,' she told the cat. 'And don't scold me for deserting you – it was you who left me.' She rinsed her hands, shook the water off them and swiped them on her jeans. Melisande sat down at her feet and began to lave a paw with a pink leaflet tongue, mute commentary on the crassness of humanity. She disdained contact with damp fingers until Sophie had dried them to her satisfaction. Then she suffered herself to be stroked.

'I must say,' Hannah remarked, looking around, 'your brewery is impressive.' It was the first time Sophie had seen her in something other than skirt and blouse – she wore plaster-stained jeans and an old man's shirt. Behind her in the passageway lurked a well-filled backpack.

'Yeah,' Hathaway said, 'but you don't want to try our cayenne sauce. I don't know what it's trying to put in there, but it's poisonous. We've got a whole bunch of other food flavouring though – peppermint, vanilla and seasonings and stuff – anything that we can get to dissolve in water. Hey, have a doughnut.' She flourished the ring of gingerbread left over from the morning's conference of medical and science staff – her own invention. Hannah took it and nibbled, a little dubious. 'Taste of home, huh, sort of? We're working on the coffee. Listen, you're welcome to stock up on anything you like, and what we'd really like is if you tried to see if your cave would replicate too.'

'I would like to do that. When we're settled again. I've come to say goodbye . . . after a fashion. Some of us are leaving.'

'Leaving!'

Kent Hughes passed behind Hannah with a nod. She waited until he had gone, then eased her backpack inside the doorway. 'We're moving over to Erehwon – Maggie, myself, Astarte, Barrett, Lillian, ten or eleven of the others. Dove and Lisa and Helen and the children are staying with the rest, in the cave.'

'What happened?' Sophie said, restraining Melisande from leaping up to investigate the benches.

'I'm still working it out. Maybe our group was just too diverse. Or maybe this was simply not a good place to be, with so large and focused and expansionist a neighbour. Some of us were troubled by the military presence. Others are troubled by the fact that the men are the ones who seem to have taken charge. And you just kept pushing.' She took a deep breath, 'We were starting to work things out between ourselves, figure out how we wanted to do things, and then suddenly we were having to cope with the question of whether to assimilate, or not to assimilate, or how much to assimilate, whether to let you in to search, or not. Yesterday was just the last straw. We've been up most of the night trying to resolve it, but in the end those of us who don't want to coexist on your terms have decided that as on Earth we have no choice but to walk away. Erehwon looks to be trying to live up to its promise of being an anarchy – there are a number of small groups, coexisting, including a group of women, lesbian separatists. We may join those, we may not. But at least we'll have more of a choice.'

Sophie said nothing, until it seemed unavoidable that she must, that Hannah was waiting. 'I can't pass judgement. I'm not a political person.'

'Everyone is,' Hannah said. 'And every act is a political act . . .' She held out a small piece of paper. 'This is a map of where we'll be. We'd be delighted to see you, any of you. You are all associate members, so to speak.' Politely, she did not make a point of excluding Morgan. 'And Sophie, before I go I have a couple of confessions to make,' she said, a little shamefaced, but more lightly. 'Melisande's started eating gingerbread – before we noticed a new drift had started, she'd got into it. It's not the same as ours, not nearly as sweet. We're hoping that since the ship has been providing for us, it's providing for her, too. She doesn't seem to be suffering any ill-effects. The other thing is . . . she came into heat between the outbreaks, but she ran off –' Hannah gave her a rueful smile. 'You're not the only person to have brought a cat on board. I know the look of the female animal who has been thoroughly romped and rogered. I had a college room mate who used to come back looking just like that, and it's all too likely, Barrett says, that like my college room mate Mel's pregnant. I know I should have told you before, but there was just too much else happening – I'm sorry, I feel we've been terribly negligent, and you did trust us with her . . .'

'Kittens?' said Hath, dropping to her knees and reaching out. '*Neat*. Here, cat; here kitty-kitty.'

Melisande gave her a look of utter disdain and sidled behind Sophie. She certainly did not seem to be poisoned or malnourished; her dark pointed, creamy coat was glossy and her eyes clear. She stretched out her front paws, spreading claws, and hitched haunches and tail ceilingwards, purring her contentment.

'Melisande has been spayed,' Sophie said, 'so it can't have been heat.'

Hannah said, 'Barrett was quite certain it was heat. All the behavioural signs were there. If it's recent, there may be some residual –' She trailed off as Sophie shook her head firmly.

'It was nearly three years ago.'

'Stranger things have happened here,' Hannah observed mildly.

Sophie stooped and held out her hands. Melisande wound her silky length between them. Sophie ran her hand along the soft fur of her abdomen, feeling the double row of nipples. Might it show so soon? She did not know. What she remembered of feline reproduction she had read a long time ago; it had, after all, been academic. She gathered the cat against her, probing for the scars from the operation and then more deeply, feeling for fullness inside her belly. Melisande hissed resentment, and turned to close her teeth around Sophie's intrusive hand, not breaking the skin, just making her point, until Sophie eased off. She settled and pointedly began to lick flat her disordered fur.

'Sophie –' somebody said.

She got to her feet, very collectedly, not yet acknowledging the idea that had come to her, and went to Marian. The old chemist was still making notes on her 'blackboard', but she had this morning exchanged her brush for a still finer one. Her inscriptions had grown smaller and neater with each passing day, and last night Sophie had noticed she had been closing her bad eye to examine her cards. The old woman looked at her, with one eye small and steady in its puckered pocket, and the other shifted slightly off true – then Marian blinked, and narrowed her eyes slightly, and the damaged eye shifted to align with its partner. 'May I?' said Sophie. She lifted one of the blank sheets of paper, folded it and covered Marian's better eye. Marian's blind eye, she found, could now perceive light, darkness and motion in all quadrants. Her better eye, formerly limited to peripheral vision, had regained enough central acuity that she could read phrases printed in Sophie's hand beneath her own.

Sophie laid down the brush and reached out for Marian's hand, saying again, 'May I?'

Marian accommodated her, saying, 'It's no different. It's only my eyes.'

All four were watching her now, as she examined Marian's maimed hand. There was no change there. She looked back at Marian, looking at her, both small, blue eyes steady for a long moment before the blind eye faltered. She felt as though she were balancing on the edge of a long fall, or a high flight. If she dared disbelieve in gravity, and leap. 'I need air,' she said, and pushed past Hannah, making the turns through the maze more by instinct than sight. Outside on the slope, she stumbled to a halt on the slope. Everything seemed to be in slow revolution around her.

'Sophie,' Morgan said. They had followed her, and stood watching her, Morgan with helpless perplexity, Hannah with simple perplexity, Marian with concern, Hath's expression declared 'She's lost it'.

Hannah said, 'Sophie, I think you need to sit down.'

'No,' she said. 'No. I don't have time.'

She felt the woman's hand on her arm, tentative. Hannah eased behind her, supporting her, one hand on her arm, one on her back. She stared out across at the long flow of grass, towards the graveyard where the swell of the sinking barrows barely broke the flatness, and past it to honeycombed grey walls glistening with water. The strangeness bore in on her. Hannah spoke; she did not hear what she said. The low, dark voice said again, 'Why don't you have time?'

'I didn't,' Sophie said. 'I might now. I don't know. I thought I'd know. I thought it would be something that I did, and that I'd know. I might, I might now. I don't know.'

'I'm not understanding,' Hannah said.

'Familial Alzheimer's,' she said. 'An inherited form of Alzheimer's dementia. It runs in my family; the people who have it develop it in their forties. My mother had it, they did the linkage analysis, we were the subject of a study, but I wouldn't let them test me, I didn't want to know. People say, "Have a test," as though tests are never positive and people never find themselves going from fifty per cent glass half-full/ glass half-empty to a hundred per cent glass smashed, beyond repair, never to be filled again. Have a test, they say, isn't it better to know, aren't you a scientist . . .? No, it's not, better to be all the time watching yourself, watching myself for changes you can't see in the mirror, picturing what was happening in my mind – knowing every time I saw a pathology specimen, an MRI with temporal and frontal lobe atrophy, knowing that might be what was happening inside my head, to me –'
She turned to, on, Morgan, 'I switched my stones, exchanged white for black, put myself in the control group. I thought I'd contaminate it less that way. I'm used to not talking about it. It changes relationships; whatever happens they're never the same after the other person knows how you will die, and if it's a man – the children, the chore of caring –'
He didn't understand, she saw. Too young to think of children, or being fifty with a demented wife. It was all an abstraction to him.

'You came looking for a cure,' Hannah said.

'Melisande goes into heat, maybe pregnant, though she's spayed. Marian starting to see with an eye that's been blind for years. There are other people who have chronic diseases – we can collect the data –' She gave a choked laugh at the sight of Morgan encountering an idea too bold even for him, like a python trying to swallow a pig. Hannah put a hand on her shoulder, massaging it gently. Sophie leaned forward, bracing hands on knees. 'Oh, God. I thought it would be something I did. I thought it would be a reward. I thought I would know when it happened.' Her attention was caught by her hand. She envisioned it like Marian's, an old woman's coarse-knuckled, ugly hand. The thought filled her with joy, that she might live to consider it with a clear mind. She wanted to vault over the years between – to flip to the end of her life as though it were a novel, to read the last page and learn how everything came out in the end. She had never felt this way before. All those years she had gone on, so bravely defying her doom by refusing to curtail her education, curb her intellect, all those years she had believed she had no fear, she had been living blind. She had not dared look forward. 'We have to take this back to Earth.'

Hannah said, in a still voice, 'It is far too soon to be thinking of that. We don't know nearly enough –'

Sophie straightened. 'And without the equipment and knowledge on Earth, we never will. We have to study this ship at the molecular level. We have to find out what has happened to us. It has to do with the insects, I'm sure of it – that's the reason we weren't just inoculated through the foodstuff or the water – it needed some kind of recombinant virus, possibly tailored to ourselves, although with each one of us being bitten only once, but we shed cells in our faeces, with our skin. The problem would be attributing ownership –' She was panting slightly, as though it was a physical effort to keep apace with her thoughts. She had always been fastidious in her reasoning, a meticulous respecter of details, profoundly distrustful of intuition. She did not have time to redo what had been ill-done. She had no time to waste on odd notions and scientific whims. She must do her work properly, first time, there would be no other. She knew – she had heard it said within her hearing – that her carefulness, her unwillingness to make leaps, to freewheel, had kept her from the front ranks in her field.

They would not know her now, those critics. She felt the very shape of her mind changing, even as she tried to argue with herself, to remind herself of the absurdly slender evidence on which she based her insight. But after a whole lifetime of denied hope, hope had lifted her up, ravished her, borne her away.

Morgan said, 'Maybe it's not a virus at all. Maybe they haven't affected genetic structure, only molecular structure – maybe they're – whatever they are, the ship or the aliens – correcting us molecule by molecule, atom by atom, almost rebuilding us from inside, with the knowledge they gained from . . . taking apart the bodies of the people who died, and they'll have constituted a template for what the human body should be –'

'But there are still scars on Melisande's skin, even if she is functionally female, and Marian's eyes may be better, but her hand –'

'You're thinking of them as automata,' Morgan said, 'without intelligence, without an appreciation of what is important and what is not important about the human body. But they must know and understand since they've taken us on –'

'But after death the breakdown begins almost immediately, enzymic degradation, DNA degradation, and the growth of the shroud is –'

'No, no, no, you're treating the shroud as the first and necessary constituent. It's not so. The information could be being gleaned from – oh, hell, the information could be being gleaned from the living. Individual assemblers could be inside us, learning us, right now – it's been part of the concept all along, nanoscale medics –'

'Then they could teach us that way,' she said. 'If they can read our physical structure, change our physical structure, then they could change the physical underpinnings of memory –'

For the second time she saw him halted by a thought too radical even for him. On impulse, she leaned forward and kissed him. He received the kiss with open hands and wide eyes.

Hathaway, standing at the entrance to the massif, started to applaud.

'– assuming that they understand us well enough –' she said, lifting her lips from his.

He put his hands on her shoulders, 'Then why not do that from the start?'

'Needing time for analysis maybe. Needing time to learn – or whatever their equivalent is; let's just use learn for the sake of convenience – the detail of the physical correlates to the memories created. It's your hypothesis that this environment is working on us to some purpose or wishes us to work on it to some purpose –'

'That's right, blame me,' he said, laughing. His breath smelled sweet and slightly grassy, of gingerbread. He shook her slightly, uninhibited, his dark eyes luminous with wonders. 'So what you're saying is that by making us learn, the ship, or the aliens, or whoever is driving these assemblers, is finding out what changes take place in our memories as we learn –'

'The biochemical and biophysical correlates of memory, yes. Maybe even the electrophysical correlates of thought –'

'So it could use that information to teach us directly. Sophie, you're a genius.'

'You're not half bad yourself.'

They grinned at each other until, suddenly a little self-conscious, he let her go, and they each took a step back, grinned at each other again, tried to speak at once, stopped.

Sophie said, 'It might explain the appearance of the fatal form of the illness manifesting as an encephalitis, with seizures, and the swelling in the temporal lobes – that's the focus of human memory – but in the pathology specimens I never saw anything, although their preparation was admittedly far from ideal –'

'Well, you wouldn't, if the assemblers were too small to see or did their crumble-into-dust trick on contact with air –'

'Or once their task was finished. Which makes me wonder about the bugs again – they seemed to fall apart after they had bitten, which suggests they were delivering a load, not collecting samples, odd that.'

'Tagging us. Or loading us with assemblers.'

'Or inoculating us with some desensitising agent to prevent an immunological reaction to the assemblers – maybe the illness was the failure of that desensitisation and manifested when the assemblers either moved in or switched on –'

'You know, Sophie, it makes sense now that all our electronics fell apart, aside from not wanting to keep contact with Earth. I mean, how many of us brought reference material up with us, memories on silicon? Losing them has made us work our organic brains overtime, so anything that's watching or monitoring the way we work could see us working to retrieve stored knowledge – and if what they're ultimately planning to do is introduce a physical correlate to the memories we need to operate this ship, then that was exactly the information they need.'

Hathaway cleared her throat meaningfully and they looked round at a loose circle of staring faces – Hannah, Marian, Hathaway, Dominic, Victoria, Altman Meyer and members of the medical staff, several of the science staff, A.J. Lowell and three of the ODA. Morgan laid his arm across her shoulders. 'Have we got a theory for you!'

40 Hathaway

Has this ever been a crazy day. Well, I mean, crazier than usual. I'm in the lab where they've got these neat lights on the walls with glass bottoms. Marian nixed the idea of burning oil right in wells of claystone – she said burning makes carcinogens and she didn't want them being replicated. So we use bits of bottle in claystone rings. Anyway, the craziness all started when Hannah told Sophie she thought Melisande was pregnant which Sophie said she couldn't be because she was spayed. And then Sophie got this kind of white and fixed look and felt up Melisande until Mel bit her and then went and looked over Marian's eye (Sophie, I mean, not Melisande) – which is way better than it was – and started talking about how she thought she was going to die from some genetic disease and had now decided she wasn't and going on about the same kind of stuff Uncle Stan does about little bits of the ship getting inside of us and fixing things that are wrong with us and teaching us about itself by tweaking our brain cells around. Somewhere in the middle of that she kissed him – he's so cute when he blushes even if he is my uncle – and they both got into it, standing face to face like they were singing a love duet with their sentences climbing all over each other. Needless to say that attracted attention and they were talking about it to everyone even though Dominic tried to get them to stop as soon as he cottoned on to what they were saying. I think he thought people would freak at the idea of the ship putting bits inside them. But it was way too late by then because other people were every bit as smart as Dominic and not entirely crazy about the way Arpád and Dominic like to control things and they weren't about to let Uncle Stan and Sophie be hustled away into conference. So there was a lot of craziness for a while with some people freaked out about having little ship-bits (assemblers is what Uncle Stan calls them – I can't say I'm wild about them myself) inside of them and other people talking about how they'd been sick before and weren't now like some kind of revivalist meeting with everybody jumping up and down with their eyes all shining and waving their arms and talking all at once and trying to outshout the next guy. The other doctors and scientists started saying the ideas were crazy and where was their proof and how were they going to falsify the hypothesis blahdeblahdeblah. I'd say they were just jealous that they hadn't thought of it first. But they started thinking up experiments and taking samples and trying to prove that people were better. They're still doing it. I can hear them from where I'm sitting and every so often a bunch of them come barrelling into the synth lab to ask me another gazillion questions about my cave and how I made the colours – because Uncle Stan blurted out about me and it right in the middle of the revival meeting. Something else I was not thrilled about. At least he didn't say anything about the owls. And now I can come out of the closet about the painting instead of having to casually sneak over and fondle the walls the way I've been doing and there are artists who are keen on doing the wall painting. So we'll find out if other people can do it. I don't want it to be something special about me even though Uncle Stan and Sophie are talking about the ship getting farther on with some people than with others and Uncle Stan has made me promise cross my heart with bells and Xmas lights on to tell him if anything strange happens to me like funny dreams or sudden understandings. I'd have thought with all his and Sophie's zinging off the walls they'd have been much better candidates for having a direct pipeline to the ship but he doesn't seem to see it that way. I really don't want to be something special with the ship because of the other craziness that's started up. Sophie started it because she started going on about how this was a great discovery and they should take it back to Earth and it's grown up into a huge row with people saying that it should be taken back and shared and other people saying that if the people on Earth had had the guts to come then it would have been theirs too and it was given to us and we should be the ones to decide what happened to it. It got so it sounded like a bunch of kids and parents saying Mine! and Selfish! even though hardly anyone used those words and everyone talked like professors and politicians and dressed it all up pretty. I got the creeps when they started talking about how to control the ship like the only reason they wanted to communicate with the ship was to tell it what to do. And I'm the one who has been doing most of the communicating.

I just moved to hide. I could hear the green beret guys coming and I decided I didn't want to answer their questions. Now they're standing around in the corridor talking to Uncle Stan about the dark place that Uncle Stan thinks may be some kind of control room and whether it's safe to go down there now or not. They're really hot to trot about the idea of taking the ship back. I suppose the one good thing all this has done is it's stopped people talking about hunting down Stephen. Even if he did nearly kill that woman it doesn't bug me half as much as listening to people like her sister go on about how they have to find him and punish him. Marian thinks it's all political and she's out to make Arpád and Victoria look bad so they won't get the Montreal Accord organised to be signed. She's going to keep the lawyers busy dealing with the criminal stuff for ever. The black lawyer who is going to represent Stephen thinks that they don't have enough of a case against him under Earth law because all the evidence is back on Earth and it's just her word against his and enough irregular stuff has happened – like his sister showing around that photograph that's probably from the foster care or juvenile files – that she can nail them on technicalities. I like her and I've told her more about me and Stephen than I've told anyone else. I still don't know why after Peta I'm not more sympathetic but I guess it's because I know Stephen – he tried to save my life after all. I'm sorry if that makes you mad at me, Peta, that I won't automatically take her part but she's not like you.

41 Morgan

'I don't wanna go back to Earth,' said Hathaway. She stood with arms folded and hip against the jut of the laboratory bench, watching him pack his supplies. 'I don't see why a bunch of people who never bothered to come, who just wanted to stay home safe, should share something some of us died for to get.'

'And your mother?' he said, mildly. 'Peta. Dave. Jack. Joy. What about them?'

She turned her head into half profile, saying sullenly, 'They could of come, couldn't they?' And brought her dark angry eyes up as another thought came to her. 'And anyway, who says they'd get anything? We take the ship back, you can guess who'll take it. The government. Big business. Ordinary people won't get a look see. And you're going to help them to do it. Doesn't it bother you?'

'Yes, it bothers me,' he said briefly, a little angrily. 'But that's the way things get done. You think we should be like that group next door – just leaving everything as we find it, and touching nothing.'

'Better than give it over to people who'll lock it up and give it out in little bitty bits for the right price,' she said, unyielding. 'Uncle Stan, you don't owe them nothing now. They're not paying you. OK, so maybe they're paying something into a bank account back on Earth but I haven't seen a whole lot of ATMs around here. They're not buying your food or your clothes or giving you health coverage. They've not even bought your equipment. It's you whose doing this work, with your own brain. You have a right to decide what you're going to do with it.'

He paused in his packing to watch her. Even now, knowing that there was an able mind beneath that recalcitrant exterior, she could surprise him. He sighed and said, 'Hath, I still regard myself as having a debt to society back on Earth.'

'For what?' she demanded, looking suddenly very like their grandmother, for all she had several inches and fifty pounds on that peppery little woman. 'For all the help society gave you you'd have wound up collecting garbage or fixing cars because that was what was appropriate for your socioeconomic status,' her tone pranced mockingly around the last two words. 'Jeez, Uncle Stan, what you got you got from people, not society, people like those teachers who helped and covered for you – I mean two report cards so that the guys on the street wouldn't have that reason to beat you up. It's ordinary people who cared, not society, not big shots in Boston or New York or Washington, and it's ordinary people who'll get cheated if you help those army guys take this ship back to the military. Sure, you got scholarships, but it was your own skullsweat that got you them and don't you forget it.'

He cinched the straps on his backpack, alert to fragile objects sliding and rubbing together inside, checked the list in his notebook one last time and slid the notebook into his pocket. 'Hath,' he said, quietly, 'I know my worth. I also know the military answers to the government and the government to the citizenry of the nation and to the other governments of Earth, and there is no power on Earth that can stop this many people spreading the word about what this ship might be able to do. The Montreal Accord explicitly forbids any nationalistic claims and monopolies because people like you have foreseen what could happen. Hath, we need the equipment and expertise that there is on Earth –'

Her eyes narrowed. 'That's Sophie's schtick. Is she why you're doing this? For her?'

He made his hands rest atop the backpack. Resisted the urge to shoulder it. Any time they trod close to matters of heart and sex he had the uneasy sense of being at a disadvantage in awareness and experience. She made him feel again like the bookish sixteen year old who had blundered so humiliatingly through his first and only encounter with a prostitute. And something about her, the tough resourcefulness, the tendency to scratch rather than cry, reminded him of that woman. She could not hate Earth as much as she pretended, he thought. But better hate than cry. Tough lessons from a life of poverty and struggle. Scar tissue is strong tissue, particularly in the young. She was the wrong age to see that there were more than one kind of scar.

He said, 'I'd like to say that I'm doing it for Sophie and her family. I'd like to say I'm doing it for people like your father, young men and women who would sicken and die in their prime.' She flinched a little at that, and scowled more deeply. 'I'd like to say I'm doing it for old people like Marian, whose lives could be improved by the ability to cure blindness and infirmities. And maybe I am, at that. But what I'm most aware of is that I'm doing it for me. Because I want to know.' He leaned sideways to slide his arm through his pack and ease on to his shoulder, though it was not particularly heavy. He did not want to disturb the contents. He straightened and shouldered the other strap and eased the buckles tight. Then he lifted the breathing apparatus. Her eyes followed it.

'You think that's going to work?' she said.

'It runs on bottled air. It doesn't rely on filters – so it doesn't matter what the gas is.' Within reason, he added to himself, 'Chemistry's chemistry throughout the universe. Spectral analysis of heavenly bodies tells us that.'

'And suppose,' she said, going for his argument's weakness like a Rottweiler for a limb, 'the ship's little assemblers get into it and take it apart.'

He smiled. 'Just wish me luck, Hath.' She drew breath; he answered it a little sternly, 'As you yourself would say, "It's my life." I'll see you when we get back. I'll give you a good argument then.'

A.J. and his team were waiting none too patiently at the main thoroughfare. Morgan made best possible speed to join them without jarring the backpack, afraid his permission to go downstairs would be rescinded. A.J. merely looked him over; it was Raho who remarked, 'Said goodbye to the girlfriend, Prof?' His only answer was a wry smile; he had grown circumspect in mentioning Hathaway in their presence.

At the entrance to the dark area, watched warily by the cavern's inhabitants, A.J. gave them a short final briefing, intended, he knew, for his benefit. They would deploy as they had deployed before, but this time he intended them to wait out the release of gas, if there were one, and see whether their precautions sufficed. And this time Morgan would be going down.

They donned their masks, A.J. checking Morgan's, running a finger around seals and checking straps. Raho entered first, followed by A.J. Morgan came third and Deforest Piett brought up the rear. Raho carried a single lantern, lit, and Morgan, two, unlit. The single lantern cast back compact and oddly unsinister shadows of the two slow, smoothly moving leaders.

Having not descended before, Morgan had no idea what to expect.

He had no sense of distance. He concentrated merely on finding places to step outside A.J.'s shadow so he could see to avoid the ridges which knotted the floor of the tunnel. So intent was he on this that he all but collided with A.J. as the team sergeant held up his hand and stopped, looking past Raho at an ellipse of dim, yellow light. He signalled to Raho and took the lantern from him, and the other crept noiselessly forward and eased himself around the edge of the ellipse, so that he showed merely as a roughness to its curve. Then the roughness melted away and Raho's silhouette showed briefly against the light as it flickered a hand. A.J. said, in a murmur, 'Quietly, Dr Morgan,' and Morgan, who had thought he was being quiet, became excruciatingly aware of every chink of glass and metal from his bag, every creak from his boots, every gurgle of air in his gut, and the breath sawing in and out through his helmet. He followed A.J., feeling like the 4 a.m. train through the slumbering suburbs. A.J. halted him yards shy of the lit exit, and nudged him down into a crouch so Piett could look over him. Through the aperture he could see a large chamber, yellow-lit, an expanse of floor densely woven with stone cords and ropes. Raho flowed from one side of the exit to the other, weapon at ready. A.J. moved in to the side he had vacated. They eased out of the exit, Raho first, then A.J. A moment later A.J.'s head reappeared to wave them through. Morgan shuffled the final yards, craning his neck to keep his eyes on the expanding view of the yellow lit chamber. But even that expanding view did not prepare him for what he saw when he stepped out. Quite forgetting himself, he simply stood until Piett put a hand on his back from behind, and then he took a further few steps forward, just remembering to feel out the floor with his feet. He slowly turned, following the long, long curving ramp upwards to the first crossbridge and then across to the huge spindle which reached almost to the floor, and down around its blunt curved suspended base, and up again to another crossbridge, simply absorbing with his eyes the shape, texture, colour and size of it. In a little while he would start reducing his experience to words, making descriptions, and then he would start having ideas, drawing analogies, formulating hypotheses. In a little while he would start to behave like the highly educated scientist he was. But for the moment he felt like a small child, all eyes, ears, nose and wordless awareness, for whom everything was new. He was hardly aware of the three men flanking him.

His foot catching on a ridge, he tripped and just managed to right himself against the weight of his backpack. Its contents rattled. The lantern sloshed. The three men around him were still and tense, weapons readied, waiting. Nothing happened, and more nothing. Raho gave him a look of faint disgust, slightly reminiscent of Hath. A.J. relieved him of the lanterns and lit all three. He and Raho and Piett conferred briefly in the barest of whispers, while their eyes looked everywhere but at the others' faces.

'You and I'll go up the ramp, see what we can see. Piett and Raho stay down here, cover us. We stay in sight of the ground at all times.' One lamp he set by the exit and one he gave to Morgan, and the third he would set at the base of the ramp. Not for light, for warning. And then he and Morgan started picking their way up the ramp. Morgan's thoughts came in shorthand, dense pellets of concepts reduced in a single word, or less. Cables, he thought. Nerves and plexuses. He strained for an analogy, rejecting any that came. Distrusting too deeply anything from Earth. Making assumptions too soon would limit him. He would not see what he needed to see. And thinking so deeply, did not see it – until A.J. snapped out a hand like a turnstile bar and halted him hard. He gestured with the tip of his weapon up and across a quarter turn, to where the topmost edge of distorted colour showed over the edge of the ramp. Morgan started to back towards the wall to better his angle, and A.J. stopped him, 'Stay in sight,' he said, very low, indicating Raho and Piett who were shifting to keep them in view from either side of the spindle's bulging base. He started ahead, indicating that Morgan should stay, but Morgan let him move a few steps and began to shadow him, step with step, stopping as A.J. glanced behind. He was scientific adviser to this team, and he *would* see. With every slow step he saw more of the colour, a smoothed flattened wall like the ones Hathaway had used, but much larger than any she had painted. He could not quite make out what the pattern was, distorted as it was by the angle: there was green in it, and gold and blue, and the expectation drove him upwards, after A.J. Lowell, following openly now. And then A.J. stopped, with an unambiguous hand signal. Did not turn. Morgan saw that in the centre of the colour had arisen a round dark blemish, moving obliquely across like a bubble, bringing with it shoulders, a torso – A.J. said, very quietly, 'Hello, Mr Cooper. We wondered where you had got to.'

Stephen Cooper walked up to the edge, the expression on his face distracted, unsettled, and a little petulant. He said, whispered really, 'What are you doing here?'

A.J. said, 'The same thing you are, I expect. Exploring.'

'Go away,' Stephen Cooper said. And he knelt, facing A.J., his hands seeking the ridges on the brownstone, gripping them as though he would fuse skin and bone with them. Morgan saw his fingertips blench with the pressure. 'Go away.'

Across the cavern, beside the exit, the first of the lanterns flickered and went out. Then the one at the base of the ramp. Stephen Cooper said again, hoarsely, 'Go. Away,' his brow drawn as though in hard concentration, or pain.

Below and behind him, Aquile Raho brought sight to eye, barrel to bear, and fired a single shot. Morgan would later recall the detached thought that Cooper must have indeed be gripping hard, so as not to have been thrown forward. He was not aware of being surprised, or appalled, then or later. Then Cooper rolled slowly sideways off the ledge, straight down to the hard surface below.

A.J. pointed, hard, to his own mask. Morgan fumbled, closing vents, switching on the gas, his eyes watering. He could all but feel the creep of the gas around his temples. He would have to breathe soon. The straps were tight, but tight enough? Had he seated it properly? Were the seals sound? In the claustrophobic confines he felt sweat and paranoia mingle. Adviser or not, he was not a member of the team. Would they have taken the same care with him they would with one of their own? A.J.'s movement towards him made him start violently and gasp. The oxygen released a burst of white speckles across his vision, and for a moment he waited to collapse. But A.J. passed him with the still-burning lantern, and he breathed again.

On the last quarter turn of the spiral, higher than head height, A.J.'s lantern began to flicker. Raho and Piett were still standing. A.J. paused, and the lantern dimmed to near extinction, and so he stayed where he was, mapping out the ascent of the gas. Waist, shoulder, neck, eye level – his eyepieces were twin blank orange discs – he turned again and let himself rise with the gas, step by step, carrying the lantern before him, passing Morgan again, leaving Morgan behind. Morgan's breath was a gale in his ears. His sinuses began to ache from the pressure on them. His eyebrows itched. He watched Lowell ascend, flickering lamp before him. Another quarter turn, and a few steps beyond, and then Lowell took a step and the lantern flame steadied somewhat. He paused, and the flame burned brighter. He dipped it, and brought it to waist height before it dimmed, waited a moment longer and lowered it to hip height. He turned and step by step, mapping the gas's retreat, descended. Morgan worked a quick back-of-the-eyelid calculation as to how fast gas might be cleared by adsorption on the walls of the chamber, versus ventilation. The apparent rate of dispersal required some form of ventilation, though he could feel none. He crouched where he was and peered at the coarse floor of the ramp, looking for any signs of vents or pores, and then unshouldered his pack and pulled out the microscope case, unpacking the 'scope before he realised that masked as he was he could not put the eyepiece to his eye. So as A.J. drew level to him he said, his voice muffled, 'I can't see a damn thing unless I take this mask off.'

'Wait,' said A.J. and continued down.

Near the base of the ramp was Stephen Cooper's body, laid out surprisingly tidily on its back with legs straight and only slightly spread, one arm thrown above his head and the other clutching the torn shirt beneath the exit wound, as though to hold it closed. The middle of his chest was a bloody ruin. His face was caught in its rictus of shock and pain at the bullet's tearing flight. Deforest Piett's fingertips on his carotid were quite redundant. A.J. walked over and looked down at the dead man, then at Raho. Whatever passed between them, through the polished lenses of their masks, was not to be shared; whatever reckoning there might be was to be deferred.

A.J. laid the brightly burning lantern on the floor and signalled to him that he could close off the air supply and open the vents on the mask. They watched him do so. The miner's canary indeed, he thought wryly. His fingers were trembling, a vibration like a high tension wire. He felt no revulsion, no outrage. He recognised the anaesthetic which had carried him through his teenage years. He had lost two friends to drive-by shootings by rival gangs. A third had been killed by police during an armed robbery. These things happened, and to get upset about them was only to invite contempt. Stephen Cooper had – somehow – used the ship against them. He had offered a threat and Raho had responded. Morgan would have to go up the ramp again and study the place Cooper's hands had gripped. That was the job he was here to do. They would despise him if he could not do it. There was that brilliant green – a picture wall. There was the gas – where had it come from, and how had it been so quickly drawn off. And its inertia and density . . . A.J. signalled across to him that he might now remove his mask, and so he did. Shivering a little, and hiding it, he set to work.

FOUR

FIRE

'You mean they're not going to do anything?' Hathaway demanded. 'They shot Stephen dead and nobody's going to do anything about it. You're just going to say, oh, fine, fine, no hard feelings, awful pity, terribly sad, but after all he was a criminal and a threat and an inconvenience and really it's for the best because he would just have upset our happy little family.' She looked furiously from Morgan's face to Victoria's, Sophie's, Marian's, 'Well, *fuck* your happy little family!' She swept through the door, looked back over the claystone wall as Morgan and Victoria both rose. 'Don't bother!' she threw at him. 'I don't want to *talk* to you. You cold blooded bastard!' She departed at a lumbering run.

In the silence, Marian lifted a shallow dish of steaming water from the improvised retort stand, and poured it into a mug, spilling only a little. She wiped it off and passed it over to Morgan. 'Get that into you. Only tea, I'm afraid.'

He looked down into the coffee stained depths of the mug, wondering how he could possibly refuse to drink it, when it was almost the last of Marian's hoarded stock. 'Dreadfully English, I know,' she was saying, 'but a small comfort in terrible times.' She nodded slightly as he looked up, confirming that she had indeed seen terrible times.

The smoky brown coiled out of the tea bag, sinking with its own cooling density. The dried leaf odour of it was intense, Earthly, alien. He said to it, 'I should have gone after Hath.'

'And what done or said? Let her work herself into a passion over something which was not your doing or your fault – something which you could not have prevented and cannot alter. Sergeant Raho acted according to his training and judgement in shooting to kill someone who was offering a threat whose measure they did not know, in a place where, remember, they had already lost four men. She's a tough youngster, and there's nowhere she'll be alone.'

He felt disorientated. Hath – Hath was his own kind. She should have understood. This was the way one survived. Not getting involved. Walking away.

But he had seen shock in Sophie's eyes as well, shock that he would accept this. He remembered his early years at university, all the little ways he became aware of being different from others, from his attitudes to money, to women, to violence, to safety. All the little ways in which he had learned to pass, to take on their attitudes and assumptions as protective coloration. And yet it seemed he knew nothing. The mug in his hand trembled; he set it down jarringly.

'Would you have shot him?' Morgan appealed to Marian. It was the surest measure of such things he knew. In science, he believed in abstractions, nowhere else. One's own actions were the touchstone of oneself.

She looked steadily back at him, small eyes the colour of the forget-me-nots painted on his American grandmother's wedding china. She said, quietly, 'I do not know how many men were killed by the explosives I prepared. I did what I was ordered to do, because I believed it necessary.' She fell silent a moment. 'Once, only, I acted outside orders. I found out that one of my group had betrayed or was intending to betray us to the Germans. She denied that she had done anything, though I had the evidence in my hand, the message she had left in a drop for them. She said they had made threats against her family and what did I know of that, when my family was safe across the channel. I realised that I could not leave her alive – if she had done nothing, I could not trust her, and if she had, well.' She looked down, at her ill-matched hands. 'I believe,' she said, 'if I am to be damned for this, I will find hell already a familiar place.' Raised her old, patrician face. 'And in answer to your question, yes. I do believe I would have done the same, as a soldier, in a dangerous and uncertain situation. But whether I shall countenance it now . . . as a civilian –' She shifted slightly, turning her attention to Victoria. 'I have been thinking on this,' she said, 'for quite some time. Most of you here are much younger than I am. You come of a generation raised to hold the military in contempt. Now you find yourselves in a new relationship with military men, a relationship I believe you do not understand.'

She paused, gathering her thoughts. 'Historically, in a democracy, the army is an instrument of the state, and ultimately comes under civilian control. That is sometimes not a happy situation, but it is the best solution possible. Weakness in a civilian government is no excuse for military intervention. But as a corollary your weakness cannot be used to excuse or to shift the blame. *They* are not the government, you are; they act and will act for you. Fail to understand that, and you will fail as governments have failed throughout history, allowing crimes and perhaps even atrocities.'

Victoria listened with a smile of rueful understanding, 'Ah, but whose government do they serve? Ours, or the government back on

Earth?' She looked, suddenly, at Morgan. 'Do you know, Dr Morgan? What are their orders and do they intend to carry them out?'

Marian said briskly, 'You understand as well as I what their orders are. Had they been otherwise, they would have had an identified civilian authority aboard this ship. They look to Earth, and in particular to the United States. They would not do otherwise.'

'Would they,' Victoria asked in a quiet voice, 'force the return of *Tevake* to Earth?'

'They're not alone,' Sophie said with force. Though pale still, her face was controlled and determined, and her upswept hair as exquisitely ordered as before. 'Don't put the onus on them. There are quite a number of ordinary civilians who would, given a chance, go back to Earth.'

'And as many who would not,' Victoria said.

Morgan set down his untouched tea, excused himself, and left the laboratory. Outside on the slope beneath the massif he squinted against the brightness, looking for a stocky figure in an acid green and black shirt. He should not have let her go alone. He supposed he was still in shock, the slow-dawning shock which comes when moral sense finally overtakes the most sophisticated of rationalisation. He remembered the first time he had seen a dead man, a black youth slain in a drive-by shooting, and how he had bragged to his friends about it until his mother had slapped his face. He had been – six? seven? He remembered that same sick, oppressed feeling of waking up to a whole weighty universe of meaning.

He started violently at A.J. Lowell's approach. The team sergeant affected not to notice. 'What do you make of this?' Lowell said, handing him a small sketchbook. He nearly dropped it as he realised whose it was. A quarter of the pages were filled with maps, sketches of the caves, with paced out dimensions carefully printed in an uneven hand. The printing gave the impression that Stephen had been unused to writing, an impression confirmed on the latter pages. The notes outlined Stephen's growing belief that he had begun to communicate directly with the ship. Morgan found his hands unsteady, and so he knelt on the matting beneath the massif, propping wrists on thighs, notebook on wrists. Stephen had written of a grey fuzz which he had likened to velcro which snagged head and hands, of conversations with a voice in his mind which sounded like the dead Adrienne LaFleurette. He seemed quite trusting in it, if frustrated by its reticence. You do not have the language, it told him, and promised to teach him.

Lowell said, 'How much of that is for real?'

Morgan did not look at the soldier. 'If the assemblers could figure out the exact set of circuits to excite, they could in theory convey whatever information they wished, in whatever form they wished, as long as . . . as they seem to have said to Stephen, we have the language. It may be the language that has been the problem. Sophie could tell you more.'

'And what about them?' He reached down and flipped the pages of the notebook to turn up Stephen's annotated sketch of the alien creatures, recognisable as Hathaway's owls, including lower bodies and feet. 'This, for instance. Was he planning some kind of con? Or did he draw these from life?'

He gave the notebook back to Lowell with what he hoped was a rueful smile, but which may have simply been cold and stiff. 'When I meet one,' he said, 'I'll let you know.'

Lowell nodded. Morgan waited a moment and then said, 'I'll get back to work,' with what he hoped was the right amount of anticipation, even impatience. As he turned away, Lowell said, 'Dr Morgan, have you spoken to your niece about this?' He lifted his head from the notebook as Morgan looked back, swiftly enough to observe Morgan's expression without giving the impression he had lain in wait. 'This', Lowell said, passing up the sketchbook, 'bears a more than passing resemblance to Cooper's painting on your niece's wall. Except that, on the wall, there are no aliens.'

'Or the wall illustration was never finished before Stephen was driven underground,' Morgan said, with a shrug. As a good boy in a bad neighbourhood, he had encountered police angling for a tip or a lead in a case; he knew how to stonewall. 'I saw no reason not to take her word for it that Stephen occupied the cave while she was absent. Hath has always been truthful with me.' Which in itself was true enough. 'But I'll speak to her. Find out if there was any overlap, if Stephen talked to her at all about –' He tipped his chin towards the sketch, feeling the sweat at his hairline as his hair shifted, and hoping that Lowell could not see the damp strands clinging. He said, 'Have you seen her, by any chance?'

'She went off to Erehwon, a little while ago.' A beat. 'One of the scouts is keeping an eye on her,' he said deliberately. 'She is close to you, after all. Dr Morgan,' he said by way of leave taking, and turned and walked off. 'Sergeant Lowell!' Morgan said, sharply, and before he thought better of it. The sergeant turned. Morgan said, 'We were wondering. *I* am wondering. When your loyalty to the US government will end? If there is no going back.'

The sergeant said simply, 'It is our duty to get home.'

43 Hathaway

Totally creepy, knowing you're being watched. I didn't know it was happening until Astarte (who's a cop and one of the women who left the women's group) pointed it out.

It's going to be lights down in about an hour or so. One of the women here (in Erehwon) has made this really neat candle-clock which burns up only so fast and lets everyone more or less tell time by it. She's this *intense* woman who used to be a physicist but got totally turned off it because it was all egos and politics and there was no *purity* in it – like it was religion and not science. She's completely into her candles and trying to make them perfect with the oil filling up the wells just so and the wicks cut out of this pair of denim jeans just so. I know what Marian would say about her burning the oil actually in the wells. Aside from the lanterns they haven't done anything at all to their cave because they believe the ship should be left alone – not even given a name. That's kind of sad when I think about everything that Hannah wanted to do in hers. She's not the same person – sort of like some of her stuffing is missing and her seams need stitching.

Hannah's going to keep this letter here and they've promised to put it with all the others if something happens to me. They weren't real happy about me writing it like I was leaving evidence or something or like I was in wa-wa-land thinking that these letters were ever going to reach you. I guess that they're wondering too if I really want to go on when I'm writing letters to my family back home. But so far as I'm concerned they can just suck it in and sit on it. If there's any way I can do it these letters are going back to Earth. (But those letters belong to me, and if anything happens to me they belong to my family – so if you're reading them and you aren't me or my family, that's OK, but if I'm dead you have a moral obligation to see that they get to Mom and the kids, right?)

I *really* hope this isn't the last letter in the pile because what I'm about to do is go on a spying mission. I know A.J.'ll let me down into the control room since I'm the one the ship painted for and everyone knows I taught Stephen wall painting. A.J.'ll be watching me close in case I do like Stephen did but I think I can get Uncle Stan to convince them all that I can maybe help. The people here in Erehwon have told me all about what I need to look for. They want maps of the downstairs and to know all equipment and weapons of the guys who're down there and who's on watch and when the watch changes over and how many other people are trusted to come down. Once they've got that they're going to come down and take over.

Maybe if I'd thought about this more I wouldn't of done it. But I was just so upset about Stephen that I didn't exactly think about anything except getting away – and my cave had been kind of taken over and turned into a sightseeing thing so there was nowhere else to go than to Hannah. I started out by crying all over Hannah and telling her about Stephen getting shot because Uncle Stan thought the dark room could be some kind of control room and about all the miracle cures Uncle Stan and Sophie thought were happening and how people were getting all worked up to take them back to Earth. I knew the women wouldn't want to go back to Earth on the Camp and the army's say so. Hannah got upset and angry and brought in all the other women, which was when Astarte said about my tail. It was because of him that the *others* got into the act because they wanted to know why I was being followed. They're the ones who scare me. There's Eilish and her sister Rosamond. I still can't figure out whether Rosamond is really wet and pathetic or just trying to make people feel sorry for her and I found it real difficult to be near her. She gives me the creeps. Eilish is scary in an argument because she never gives up and it's really no holds barred. She really knows how to use people's emotions and insecurities against them. She's got Hannah kind of hypnotised. I don't think it's sex though. More a kind of brainwashing because she's got this smart, twisty brain. Then there's this guy who looks like a monk and has the gentlest eyes you think you've ever seen until he looks at you. And then you see that they're only gentle because you're not there to him. I mean – nobody's mean to the air. And it's as though that's what everybody is to him. Just air. Some of the other people here were involved in liberation armies and even terrorism and one or two of them have been thrown out of other caverns. Once I'm gone they're ever so casually going to go out and start talking to people in other caves and find out what they feel about having the American army decide what happens to everyone. They're talking as though everyone in the Camp is following the army and as though people like Uncle Stan and Sophie and Marian didn't even exist and didn't even try to help during the Centauri 'flu. Which I guess is the way to do it to make sure people are mad. But now I'm writing this I'm thinking maybe I should of thought more about how I felt about turning Stephen over – like how I'd be responsible for anything that happened to him. I don't want anyone being killed.

I don't have time to write this any more. I don't think I want to. Now I got to get back to the dark place and have a look and think how I'm going to get Uncle Stan out before everything goes down or the balloon goes up or whatever that expression is. I did get what I wanted which was somebody to do what I couldn't and fix the people who killed Stephen and want to drag us all back to Earth without giving anyone else a say so – including the owls and the ship. So I guess maybe this is like some kind of deal with the devil and I'm just going to have to live with it on my conscience.

44 Morgan

The inscribed wall had now spread past and over the tunnel, though the cavern's occupants' zeal had diminished somewhat and from having a pen thrust at you immediately on entering, you were left to lift your own from the little ledge made for it. Morgan's eye was snagged by several thick black bars and he found one at eye level to inspect, thinking of the black in Hath's cave. But it was not ship's black, rather an ordinary black paint, almost obliterating a name. It took him too long to realise that the name must have been the name of one of the casualties of the outbreak – what he and Sophie had now termed 'adaptation sickness'. With a fingertip he inscribed single strokes at one of the small clear patches on the wall, lightly, then forcibly. But the wall remained unchanged, granular grey. No colours appeared at his touch? What was different about Hath's wall, and why? He rubbed briskly at it with a practised hand, and a groove deepened beneath his fingers. But the plastic properties were unchanged . . .

And then he caught sight of the figure sitting beside A.J. Lowell in front of the nearest entrance to the spire, and all speculations went out of his mind. He crossed the expanse between them at a flat out run, and came upon them as Hathaway was saying, '– I guessed I should come tell you before you came looking for me. I didn't want my uncle getting in trouble because I didn't tell him either.' She slanted a sideways glance at him out of dark, unreadable eyes.

Her coarse, glossy hair was neatly parted, showing pearly scalp in a line, and bunched in a pony tail tied with a white ribbon. Gone were the handmade beaded buckskins and plaid shirt. She wore her weathered maternity jeans, and a pastel blue smock he had never seen before, with a yellow duck appliqué and a round collar trimmed in white. She did not look up when Lowell passed the sketches up to him. They were not her originals. She had redrawn them. He had to restrain himself from dragging her away and demanding what the hell she was doing here. Everything about her appearance was wrong. Except for her tone, which in answering Lowell's questions was pure Hathaway. 'I told you, I saw them when I was sick. I drew them when I was sick . . . No, I didn't see their legs. I can't tell whether Stephen was jerking off when he drew them like that . . . No, I don't know for sure that he saw my sketches, but I guess he did . . . Why? Because I wasn't thinking about hiding things before he found me. I was thinking about dying. So he could have looked through them . . . No, we didn't talk about them . . . Yeah, I saw his drawing. I guess he did it after I left . . . Why did I leave? He creeped me out, putting that body in the back of my cave . . . Nah, I haven't communicated with the ship. How do I know? Well, I would know if I had been sticking to bits of it, or if dead people were talking to me . . . Nah, my paintings were all made by fingers, like I wrote . . . Sure I wrote,' she said, defensively, 'letters to my folks at home. Listen, I know it's dumb, maybe, but I'll send those letters if I possibly can. No, they're *personal* letters. About what happened to me. OK. I'll let Uncle Stan read them. Then he can tell you the bits you want to know . . . Why am I here? Because Uncle Stan's my only family. And maybe I made a mistake leaving Earth.' Now that, he thought, should have choked her, if it were the truth. 'Maybe I miss my folks and want to get back home. I'm going to have a baby, y'know,' she said, pointing out the obvious. 'Uncle Stan's my only family. So maybe I want to be with him. Help him. He's real knowledgeable.'

'Dr Morgan,' Lowell said, his blue-marble eyes mild. 'Your niece believes she can be a help to us.'

'May I talk to her a moment?' he said grimly.

Lowell released her to Morgan's recognisance. Hathaway trudged grimly away with him, her mouth set, in expectation of his inevitable outburst. Which he muted into the most temperate, 'Hath, what are you doing here?' he could muster.

'You *heard* me tell him,' she said. 'I came because I knew about the drawings in Stephen's notebook and I thought you would get into trouble if –'

'Hath, you could not have known about Stephen's notebook. At least, you should not have known about Stephen's notebook.'

'– if they thought you were keeping things from them, so I wanted them to know it was because of me not telling you and you not telling them, and I did my best, even putting on proper clothes and everything – but isn't this smock gross? It makes me look tri*ang*ular.' She turned into profile to demonstrate, hands coyly folded under belly and a poster-child simper on her face. Her eyes were still angry, savage, even.

'Hath,' he said, quietly, 'why did you come?'

'And when the baby kicks, the whole thing jumps up and down –'

'Hath.'

She looked up at him from beneath her lashes. Her lower lip quivered. 'I wanted to see if they'd actually killed him. I thought maybe they were just keeping him prisoner.' In the midst of her performance, she was overtaken by genuine emotion. Her face set into the stubbornness with which she met it. 'Why are you still working with these fuckheads?'

He said, 'I'm their adviser on alien habitats; I'm here to make sure they don't run into any avoidable risk, and maybe, just maybe, I can prevent what happened to Stephen from happening to anyone else, because people don't understand what exactly the ship does or could be made to do.' A lousy rationalisation, he would have said, listening to it. Speaking it, he almost believed it. She didn't. She started to turn away, folding her arms.

He said, 'There's something I want you to take a look at, something Stephen left. Think about it a moment, while I clear it with A.J.' Leaving her, he went back to Lowell, who was leaning against the mouth of the tunnel, watching them.

'I'd like her to take a look at the image,' he said. 'She was responsible for the discovery of the imaging properties of the upper side caves.' He paused. 'It'll give me a chance to find out what else she knows . . . that she hasn't told anyone about.' Mendacity tasted bitter in his mouth, but he did not know whom he was deceiving. Hath, or them.

'So, Prof,' Lowell said, and the tone made it a test, 'you believe in good fairies.' He flipped open Stephen Cooper's notebook and unfurled Hathaway's paper and let him compare the two, the roughly drawn complete sketch and the finer head and torso study.

'I believe there are aliens,' he said. 'But good –' And for the first time he engaged Lowell with a frank, challenging stare, 'That might depend entirely on whether *we* are good. Or not.'

He felt his pulse pick up, as it had picked up when he defied his brothers or his father, or any of the alpha males at school, waiting for the forgiving laugh, the affectionate clout, or the fist. Lowell merely gave him a smile that was no more than a tucking in of the corner of his mouth. 'Take her down,' he said. And then, with no smile whatsoever, 'But whatever she does, make sure we know it's going to happen first. Understand?'

She listened with eyes as unreadable as obsidian as he gave her the warning. As Lowell forbore to spell it out for him, he forbore to spell it out for her. Though he would have dearly liked to. Given the least intimation it would have had some effect he would have thrown himself down on his knees to beg her to caution, and to resist all vengeful, reckless or showy impulses. But 'Sure' was all she said, and there and then he promised himself that at the first sign of anything untoward he would personally hit her over the head with anything that came to hand, as hard as he had to.

That resolved he decided to reinforce the warning by walking her past Stephen's shroud. He had been enshrouded with almost unnerving rapidity – supporting evidence, Sophie had said, for internal infestation by the assemblers. He let her stop and stare for as long as she must at the silver grey shroud, now so dense that Stephen's features were just peaks and depressions in a fine-woven curve. The blood and tissue shaken loose by his crashing fall had, Morgan was relieved to see, also been sheathed. Quite likely she would not recognise the little nodules on the surrounding ridges for what they were. He told himself grimly that any trauma caused by the sight would be far less than the trauma caused by Aquile Raho's bullet – and it was he who turned away first, nauseated at the thought of Hathaway under that shroud, stubborn face, strong hands, heart and belly full of life all to be dismantled molecule by molecule to add to the ship's chemical pool. He heard her whisper, 'Bastards,' and then she deliberately stepped over him and started across to the base of the ramp. As he caught up with her she said, 'And you're one, too, Uncle Stan.' She jerked a finger up, making the gesture look as much as possible like obscenity without being one. 'Up there?'

Her face changed as she came in sight of the brilliant splash of green, Stephen's final and most improbable artwork. She trotted forward, scanned it, backed away so absorbed and heedless of trips underfoot and drop behind that he jumped forward to catch her. She looked down, back and at him in scorn – she had body lengths still to go to the edge – 'Wow,' she said. '*Stephen* did that?'

'Yes.'

She went up close and inspected it, a green shimmer on her skin. 'This is like a photograph. He didn't paint it at all.' She swung round. 'Didja find where he was lying when he was thinking this?'

'I think here,' he gestured. 'This is where his sleeping bag was.'

She followed his gesture and the light went out of her face. 'Shit,' she said. 'I'm just a ghoul. Like the rest of you.' Before he could stop her, she reached out and swiped her palm across the forest scene. 'Hath!' But instead of a wide arc of yellow, the forest remained unchanged, the hazy shadows, the gilded spires. Hath cast a twisted smile over her shoulder, and went to the edge, stepping high and with pointed care. She stood looking down. After a moment, carefully, Morgan joined her.

'He was up here when they shot him and he fell' – she gestured – 'down there,' she pointed out the shroud.

'Yes,' said Morgan, and swallowed. The shroud did not look man sized any more. More Hath sized. 'Hath, would you please come away from the edge.'

She gave him a long, slow look. 'OK.' And turned and walked back to the shining wall, stumbling once – accidentally, he thought, because she could not see what lay directly before her feet. But she gave him her best, 'Had you, didn't I?' look, and he let it be. She slid down the wall, and sat cross-legged, hands upturned on her knees, in meditation pose.

'That smock is just not you,' he ventured, joining her.

'It was something one of mother's so called friends gave me, you know, one of those *little messages* about what's *appropriate*. And you know I can't toss clothes; I was poor too long. So I was going to dye it Scarlet Letter red and take off the ducky-wucky. But I thought it would do to dress conservative like here.' Her eyes were flat and black, shadowed from the brilliance of the screen behind her. She had a silver-green halo, as light caught the weave of her hair.

She was so young, he thought, forgetting there were less than ten years between them. But even young, his loyalties had never been so fiercely personal and resolute.

He said, 'Yes, I wish they had found another way. But I think to maintain order, we need people capable of using force.'

'There's using force and there's killing,' she said in a low voice. 'And I don't want to be in a place where people kill to "maintain order".' She shrugged, closing down. 'But I guess you got to do it your way,' she turned her head into profile against the green. 'So what've you found out?'

He looked at the set profile with great unease. He had heard all too clearly the unspoken 'and I've got to do it mine'.

He said quietly, 'Hath, what are you really doing here?'

She didn't seem to hear. Or made a point of not hearing. 'C'n I use your microscope?' She reached for it, came up short, impeded by the solid bulge of her baby, and heaved herself up on to all fours. He leaned over and put his hand over it, making her look at him. He said even more quietly, 'Hath, if you have the idea that you're going to try and establish contact with the ship and then use it against us, please, give it up. Stephen surprised them. Nothing you do will.'

She pushed herself back on to her heels, and flounced her smock. 'And if they killed me, what'd you think then?'

'It'll be over my dead body that they do anything to you.'

She went very still, staring at him. Her lips parted as though to say something, but instead she leaned forward to peck his cheek. 'Thanks,' she said, 'Now gimmie the microscope.'

'Uncle Stan.'

'Mmm.'

'The light in this place ever go out?'

'I don't think so.' Stephen had written about his efforts at trying to turn it off, and in sheer desperation the night before Morgan had tried rubbing the claystone as though it were a magic lantern and thinking, *Off*, without avail. He had thrown his T-shirt over his eyes to mask the worst of it.

The sleeping bag next to him humped and rolled, dragging a brush of black hair. 'Oh, Jeez,' she mumbled, from its depth. 'I got to pee again. Every time I move I got to pee again ... Don't these guys ever go to sleep? I don't want them watching me as I go down.'

'No one will see you if you go up here.'

'Oh, gross. I mean, Arpád has some funny ideas, but living in Skunk Alley you sure appreciated not having the stink of pee everywhere.'

He groaned slightly, remembering the walk-up she called Skunk Alley. 'I'll come down with you,' he said.

She threw back the sleeping bag, showing a flushed face. 'No *way*. Like I'm two years old and potty training. I want to be incon*spic*uous. I just wanted to know if there's any time there won't be some of those guys watching.'

He propped himself up on his elbow, thinking, *teenagers*. But being young was mortifying, even without being young and very pregnant and embarrassed. 'Hath, they set watches, day in, day out, regardless of who else is around.'

'OK,' she said, 'then when're Loco Raho and Sarge Psycho *not* going to be on watch?'

'I thought,' he said, after a moment, deciding *not* to take up the matter of nicknames, 'you needed to go now.'

Her eyes flicked to his face and away. 'Now, and again and again and again,' she said, heaved herself over and said, 'Oh, Jeez,' and clambered out of the sleeping bag, pulling on plaid shirt over the dungarees she had not removed. She shuffled barefoot down the ramp.

He rolled over and caterpillared his way to the edge of the ramp, looking down to see her staring down at Stephen's shroud a moment before disappearing under the ramp into the latrine area. Across the corded floor, A.J. Lowell raised his head from stripping down his weaponry to follow her movements with impersonal interest. His eyes drifted up to meet Morgan's, and he raised a hand in a wave. Hathaway reappeared, scowled across at A.J. and tramped up the ramp. He humped back to where he had lain before she hove into view. Bundled in the sleeping bag, she squirmed and shed the plaid shirt, dropping it beside the sleeping bag with a flourish of a long pale arm. 'G'night Uncle Stan.'

Twice more that he knew of she tossed and moaned and clambered out of the sleeping bag to shuffle down the ramp. Once she complained of thirst and went down for water, which the detachment stored in a collection of bottles and small drums. He knelt to watch her filling her own flask under the eye of operations officer André Bhakta. The compact black man – more bushman than Zulu – made her laugh, and she spent longer at the water store than she might have done. Like the others, Bhakta was unmarried, though he had a two year old son by a previous, difficult relationship. Morgan had come to wonder whether that was a deliberate strategy, to send men who were single, but not unattached – if, Morgan reflected, a little sourly, any red blooded male over twenty could be said to be unattached. These days it was the women who were unattached, judging men more liability than asset, if they needed them at all. Like his niece, dismissively forgiving of the boy who'd fathered her baby.

'Hey, Uncle Stan,' she said, returning, and offered him a tumbler of water, which he declined. 'D'y'know there are six ways in and out of here? D'you know where they all go?'

'*No,*' he said, feeling beleaguered. 'Good night Hathaway.'

She sighed.

'I know where some of them go,' he said, after a moment. 'I'll tell you in the morning.'

'What's morning,' she grumbled.

'Good night, Hath.'

But she woke him again, whimpering and grinding her teeth in her sleep. He lifted his head to see her tossing, her face flushed, and the sleeping bag flap thrown back, showing the solid white cone of her maternity bra and her cleavage slick with sweat. From below came Lowell's voice, 'Dr Morgan.' He shuffled off his sleeping bag and bellied down over the edge. 'It's OK. Nightmare,' he said. 'Thanks.' Bhakta and Hughes were already deployed on the lower slope of the ramp; on the far side of the cavern Piett and Raho had rolled from their sleeping bags with arms at the ready. Lowell watched him a moment longer, then waved them down.

'Uncle Stan,' said Hath's voice behind him. 'What's going on?' She pushed tangled hair out of her face. 'Jeez,' she said, 'I was having horror movie dreams.'

'We gathered that.'

'Oh fuck, was I yelling?'

'No,' he said, and paused to consider the implications, that quiet as she had been, A.J. had still been aware of her. Sound must carry better than he thought.

'Oh,' she curled up on her side. 'Somebody turn the lights off. My eyeballs feel like they've been sautéed.'

'What's a child of TV dinners know from sautéed?'

'It means toss around in a frying pan in a bit of marg,' she said, haughtily, 'for all you deprived bachel –' She caught her breath with a gulp. But whatever had startled her brought silence, not exclamation.

He rolled over and sat up in one movement. He found her propped on her elbow, holding the sleeping bag to her chest, eyes wide as she stared at the wall. Orange sparks glinted in her eyes; the sheen on her face had an orange lustre. He followed her line of sight. The entire wall was a sheet of flame. A forest fire, frozen in one single instant, so intensely coloured and realised that Morgan all but felt the heat on his face. A tree, no more than a charred line, frozen in mid fall. Flames, rootless, caught between leap and extinction. Sparks, here now, here for ever.

'Have you ever been in a forest fire, Hath?' Morgan heard himself say.

'What? I've seen them on TV,' her voice faded. 'It's like . . . on top of us.'

Morgan said, 'I'll be back in a moment, Hath.'

Hath twisted to follow them. 'It's not any of them!'

'In all likelihood one or more of them have fought forest fires.'

'It's Stephen!' Hath said, with utter confidence. She scrambled out of her sleeping bag, throwing on plaid shirt, buttoning it askew, hop-shuffle-tugging on shoes as she started down the ramp. He pulled on his shirt and ran after her, barefoot, jeanless, feeling panicked and absurd in equal measure. He hit floor as she reached the shroud, but had already seen that it was unchanged, the fine grey cocoon uncut, untorn, undisturbed. He had no idea what he had thought, only that here anything was possible, and he did not want Hath in the middle of it. A.J. Lowell and Bhakta arrived on the trot, weapons balanced in hands, Lowell's mouth drawn in a thin line. Before he could say anything, Morgan said, 'Go take a look at the picture.' A.J. gestured Piett and Hughes to cover, and he and the dark man went up the ramp.

Hath said in a small voice, 'I thought –' She too thought of possibilities, of miracles. Morgan put a hand on her tense shoulder. 'In all likelihood it's an image the ship picked up from Stephen at the same time as it did the first one.'

She turned against him, taking a handful of denim in each hand, and pulling her face against her jacket. He had a sudden mental snapshot of Hathaway, aged three, taking a two fisted grip of absolute possession on her teddy bear and pulling it against her, burying her face in the ragged fur. He let himself be possessed. 'I miss them,' she gasped, into his chest. 'I miss them all so bad.'

He put his arms around her, silently wondering why now. She answered the silence, 'Mom. Peta. Dave.' And then he thought he understood why now, why here. He said, quietly, 'You said Stephen reminded you of Dave.'

She nodded against his chest. 'Don't tell me that's dumb,' she said, fiercely.

'I won't.'

She pushed him back from her, her face smeared with tears and set stubbornly.

'Hath,' he said, 'we'll get back.'

She turned her head away. 'It was all ruined anyway,' she said. 'It wasn't the way it used to be.'

'Hath,' he said, 'the way it used to be was hard.'

She hiccoughed. 'And now they've ruined this, too. I hate them, Uncle Stan. I hate them all.'

He thought: I'm no use at this. Slid a hand around her back and exerted a gentle pressure trying to turn her away. She resisted. 'Hath,' he said, 'I think it would be a good idea if you went upside, back to Kastély. I just . . . don't feel right having you down here when we don't know what's going to happen.'

She gave him a wide-eyed look, her lashes wet and drawn to points. 'OK.' Sniffed. 'I guess I found what I came for, didn't I?'

45 Sophie

Morgan looked unmistakably drawn when he arrived in the company of his niece, in maternity smock and scowl, Hathaway saying, 'I'm *going* to see Hannah, OK.'

He said, wearily, 'It's not really OK, Hath. But can I stop you?'

She frowned, with equal irritation and concern. 'Jeez, passive-aggressive is not *you*, Uncle Stan.'

'I thought I was merely giving you an honest answer.'

She folded her arms. 'It's light. The way there's safe. People know me. And I haven't done anything wrong like I should be confined to camp.' He shook his head, slightly. 'Besides,' she added, 'you want to talk to Sophie alone.' She smirked at him a little.

Morgan opened his mouth, but, honest man that he was, could not muster a lie.

'In which case,' Marian said, rising from where she sat, cane in hand, 'I will accompany you. I, too, would quite like to see Hannah.' She gave Morgan a witchy smile, and turned a glinting eye on Hathaway – whose expression, Sophie noted, mirrored her uncle's guilty embarrassment. 'Oh, Jeez, Miss West,' Hathaway began, and stopped, biting her lip. 'Sure,' she said, valiantly. 'Sure.'

Morgan sat down and buried his face in his hands. 'I can't handle her,' he moaned. Sophie smiled at his bowed head, and went back to her work. She listened to Hathaway's and Marian's voices slowly moving away.

Morgan took an audible breath like someone about to dive into cold water, and straightened up. 'A.J. wanted me to talk to you about something and I didn't want Hathaway to overhear. He'd like you to come downstairs and open up Stephen Cooper's shroud. He'd like to know if there's any possibility of anything still living – under there.'

'What's got him thinking that?' she said, disguising her excitement. She had wanted to exhume one or more of the shrouded bodies since the first death, but everyone in their burial yard had had survivors, and none of them had wanted so public a revisitation of their grief.

He described for her the forest scape, as realistic as a photograph, that had changed in the night. He told her about Stephen's notes, the dreams which he had grown to believe were not dreams, the feel of face against ground, sticking. She frowned. 'You haven't experienced anything like that?' He shook his head. 'Has Hathaway?'

'She said not.'

'Mm,' Sophie said, envisioning instead the fine black and sepia, black red and blue diagrams of her textbooks, the neural structures and pathways connecting them. Models and theory and order; the best of human knowledge. How very strange, she reflected, that there had until so recently been no qualification. Merely the best of all knowledge. She wondered what the aliens knew, and how they had learned it, whether, as Morgan conjectured, they already might possess full awareness of the structure and function of the human body and brain, from the ship's particulates.

Morgan said, 'Do you think she's telling the truth?' She looked at him blankly, backtracking thought processes. But before she had completed the backtrack he shifted and said, 'I really don't want her to be the one. And I certainly don't want to be the only one.' He shifted his shoulders. 'I feel like a cat with one kitten, Sophie, I really do.'

'She's hardly a kitten,' Sophie said, drily. 'And of course she won't be the only one.'

'Sophie,' he said. 'You don't know that.'

She drew breath, and stopped, recognising she had indeed spoken as much out of presumption of right as a wish to reassure. She could not imagine the ship wishing to talk to the ill-educated Hathaway and not to herself. Morgan smiled, slightly, forgiving her.

'It would greatly help,' she said, somewhat sulkily, 'if she would share her understanding with us.'

He shook himself. 'Sophie, is it possible? That the ship could establish a direct mind to mind link? That Stephen Cooper, or something of Stephen Cooper, could still exist? Somehow. Sophie, he could not have survived.' He put fist to sternum, marking place and size. 'It wasn't small calibre. He was dead. But it's not impossible, is it, given the seeming restructuring that seems to be going on in the living? What would it take to keep someone's brain alive, maintain it until – until all the necessary information had been transferred?' Beset, he took refuge in the scientist's ubiquitous passive. 'And how might that information be stored? Have all our dead been – deconstructed and stored?'

She murmured, 'I would not speculate upon that too loudly,' and turned to collect her instruments.

But kneeling beside the grey shroud which enclosed Stephen Cooper, she found herself uneasy. She had a pathologist's rational understanding and deep familiarity with death. She knew its boundaries and its properties. Even as a teenage girl she had been impatient with empty-grave, dead-walking horror – positively tiresome on the subject to her friends. She did not care for such irrationality, even mooted as entertainment, escape, fantasy.

She could feel herself being watched. Not merely watched, guarded, two men seated at the two corners of the shroud, head and foot, stood back on her insistence, but nevertheless with arms at the ready. The other spectators were in a loose arc behind her, at Lowell's insistence – he wanted his men to have a clear shot. She felt absurd, and more than a little resentful. Damn them anyway – this was a simple exhumation.

But if it were simple, would her hands be so cold? A rotation at the medical examiner's office had almost inured her to decomposition, maceration or dismemberment. And if something took her by surprise, what of it? Her dignity could withstand a public attack of nausea. And she hardly imagined she would peel back the shroud and Stephen Cooper would open his eyes and sit up.

But wouldn't that make a lively scene.

She allowed herself a moment to think on it as she pulled on her gloves, her plastic apron, and fitted the improvised face shield over her pinned back hair. She laid out her instruments, the set which would take her through the shroud, the set which she would use in her dissection of the body; the glass vials filled with saline and preservative; the small plastic bottles of silver stain and ink; the plastic specimen bags. Most had already been once used, washed in water and alcohol, dried. She said, looking over her shoulder, 'Morgan, would you mind,' and offered up her clipboard and notes. 'You don't have to look,' she added. 'Sit back a bit; I don't have protective equipment for you.'

He gave her an odd look, plainly wondering what she was envisioning. She was not sure herself – habit had made her say that, habitual awareness of the commonplace dangers. She held his eyes and he gave in, shuffling back behind her.

She said, 'Do you remember how he was lying?'

Morgan swallowed. 'I think his head was at your right.'

She nodded, and looked down at the shroud, focusing her attention, slipping into working mode. She spread a measuring tape and measured the dimensions of the shroud, length, width, depth and semicircumference. Inserted a thermometer into the shroud. Temperature was ambient. She dictated the results, hearing the tiny scratchings of Morgan's pencil like a fly rasping against a wall. She bent close to examine the shroud. First by eye, seeing no difference but the colour, then by microscope, resolving the fine interlaced fibres, similar to those on the shrouds and dirt-balls in the green-lined caverns.

Face or chest or abdomen, she thought, but her training told, and she made her first opening where she judged the sternum to be, using scissors and fingers rather than scalpel. Against the latex gloves the shroud felt like glass wool. Her fingertips itched, more with anticipation of injury than discomfort. They always did when she worked under infection precautions. She debated stripping a wide area initially versus working through a narrow incision, and went in the end for the stripping: the light was not so good that she could work in self-inflicted shadows.

The shroud came away in layers. There were definite cleavage planes where the interlacing was less dense. She followed the layers and the lie, using blade, scissors and fingers to separate them and peel them back. There was no smell of decay, only the musty cumin-like odour of the shroud. She asked Morgan to note that; he did.

The inner shroud was moulded more finely to Cooper's form. Through the gauze she could see the shape and blanched colour of his wrist, and the ragged end of a red plaid shirt. She paused, settling back on her heels, and slowly dictated to Morgan what she had so far done. She sensed a shifting impatience behind her. Tough. There were no reprises in autopsy, and this was uncharted territory indeed.

She worked her fingers through the innermost layer, and around Cooper's wrist. It did not shift with her touch, as it should with rigor passed – bound down, she surmised, and, pushing further through the stiff gauzy strands, she took a firm grip and moved the wrist from side to side, tested the binding gently. It moved only a little. She eased her fingers over the radial artery, checked her watch, and waited, ten seconds, thirty, sixty, ninety. At two minutes she said to Morgan, 'Note no radial pulse.'

He gave her a profoundly dubious look but wrote it down.

Delicately, she shaved grey fuzz from the skin of the exposed wrist, noting the pallor of the skin. She would have expected more discoloration after three days. Still no odour of decay. Thoughtfully, she opened a packet of swab, took up sterile tweezers, swab – one of their last – and swabbed the skin. Morgan opened a sample back; she directed him to a sterile one. 'What is it?' he said.

'I'm not sure,' she said.

She was even less so when she tested the exposed skin with her fingertips, and found it stiff to touch. Blanched already it did not

221

change colour further, but the impressions of her touch slowly filled in. 'No sign of capillary filling,' she said, 'skin pits to pressure but pitting is transient.'

She remembered one slow night with two techs and an intern discussing the perfect crime and how one might sterilise a body so as to invalidate all markers of decay. Liquid nitrogen, autoclaves, premeditated doses of antibiotics and gamma radiation had all figured. She felt the corner of her mouth tuck in slightly. No matter how sleep deprived and coffee-crazed they were, alien nanotechnology had never entered the discussion.

She said, 'Decomposition's not advanced as far as it should at this temperature. His skin should be discoloured; but it's not. He should be soft; he's not. It may be the binding down, but –' As she spoke she was dissecting around Stephen's index finger.

Morgan observed, 'This is the moment, you realise, for a wizened arm to shoot up and grab you by the throat.'

She bit back a sharp reproof. She had never had much patience with juvenile humour in the autopsy room. He took the reproach from her face and murmured, 'Sorry.'

She freed the finger, picking away the grey web between it and finger and thumb with the tip of her scalpel. The grey fuzz seemed thickest over a dark old bloodstain on the fingertip. She laid down the scalpel, braced the finger with her left hand and tried to bend the fingertip with her right. It did not bend.

The hands, she thought, might be an anomaly. But still there was sweat beneath the headband of the face shield and inside her gloves. She folded her gloved hand around the cocoon encasing his and tried to curl his fingers. They resisted.

'He's still stiff,' she said to Morgan, 'at least in his hands. It could be rigor, or it could be infiltration. I can't tell without dissecting tissue samples. If it's rigor, it argues for enzyme degradation and tissue damage proceeding after death, but it argues against decomposition . . . I think – I think before I do that I'm going to have a look at the chest wound.'

There was a whispered conversation going on behind her.

'Dr Hemmingway –'

'Later, please,' she said, the words out even before she had thought of them. Morgan slanted a glance towards her, with a half smile. She said, loudly enough to be heard behind, 'I can't afford to miss anything.'

She took up her scissors and began shearing away the layers of shroud over the chest. It took a little while for her to realise what it was that seemed strange; it was that there was no staining. She was still thinking in terms of bodies that oozed and fabric that stained. She shook her head slightly. She could not afford prejudice and blinding assumptions. With scissors and scalpel and fingers she worked the shroud away from Stephen's intact chest on the near side of the wound.

Stephen's bare chest, she realised. 'Morgan,' she said, 'did someone open his shirt?'

'No,' Morgan said, with averted eyes.

With her fingers she probed centrewards between shroud and chest wall, following the curve of the rib towards the sternum, and across the sternum's narrow plane. The shroud was denser here, hard to force her hands through. But at what might have become the very limit of her reach she felt a dip in the chest wall where none should be, a falling away of the stiff skin. She took up her instruments and began to cut along the line her fingers had probed, snipping at the thick, knotted growth. As her cuts became cleaner she could see that, beneath the whorls and knots, the grey fibres were both thicker and as well aligned as though they had been combed, sweeping down and away from her. When she reached the lip of the wound, her suspicions were confirmed. The fibres bunched through the opening in the chest. She continued to cut and trim, until she had exposed a narrow ledge of bloodless skin. Bloodless, again, but not decomposed. And peculiarly smooth-edged, like a waxwork that had been melted. She could see no old blood, no splinters of bone. She explored deeper with her fingertip, meeting resistance and pressing through, until she came upon a firmer structure, yielding but nevertheless with a shape. She leaned forward to see, but saw nothing distinctive, except maybe a denser area of grey fibres. All she could smell was mustiness. Slight spice. She let her fingers guide her, following the buried firmness to the edge of the wound, where it met a rib. With very small, almost timid strokes she cut her way up to where the bullet had sheared and distorted the rib above, and felt into the shroud, feeling the same firmness.

She sat back on her heels, scalpel held before her. She heard Morgan say, 'Sophie,' and told him, 'A minute. Just a minute. Let me think.'

She had noticed a slight resistance as she cut at skin level but had not thought anything of it, working in unfamiliar textures. Were those structures meant to be skin, ribs ... replacements ... or merely a framework on which new structures should be grown? Was there, beneath the ghostly ribs, a coarse grey ghost of a heart? There were so many possibilities to explore. Yet she hesitated even to voice them.

Proceeding with such explorations required certainty of death, certainty that Stephen Cooper had no interests to safeguard, nothing left to lose. And she was lost without map or signposts in a country she had once known so well.

Was Stephen Cooper dead? No respiration, no heartbeat, no reflexes. She might wish for an EEG, an ECG, even an electromyelogram to examine the state of these rigored muscles, but if wishes were horses beggars would ride. And that was not the question, anyway. The question was not that was he dead, for he was, or had been. The question was would he remain dead. And of that she was no longer as sure as she'd been.

It was not merely the blanched skin, the rigor, the apparent sterility – which she hoped to Christ she had not compromised by her examination – it was the bloom of grey fibres from a wound that, were it not on a dead man, she might say was showing signs of healing. Something that did not look like either a premortem wound on a decaying corpse, or a healing wound on a living person – assuming that any wound on the living might be left gaping so. It was most of all the shadowy resistance at the level of the skin, the sketched in projections of the ribs.

But, she thought, staring at the blanched, stiff hand, it is one thing to rebuild structure, another to restore function. One thing to follow the architecture of the heart, another to start it beating, to reliquify or resynthetise the blood, to orchestrate the conjunction of oxygen, ions, ATP, actin, myosin . . . to have all these elements together, ready and primed for a single animating impulse. And what of the brain, beginning to die within four minutes of circulatory collapse? How swiftly might these fibres penetrate, to preserve? And if they failed to preserve and must reconstruct, how would they know, from dismantling cadavers, the structure of a living brain?

But they have living models, she thought. Ourselves. Stephen himself, when alive. She shuddered slightly, a wisp of damp hair brushing chill on her neck.

And what of her examination? Had she, merely by opening the shroud, seeded rot? If she were to continue to cut away the grey fibres, down to the ruptured heart, would she be cutting vital – what – connections? conduits? frameworks? Would she be perturbing the intricate molecular dance? She was beyond her competence as a doctor, into the uncharted terrain which the scientist inhabited. But she had the same ethical constraints, constraints which would not have allowed her to proceed with risk to any living, non-consenting human being. That Stephen Cooper was not presently living, she had little doubt. But whether he was beyond further harm, as Earthly definitions presumed, she did not know.

She made her decision quite suddenly, almost as though the questions themselves contained the answer. With gloved hands she relaid the dissected shroud layer by layer over the punctured chest. When she turned to the first incision she had made she could see that the shroud was already reforming between the pallid fingers, and resprouting in the patch she had shaved. She laid those cuttings back in place, too, and sat back on her heels. 'I don't know what's happening here.' She turned, climbing to her feet as she did so, and walked back to the men and women who had been watching her.

She said, 'He's not alive, I am as certain of that as I can be without any kind of bioelectrical monitoring. But whether he will never again be alive I cannot be so certain.' She paused, to let them take her meaning, obliquely phrased as it was. 'He's not decomposing – there are universal markers of the decomposition process that are based on bacterial consumption of tissues, and those are completely lacking. His muscles are still rigid, as in rigor, and his skin is blanched and somewhat resilient in texture. There does not seem to have been any bloating of his abdomen. He is extensively cocooned and infiltrated, and his clothing appears to have been absorbed, but his skin and those structures I exposed – hand and a portion of his chest – appear to be entirely intact. I have, however, not had opportunity to open a shroud prior to this, so I do not know whether that is normal or abnormal at this stage in the process. All I have to proceed on is that the shrouds lost volume with time over five or six days. Note that all previous shrouds have formed on bodies lying on matting, not on claystone, so there may be different characteristics, although upon examination by low power microscope at least they appeared superficially the same in structure.' They begrudged the digression, so she said what they were waiting for. 'I checked the wound. The edges showed signs of reabsorption, but the reabsorption was limited to fragmented bone and tissue. The fibrous outgrowth from the ship's floor is densest leading into the wound, and it appears to be structured to a degree to follow the anatomical structure of the bone and tissue removed by the bullet. There seems to be no recognisable reconstruction of tissues, not as yet. There are many unanswered questions. But I do not believe I can in good conscience go on. I have no means of knowing whether or not I would be interfering with the process of . . . reconstruction.'

There was a silence. 'You're saying the ship's rebuilding him somehow?' The speaker was the middle aged man who had argued law with Amanda Sumner – himself a lawyer, Laurence Chandler.

'I am not ruling out the possibility.'

'You can't just stop now.' He flicked a hand towards the shroud. 'Keep cutting.'

'I *have* to stop now,' she said, keeping the dislike out of her voice. It had, after all, more to do with that presumptuous handflick than anything he said. 'I have no idea whether cutting into the shroud, even taking tissue samples, would be doing harm. For one, he appears to be in a completely aseptic state. Have I already introduced bacteria which will start tissue degradation –?'

'Or are we also free of bacteria?' remarked Morgan at her shoulder.

'For pity's sake,' Chandler turned to Arpád, 'the man's dead. She said so herself.'

Sophie said calmly, 'Dead at present, yes. But I'd like to see what the ship makes of him. Since we do not understand what is happening or how sensitive it may be to being disturbed, I advocate – in fact, from an ethical standpoint I insist – we let it be.'

'And I think increasing our understanding is more important than any individual life.'

There was the obvious rejoinder: even yours? In all likelihood the discussion would have degenerated from there. 'What lies in that shroud is not life, but may have the potential to regain life –'

'How can you know that?'

'How can any of us know it is not so? If Cooper is dead he should be left to rest in peace. If he is being reconstructed, then he should be accorded all the rights of a foetus in utero, that being our closest parallel, except that unlike a foetus Stephen has no mother whose rights might conflict with his –'

'You are not a lawyer, Doctor –' Chandler pointed out.

'I am not discussing law,' Sophie said, narrowly, 'as much as medical ethics, and perhaps you will claim I am not a medical ethicist, either – but I am a medical researcher, and as such I am well acquainted with the principles guiding experimentation on human subjects. I do have a platform to argue from, and tools to argue with.'

'And what about the rights of a society that might not want a dangerous criminal introduced?'

'Does anyone happen to recall whether one's criminal record is cleared upon death? I believe it is. But that is another issue on which our Earthbound laws are going to need revision.'

'If you think –'

226

'Wait,' Arpád said, stepping forward, 'please.' To Sophie, 'Are we to understand then that you believe that Cooper's death may not be permanent?'

Chandler said, 'We've seen no sign that the ship is capable of making anything more complicated than simple organics, never mind DNA and proteins. And the notion that we've been healed of all our ills is just that, a notion.'

Sophie said, 'I realise that we have had no opportunity to present our findings in a formal forum, but you are very welcome to come and examine our data.'

'You can keep your data,' Chandler said. 'I want an explanation.'

This man, Sophie thought, with a sudden, unwelcome insight, is frightened. With insight came compassion; and with her wrist she pushed at the damp roots of her pulled back hair along the edge of her forehead, letting him see that she, too, was sweating.

'That's simple enough,' Morgan was saying. 'The ship's done *to* us anything it is capable of doing. But it's done *for* us only what we've been capable of asking it to do. Just because you sit on the floor and play blocks with your three year old doesn't mean you're not able to do double entry bookkeeping. But double entry bookkeeping's no use for a three year old. It can't learn anything from seeing a complex task done. But it can learn from putting blocks one on top of another.'

'And we're at the stage of stacking blocks,' Chandler said, but with less hostility.

'Yes. I believe the ship – and whoever's in control of it – is trying to teach us about itself by responding to the stimuli we give it.'

'In other words,' Dominic said, very drily, 'an interstellar Montessori.'

Morgan grinned, showing crooked, gold filled teeth. 'Never went there.'

'Well, why's it bothering to put him back together and none of the others? Surely some of them have made a much greater contribution to this society and the ship than he has,' that with an angrily protective glance towards Victoria, who endured the attention drawn towards her.

Morgan said, 'There are hints in the notebook he left that he might have made a direct mind to ship contact, which produced the image up on the second level. It may be trying to rebuild him because it needs him to be a mediator.'

A.J. Lowell said, almost gently, 'Dr Morgan is judiciously omitting the fact that the best demonstration of Stephen Cooper's "mediation" was his use of the control room's defences against us. What may be happening may be a miracle, but it may be a dangerous miracle, nevertheless.'

Arpád said more brusquely, 'This is not to be discussed, even between ourselves when we leave here. If something comes of it, then there will be time enough to decide what to do. If not – we would create needless unease. Doctor, you will advise us all as soon as you know more?' She nodded. The non medics and non scientists left with Arpád; the medics and Morgan closed round her and the shroud, asking questions, probing the shroud, trying to see into the swift-closing rents in the shroud. Sophie answered them as she gathered up instruments and specimens, and took her notes from Morgan. He looked shaken, as shaken as she felt.

She found Victoria Monserrat beside her.

'My husband,' she said, quietly. Paused, as though reflecting on the words. 'He was not . . . similarly preserved.'

'I cannot say,' said Sophie. 'Not until I have seen what happens with time here.'

Victoria shook her head. 'After three days, Ellis's mound was quite noticeably shallower.' She had a small head, quite finely shaped, seen now that she had had her hair cut quite short. It lay around her head in short, two-toned ripples, as the dyed length grew out. She had divested herself of dye, styles, suits and the careful postures of professional womanhood. 'I haven't anyone left to let down,' she had said to someone who remarked on it, 'or anyone left to impress.'

'One wonders,' she said now, 'that a petty criminal should be so – honoured?' the slight lilt to her tone made that a question. 'While far better men – and women for that matter – have been disassembled,' she glanced at Morgan, with a little grim humour. 'But perhaps I should wait and see what *Tevake* intends for him, before I bear any grudges on my husband's behalf.' She sighed. 'He would have enjoyed this so much. He would have been at your elbow every moment, or he would have had you at his. He had quite a dominating personality, when his intellectual passions were engaged.' She looked down, seeing, Sophie was sure, that earlier shroud. 'I, on the other hand, am afraid of chaos.' She sighed, smiled. 'Which is why I make law. I must admit it is with more than a little trepidation that I consider the possibility of having to rule on whether a person's crimes should outlast death, if death looks less than permanent. Still, that will be another day's trials, as my father used to say.'

In the laboratory, as the questions and speculations went on around her, she rummaged in their accumulation of chemicals, pills and foodstuffs not yet used for priming synthesis. What she would like was a substrate for bacterial growth that had not been made by the ship – that ideally had not been in contact with the ship, that on Earth would grow bacteria swabbed from skin or body orifices. 'Has anyone got any microbial knowledge?' she asked, from her knees, raising her voice to cut through the chatter. 'I took some sterile swabs. I want to know if they're growing anything.'

'Of course they should be growing –'

She shook her head. 'No bugs, no decay . . .'

Emilie Linn came forward – she had majored in microbiology, many years ago now, she said, with a smile. Not that Sophie had anything sophisticated in mind in the first instance. She merely wanted to know if there were any bacteria on Stephen Cooper, and if so what kind. Was he preserved simply because he was not decomposing? She left Emilie picking out packets of sugar and vitamin pills and murmuring to herself over the conundrum posed her, and re-entered the fray, 'Has anyone seen Stan Morgan?'

Somebody had: on the way back he had been waylaid, offered a note, and had headed off down one of the other corridors. Sophie sighed. Morgan would have fallen on her idea like a pup on a brand new slipper and worried it up down and across in every direction. He had a gift for asking productive questions, a gift she could have done with to clarify her thinking. Everyone else was far more interested in arguing her decision not to explore Cooper's shroud further. Arpád's injunction towards silence, agreed with in principle, was being completely disregarded.

Arpád himself appeared a moment later and they all fell silent, residents, postdocs, department heads, and hospital chiefs, like guilty children. He contented himself with a glower, but his heart was not in it; he had the curious tranquillity about him which marked Arpád in crisis. 'Dr Morgan?' he said, flicked dark eyes across them to obtain his own answer, 'The girl? Miss West? . . . Not here,' he said briefly over his shoulder, and Sophie saw Sergeant Lowell, his face as still as Arpád's. Arpád turned to go – and she shouldered her way forcefully through her colleagues to catch him in the corridor. 'What's happened?'

Arpád glanced at A.J. Lowell, who said, 'Best bring her. They'll all have to know soon.' The set of his mouth passed brief, silent comment on what he thought of the medical profession's discretion.

They went through the knotted passageways of the Citadel rather than out and round on the apron, presumably to avoid attracting attention – although having scouts posted on all the internal approaches and diverting anyone passing within earshot on the apron was hardly calculated to avert curiosity. And the conversation which greeted them was anything but classifiable.

'So what's that poem where the guy comes to on the side of a hill, and is thinking about this mysterious girl?'

'Keats,' supplied A.J. ' *"La Belle Dame Sans Merci."* '

All the special forces team was there, squatting or seated on the ground or the main slab, and there was an energy in the air about them she had not seen before.

'Sounds like a girl I knew in Boston,' Greg Drover said.

'Sounds like all the girls in Boston. Merciless, the lot of them.'

'Whatja do, sleep through French? Means thanks.'

'They weren't thankful, either.'

Short lived derision greeted that remark. Kent Hughes and Edward Illes rose as one to offer her their seats, moulded claystone outcroppings. She took the nearer one, and Ed Illes sat down beside Drover on the matting. Arpád settled back into his chair and steepled his fingers, placid as though shaped from claystone himself.

She noticed then that among the special forces team were two new faces. Cumulatively, she thought, they had such presence and energy – particularly in the mood that they were in – that it was difficult to simply *count* them. But those were new – a dark-haired man with a fine, Semitic profile and a lanky man with a stubble of white-blond hair. Above one ear he had an indistinct tattoo, possibly a mushroom, or a rose. She remembered that tattoo, remembered seeing it on the first day, when he was shaven bald as marble. It was a rose. She said to A.J., 'You found your missing men.'

'They found us,' A.J. replied. 'Came to on the other side of the ship and been working their way back ever since.'

'Did all of you ... make it through the outbreak?' she asked, suddenly feeling very much like one of those prim Boston girls. Her ankles were pressing together by reflex. It was all that male energy.

'Yes, ma'am. The Captain and Raphe – the medic – stayed behind with the group we've gotten in with. But we're birds of ill-omen, I'm afraid.' He glanced at A.J. briefly, and some message of approval passed between them. 'Just to fill you in, we think you're in for trouble with your neighbours. We were several cells out a couple of days ago, when we happened to overhear a couple of people coming through recruiting for an armed takeover of some supposed control room from some supposed army team. Pretty slick, actually; someone'd given them

230

some idea of contact protocols – sorting out friendlies from unfriend-lies,' he footnoted. 'They established that we were new to the area, so we didn't hear much more. But we caught the general drift – their agitation tactics aren't bad, either – and the next couple of cells over we managed to make like we were recruits who'd got lost and get directions, mainly to send us on our way. Anyway to summarise a lot of sneaking around we had a saunter through this cell next to yours. There's a big no go area behind a ridge and they're working hard to lure people away from it until they've been properly chatted up and giving the right signals. We just played big dumb farmboys passing through. But we'll go back if you need. Though signs are that it's coming to a boil.'

'The cavern,' Victoria supplied, 'is Erehwon.'

A scout came running up the slope and through the wide right hand entrance to the crescent. Panting slightly she said, 'They've been reported – Stan Morgan and the others – five, six caverns over. Heading away from here through the tunnels.'

'Well,' Chandler said, 'that changes things.'

'Not necessarily,' A.J. said. 'Doc,' to Sophie, 'you know if there are any photographs of the prof or the girl? Or Miz West, for that matter?'

'Stan carries them. Of Hath.' Sophie said, bewildered. 'I don't know whether he has them with him.' She started to rise. 'I can check.'

A.J. stopped her. To the scout he said, 'You know where the prof's berth is? Look through his stuff, and the girl's. Then Miz West's if you have to. I want a picture shown to these people who say they saw them. I want them to swear hand on heart that those are the same people they saw before we go tearing away through the tunnels looking for them.' He paused. 'If there are any notebooks, letters or anything like that, bring them over, too.'

Deforest Piett said, after a moment, 'You think they've gone to the trouble of sending out ringers? You think it doesn't make better sense that he's taken his niece away before anyone came down on her about what she could do with the ship.' A small pause, weighing his next words. 'You haven't been so sure about the little guy yourself, lately.'

A.J.'s lips thinned, but whether at the accusation against Morgan or against himself, Sophie did not know. She was very angry, but before she could find something suitably cutting to say, A.J. shifted in his chair. 'I should have had someone detailed to watch him. For his own protection. I shouldn't have let the damn niece downstairs, either. I knew she was up to something. Got curious, dammit.'

'Been hanging around scientists too much, Sarge,' Aquile Raho opined, comfortingly.

The sergeant gave him a wry look, and then said to the rest of them, 'I'd much rather think the prof's bundled his niece off than think the lot next door have him. But I've got to work with the worst case scenario and that's that, willingly or unwillingly, he's with the lot next door. He knows too damn much. And the niece, maybe. Smart people could use them to cause us a whole hell of a lot of trouble.'

Sophie felt the blood drain from her face. An extraordinary sensation, as though the skin itself were chilling and shrinking on her skull. 'Morgan would not help anyone who is planning to attack us.' Her voice was shaking. 'He grew up in a very bad, gang-ridden, crime-ridden neighbourhood, and he did *not* join the gangs, he did *not* take to crime. He got out. He won't do it, I tell you.'

The marble pale eyes regarded her with genuine sympathy. 'Doc, someone who knows what they're doing and why they're doing it – as opposed to just screwing around because they like to hurt people – can break just about anybody down, no matter who they are, where they come from or what they believe. You got to be more than a little crazy to stand up to torture, no matter how well trained you are – and the prof doesn't strike me as crazy.' He paused, and said if anything even more gently, 'If they've got him, and if somebody's there who knows what they're doing, you'd better get ready to be kind to him when he comes back, Doc. He won't be the same man. Not then and not for a long time after.'

46 Morgan

In the sunken area of Erehwon, hidden from the main cavern, Eilish Colby and two other women gagged him, then stripped him to his underwear. He could not find the wits either to resist or to cooperate. He had thought to meet Hath, in response to her urgent note, and when Eilish pushed a gun into his back and told him to be quiet and walk, his mind had simply shut down, as it always had under threat. He watched Hathaway come stooping from one of the pockets in the wall, face hidden by her battered hat. He made a muffled, desperate sound of appeal – and she straightened up, hitching up her belly, and he saw it was not Hath at all, but a girl of similar build, stature and colouring. He did not understand. She regarded him impassively for a long moment, shrugged, and turned away. The three who were stripping him dumped him painfully on his shoulder on the turf and hauled his jeans from his hips. Through tearing eyes he watched a silver-haired stranger in Marian's blue coat, skirt and trainers emerge behind the ersatz Hathaway, hold a small compact before his face and start to sketch age-lines into a fiftyish, *male* complexion with a make-up pencil. Eilish tossed his clothes to a slight, dark, olive-skinned young man, not the least like himself, but seeing the stranger pulling on his jeans, he felt an almost superstitious dread.

Eilish and the others lifted him to his feet and forced him, barefoot, down to the bottom of the hollow and into one of the small side caves. There he found Hathaway and Marian, stripped and gagged as he was, each bound at wrist and ankles with a single length of rope which was then tied in a noose around her neck. Marian was sitting upright, hair disarrayed, face bluish white around the gag and a bruise forming in the fragile, old skin of her cheek. They had at least left her her sweater. Hath had been stripped to bra and underpants and was lying on her side, her hair sweaty and tears leaking out of her eyes. Eilish crawled past him and heaved her up to a sitting position with her back against the wall, and now he could see that the skin of her feet, thighs and belly were scraped and beaded with red from her efforts to push herself towards the cavemouth, and there were deep red and bluish lines on her throat where the noose had jerked taut. Above the gag, her eyes sent a silent, desperate message – but whether begging forgiveness or sending a futile warning, he did not know. But he let her hold his eyes as they tied him, hand and foot, trying to reassure, and failing. Why had she sent the message that had brought him here? Under duress? Or taken by stealth? Her eyes became even wilder when Eilish started to leave. 'Mmm! Mm-mm!'

'You know you're supposed to be quiet,' Eilish said, in her husky-sweet voice. 'Or we hurt the old lady.' Marian's sunken eyes flickered slightly. 'And that goes for you, Dr Morgan. Make a sound and the girl suffers. I do mean it.' She slid out of the cave. Morgan looked after her, but only the narrowest slit of the outside showed, and he doubted they could even be seen from outside.

Hathaway began to sob, small mewing sounds. She was sitting huddled against the claystone, her chin down, eyes tight shut. Then he smelled urine, and understood, and ached for her. With his bare foot he touched hers, getting her to look at him, trying to smile behind the gag, trying to convey that it would be all right. She shook her head violently, her face twisted with shame and anger, and avoided his eyes.

233

Beyond Hath's feet, Marian's were mottled with chill, scarred and misshapen with age. Or not with age, he suddenly realised. Several of the horny nails were twisted in their beds. The skin pulled against overlapping seams in itself like an ill-laundered appliqué. The seams curved up from beneath her sole. Those were not old feet, they were scarred feet. He sensed her looking at him and met her steady, faded forget-me-not eyes. There was no expression in them, neither resentment nor resignation. And then the eyes shifted, at a shadow beyond them. Hannah crawled into the cave, dragging several folded blankets. 'I brought you blankets,' she whispered, and spread them carefully around Marian, tucking them under her mutilated feet. She started to cover Hathaway, stopped at the realisation she had wet herself, and said, 'Oh, Hath.' The girl just stared back. 'I'll see if I can get you some clean pants.'

Marian suddenly banged her head back against the wall. Hannah looked at her. The old woman did it again, eyes fixed on Hannah. Hannah breathed, 'Marian, don't.' Marian threw her head back a third time. Hannah stopped her from doing it a fourth with hands on both sides of her head, and hesitantly reached behind Marian's head and loosened the gag. With a little toss of her head Marian freed herself of it. 'Thank you, my dear,' she said. And then urgently, 'The presumption that that area represents some kind of control room is tenuous. The inference that we can gain control of the ship is premature. And mounting an attack on a special forces ODA in an entrenched position is reckless in the extreme.'

Hannah glanced towards the mouth of the cave, hands on Marian's gag. Then she leaned closer, whispering, 'We left Earth to explore the possibility of building something different from what we had always known. We were counting on the aliens' continued help in dealing with those who had power and are accustomed to using it. Who don't know how to achieve anything without organisation, regulation ... militarisation. Your special forces unit is trained for that very purpose. From the core of a few, how many are now involved in guarding that 'control room'? Twenty? Thirty? How many more are directly or indirectly involved in servicing them? The cavern walls should be a natural boundary for any organisational unit. But already your – what is it? community? organisation? dictatorship? – has moved beyond your walls. They have defined another individual's territory as being something they are entitled to. And they have moved in and taken it. That was, after all, the way of Earth.' She drew a tight breath. 'We will not commit the hypocrisy of saying "We have no choice." We do have a choice: it is submission. And we have decided to reject that choice.'

'And the only way of rejecting it,' Marian said, 'is to fight? Does that not place you at risk of becoming what you reject?' She shifted slightly; if the intensifying discomfort in his own newly bound arms and wrists was anything to go by, she and Hath must be in considerable pain. She did not show it, but for the fixed determination in her face.

Hannah breathed out, a harsh, rough sound, but did not raise her voice above its murmur. 'I do know that, Marian. We'll be obligated always to respond. We won't be able to control. We can't play to win and we can't afford to lose; we'll have to play for stalemate, over and over and over again.'

'Battles may end in stalemate. Wars do not end until one side can no longer fight, or is forced to capitulate.'

Hannah sighed. 'We shall try. But we also hope that there are enough people on the other side who are not willing to be part of this war –'

'And who will force capitulation,' Marian concluded for her. 'Yes, that is possible. But there are also people, ordinary people, who want to learn the workings of the ship and take it back to Earth.'

'That wasn't the arrangement,' Hannah whispered, her face hardening. But the hardening was a kind of despair; she was anything but a hard-hearted woman. 'The aliens said that it would be a one way journey.'

'They said nothing of the sort,' Marian whispered back. 'They were extremely brief and more than a little ambiguous; they never said how long the journey was destined to be. They said they themselves would not return to Earth; they did not say whether we would.'

Hannah gave a low, despairing laugh. 'And you think we might drop by Earth, let off our unwilling passengers and tell them all our wondrous discoveries and then just fly away to see the universe? You think any government on Earth would allow us? We'd have fifty armies fighting it out among themselves for possession, rules, regulations, admission criteria . . .'

'You are whining,' Marian hissed. 'I find that disagreeable in children and intolerable in women. Pray tell me how these fifty armies will come aboard? By rubber dinghy? Parachute? Launched from cannons? Nobody can come aboard without the cooperation of the people aboard this ship. The majority of us would gladly divest ourselves of the unwilling, the pathetic and the disaffected, secure in the knowledge that we *have* the knowledge to control the ship and our own lives. You do not need to go to war – which I can assure you is a costly and bloody exercise in, what is that exceedingly useful word, *machismo* – and not at all like it is in films . . . Where was I?' she snapped, irritated at the lost train of thought. 'You need not go to war to attain your goal. With knowledge and numbers, you can dictate terms to Earth, honour any remaining loyalties and still undertake your voyage.'

Hannah showed signs of a slow kindling anger. 'The fact remains that Stephen Cooper was shot out of hand when he tried to resist them. The fact also remains that your scientists are putting more and more knowledge into their hands. We have only the weapons and ammunition we brought with us. When that is expended –'

'Mankind slaughtered each other for millennia before the gun,' Marian said. 'Hands, fists, sticks, clubs, knives, slings and stones, bows and arrows, throwing sticks, garrotes . . . I learned unarmed combat in field school, which lasted all of a couple of months.' She met the other woman's eyes. 'I have killed other human beings, Hannah. I make no apologies; I did what I had been sent to do; I recognised it was necessary. But to this day I curse the megalomaniacs, sadists, conciliators and fools who made it so. You have not been invaded. You have not been threatened, except in your own minds. You have no just cause.'

'We are afraid,' Hannah murmured, 'of having all the choices taken away from us again.'

'Death will most certainly do that,' Marian said.

Hannah caught her breath in a shallow gasp, and then took the gag and started to pull it up. Marian jerked her head back. 'Tell me you will take no part in this madness.'

Hannah stopped. 'They need everyone who can handle a gun.' And gently but nevertheless inexorably, she forced the gag back over Marian's mouth.

They had no more visitors until after darkness fell. Outside the cave they could hear vigorous activity, argument, snatches of conversation. The decoys were working – people from the Camp were following them. The decoys had failed – the members of the Camp had been showing photographs. The discomfort in Morgan's arms became a burning that all but made him groan aloud, and then a smouldering numbness. His legs cramped, but he could not straighten them against the noose. He envied Hath her ability to sit tailor-fashion. The fullness of his bladder added another misery.

They had tried to communicate with each other by toe-waggles, but although Marian was expert in Morse, Morgan's knowledge was sketchy and Hathaway's nonexistent. He tried to outline letters on the claystone with his bound feet, but the effort was exhausting and neither of them could read it. They withdrew into their individual miseries. Marian seemed at times to be dozing, leaning against the innermost wall – but Morgan noticed the way her eyes unhooded and fixed every time people came close enough to the cave for her to hear their conversations. She listened intently, while he found himself increasingly unable to make out what they were saying over the beating of his heart and presently stopped listening altogether. Hathaway shuffled over until she could lean against his side and he found himself humming softly to her behind the gag: lullabies, love songs, snatches of popular classics, anything he could think of – except when a flash of Marian's eyes warned him to silence so she could listen. He let his world contract to this white, somewhat chilly cocoon and its discomforts.

Darkness dropped upon them. Hathaway, who had been dozing, woke with a start, the whites of her eyes barely visible in the indigo dusk. He made a soothing sound, but the cocoon had been rent and he was again aware of the outside. People were moving, giving each other whispered instructions and acknowledgements. He could hear the sounds of weapons being checked and readied and laid down upon each other – the sound he had heard so often in his time with the ODA. He heard the names of Arpád Jurassic, Dominic Peltier and Victoria Monserrat spoken, and descriptions given of each. A rustle of paper laid out; a map, perhaps, for someone was saying, 'There and there.' He heard the gradual thinning of sounds as people moved away. His heart beat hard with hope – hope that they would be forgotten now the hour was at hand. His heart beat hard until it tired itself and him, and he himself slid into a miserable half sleep.

He was awakened by the touch of a hand on his ankle, by the striking of a match. A hand carried match to storm lantern, and two hands set the lantern on a ledge in the opposite wall. The lamplight curled around a shorn head, just caught the edges of a row of ear studs, and the corner of a gentle monk's eye. The man considered them gravely.

'The time has come, the walrus said,' he said softly, and laid out beside Morgan's feet three small-bladed scalpels, a filleting knife, and a curette – instruments like Sophie's. But we're alive, Morgan thought, stupidly, his mind refusing to go where the sharp tips pointed. Marian's violent reflexive jerk startled them both, as she tried to scuttle her feet away from them. The blanket slid from her maimed feet. Seth lifted the lantern down from its ledge and raised one of her feet to examine them more closely. Marian struggled against the gag, noose and binding. 'Gestapo?' he said, laid her feet down, said gently, 'You needn't worry, Miss West. It was just unfortunate that you were suspicious enough to come with Hathaway, here I am afraid.' He leaned forward and reached for Morgan's head, past Morgan's head, fastidiously making no more contact than he must to untie the gag. 'Please make no loud noise,' he said, his face close to Morgan's. 'Or I will have to kill all three of you.' He looked into Morgan's eyes for assent, and then took away the gag.

Morgan's mouth was vile and gummy with thirst. 'I won't tell you anything,' he said.

'Yes, you will,' said Seth. 'This is my profession.' He considered Morgan a moment, and then reached past, still with that fastidious care, and retied the gag. Morgan bunched his muscles to try a head-butt, but could not find the moment, could not make the moment, and then the gag was back and Seth was loosening the bonds on his wrists. Morgan thought, I'll get the knife, I'll have to, I won't have another chance . . . steady, steady, wait . . .

And Seth took the middle finger of Morgan's left hand and broke it like a twig. He had an instant to think – No! – as he felt the hard fingers close upon his and force it backward, and then his arm, shoulder and neck seemed but hollow channels for a fire storm. He howled out behind the gag, the sound reverberating with the agony in his skull. He felt his head taken and pulled forward, and Seth said quietly in his ear, 'That's quite enough noise, Dr Morgan,' icy breath upon the fire storm. He waited, holding Morgan close, until dread and revulsion silenced Morgan, and then he loosened the gag again.

'Who are you?' Morgan gasped out. The other, though light skinned, spoke with no accent whatsoever, a pristine generic English that suggested the language had been studied and not learned native.

'Only a man with a particular training.'

'A terrorist,' Morgan panted.

'To some. To others a freedom fighter. Or a liberator.' He was mocking him, Morgan thought, and the thought made him angry. 'I've got nine more fingers,' he rasped out, though the very thought of re-experiencing that agony made him retch. But he thrust out his shaking hand, with its twisted finger. 'Get on with it.'

The torturer looked at him with respect and pity. Feigned, he told himself, feigned. The game was as much psychological as physical. The infliction of suffering creates a terrible intimacy. He thought, there were people like him in the neighbourhood, in the gangs. I survived them. But he had survived them, he knew, by not letting them notice him. By not having anything they wanted from him. He could not hold his hand up any longer, nor look at his swelling finger. He let it down, trying not to jar it as he laid it down. If it hurt any more he would surely faint. He said, 'I'm just a scientist.'

'You are too modest, Dr Morgan, and I don't have time to deal with your disingenuousness.' He set the gag back in place, tied it. Morgan, shaking with cold, tried to brace himself for another fire storm. He tried not to, but he closed his eyes.

Hathaway's whimper made him open them. She was staring down, huge-eyed, sweat gathering on her brow, as Seth's scalpel incised a fine red line on the taut skin of her abdomen. Morgan lunged, noose snapping across his throat, falling more against her than against Seth. Hathaway gave a series of twitching jerks, her eyes frantic, and Seth righted Morgan, jarring his broken hand, and untied the gag from Hath's mouth and let her retch up bile, saliva and half-digested gingerbread over Morgan's leg. 'I'm sorry, Uncle Stan,' she gasped out. 'I'm sorry. I told them about you. I told them about the control room.'

With shaking hands, Morgan pushed the hair back from her forehead. The cut on her abdomen was long but paper-shallow – but the scalpel was still in Seth's hand as he watched Morgan's face for his decision. Morgan knew that all his years of furtive planning, of careful ascent one inch at a time from the place he was born, the poverty, the violence, the physical and emotional filth, had not brought him to a cleaner, safer place after all. The bullies, the thugs, the gang warriors – all of them were only little monsters who did as their appetites, urges and fears dictated. They were victims of themselves, first and foremost. But in the wider world, the monsters grew so much larger. In the larger world there were men who had made themselves what they were, assassins, torturers. And so everything he had hoped for, everything he had worked for, everything he had believed, was a lie. From his great desolation he regarded in wonder the small part of him that still said, I won't. I won't. What choice had he? What hope had he? He drew breath to voice his capitulation, though he did not know what words he would use. Absurdly, he was terribly concerned not to seem foolish, or weak.

Hath bucked her head against his hand. 'Don't –' she gasped out. 'Don't let the bastard win.'

He looked at the torturer in dread, and found the simplest words. 'I'll tell you what you want to know.'

And after that, Seth did not touch Hath again, except to retie the gag as she began to sob and curse them both, indiscriminately. He left

Morgan's mouth and hands free, as he questioned Morgan about the control room, why he thought it was a control room, its layout, its occupancy, the ODA and its personnel, the scouts and their state of training and deployment, the Committee, its members, constitution and influence – and Morgan answered the questions, answered them all, letting the white cocoon close around him so that the only people who mattered were Hath, Marian, Seth and himself. And once he was done Seth retied Morgan's hands, on his lap this time – a small mercy for which Morgan was hideously grateful – rebound the gag, took down the light and blew it out. In the darkness his accentless voice said, 'You'll be safe here, until it's over.' He offered no thanks, made no more promises, did not mock Morgan with an assurance that Morgan had done the right thing – and for all of these Morgan was again grateful. Hathaway's muffled sounds had stopped some time ago; she huddled against Marian with her eyes closed. Marian had watched throughout, dispassionate intelligence and no judgement in her faded eyes. But he was glad of the darkness, that he need see neither of them. He would be glad if it never came light again.

47 Sophie

So they made ready for war.

Raphe Tejada, the A-team's senior medic, had remained behind on the far side of the ship. But they had Greg Drover, and Altman Meyer had served in the early years of the Vietnam war, as had two of the other physicians and the senior nurse, while a third of their number had been involved in civilian disaster planning and a fourth had flown into disasters in several countries with Médecins Sans Frontiers. To them fell the organisation of the medical response, retrieval of casualties, triage, surgery, nursing support, recovery.

In Marian's absence, Sophie found herself appointed pharmacist and production manager, priming wells of all their available pharmaceuticals and fielding as best she could the inevitable questions about purity, reliability, concentration and sterility – to which the only honest answers had to be: unknown, unknown, unknown, and you have to be kidding. Had anyone asked her she was not sure she would herself have consented to have the ship's preparations injected into her veins – but that was now, while she was hale, whole and feeling no pain. And nobody did ask her, and nobody offered to obtain advance consent from the troops in the field, the A-team and the green shirted scouts, which she thought might have been appropriate. But Dominic was fiercely protective of his company of law enforcement officers, territorial army personnel, backwoodsmen and hunters; he would not have them forced to think about their death by any ethical nicety. So she inoculated, decanted and labelled, inoculated, decanted and labelled, setting up row upon row of the motley collection of cleaned out and alcohol sterilised specimen vials, pill-bottles, cosmetics pots, baby food jars, labelled with tape and pen, or masking tape, or grease pencil on lids and side. She had replicated every solution – volume expanders, steroids, morphine, antibiotics – from the A-team's medical kits; had crushed pills – common pain killers, sedatives, sleeping pills and others – in measured volumes of water and decanted the resulting solution, calculating a predicted concentration, and wishing she had Marian with her to check solubilities. Those solutions which she knew would tolerate boiling, she boiled. Better than nothing. She labelled, numbered batches, noted origins, tracked each solution through the process in her notebook in a rapidly shredding scrawl. Every so often someone would hurry in from the medical area, press a clipboard into her hand and carry off the rattling tray of pharmaceuticals. And she would frown at the felt tip scribble on the plastic of the clipboard, sigh, take note of those drugs they lacked a priming stock of, and mould new wells of the others. She had far too much to do to think about anything else, and for that she was truly grateful. Underneath the bench, as far underneath as she could push her, Melisande yowled in her cat-carrier and rattled the mesh door. 'I'm not letting you out,' she said, at intervals, as the noise peeled away her nerve sheathing, layer by layer.

Some time during cyan a runner came to tell her to report to triage where she found the medical team assembling stretchers and laying out sheeting and towelling to be torn into non-sterile bandages. Greg Drover and the two physicians with recent field hospital experience huddled against one claystone pillar to refine their criteria for triage and the four residents huddled against another over two pocket surgery guides. In the middle of the area stood a slight woman in an olive green shirt, with a rifle held in one hand, barrel down, and a bear-bell held in the other. She had the weathered face of someone who had spent much of her life out of doors, incongruous with the expression of an elementary school teacher.

'Is everybody here now?' she said, testily. 'I've got several more groups to see after yourselves.' The huddlers unhuddled, reluctantly. 'Right, this is to make sure that everyone knows what kind of alarm signals to listen for. We've three entrances, and the warning signals for incursions will be, lower entrance,' she pointed, the bear-bell giving a muted rattle, 'single bell,' she swung the bell in hard, even strokes, 'Right entrance, double bell,' she demonstrated, 'Rear entrance,' she pointed at the less used entrance behind and to the right of the Citadel, 'triple bell. These bells will sound when possible hostiles have been sighted approaching the entrances. If any warning bell is followed by a short continuous ring, that indicates that the force is definitely hostile, that they have fired on the guard posts. If they get into this cavern, we shall do our utmost to warn people of their positions so they are not obliged to expose themselves to learn what is going on. So, for our purposes, assume that the lower entrance is due south. Then incursion in south west quadrant is indicated by –'

Someone behind Sophie murmured, 'Never thought you'd be needing a course on campanology, did you?' There was a muted ruffle of pages, followed by a whispered, '*Bell* ringing, sweetheart. It's not in there.' 'Call me that again and it'll be –'

The scout looked sternly past Sophie at the mutterers. 'And finally, if it looks like they are going to reach the Citadel, you will hear a continuous hard ringing,' she demonstrated vigorously, 'at which point I would advise you to keep your heads down as much as possible, because you may come under fire.' She viewed with reserved approval their conspicuously displayed red and white crosses. 'I will add that the signals may not necessarily be given by bells, but could be given by drums of various kinds or indeed by any noisemaker that comes to hand. And should you find yourselves surprised, we would appreciate if you would be prepared to sound the warning. We have prepared a number of trenches or shelters – this will be particularly pertinent if any of you find yourselves caught in the open while retrieving wounded – and there are, of course, the side caves. The trenches are –'

'Gung ho, isn't she?' muttered the campanologist behind Sophie. Sophie herself had a grotesque impression of an air hostess pointing out exits, floor lighting, flotation pillows and other safety features 'in the event of a forced landing', i.e., crash, as the scout described where the refuges might be found. She was not sure whether it was suppressed laughter or suppressed sobs building up in her throat. Fortunately, the briefing ended with a last ring of the bell, a vigorous 'All clear!', and the scout moved briskly on. A few voices were raised in brazen mockery, but more held their peace. People hastened to reassure the frailer nerved among them that it was the spire that would be the target, not themselves.

She would have gone back to her lab, but one of the emergency physicians, a small, formidable Egyptian, cornered her to demand what they were going to do about *blood* – and she had to explain at some length that she had filled a well earlier that day with her own blood, and had watched the surface cloud with a fine silvery mesh of reabsorption fibres. She did not know why; she had no idea how the ship discriminated between matter to be reabsorbed and matter to be synthesised. Maybe it was the sheer complexity of the mix, maybe the presence of macromolecules, maybe there was some biochemical marker present, either naturally or introduced. But the ship would not synthesise blood. Plasma, then, he said, fixing her with a dark, glittering eye. Clotting factors. *Anything*. And in the meantime what was her blood type, was she a donor in good standing . . .? She escaped, having mortgaged the contents of her veins, only to be accosted by one of the trauma surgeons wanting to know whether she would be prepared to stand by as a relief assistant surgeon. Only as a last resort, she said, feelingly . . . The redheaded emergency nurse Dove, in charge of recovery, wanted to know what basis she had for assuming the calculated concentrations for the drugs she had dissolved. Sophie had to say, none; it was merely an assumption, based on the apparent fidelity with which the ship reproduced mixtures. Dove looked pained at such cavalier reasoning. 'We'll be titrating, then,' she said. 'I wish to God we'd had a chance to test some of these preparations. And I hope to God we don't have to use them . . .' One of the residents presented her with a doughnut, vanilla flavoured. The smell reminded her painfully of Hathaway, and so of Stan. She could not finish it. She carried it back to the laboratory and set it aside for later.

Cyan pennant was drawn in and replaced by blue. She tidied the lab. She covered the wells. She tidied the lab again, moving vials to lower down nooks on the walls. In case. She reviewed her notes for clarity, trying dispassionately to decide whether, in the event of her death or disablement, people would be able to find all they needed in them. Dominic visited her briefly. He was like an overwound spring, though he tried not to show it, his words coming in snatches, their ends bitten off. Crisis did not soothe him; it merely made him more alert to all the possible things that might go wrong. He worried about infiltration, about agents in place; he worried about panic; he worried about people failing to heed the alarms, failing to take cover and stay under cover. If he intended to raise her morale, he failed, singularly. He did tell her one essential, terrifying piece of information: the three people who had been seen travelling away from Kastély, wearing Morgan's, Hath's and

Marian's clothes, were indeed impostors. Which meant that the three were probably being held in Erehwon. If they lasted the night, they would make provision to rescue them.

She went back to triage. She listened to discussions of modifications to emergency procedures to accommodate their conditions. She contributed, minimally, to decision making on drug regimens. She smiled politely at suggestions that the synthesis of coffee ought to take higher priority. She tried not to hear whispered speculations about what the Erehwonites might have planned, and hissed arguments about whether or not there should have been more attempts made to negotiate.

She went back to the pathology lab. Decanted the contents of wells – more morphine, more steroids. Covered them again. Looked at her notes. Thought they might have made sense, if not for her state of mind. A scout looked in on her and suggested that she stay within the Citadel overnight. They doubted that there would be a night attack, but you never knew; the enemy might prefer to use the darkness, despite the handicap. When she asked to go for her bedroll, the scout had it brought. She considered joining the rest of the medical team in triage, but in the end unrolled her sleeping bag beneath the bench, beside the cat-carrier, and lay upon it, listening to Melisande's intermittent lament and feeding her the last of the cat treats through the mesh.

The drum roll sounded. Darkness fell. The worst hours began. She did sleep, some time. Her dreams were vile.

The light came up at last. She groaned, sticky-mouthed and sandy-eyed, and started to ease herself stiffly out from underneath the bench. In the cat-carrier, Melisande hissed. Half way up, she paused – was that bells? Quite faint and distant, quite unlike the cacophonous demonstration of the night before. Probably it was a test, a trial warning.

And then she heard the first shots. Sharp, little testing reports. Adrenalin ignited a smoky fire in her blood. She felt it flare out along her nerves, burst and spread on her skin, imparting a disconcerting sensitivity. She could feel her clothing abrading wrists, underarms, inner thighs. She could feel the air chill her skin as she moved. She caught up her equipment bag and ran for the medical area, by reflex taking the fastest route, out on to the apron. 'Doc!' A scout sprinted up the slope. He threw his weight against her, pushing her back and down among the claystone boulders and crouched down beside her, staring at her in disbelief. A heavyset, middle aged man, he was breathing so hard that she went from being alarmed at his behaviour to being alarmed for him. 'For Chrissake,' he managed at last. 'Stay under cover. This is the real thing. They're in the cavern.'

'I'm a doctor,' she said. 'I have to get to medical.'

'Through there,' he pointed. Looked out into the main cavern, said, 'Shit. *Get down! Get down!*' And ran, scuttling on all fours towards a woman and three children who were crossing the base of the apron towards the latrine area. '. . . need the toilet . . .' Sophie heard her protest and then, 'Hey!' as without ceremony he hefted two of the children and started with them towards the nearest shelter trench. She dragged the third child after, 'But they need the *toilet –*'

At the far side of the cavern near the secondary entrance, Sophie could see figures swirling like leaves in an eddy, like ice flakes riding meltwater down a drain. The leaves were the green shirted scouts, the ice crystals light-clad figures pressing inwards from the two south entrances. The enemy, thought Sophie, putting quotes around the words. The other tribe. The rival team. It was all so absurd and so far away. She could hear screams, shouts, the snap of gunfire, a short burst from a machine gun, and over it all the ringing of those ridiculous bells, signals quite forgotten. The figures ran, crouched, rolled, dropped, scrambled up and ran again, in short starts like insects over a pond. One or two, having fallen, did not get up. It made no sense. Her teeth were chattering. She could see other people, their people, standing in twos and threes along the base of the apron and the shallow upslope. Spectating. She could not moisten her mouth or steady her jaw to call to them. In the trench to her right the middle aged scout was shouting to them, his arm windmilling, while the woman at his side held on to him, her eyes looking wildly around her with the beset expression Sophie had once seen on a woman trying to find a taxi before her drunken escort embarrassed her further. And then the woman saw something to the rear of the massif that made her haul back on him, turn him bodily to look.

From the pennant tower the drum began to beat, hard, panicked. Sophie looked back and up in time to see the yellow pennant jerk as a bullet struck it. The drum hesitated for a breath, and then resumed. Three people ran past, stone-clad, crouching low, a woman and two men. One of the men glanced her way and she glimpsed gentle monk's eyes behind small silver rimmed glasses. The woman called out, shrill with panic, 'Arpád! They're in the Citadel. *Arpád.*'

'Here,' said the accented voice from further along the massif, and the third man dropped smoothly to his knees, brought his rifle up and fired. Sophie heard a grunt and a slither of a body falling. The woman gave a gasping cry of triumph, looking right and left, hair whipping across her face. It was Eilish Colby.

Behind them the middle aged man levered himself from the trench, handgun in his hand. Sophie had a brief, vivid impression of desperate resolution and strain, of an ordinary man steeling himself to a repugnant heroism, before his face vanished for ever in a bloody implosion. The monkish man spun from his assassin's crouch, calling out, 'Victoria! Arpád's hurt. Victoria, help.'

Sophie cried out in a voice that astounded her with its power. '*Don't! Don't answer. Murderers!*' And for an instant she herself looked into death behind silver glasses as the man turned his head her way. Why he did not fire, she did not know; it did not occur to her until much later how well she was concealed among the outcroppings of the massif. He flicked his glance away towards the dozen or so green shirted scouts running towards them across the cavern. He caught Eilish's arm when she would have stood and fired, and pushed her on, fired several rounds himself, dropping three of the oncoming figures, and disappeared around the rear of the massif. The scouts stormed past. With them went all sound, it seemed, but the sound of a child screaming in the trench where the scout had fallen.

Victoria suddenly appeared, scrambling through the claystone, leaving faint bloody smears. 'Doctor,' she said, glassy eyed – perhaps at that moment she did not remember Sophie's name, only her profession. 'Arpád needs a doctor.' There was blood on her hands. Sophie started to gesture towards the trench, started to indicate a prior need, but saw that one of the scouts had returned, drawn by the child's screams. So she let Victoria lead her through the mounded stone and into the back door of the crescent, dreading what she would find.

Arpád was not dead. The bullet had ripped through his shoulder and embedded itself in a halo of blood and tissue in the claystone column at the entrance to the crescent. He was sitting slumped at the base of the column, blood smear mounting like a standard over him, swearing to himself – there was no mistaking the tone – in what she presumed had to be his native Hungarian. That he was conscious still he owed to Victoria's attempt at applying a pressure bandage. Sophie left it in place and applied another, feeling shattered bones – collarbone? first rib – grind beneath her fingers. 'Get a stretcher,' she said to Victoria, who went feeling her way through the claystone maze with outstretched hands and urging herself on in broken whispers. Arpád groaned, his litany faltering, his face glazed with sweat. She spoke to him; he did not respond; but she kept talking, telling him that he would be all right, that it did not look too bad, that Victoria had gone for a stretcher. Dominic stumbled through the other entryway, looking even paler than Arpád, and said, 'Dieu, I thought they'd killed him.'

'They gave it a good try,' Sophie said, briefly.

Dominic spoke to Arpád in Hungarian and got a few words in response, and then Arpád closed his eyes and leaned his head back against the column, rolling it back and forth, back and forth. Dominic said, sounding a little helpless, 'Don't worry, I'll take care of everything.'

'Is it over?' she said.

'Oh, yes,' he said. 'I think so.' He got to his feet and stood framed in the entry way, an exquisite target for any sniper until André Bhakta rose up before him and rolled him back in, around to the rear of the pillar, almost tripping him on Arpád's outstretched legs. The soldier stood before him and fixed him with a look and waited until the message penetrated, and then to Sophie, 'Did you see what happened?' The stretcher bearers arrived then and she surrendered Arpád to them. Bhakta waved in two of the more experienced scouts and sent Dominic off with them under escort, then turned back to her, expectantly.

'Is it over?' Sophie said again.

'Maybe. We haven't heard from the party downstairs yet. Tell me what you saw.'

As she told him, briefly, she could look past him and see the stretcher parties returning across the bowl of the cavern, four or five of them, coming at a steady walk or a stumbling run. Scouts, mainly, some with bloodied uniforms, some flushed with effort, some white-faced, intensely concentrated. Most of the stretchers were flanked by two or three others, scouts, civilians, friends or family. She saw a man supporting a woman whose right arm was lumpy with bloody cloths to the elbow and still dripping blood from the fingers. He leaned under her, pulling her good arm over his shoulder so her breast rested on his bowed back, speaking up into her face, while she shook her head to his words, eyes half closed and running with tears of silent pain. Then two others reached him and they gathered her up in a two handed chair. Sophie said, numbly, 'I'd better go and see if they need me.'

As she reached triage, which had spilled out on to the rear apron, two people passed her carrying a stretcher with a figure covered by a bloodied blanket. Only the boots showed, and a brown trouser cuff. She wondered who it was – the man who had died trying to stop the three assassins. Or someone else. Dove caught her arm as she looked after it. 'We need to get the dead out of the way. We don't want anyone

247

bound down underfoot,' she said shortly, by way of explanation. 'That blood yours?'

'No,' Sophie said, and the redhaired woman pushed her towards a side cleft where she found two young girls with water basins, disinfectant soap solution and towels. In silence they poured for her and watched her wash the blood from her hands. Sophie sought for something to say that might comfort them, but she found herself intimidated by their sharp boned, remote young faces, by the efficiency with which they anticipated her needs even before she thought of them – water, soap, rinse. She was joined by their orthopaedic surgeon, Dinesh Ramachandram, who did not look at her as he stood at her side to give himself an abbreviated, vicious scrub, saying, 'Why the hell I'm doing this I don't know. Nothing's sterile.' Then he looked at her. 'Get gowned. We need you.' The silent girls produced a tattered plastic gown and gloves and helped her into them.

The operating theatre was a walled area, roughly L-shaped, with four claystone slabs raised like altars. It had been intended as part of their permanent infirmary. Sophie found herself assisting Ramachandram while he swiftly amputated the woman's arm. They did not have the blood to support her through attempts at reconstruction. Nor did they have the time, with other casualties still arriving. But to have done this, when he could have done better, enraged him. She did not take his bitter observations on her technique personally. But at the end of that operation, Altman Meyer, who had been at the table behind her, quietly exchanged his own assistant – a surgical resident – for her.

She was not sure she was grateful, for all his calm authority. She found chest injuries the most frightening of cases. She remembered one night on emergency services during her internship, a 'domestic' with a woman and her brother arriving together with knife wounds to the chest inflicted by the woman's estranged husband. As she and the attending physician struggled with the brother's spitting haemorrhage and panicked outrage, the woman herself had gone quietly into shock and died. The knife wound was a small, purple slit through the underside of her left breast, half the length of Sophie's thumb. No other injuries were as frightening, as subtle and as swift.

Triage's next patient, a white-clad man, came bubbling blood from nose, mouth and a puncture high in the chest. She lent her strength to the surgeon's in cutting through ribs and held the wound retracted while he tracked the bullet deep into the bloody chest cavity, ligating bleeding vessels as they went, at intervals murmuring something that sounded perilously close to a prayer. But the man left the table alive, with a chest tube in place and a brusque recitation of instructions. Meyer stripped off his bloody gloves reflexedly and then gazed around him like a man who had found himself on the wrong side of the looking glass. For a moment he had lost track of where he was; perhaps he thought himself back in Vietnam. A nursing assistant took the gloves from him with a sigh, bearing them off on a plastic sheet like a stray wise man with offering. Sophie pulled off her own gloves by the fingertips, so they could be cleaned, sterilised, reused. Sutures, latex gloves, needles; their supplies were all finite. The plastic sheets, scavenged from all over Kastély, were ragged. She leaned against the claystone behind her as the nursing assistants swabbed down the table and draped it for their next patient.

A scout came and stood just inside the entryway, clear of the traffic of patients and doctors. He wore a police badge on his green shirt; one of their seasoned ones. 'Just so's you know,' he said. 'We've just had word from downstairs: the ambush was successful. We've cleared them out of here. Our people are moving into Erehwhon now.' He looked at them looking at him. 'Just so's you know.'

A flicker of yellow caught her eye. She looked up, towards the clock tower. The timekeeper was just pulling in the bullet holed yellow pennant. He unfurled the green. They were three hours into the morning.

48   Morgan

And after the distant gunfire, distorted by the tunnels and caverns, came a silence. He thought, when the silence became unbearable, to slide on to his side and inch further out of the cave. But as he did so, Hathaway jammed her calloused foot into his ankle, and he looked at her and saw Marion's frantic head shake. He stared a question at her. Hathaway added her own head shake in support, looking frightened. And so he did not move. He listened.

Running footsteps, pat-pat-pat, scuffle, slide. A woman's voice, Maggie's: 'Get going. Get clear if ye want to live. They'll be here shortly.' Just outside the cave she rummaged and scuffled. 'They were ready, more than ready. They were dug into the walls. It was an ambush. It was a damn massacre.' Eilish said, 'Seth, have you seen Seth?' A pair of stone coloured, bloodied trousers were flung into the mouth of the cave. 'I don't have t'do anything!' she said, in a breaking voice. 'I didnae go tae fight; I went to help. They've taken all the wounded. An' I'm not staying to be tried and shot.'

A woman said, 'We'd better go and see what happened.'

A man said, 'We'd be better off going after Maggie.'

Eilish said, 'I'm waiting for Seth.'

There was another brief flurry of activity, a briefer argument, running footsteps and then quiet. Except – or maybe he imagined it – a lone woman's whispery breathing.

Marian had her eyes closed, holding very still. Hathaway drew her knees up against her abdomen and bent her head forward. He understood then that they feared reprisals if anyone recalled their existence.

Then a gun fired like a thunderclap; a bullet struck just inside the lip of the cave. Perhaps Morgan glimpsed the flicker of it in flight an instant before the wall burst grey – perhaps not – but a moment later he saw the much larger, slower shape of a body twisting as it fell. A small spray of blood anointed the lip and floor of the cave mouth.

Hathaway had jerked back and cried out, muffled, at the first report. Marian had made no sound. Now she leaned hard against Hathaway, pressing her bony shoulder against the girl's, holding the girl's gaze. Morgan could see Hathaway's ribs rising and falling beneath her skin, short, shallow breaths.

The silence returned.

Footsteps came, slowly, rasping on the matting. They listened to them softly pacing outside. Pain sawed through his hand, one stroke for every heartbeat. Someone filled up the entrance to the cave, moving very slowly, leading with his rifle. He watched the armed man come with a dumb animal fear, incapable of recognition until he spoke.

'It's the prof.'

Cautiously still, Kent Hughes eased over to look past him. 'And the girl and Miz West. You OK, Miz West?'

Astonishingly, the creases at the corners of Marian's eyes deepened slightly and with great dignity, she nodded.

Hathaway whimpered behind her gag.

'Hang tough, kid,' said Hughes. 'Miz West, have they booby trapped you? Explosives, wired ammunition – you know. Did they leave anything around you?'

Marian shook her head.

He unsheathed his knife. 'OK, I'm going to take you out one at a time. When you get outside just stay down. We think the area's clear but we're still checking caves. The prof first, sorry, ladies.' He sliced gag, noose and ankle and wrist bonds. Morgan wiped at his foul mouth with his sound hand, wiped at it again. 'What happened?'

'Prof, that'll have to wait. We just want to get you out of here, OK.'

Hughes had to drag him out of the cave. He could not even crawl. Beside the cave a woman lay on her front, face turned into profile, the thin bone of her temple blown out in a bloody mulch of tissue and bone shards. One green-brown eye stared upwards at an impossible angle. He evaded its line of sight. On her outstretched hand was a silver skull ring with emerald eyes. He thought he should know her. But he could not bring himself to look long enough. Raho stood guard over him as he crouched on the grass, head averted. 'The docs'll fix that hand up, Prof,' was all he said.

Hathaway came out struggling weakly, and cried out, a little gasp, at the sight of the dead woman. She took a few steps on uncertain legs and fell partly atop him. Under her blanket she was naked below the bust, stained underwear torn off by the claystone. She got her arms around him and held on, held on with all her trembling strength, whispering, 'I'm sorry, I'm sorry, I'm sorry.'

Hughes was longer removing Marian, trying to be gentle with the old woman, who was saying, through chattering teeth, 'Don't mean to be such a bother but it was just so long –' Her face was grey beneath the bruise. 'If I can just get a minute or so to pull myself together I'm sure I can supply some kind of useful intelligence. They did talk rather a lot just outside.'

'I'm sure A.J. will want to know, but what you need, Miz West,' said Hughes, shifting his grip to lift her, 'is a nice cup of tea.'

'Oh that would be excellent,' she said, gamely. 'Quite excellent.'

With help from one of the scouts Morgan managed to get and keep his feet. There were quite a number of their people in Erehwon now, working systematically along the walls, searching caves. All were armed. Besides the woman there were two other bodies, one quite dead, one still moving feebly. Before they reached it a pair of scouts with a stretcher between them arrived to transfer and lift it.

He stumbled on some unevenness on the turf, almost turning his ankle, and looked down. Beneath his foot was a circular grey patch, perhaps eight, nine inches in diameter. He toed it, and grey filmed his skin. For the first time since Seth had broken his finger, something of the old Stan Morgan stirred him, the Stan Morgan who was a scientist and not . . . whatever Seth had reduced him to. He started to crouch, and Raho said, 'Hey, Prof. Not now. This is not the time. And this is sure as hell not the place.'

There were bloodstains, but no bodies, inside Kastély; the dead had been removed to the burial yard as soon as they were pronounced dead. The wounded were in the medical unit; he could hear their groans and cries across the cavern. 'You don't want to go there,' Hughes decreed, and instead took them to Morgan's cubicle and sent for one of the medics to come and check them over, and one of the scouts to collect clothes and more blankets for them all and hot water and tea bags. Emilie Linn appeared, examined Hathaway, Marian, and was looking at Morgan's finger with her brows pulling together when a scout stuck her head through the door, 'Dr Linn, they need you in triage.'

Hath, seated on the low wall, lifted her head to give them a twisted smile, as the doctor left. 'I guess we're not going to die,' and then her eyes filled. 'Oh Uncle Stan.'

'Please,' he just said, exhausted. 'Hath, please.'

Marian, lying on the bed, sighed. 'If you would cease to presume that the universe turns on your whims, my dear, you might register that this was an inevitability. Although you were exceptionally foolish to involve yourself with these people, and should certainly learn from it, you did not cause this.' To Morgan she said, 'That note they lured you with? The child herself did not write it; it was forged using a letter she had left with them.' She swung her legs off the bunk and sat up. 'Come,' she said, imperiously. 'Sit by me.' He did. 'I would like to talk to you about what happened back there.'

If he looked down – because he could not look up – he could see her scarred feet with their twisted nails. 'What is there to talk about? I told them,' he said – whimpered. 'I told them everything.'

'Yes, my dear, you did.'

He felt as though the quiet old voice was a knife, being slid slowly into his guts. He pressed himself against it. 'Everything they asked –'

'So did I,' Marian said, 'Not the first day, or the second. But I told them. Why they did not then shoot me then I will never know. I feared then it was because they thought they might still wring more from me.' Her vision had gone inwards; she shuddered briefly and with an effort focused her bleached blue eyes on him again. 'From the moment that an agent is known to have been taken, those in command must assume that the enemy are in possession of everything he or she knows.' She patted his hand lightly; it jarred his nerves, so much so he could hardly resist jerking his hand away. 'But although you told him everything he asked, you did not tell him everything you knew, and judging by what we heard the key questions may have been the ones they did not ask. In their disdain for mankind's manipulation of their environment, they failed to appreciate the tactical uses of such an environment as this. Their hubris may have doomed them, my dear, their hubris, Sergeant Lowell's cunning, and your bravery.'

'Bravery?' he said, in a thin whisper.

She laid a hand like a dried leaf along the side of his face, turning his head towards her. 'There are people who offer up under torture everything that is in them. In your case that was considerable – and if you had offered them that, if you had illuminated their blind spots, the outcome might have been quite different. I do want you to know that in my eyes – in the eyes of someone who has been put through torture – you have nothing to condemn yourself for, young man. You gave up no more than you had to; you survived, and you kept the two of us alive. That was the best you could hope to do.'

He leaned his head against the end of his bed cubicle and began to cry.

A white-faced Sophie appeared some time later. By that time they were all fully dressed and nursing cups of extremely weak, heavily sugared tea. Marian's colour and spirits were better, and Hathaway had recovered enough to complain again about the ship's inability to make soft drinks. Morgan was feeling increasingly nauseated with the thundering pain spreading from fingertip to shoulder, and was sitting huddled on the bed, legs drawn up to support the mug and the steam moistening his forehead when her voice said from the doorway, 'Stan?'

He lifted his head, looked fully into a human face for the first time since his rescue. Her hair was coming down from its French twist, she was wearing a sweat-stained black T-shirt with a garish rock group logo which was at least a size too small, there was a bloodstain on her jeans and she smelled of sweat, latex and blood. And she looked like she was about to throw herself on him, her eyes fierce and a little wild.

He got to his feet, handing the tea off vaguely to Marian, and she did, pushing him back against his clothing shelf. He concentrated hard on not retching in her ear, and wished he could enjoy the sensation of her hands fisting on the fabric across his back and the impression of her nose and brow into his collarbone and shoulder, the feathering of her hair against his chin. He had never appreciated how a tall woman could tuck herself against a man.

'This is such a damn cliché,' she said, a little while later, releasing him to swipe at her eyes and rub at the damp patches on his shirt. 'But I swear to God it was only when I understood what A.J. was saying about what these people having hold of you might mean – what they could

do to you – I swear it was the first time that I knew that you – that I –'
Her hands fluttered around his finger, all her professional assurance
completely gone. 'Oh, God, Stan,' she said. 'Oh, God.' Her eyes
searched his face, imploring him to answer the question she could not
ask.

He said, 'You'd better hear it from me. I told them everything they
asked.' He swallowed nausea. 'Everything.'

Somehow, that calmed her; that had not been the worst possibility in
her mind. She took his thumb in one hand and the other side of his
palm in the other, steadying it between them. 'A.J. said you wouldn't
have any choice.' She swallowed. 'I know – I know this doesn't help
you right now. I have enough imagination to know that – but I'm glad
you didn't let them hurt you any worse than this.'

She seemed, he thought, quite unaware of the absurdity of her
words.

Hathaway said, 'It was me, Sophie. He wouldn't let them hurt me. He
said – after that guy broke his finger – he held out his hand and said,
"I've got nine other fingers. Get on with it." '

Sophie's expression was more appalled than impressed. She looked
from Hathaway to Morgan. 'I really', she said stiffly, 'don't understand
you people sometimes.'

'Californians?' Hathaway said, dangerously.

'The two of you,' Sophie said, rescuing herself. 'The two of you.'
Some associated thought made her flush slightly. 'Stan, I – I mean,
you're not obligated to reciprocate – just because I – Oh, damn. You're
feeling awful – you look awful – and I'm expecting – I don't know what
I'm expecting – I feel about seventeen –'

'Gee, ta muchly,' Hathaway put in. 'I'd say thirteen. Look, Soph,
maybe you ought to see someone does something about his hand.'

'Yes. Yes, I know.' But she did not move for a moment, gazing at
him, lost to herself. Then forcibly recalled herself, muttered, 'This is
crazy.'

'Right,' Hath said. 'He's not *that* good looking.'

She ignored that and sat him down again, still holding Morgan's
hand. The physician was in control again. She turned it, peered at it,
brushed the bloated skin lightly and asked if he could feel her touch, if
he could move it, if it felt hot, cold . . . 'It's going to be a little while
longer,' she said. 'Our orthopod is still working on someone, and I'd
want him to take a look at this. It looks like there's a dislocation at that
middle joint as well as possibly a fracture – but without X-rays we'll be
working in the dark to a certain extent. Still Raman will set it and the

worst that should happen is the joint becomes arthritic in time. There's nothing to suggest nerve damage.'

He tossed out the old saw, 'Will I still be able to play the piano?'

She looked into his face, her expression quizzical. He could see the spiderweb glitter of sweat trapped in the fine lines around her eyes and her mouth. Her irises were more blue than grey from this distance; it was the dense hazel flecking that neutralised their colour. Her eyebrows were slightly darker than her hair, and in her left, he could see two white hairs. She said something; he watched creases form and relax in her lips. He had always thought that human lips in close up looked a little like earthworms. Hers were too pink.

She said, 'What are you smiling at?'

'I'm just remembering how I used to turn girls off.'

'Intentionally or unintentionally?'

'Unintentionally. Most girls weren't scientists.'

'I'm a girl,' she said, leaning closer. 'And a scientist.'

'But your lips don't –' he said, against them.

'Don't what –' she mumbled.

'Look like –'

'Damn, but it does the old heart good when a woman takes my advice,' A.J. Lowell said from the doorway.

They detached, Morgan reluctantly, Sophie blushing and promising, 'I'll go and see if Raman is done with his case.'

A.J.'s chuckle followed her out. 'Just like a teenager caught making out in the parlour.' Hathaway made a sound rather like a feeding goldfish, but wisely did not say anything. Then his expression sobered, and he sat down on the low wall. 'Right, people. Good to see you back, more or less in one piece. I need you to tell me what happened to the three of you. I'm particularly interested in who was in that cave, who was involved in the attack, who you know escaped, and so on.'

Morgan's nausea, which had briefly abated, returned. It occurred to him that the nausea was as much spiritual as physical, the need to bring up again and again his deeds until he was purged of them. 'I told them everything.'

'Thought you would, son.' A.J. said, simply. 'There was too much good planning about this for them to be amateurs.'

'He told them to protect me,' Hathaway said, stubbornly.

'And he did not supply them with information beyond the direct answers to their questions,' Marian defended him.

Morgan said, to the claystone, 'I grew up in a lousy neighbourhood where you volunteered nothing, to anyone.'

'A lesson well learned,' Marian said. 'Am I to understand,' this to A.J., 'that you exploited the claystone as camouflage and armour? They said you had "dug into the walls".'

'Miz West,' A.J. said, after a moment, 'I'm kind of glad they started on the prof, and not you. Though,' he leaned forward, 'it looks like they had a go at you, too.'

She brushed her face with fingertips that wavered slightly. 'Had I known they would have been needed, I would have kept up my unarmed combat skills as well as my . . .' Her face clouded. 'They took a weapon from me,' she said, in a thin voice. 'A Walther PPK. I was carrying it when they took me hostage. Will you tell me –'

'We have it,' A.J. said. 'The woman carrying it was killed before she could use it.'

'Thank you,' she breathed, and Morgan stared at her; so she, too, was carrying her own burdens.

'Woman?' Hathaway said.

'Yes, the leader of those women in the side cave. Big girl, brunette.'

'Hannah,' said Marian, in deep distress. 'Hannah, dead?'

'By the time we got her into triage, yes.'

Marian sat just breathing in and out for a minute, tears moving in an erratic creep down her age-seamed skin, while they watched her, worried, or tried not to watch her, tactfully. 'How many?' she said, hoarsely.

'Fourteen dead so far; twenty-three wounded badly enough to need surgery. We don't expect all of those to make it. Of the dead three were ours, scouts – killed when the enemy broke through into this cavern. We expected the attack on the control room, and we had a pretty good idea, just judging from the degree of sympathy in the caverns above, which routes they'd have to take. We dug ourselves into the walls after dark, concealment and shielding, and just waited for them. Caught them in a crossfire. What we didn't count on so much was a serious break in up here, going after members of the committee. That was when the scouts were killed. Arpád's down, shoulder wound.'

'That was why the names,' Marian said, to herself. 'They had a "hit list".' She put the words neatly in quotes. 'They intended not only to take over the control room but to eliminate our leaders.' She nodded, almost in approval. 'But tell me, Sergeant, how did you come to anticipate all this, when as of early yesterday I at least had no intimation that anything extraordinary was to happen? I suspected the child might be contemplating something foolish, but I never thought to be captured. Foolish of me.'

He grinned, his face suddenly losing a tension Morgan had not noticed was there. 'Two little birds told me. Two little birds by the name of Metzner and Lecce.'

She raised a white brow. 'Your missing men?'

'Gassed and dumped way the hell the other side of the ship. Practically walked all the way around the whole damn thing – sorry, ma'am,' Marian tipped her head graciously, 'finding us. Helped at the end by the Erehwonites' recruitment drive. The captain and Raphe are still back helping the people they wound up among. Pity; we could have used Raphe.'

That Morgan appreciated. In the field a medic was gold, an officer merely brass. A.J. settled in, hands folded. 'Right, people, I need as much information as you can give me on the number of people you saw at your end, their names, who got away, where they were headed, that sort of thing.'

After A.J. was done with them they went to the graveyard. Morgan would never know at whose instigation, his or Marian's or Hathaway's. The bodies had been laid out neatly, in a row, along the far edge. A move not welcomed by all, judging by the angry eyes that watched them. Or maybe it was the fact that someone had shown a little respect, covering wounds and faces with portions cut from their pale clothing, folding their hands, ensuring that their jewellery remained untouched. The shrouding had already begun, the thin grey fungus coating hands, stains, features. But they were identifiable. They found Hannah, knowing her from the height, the broad shoulders and big hands and the spreading hair that looked reddish against the grey. From the stain from breast to hip, far from covered by the napkin of fabric laid on her belly, she had been shot in the stomach and lived a while after. 'Oh, my dear,' Marian murmured. Morgan left her standing there, Hathaway beside her, and moved down the row, looking at one face after another, mostly men, but some women. Beyond the last of the row he lifted his eyes from the flat, empty place and gazed across the cavern to the bright maw of the nearest tunnel. A.J. had said Seth was not among the dead, nor among the wounded. But he had had to see for himself. He had to find for himself that empty grave that should have contained a man.

FIVE

ASH

49 Morgan

Morgan woke, cold, in darkness, in pain. There had been ashes in his dreams, smoke and ashes. One handed, he pulled the sleeping bag around his ears, muffling his face against the chill. Through half closed eyes he saw the gauzy flame of one of their lanterns, and Sophie's face with tinted highlights along cheekbone and nose and following the curve of her elegant French twist.

She crouched beside him. 'Morgan, we need to talk.' In the three days since the raid, neither of them had alluded to her outburst in the cubicle. If anything they were more tentative with each other than before, keeping their sufferings to themselves in the aftermath of the raid. Sometimes when the pain kept him awake, he could hear her grinding her teeth in her sleep, beyond the partition and, for all her impeccable grooming, there were mauve and ochre smudges under her eyes.

He eased himself to a sitting position on the bed, ducking his head to avoid the overhead storage shelf. She carried a candle in one hand, the thermometer and her watch in her other, and he wondered at her having secured two of Kastély's treasures. She arranged the three items on the bed beside him, in a triangle, so that the light caught the dull thread of mercury and the enamelled watch hands which stood at 3.37. He could not quite read the thermometer, and Earth-time was no longer meaningful to him. He looked questioningly at her.

'The ambient temperature's twenty-two degrees. And by our tabulations the light should have come up five minutes ago.'

He had disregarded his chill as a consequence of pain, sleeplessness and pain killers. But until four days ago he himself had recorded those measurements. 'The temperature and length of day have been invariant within the errors of our instruments since we got here.'

'According to the records there were no changes until this morning.' She made an impatient sound, 'But when I asked the person who had made these readings, it transpired that yes, indeed, he did see a slight drop yesterday, less than a degree, and yes, indeed, lights up yesterday was late and lights down early by a couple of minutes. But since everybody knows ambient temperature is twenty-six degrees and the light/dark cycle is exactly half of a thirty-hour, nineteen-minute day, he decided none of those meant anything,' she said, with acerbity. 'But that's not all. Marian and I were in Erehwon yesterday. There are areas of what look like breakdown of the matting, roughly circular hollows reduced to that fine grey dust lying on bare claystone; I counted twenty-four of them around yellow interval. It's difficult to tell if the walls are deteriorating as well because any dust will slip off vertical surfaces, unless the deterioration actually creates hollows. But the water's faintly turbid, suggestive of colloidal suspension and, while the gingerbread is still being produced, it has dark streaks in it.'

Morgan shoved back his sleeping bag and fumbled up on to the above-bed shelf for his clothes. 'I'll come.'

'We can't go over until lights up. A.J.'s orders,' her mouth twisted a little. 'He was appalled when Marian and I went alone yesterday – though it was Astarte who asked for us . . . She and her partner are former police officers. They weren't involved in the attack and they're trying to pull what's left of Erehwon back together – ah,' she said, as suddenly they were drenched in light. 'Eight minutes late,' she added, blinking, and noted it down. 'You get dressed; I'll return the watch and tell the others we're going over.'

Morgan said, 'I don't want anyone with us except scientific staff.'

She turned in the doorway, her flaxen head just level with the walls, and smiled at him, approving his self-assertion. 'I'll do my best.'

Dressed – a frustrating process with one hand splinted and throbbing with every movement – he went by the lab to pick out the instruments he thought he might need, and since Sophie was still not yet back he summoned his courage and went in search of her. It was getting easier to be among people, which was as well, because he found her in the crescent, amidst a cluster of its usual occupants, saying a little testily, 'If you would give us a chance to take a good look at the problem we might be able to give you a better idea of what you should do about it.'

Victoria said, 'I do not think we would be in any way justified in forcing an evacuation. The remaining people in Erehwon should be allowed to decide for themselves whether they need to leave their home.'

'And supposing they did this themselves,' Lowell said.

'That', Sophie said, 'is exactly what they suspect of *us*.' She ran the flat of her hand over her hair. 'They are wondering if we are responsible, that it's retaliation, or us trying to disperse them, or get them off our borders. Suspicion works both ways. Would you please give us a chance to find out exactly what's going on – to our best ability – whether it's, I hesitate to say natural, but normal. A seasonal cycle maybe – well, *Tevake* has had a go at providing us with day and night. Or a maintenance cycle.'

'Suppose', Victoria said, 'it has something to do with our distance from the sun ... or wherever we are.' She gave a short laugh, and explained, 'I had a high school boyfriend whose favourite movie was *Silent Running*.'

'Ah,' said Marian, unexpectedly, 'the one about the gardener and the last trees. Interesting film, albeit of somewhat muddled morality.' She raised a snowy eyebrow at their reactions. 'One must have something to offer in conversation with grand-nieces and nephews besides intrusive queries about the progress of their education ... But one would think shipbuilders so advanced would have devised a battery.'

'And what is your feeling, Dr Morgan?' said Lowell, having seen Morgan before any of the others. Probably, Morgan thought ruefully, through the claystone itself. 'Could this be a normal occurrence?'

Morgan debated a moment over how honest to be. To a large part he trusted these people's rationality and, even more, their common sense. He said, 'If I saw this kind of sudden breakdown in one of my experiments I'd be very worried. The trouble with any complex system – like a closed environment life support – is that the tight coupling of the various parameters and all feedback loops means that if one parameter changes abruptly it tends to set up oscillations in others. The fact that environmental parameters have been so stable until now suggests fine control – but whether that control is also robust and tolerant of fluctuations is another question.' He drew a deep breath, 'So no, I don't think it's normal. I do think it could be very serious.'

They felt the changing air as they walked the final length of the passageway, a deepening chill, an aridity, the slight spice taste of dust. In the cave mouth Morgan halted, involuntarily. Sophie's description had ill-prepared him for this; indeed, she herself looked taken aback. The light was dimmer, as though shining through ash. The matting was patched with circular grey-black wells, eaten down to the bare claystone. The green itself had an dull, ashy overlook to it. The waterfalls were reduced to fraying threads which left dark stains behind them. Marian swiped a finger on a ledge beside her, and brought it up black. She rubbed more briskly, with the deft wrist motion they had all developed with experience. The claystone remained inert, though her finger blackened.

Sophie said, 'This is much worse than it was, even yesterday.'

'Where are all the people?'

'Perhaps over there,' Marian said, tilting her chin in the direction of the curved rise to their right. 'There's quite an area concealed from view.' And resolutely, she set off for it, with Sophie following and Morgan lagging behind, reluctant to revisit the scene of his captivity.

Before they reached the base of the rise, a woman came briskly over it to meet them. She wore a brown leather jacket, leather gloves, and a head scarf wound round her head and pulled across her face. She flipped it back as she set herself in their path, and regarded them with no particular welcome. Fatigue and grey dust emphasised the lines around eyes and mouth.

'Astarte, you've probably seen Stan Morgan next door, but maybe not been introduced,' Sophie said. 'He worked on environment systems at NASA. Morgan, this is Astarte, formerly law enforcement, and one of Hannah and Dove's original recruits.'

Mention of Hannah merely turned her narrow, forbidding face grimmer. 'I can't tell you much more than your eyes can,' she said, huskily. Coughed. 'It started three to four days ago, maybe further back, if anyone had been paying attention, but we first noticed it then.'

'I did see something when I was with you,' Marian said. 'But I thought it was the residue of a fire, or possibly the scorch-marks of a gun discharge. And that night seemed cold, but I remember being cold in France, with poor food. And fear.'

Astarte's eyes glanced off hers. 'We're not taking any of them back,' she said. Looked at Morgan. 'You can tell your lot that. Call it fear of reprisals if you like.'

Marian said, 'As we promised you yesterday, this isn't a reprisal. We're not capable of doing this.'

'And we wouldn't,' Morgan said.

'So,' Astarte said, turning to him, 'What do you think is happening?'

'May I take a look around?'

She waved a gloved hand.

Leaving them, he walked the few paces necessary to reach the nearest decayed area, and set his satchel down on the intact matting. As he knelt, he felt the dust in his nose and throat, an unpleasant, almost suffocating sensation. He found a handkerchief, wet it, and fumbled to tie it around mouth and nose. Sophie took the corners from his hands and did so, murmuring, 'We should have brought extra masks; I wasn't thinking.'

Marian said behind him, 'It's getting quite unpleasant here. Have you anywhere else to go?'

The area looked like the one he had seen on the morning of his rescue, but larger and deeper. With a spatula Morgan sampled the dust, scooping it into vials to examine back at the lab, and on to a slide on the stage of the field microscope. It looked very much like crumbled matting or claystone, fine granular material with a suggestion of faceting. Sophie rejoined him a moment later, leaving Marian with Astarte, and he passed the microscope up to her. She sighed and said, 'I looked yesterday. I couldn't see anything like an infectious agent. But then a programming virus wouldn't show under a microscope.'

'You mean this could *spread*?' he said in dismay.

Her mouth twitched. 'I'm a pathologist. I'm used to thinking about things being catching.' All trace of humour left her. 'Particularly since when I look at all these perfectly circular patches I think immediately of viral plaques. A single infected cell or unit, spreading its infection outwards.' She looked around her and pointed. 'Since the plaques are largest and most dense over in that area, I might rashly surmise that is where the quote unquote infection originated. And since there has been a fairly even falling off in density, I might say that it is some kind of airborne spread, rather than foot borne, or I would expect that the spread would be further along areas of traffic.'

Morgan knelt, looking up at her. It was too much effort to rise. The sodden point of his handkerchief stuck to his throat and he felt a trickle of water free itself and trickle downwards. He said, 'Did you look at the edges?'

She nodded, took a mask and gloves from her pocket and put both on before kneeling beside him. 'We don't have high enough resolution to get details of the microstructure, so I can't say for sure I wasn't seeing anything of significance.' As she spoke she was tweezering shredding matting on to a fresh slide for him. Obligingly, he bent his head to study it. She said, 'As far as I can tell, there's an order to the breakdown – you'll notice that you see strands of all different lengths, but not of different thickness. So it looks like the breakdown, or digestion, or whatever it is, happens along the long axis only, rather than from the outside in.'

He handed back the microscope and unstrapped his notebook from its pocket in the satchel, flipping through until he found the drawings he had done of matting disintegrating under the microscope. He passed it to her in silence. Speaking seemed like too much of an effort.

'Interesting,' she said. 'You've drawn them different thicknesses.'

'I drew what I saw.'

She frowned. 'So, isolated fibres of matting appear to break down from the surface in all dimensions. But this breakdown appears to be happening in one dimension only.' Her voice, Morgan thought, sounded odd. Or maybe it was listening that was an effort. 'I wonder if it's proceeding from tip to base or base to tip. And if it's proceeding from base to tip . . . what happens when the base erodes away and the signals are interrupted if as you hypothesise it needs constant input to maintain its integrity . . . Stan? What is it? Is it your hand?'

He said, 'Not pain – a heaviness.' She stared at him a moment. 'Stan, come on, get up. On your feet,' and hauled him up to standing and steadied him, peering into his eyes. 'Stan, you ever gone caving? Been exposed to bad air?'

'No. Why –' and then his eyes widened. If the matting and the little trees were part of the oxygen exchange system, aided by the pores through the claystone, and if the one was dying off and the pores were plugged . . .

She pulled him towards Marian and Astarte, who had been joined by Lillian, and interrupted all three without ceremony, 'Have you been having trouble concentrating? Feeling lethargic? Nauseous? Had difficulty waking people up?'

'Yes,' said Astarte, warily, and Lillian, 'What are you getting at?'

'The gas exchange systems are breaking down. It's worse down low, which suggests a buildup of dense gases, carbon dioxide, maybe. The matting itself could be giving off toxic gas as it degenerates. You're going to have to evacuate.'

Astarte's lips thinned. Lillian said, 'No.'

Astarte put a hand on her partner's shoulder and turned them both, walking Lillian off for a low, intense argument.

Marian said, 'The people who're still here are in a hollow on the other side of that hillock. The deterioration's not as bad there, but it is low lying relative to much of the cave.'

'We'll have to get them out of here. Preferably to somewhere nearby so if there is some kind of infectious agent we will minimise the spread.' Sophie shook her head. 'My God, what awful timing, when there is already bad blood between our communities.'

Morgan turned back towards the instrument case, with a vague and miserable sense of urgency. They *had* to know what was happening. Sophie caught his arm. She gave him a swift inspection with a diagnostic eye. 'Stan, you'd better get a message back to Kastély. For safety's sake someone should know we're in here. Marian and I will try to evacuate everyone. We won't be taking more samples without gas masks.' She frowned slightly, abstracted. 'You'd better walk back on one side of the corridor. Let's say the right. Don't touch the walls or anything else. When you get back to Kastély don't go in. Send someone for Theresa. A crops diseases specialist is the best person I can think of for something like this. Tell her what's happened here and that we are concerned about a transmissible agent. Let her decide on procedures and ask her whether we ought to seal this area off completely. We *cannot* let this spread.'

Morgan said, 'I – walked through one of these' – he gestured at the grey circle – 'the beginning of one of these – just after we were rescued.'

They looked at each other a moment, then she nodded. 'You're right. If there were lesions three days ago then everyone who was in here then could have tracked back an infectious agent. However, we can still do something to decrease the amount of inoculum, so take the precautions anyway.'

Infectious, he thought, as, still shivering slightly, he picked his way towards the door, trying not to stir any more dust than he must. 'Stan,' Sophie called after him. 'Find out who is out on long patrol. We'll need to talk to them when they get back in.' He waved; she waved back and he went on, feeling his own filthy footprints like some malignant tracker at his heels.

50 Sophie

'My conscience troubles me,' Marian said.

Sophie sighed and glanced back over her shoulder. She could see the bright green of the little, tree-lined cavern at their backs, fancifully known as Fangorn. 'It was the best we could do – and we did tell them as much as we knew.' Despite herself she pictured the feathery trees blackened and crumbling, the mats of matting grey-pitted, the walls seeping and dark, and knew that Marian envisioned the same. 'We did give them the choice.'

'With that tribe of sickly people at our backs?'

'They would not come with us. And despite being so near to this, that cave seems to have quite a healthy atmosphere.'

'Yes. That was a most astute question you thought to ask, about growth in the trees.'

Sophie hardly heard the compliment. 'I wish we didn't have to go this way,' she said as the dull grey-green iris of Erehwon opened before them.

'The alternate route would take us through four caverns, risking spread to one or all.'

'Except that the people who fled may already have spread this.'

On the threshold of the dying cavern they exchanged identical grim looks. There was nothing else to say. The light seemed even poorer than when they had left, escorting Lillith and Astarte and their band of refugees. Sophie said, 'We'll go up and along the ridge. Whatever was affecting us seems to be more concentrated down low.'

Marian nodded and, as they started upward, took a grip of Sophie's arm, as though in need of support. Sophie looked at her, checking, and Marian leaned forward and said softly, 'There may still be one or two in the upper caves. Don't look up too readily.'

Sophie swallowed, dry mouthed. The elderly ex-spy led them onwards, head high, poised and dignified for all that her hair was dusty and her hands grubby. They did not speak as they walked along the ridge. The surroundings would have been oppressive enough, without the sense of an unseen watcher. Her first words as they left the cave were, 'Was there?'

'Mm, oh yes, almost certainly,' said Marian. 'But not trigger happy, fortunately for us. In all likelihood he – or she – will now scuttle down the wall and track down his fellows, who will enlighten him as to what has happened. It is possible that some of them will try to outlast the breakdown in the upper caves. Foolish but understandable. But we shall have to make sure they are warned if a decision is made to seal this area.' She sounded quite cheerful, so much so that Sophie looked at her and thought: I'm hooked up with an octogenarian adrenalin junkie. Except that Marian seemed less octogenarian by the day. Sophie could not say that her appearance was changed; she still had the same antique skin stretched over stately bones, the same gnarled, scarred hands, but there was no doubt that she was seeing through both eyes, and that her senses and wits were working as well as Sophie's own. Better, even. If Sophie had been alone she would never have suspected the cavern was still occupied.

The sure, bright light of the tunnels was welcome. They walked, single file on the left, Marian leading.

'Whether or not the gases affect us or any of the neighbouring caves,' Morgan was saying, as they came into earshot of the entrance to Kastély, 'will depend upon the reserve capacity of our own recycling system. If that can absorb it, there should be no difficulty. If it cannot . . .' His relief at the sight of them was transparent. Sophie and Marian exchanged a sigh when they saw the congregation around Morgan – a congregation which now consisted of most of the scientific, medical and administrative staff, several of whom made a move towards the women. Theresa, the agricultural epidemiologist, said sharply, '*Please* don't go into that corridor. Yes, I do mean you! Unless you want to go through decontamination yourselves!' Morgan was sitting on a ledge. Theresa came forward, keeping to the left of the corridor. 'Sophie, Marian, I'm afraid I'm going to have to ask you to wash and change all your clothing.'

Sophie smiled ruefully, 'Somehow I knew you were going to say that.' Covertly, she looked around for one of the A-team. She needed to go back into Erehwon to obtain proper samples. For which she needed a gas mask, and not an argument.

'We've improvised a basin lined with plastic to store the dirty water, but I can't promise there's absolutely no risk of the water getting out to contaminate the environment, and the more often we have to do this, of course, the greater the risk.' The tone of that last was pointed, and Sophie inferred a very recent argument about quarantine.

Dominic said, 'Sophie, Marian, can you add anything to what Morgan's told us?'

Morgan supplied, 'I've given them a description of what we found and advised them that you think it could be contagious, but I wasn't able to support your argument,' he finished apologetically.

'There's no evidence, as yet,' Sophie said, with crisp authority. 'But I would strongly recommend that we behave as though it is until we know better, whatever the inconvenience.'

Several heads nodded agreement.

'You got the people out, though,' Victoria said.

'Where are they now?' 'Shouldn't they be quarantined?' 'Have you warned people in the neighbouring cells?' 'What about how cold it's getting in here?' Dominic waved his hands for silence. 'The ladies', he said, a little sententiously, 'need to shower and change if they are to join us. And we need to discuss what to do about this latest development, and who needs to be informed. In an *orderly* fashion, without increasing the risk of spreading panic.'

'But where *are* they?' Chandler insisted. 'Surely someone should be putting them through decontamination before they go into another area.'

'They have gone to Fangorn, and have moved into a smaller cave off the main one. That was the best we could do on short notice since several of them were suffering the effects of the bad air –'

'Bad air,' someone muttered. 'That's highly scientific.'

'– and needed to be evacuated immediately. The community leaders in Fangorn have been advised of the risk, but they were willing to accept it in face of need. But they are considering whether or not to seal the tunnel between themselves and Erehwon entirely –'

'We can't have people cutting themselves off! There are public rights of way.'

Marian gave him a look of frank disbelief. 'Young man' – well, Chandler was thirty years plus her junior – 'have you heeded anything of this discussion?'

Behind them, Piett and Raho trotted into view, looking hale, cheerful and above all clean. While Raho headed for Morgan, Piett waited to hear out Sophie's request. He said, 'I'll need to ask the sergeant.' Looked her up and down, impersonally. 'I suppose you're right to leave off changing, but the sergeant thought we should fetch you to see this too.'

'See what?'

'I'd better let the Prof tell you once he's seen it.'

51 Morgan

Down in the spire A.J. Lowell's questions were brief and pragmatic, his sharp military focus as restful as it was unsettling. There was no need to use up air convincing him of the gravity of such a breakdown. He delegated Hughes and Raho to meet and accompany Sophie, guard, assist, and ensure that she got all the samples she needed. He ordered Lecce and Bhakta to stand by, and he himself escorted Morgan up the winding spiral ramp.

Morgan knew what it was he would see. He had already glanced upwards, looking for green, or flame, and found only grey. Nevertheless, he was not entirely prepared for the impact of the changed image. The fire had burned out, and left devastation. A post-holocaust scene. Black needle trunks, charred tree skeletons, some jabbing at a livid sky, some canted against each other, some fallen and half buried in waves of ash. As the flames had been caught and suspended in their rising, so the trees were suspended in their falling, the ash in its swirling and settling, the earth in its cooling.

It was the same forest as had flourished green a handful of days ago. The same forest as had blazed behind Hathaway's dark head. The charred corpses of the same trees in the same configurations. The same alignments, the same contour to the earth. It was the forest that Stephen Cooper had described from his dream on the second last night of his life.

'So, Prof,' Lowell said. 'What do you make of it?'

Morgan swallowed, remembering dreams of smoke and ashes. He said, slowly, 'I don't know. Have you measured – Stephen's shroud?'

'No change there. Same dimensions, same temperature as yesterday.'

Morgan said nothing.

'What I'm wondering,' Lowell said, still looking at the landscape, 'is whether this could be connected with what you say is happening upstairs. Whether Cooper is somehow still alive and thinking under that shroud, or whether his brain has been let's say downloaded into *Tevake*, somehow his hostility is still influencing what *Tevake* does.' He folded his arms, the light silvery on his features. 'It's hard to believe that a man could remain sane under those conditions. Especially a sewer-rat like Cooper.' His thin lips quirked. 'I'm not sure I could, and I think I'm pretty sane. And what about the rest of them planted in the graveyard upstairs? Terrorists, snipers, guerrillas, enemy disinformation, and friendly fire, those I can handle. But aliens we can't see, technology we don't understand and hostiles who could be more threat after they're dead . . .' He shook his head, an expression of deep unease on his face, which Morgan found quite frightening, like the splitting of a foundation rock. Then the expression was gone; the assured soldier was back. 'So what do you think, Prof? What are the odds that this is just sort of happening? And what're the odds we could stop it by digging Cooper and the rest of 'em up, wrapping them in plastic and just letting them rot?'

Morgan's thoughts moved slowly, cringing and lame. 'They probably wouldn't,' he said. 'Given what Sophie has observed about our seemingly being sterilised.'

'Mind your mouth,' Lowell advised affably. 'But I get you – all our bugs have gone away. Been eaten by *Tevake*'s bugs, if I understand right. So just uprooting them wouldn't do it?'

Morgan dropped his hand. 'We don't know if it has anything to do with Stephen, or anyone else,' he said. 'We do know that this environment is not entirely benign and that *Tevake*, or the aliens, or whoever is running this show, have probably misjudged in the past – witness the deaths from the 'flu. We also know that this environment is set up to behave in a particular way, to elicit a particular response or a particular form of learning –'

'According to your theory.'

'It's consistent with the evidence we have so far. And maybe this,' he looked up, and found the scene as ominous as before, 'maybe this was *Tevake* using the metaphors that it had from Stephen's mind to communicate with us, trying to warn us –'

'Warn us about what?' A.J. said, sounding edgy.

'I don't know,' Morgan said. 'And I'm afraid what's happening in Erehwon may already be happening in Kastély.' Lowell's pale eyes came to bear. 'The temperature's dropped two degrees and the light came up eight minutes late today.'

'Prof,' A.J. said grimly, tapping fingertips to the image, 'if you're right about this being a warning, you better get us some answers, and you better get them fast.'

Lights down was seventeen minutes early, anticipating even the sunset drum which Arpád had suggested be brought forward a few minutes to compensate. As it was people raised their voices in complaint at this seeming dereliction of duty and went to their beds grumbling and unaware.

But lights up was twenty-two minutes delayed, and shortly after lights up all complacency ended with the report of the first signs of breakdown in Kastély, circles of crumbling matting in an uninhabited area between the two main exits on the far side of the cavern from the Citadel.

Morgan found Hathaway in her cubicle, dozing, curled up on her side, battered hat over her face. Yesterday she had had several severe and worrisome pains and had been put on bedrest. He went down on one knee, and lifted her hat from a flushed, scowling face; she stirred and muttered, 'Get lost.'

'Hath, it's me.'

Her eyes opened, wide and shiny. She heaved herself up into his arms and clung. Taken unprepared, he nearly overbalanced from the heft of her, and from trying not to jar his splinted hand. 'I am so *bored*,' she proclaimed, her breath warm on his ear. Sheer relief made him laugh. She pulled back, staring at his face. 'I am serious. I am going *nuts*. I haven't had a bad pain since last night and Emilie still wouldn't let me get up this morning.' She scrambled on to her knees. 'What's going *on* out there? I've been hearing the weirdest stuff through the walls. Like there's parts of *Tevake* dying off and Stephen's turning into a sort of vampire – don't look at me like that! I *heard* it that way.'

'Hath,' Morgan said, 'this is serious.'

She assumed a grave expression. 'OK, serious,' she intoned. She patted the shelf beside her. 'Siddown and tell all.'

He sat down, looked at her, wondering if he should be doing this at all.

'Hath,' he said, at last, 'I need your help.' His gaze naturally dropped to his hands on his lap, and sheered away from the sight of the splinted and bandaged left. He stared at the matting. 'I am very much afraid,' he said, 'that we may be facing a major breakdown of our environmental system. I'm . . . unable to come up with any useful ideas why.'

'Hey, Uncle Stan, give yourself a break. You've got a busted hand, you can't sleep worth beans and you're doped to the eyeballs on painkillers. You're not the only genius aboard; they'll figure it out. Sophie's coming along nicely – she sounds almost as crazy as you do at times.' She grinned at him cheekily.

'Hath,' he said, 'I think we might have blown it. The human race, I mean. I think . . . *Tevake* tried to warn us through the images it took from Stephen. And we didn't take the warning.' He looked away from the disbelief on her face. He should not be doing this. He had come to ask for her help. Not to tell her that in his eyes they were already doomed. He heard her open her mouth, close it; he heard her lick her lips. She said at last, a little huskily, 'Uncle Stan, this is just not you. C'mon, look at me.'

He did. She was frowning, hard, at him. 'I dunno what to say,' she admitted. 'I mean, I've known people who thought humans were just garbage and the sooner the bomb dropped or AIDS wiped us all out the better. But you're not one.' He looked away. She hesitated, said less certainly, 'Seth was just one rotten apple, Uncle Stan, just one really lousy rotten apple. You can't give up on the whole human race just because of him. Listen,' she continued valiantly, to his unresponsive profile, 'the aliens gave us an invitation, right, to come. Just watching the news for a few days would have let them know what kind of people we were. But still they took us along. They've treated us pretty good. They probably saved my life. They didn't kill those army guys who went messing around in the control room. They didn't kill you guys when you shot Stephen. There's a whole *ship* full of people,' she flung out her hand, 'who had nothing to do with our dumb little war. Are they going to get killed off because *we* fought? I mean, *Jeez*, Uncle Stan, you guys say teenagers are self-centred!'

Despite himself, he smiled. She hooked both strong arms around him and snuggled up against his back, a forceful and not at all feminine movement when she executed it. 'OK, so suppose *Tevake* is doing this deliberately to get us to learn something. Maybe it's not to fight. Maybe it's something else. If there's one sure way to get our attention, it's scaring us into thinking we're all going to die. Maybe they are saying hey, Earthlings, get a life.'

He laughed. 'Hath, I am so glad –' He could not finish. So glad you came. So glad I capitulated. So glad he did not hurt you. He gripped his splinted hand in the other. 'I need you to do several things,' he said. 'I need your ideas. I'm terrified of missing something I should see. Whoever is in charge has already demonstrated that they're willing to let us take casualties. We may *have* to solve the problem to keep this part of *Tevake* viable. It might *be* a warning against our aggression – it does seem to have originated in Erehwon – or it might be a deliberate strategy to break down our organisation here, displace us and force us to reintegrate elsewhere. But if there's an answer, we're not going to get long to find it.'

She pushed herself off him and folded her arms. 'That sounds way more like you. What else?'

'I need you to try and pick up where Stephen left off in trying to communicate with *Tevake* directly.'

'You mean let it into my *mind*?' she said, revulsion, uncertainty and distaste chasing each other across her face. 'I thought the army guys were kind of paranoid about me doing that. And what's going on with Stephen, anyway? Is he turning into some kind of Undead or what?'

He recognised a determined attempt to change the subject. 'We don't understand what's happening with Stephen,' he said. 'The day before the troubles started Sophie opened up his shroud a little way, enough to see that he wasn't decaying and there was a suggestion that . . . he might be being rebuilt. It's far-fetched; we can hardly imagine how he could be reanimated after being dead for so long; but Sophie decided not to risk endangering the process so we've left him alone since.'

'Wow,' said Hath. 'Is that going to happen to Hannah and the others, too?'

'We don't know. Certainly we're keeping an eye on their shrouds.'

She gave him a troubled look. 'You know, Uncle Stan, I ought to be glad, but I feel kind of creepy. We are definitely not in Kansas any more.' Morgan breathed a laugh, which evaporated as she said, 'You guys are going to be careful? I mean, it wouldn't be all that great if someone decided to put a stake through his heart.'

'Believe me, we have thought of that,' he said. 'There is a guard on his shroud, day in, day out.'

Her face clouded; his vagueness had not deceived her as to who. 'And what if they just up and shoot him again?'

'Hath,' Morgan said, 'we are doing our best to make sure that whatever happens with Stephen this time it does not take anyone by surprise. One or other of the medical staff is on call at all times, and they check for signs of life at least twice daily. They've worked out how much risk they're prepared to take to preserve him, but they're not going to reject a miracle out of hand. No matter whose miracle it is.'

Some of the thunder left her expression. 'OK. I guess I believe you. But whoever has been talking ought to be shut up.'

'I know. So what I've told you –'

'Yeah,' she said. 'Cross my heart and hope to die.' He found nothing to amuse him in the playground formula. She looked at him from under her lashes. 'I'd really like to see these dead zones. I don't suppose you could get Emilie to let me up, do you?'

The area of blight had been cordoned off with stakes and flags, and was guarded. 'Jeez-us,' was Hathaway's comment, 'is that ever ug-lee.' She squatted, with a grunt. 'It looks like some superindustrial waste has gotten to it. Except it should be glowing.' She made pulsing glow motions with her hands, glanced up, looking for appreciation, found none. 'So what's happening when you shove it under a microscope?' she said, and reached for the ragged edge with her bare hand.

'Hath!' She stopped. 'Hath,' he said, '*please* don't touch it. Aside from the risk of your transferring it elsewhere, we don't know whether that breakdown could affect any assemblers which have colonised us.'

'Say again?'

Having her so near those poisoned wells made him nervous. He said, 'Come out of there, Hath. We're still not sure these aren't giving off any toxic gases, and I for one wouldn't mind having a sit down.'

She stood up, but spent several seconds longer staring down at the ruin around her feet, with such intense concentration on her face as made him hesitate to assume she was simply, childishly, asserting her independence. Then she picked her way back to him, complaining, 'It is *such* a pain trying to see where I'm putting my feet. I feel such a *blimp.*'

He smiled, feeling stiff muscles ease into the expression. 'You are fecund and radiant.'

She blinked at him. 'Jeez, there must be some funny gas coming off those things. Let's get you away from here.' She took his arm and steered him to where an outcropping of dry claystone offered a place to sit. 'OK, what were you saying about assembly? Are we going to turn into religious revivalists or prep-school teenies?'

'Hath,' he said. She gave him her best bland stare. He said, 'This is a hypothesis . . .' And he laid it out. Most of it she had heard before, in parts – his observations of the common origin and properties of all *Tevake's* 'fixtures and fittings'; the improvement in health in the crew as a whole, including Marian's recovery of much of her vision, and the fact that he had not suffered a migraine since the day of their arrival; the absence of any bacteria on their skin, mouths or faeces – Emilie Linn's experiments had failed to yield any growth from swabs or samples – and Sophie hypothesised that the bacteria had been displaced by the assemblers.

'That's *gross*,' she said, as soon as she caught the gist, and to the cavern at large, 'Gimmie my bugs back!'

Morgan laid his head in his sound hand. After a moment, he felt her lean against him. 'Uncle Stan, what about my baby?'

He straightened up promptly. 'We all appear to be in good health. We may be in better than good health. I see no reason whatsoever for your baby *not* to see a similar benefit.'

'Maybe,' she said, 'they only know how bodies work because they took some apart. Maybe they won't know how babies work until', she swallowed, and spread her hands over her abdomen, 'they take one apart.'

Appalled – not so much at the possibility, which had occurred to Sophie and himself already, but that she had thought of it – he turned to her and took her hands in his. The slow heave of the baby's movement bumped against his knuckle. He said, 'Hath, the people who died died because of some incompatibility between themselves and *Tevake*, or possibly because of a mistake, some error made by the aliens in what we could tolerate. I don't believe that they died out of malice. If we have been seeded with assemblers, *Tevake* knows what's going on in us, with us. I have no doubt that they are observing your baby's growth. But you have also to remember that the aliens intervened when you might have died from the 'flu.'

'Then why didn't they "intervene" for that woman Fleur, and all the other people?'

'I don't know,' Morgan said; it was the only truthful thing he could say. 'But I'm glad they did – intervene. Losing you would have taken all the joy out of this adventure.' He felt the shadow cross his face, remembering.

She burped loudly. 'If they're into fixing things, they ought to fix my stomach.'

Her tough-girl guise was back in place. She fixed him with a narrowed eye. 'You're serious about maybe being able to communicate with them. You really believe what Stephen wrote?'

'Sensory input and consciousness have electrophysiological and biochemical substrates. If they have the ability to alter those substrates then, yes, they should be able to create input for us, or alter our consciousness. That does predicate a truly astonishing appreciation of the mapping of consciousness to brain structure.'

'Well, if they've been watching us think for weeks, particularly if they've been watching us work those puzzle things, you'd think they'd'a worked some of it out, if they're so advanced.'

'Hath,' he said, 'I never made a connection between the guided experience and the direct communication – but yes, it fits.'

'I gotta say it creeps me out, though,' she said, bluntly. 'Little things in your head rewiring your brain so you think what they want you to think.' She stood up, looking down at him. 'I've already gotten that on Earth from people. I'm not real keen on getting it here.'

'Hath, if you're right and *Tevake* was getting information on how we code experience into memory, then you are one of the best candidates around because your early experience was so exclusive and so rich.' She looked obdurate; he knew he was floundering, and almost pleading – 'Hath, we could all die.'

She got to her feet, looking sullen and unhappy. 'Sorry, Uncle Stan. But letting these things inside my brain gives me the creeps.'

52   Hathaway

Uncle Stan, I do *not* want to do this. I do not want to do this at all.

This letter's not really for him. It's still for you. It's not a happy letter. We're in big trouble up here. I'm writing this all wrapped up in my sleeping bag because it's so cold. Not *freezing* cold yet but cold and the light's gone this sort of greyish white and there are those big ugly pits of rot all over Kastély. Erehwon is totally dead. It's dark all the time and they think they're going to have to close it up because of the unbreathable atmosphere. Fangorn – which is the cave my cave is above – is dying. All the little trees are crumbling away. I hear my cave's still OK but I don't know for how long. Uncle Stan says the control room is still OK. Nobody's travelling far now because people in the caverns that haven't been infected don't want anyone coming in from the others. Some people think it's infectious. Others think the aliens are angry with the people from caverns which are affected and don't want to have anything to do with them. A.J. has guards on all our entrances. Afraid that some of the people who think it's our fault for making war might come and try and get rid of us to appease the aliens. Everything's getting so crazy and dark and sad.

And Uncle Stan's gotten it into his head that I could be our only hope. He looks like ten miles of bad road with his broken finger hurting and what happened to him in the cave with Seth. Which was my fault. They knew about him and captured him and got him to tell them everything all because of me. I owe him big time. But I just don't know if I can do this. I've told Uncle Stan that the idea of *Tevake* getting into my head creeps me out totally. And it does. But in another way it's exciting – being able to do what Stephen did with the picture wall. Finding out whether *Tevake*'s really alive. Maybe getting to meet the owls at last. I think he's right that somebody's got to try it. But I just don't want to be the somebody. Uncle Stan said to me not long ago about the years after Dad died and before Alan came along that those were *hard years*. I guess, while everyone was telling me how *hard* it had been and how I shouldn't have had to do it and how thankful I ought to be that it was over, that I just couldn't hear them. It was like they were trying take away my only reward for getting through them, like there was something perverted in me being proud of just having *survived*. But now I've been here for a while I can tell you that I know they were *horrible* years. They were years when I'd lie awake all night trying to think how we were going to pay the rent in a week and pay for a doctor for Joy's ear infection and look after her properly without you losing your job for being off work too often or me getting investigated for being off school again. They were the years when we were flunking grades more often than we were passing and the boys were turning into gang members and Joy was sick all the time and you were exhausted all the time and I was just – don't know what I was. I guess I was like going along a narrow concrete tunnel all the time. Just doing the next thing and the next and hanging in. Oh we had fun. We *did* have fun. But the truth is I didn't really know until I came here was how horrible it was knowing that a lot of the time I was the only person holding it all together. I know you did as much holding together as I did, Mom, and I'm sure that it's no easier doing it as an adult than doing it as a kid. I guess that was why I fought so hard about the baby being made such a heap big deal with parenting classes and people telling me I had to take this *seriously* and be *responsible*. I didn't want to *be* responsible. I mean I didn't want to go out partying and shopping and hanging out the way the kids at Laguna Beach seem to do – I mean, that's irresponsible – but I didn't want my baby to be made into this terrible burden. I just wanted to be able to love her and I knew how much I could – oh guys this is going to hurt you and I'm sorry – but I knew how much I could hate people for depending upon me all the time all the time all the time. I didn't want to hate my baby before she was even born.

So that's why I left. I didn't want to be responsible any more. But I didn't want to give up my pride either. I wanted to have my baby my way, just trying to love her and figure things out as I went along. I thought the aliens would let me do that. That's the truth, I guess. And that's why I don't want to go into *Tevake*. That's why I don't want to take on trying to save us all.

53   Sophie

'There *must* be a pattern,' Morgan said, leaning forward to jerk one sheet of the map into alignment with the others, thereby displacing half a dozen of the marker coins from their positions. He nudged a peseta with a gloved hand. 'There must be.'

The map had been compiled by Sergeant Lowell from sketches and notes made by multiple surveyors and patrols. It covered an estimated fifth of *Tevake*, a hundred or so caverns, each one of which had received a number, Kastély, of course, being 1. The Citadel itself was at grid reference 00,00, but the sergeant himself admitted the shortcomings of the grid, given they had no means of checking the distances through the walls – yet. Nevertheless, it was a minor masterwork, and the sergeant had sworn unspeakable vengeance on anyone who defaced it.

The story it told was grim. Of the hundred or so caverns represented on the tiling of sixteen sheets, fully half had been showing signs of degeneration at last report – before all corridors were closed off and their survey parties driven back, sometimes at gunpoint. The degeneration ranged from a subtle decrease in temperature and shortening of the period of light to the frost-rimed wasteland of Erehwon. Here they were in mid stage, the air still breathable, but only half the cavern still produced gingerbread and drinkable water, and the temperature was a mere ten degrees celsius, compared to the balmy twenty-six of only four days before.

Morgan rubbed his eyes. Like hers, they would be sandpapered with sleeplessness and dust. He, Sophie, Marian and the map were but the residue of a desperate inquiry/strategy session involving the governing committee and all the scientists that had started at first light – by this, the fourth day, fifty minutes delayed – and lasted until red interval without reaching either consensus about the problem or resolution about action. Arpád had been the tranquil eye of the storm, organising stockpiling of gingerbread, water and chemicals, dictating equitable distribution of winter clothing and bedding, mediating disputes, marshalling survey and scientific teams and defusing all accusations and counter accusations. For him, as someone said, disaster was as good as Prozac. The rest of them looked like Morgan – grubby, exhausted, despairing.

Sophie leaned over and began to knead the rigid muscles at the base of his neck. He shrugged, seemingly embarrassed. A long time cat owner, she knew true reluctance to be touched would be expressed with tooth, claw and stiff-tailed departure; so she kept working and felt him lean into her hands, saying again, 'There should be a pattern.' He pitched his notebook on to the map, scattering more of their coin-counters. 'It doesn't look like direct spread, because it's not contiguous. I've asked about patterns of migration and travel and it isn't going between caverns that have exchange or social relationships. It doesn't depend upon numbers. It doesn't depend upon racial mix, gender balance, number of children or animals – did you know one family brought three pigs and a goat with them?' he said, quizzically, over his shoulder. 'And I heard Sergeant Metzner say that over where they were there was part of an African tribe with a whole herd of cattle.

'As far as we can tell the first signs were here and here and here –' He tapped three coins, set well apart. 'So since there were three caverns involved that undermines the suggestion that the breakdown is some kind of divine retribution for our sinful strife.'

'Stan,' Marian said, 'you've been a proponent from the first of the view that *Tevake* is communicating with us in every modality possible. Why do you reject the view that this is not also a communication?'

'Because it's so damn – uncontrolled,' he said.

'We already know,' the old chemist said gently, 'that *Tevake* is prepared to permit some of us to die.'

There was a brief silence, nobody wanting to mention the mounds in the graveyard. Under the field microscope the fine threads of their shrouds were more linear, less interlinked. There was no smell of decay – probably there never would be, if terrestrial bacteria had been effectively exterminated – but the idea of the shrouds breaking down, of the harrowed and unchanging bodies of the dead being revealed was a deeply disturbing one. Down in the spire Stephen Cooper's shroud was as dense as ever and Sophie's last palpation had no longer detected the wound.

'I never thought I'd say this,' Morgan said, trying for whimsey and failing, 'but I'm ready to pull the cord and ask to be let off at the next stop.'

'Come on,' Sophie said, sliding off her stalagmite. 'I can't make any sense of other people's notes. Let's go up and have a look at what's on our doorstep.'

Going up involved climbing, picking their way up the reshaped mounds of claystone to the clock-tower, which careful work had doubled in height to a modest twenty feet. Having groped their way up the dusty handholds and through the crawl way on to the platform, they could survey the entire cavern. There was barely enough room for both of them, winter-clad as they were, standing half overlapping with her right shoulder resting against his mid chest. 'I've heard some people saying they want to call it Tintagel.' He looked blankly at her. 'After the castle where King Arthur was born, supposedly. It's a ruin, on the Cornish coast.'

Morgan's lips twitched. 'I was a hard science nerd, Soph. Physics, maths and computing, and a little chemistry to express my softer side.'

The near half of the cavern, where they had been raising living spaces out of the claystone floor, was still relatively unaffected. The crookedly gridded array of walls of various heights, sleeping benches, and storage bays looked much the same as it had the day before. Which in itself was an unsettling sign, for the sculptors said that the claystone had become noticeably less responsive. A dozen or so people were still working on the walls, bulky in winter coats or layered sweaters. More were sculpting and lining a pantry, where they would accumulate gingerbread in case the remaining stores died off. They could see Arpád, sheepskin jacket slung over sling, sitting on a low wall and directing operations. The laboratory's tin and bottle collection had already been surrendered to store fresh water, and Sophie could just see the water stand on the far side of the huddle of people around the pantry, including its three sentries. Scouts and three members of the special forces team patrolled the entryways and boundaries, including the one between living and deadland. The remainder of the special forces group were down in the spire, guarding their lately disputed territory.

Ribbon-decorated staves, like witch doctors' totems, marked where viable cavern ended. Initially they had marked the boundary according to microscopic change, thinking that restricting traffic across the affected areas would slow the rate of spread. But now the matting throughout the cavern was showing the thinning and loss of branching that presaged breakdown, and they no longer bothered with the surveys along the boundary. All that the totems now marked was the inward march of the grey blight. One of them, Sophie noticed, was leaning at a drunken angle, the matting beneath it noticeably darker.

'Sophie,' Morgan whispered. 'I'm afraid.'

She turned in the confined space, and put her arms around him. He held her back. 'There's something I need to see,' he said. 'And I can't see it.'

She stroked his rough, dusty hair. 'You will,' she said. 'You will.'

'And if I can't. We'll all die. You. Marian. Hath and her baby . . . It's so cold.'

'You're not solely responsible,' she chided him. 'We're all in this together.' She held him until he eased back saying, 'This is all very pleasant but we do have work to do . . .'

'So we do,' she said, turning to smooth out the hanging red pennant, which her movements had disordered. 'Why', she said, 'do you think it started at that end?'

Morgan sighed, his breath warm on the tip of her ear. 'That's where most of the traffic has passed through.'

'Yes, but we've already decided the spread is discontinuous, which argues against simple foot traffic. If we were spreading it through eating and defecating, it would have started in the latrine areas. If we were spreading it in our clothes it should have come out of the laundry. I can't see any way *we* are spreading it at all. Maybe these are all single foci of breakdown and there's no connection by spread, though there may be a connection by cause. Why is next door so far advanced? Why is there hardly any sign of it in Hannah's cave, none at all in Hathaway's, though Fangorn – the cavern below her cave – is quite badly affected?'

He turned his head slowly to look at her. Pinned so close they were nearly nose to nose, and she could almost see the thoughts rearranging behind his eyes. 'Hath's cave is not affected?' he said slowly.

Abruptly he pushed behind her, and indelicately slid down her body and past her legs and through the crawlway, surfacing on the outside with an intense, abstracted expression on his face. 'I need to go see.'

'Go and see *what*?' she said, slithering after him, legs first. He was already descending at an ankle-twisting pace; at the bottom of the tower he reached up and more or less pulled her off the wall, grimacing at the pain the thoughtlessness cost him. She narrowly restrained the temptation to snap at him. He could not know how sensitive she was to being handled as though she were incapable of handling herself. He leaped and scrambled down the unworked side slope of the massif, arms flying out for balance. On the matting again he turned to her, face pinched with urgency. 'I'm not going to say. Because I don't want to bias you. I can't trust myself to see an alternative pattern. But if I'm right – *if* I'm right, it could be the answer.' He ran a grubby hand through dusty hair. 'What we'll do about it, I have no idea because it can't be the whole answer or else they wouldn't be noticing the claystone slowing down. Unless there's some kind of threshold and we're below threshold now and to reverse degeneration we need to aspire to reach threshold. Unless it's the *kind* of stimulus – stimuli, whatever. But it fits the pattern, it does fit the pattern.'

She took a fistful of each sleeve, pinning him. 'Stan Morgan,' she said emphatically, 'if you drop dead of excitement or dash your brains out falling on these rocks *without* explaining to someone we will be up a crick without a paddle as my grandmother emphatically did not use to say, being far too refined. To hell with the need for lack of bias. *Tell me.*'

He stared at her for a moment, and then took her face in both hands and kissed her, lightly, almost absent mindedly. 'The worst affected areas,' he said, on a very shallow breath, 'are those nobody has worked on. The areas which haven't been affected – or haven't been affected yet – are those ones where people have been manipulating them. Painting, like Hath, writing names, like that naming wall next door left, building' – he tilted his head, cradling her face still, towards their neolithic village – 'sculpting . . . interacting. Marian may be right: it may be a message to us, to get on with learning.'

'There's another possibility you might not like as much,' Sophie said, feeling her jaw move against the distinct scratchiness and vague warmth of his gloves. 'Not all the neurons in a human foetus or infant are present in a human adult. Neurons which don't get the right input, don't make enough connections or strong enough connections, die off. Nervous system injuries cause cell death at remove and downstream because cells are deprived of their input.' She paused. 'What I'm saying is that this may not be a voluntary process.'

He dropped his hands. 'Then we'd better find out how we can give the surviving cells the right input,' he said.

'We think we have found a pattern to the die off,' she said to a hastily assembled coterie of Arpád, Dominic, Marian, A.J. Lowell and Victoria over the map in the Crescent. Above them, on the clock-tower, the timekeeper was hanging the cyan pennant. The temperature had dropped another degree. The hope in the eyes of their five listeners was painful to see.

Marian sat composedly, hands folded atop her cane. She was wearing her brilliant blue coat, black gloves – plainly her own, because the left was three-fingered – and a black silk scarf. 'Excellent,' she said, quietly. 'Do go on.'

'The die off is worst in the areas which have not been manipulated, and least where we've been actively working. It's worse at the other end of this cavern than at this. It's worst of all in Erehwon, where for ideological reasons they did nothing. It's quite bad in Fangorn which we initially attributed to contamination by the refugees, but now we think is because it was settled by people who liked it pretty much the way it was. But Hath's cave is still pristine, warm and with matting of normal morphology, and with a normal light cycle. We've just been there. If you look at the map,' she gestured to the map spread on the claystone table, 'silvers represent places where there's been active sculpting – the bigger the coin, the more extensive the work. Coppers represent die off – again the bigger the coin the more severe the effect.'

'My Lord,' Dominic breathed. Nowhere did copper rest upon silver, though in places they rested side by side – a large silver coin beside a small copper coin, a small silver coin beside a large copper coin. Human activity and die off were mutually exclusive. 'So,' Marian murmured, 'where human hand has touched –'

Victoria leaned cheek on fist, fist on knee, and said slowly, 'But people have been working at this end of the cave, and you're still seeing signs of decay around here, aren't you?'

Morgan looked up from the map with a hunted expression. 'I know, I know. It's just one pattern that fits, and it doesn't fit everything, and there's data we don't have. Like whether there's a threshold of engagement that we haven't reached yet. Like whether early manipulation – like Hath's – or late manipulation or constant manipulation is more protective. And what *kind* of manipulation is best.' He straightened up, balancing on his heels, his face grim. 'But we looked into Erehwon – there was a peephole left when they sealed it. It's completely dark in there, and it's what – just turned cyan here, an hour and a half past midday. I would have thought there would have been some heating effect from all the caverns around, but I'd say it was well below zero. We lit a candle and pushed it through and it went *out*. And an atmosphere that won't burn a candle won't support life. Their die off started what, four, five days before we saw the first signs here. We don't have time to collect data before we act.'

'What are you suggesting,' Arpád said, calmly.

'We get everybody here, and I mean *everybody*, working on the construction, over as wide an area as possible. We get all the artists and designers aboard working on dry areas of wall, the way Hath started, and we get them going up into caves and drawing and painting on every surface they can reach. We do everything we can think of to tell *Tevake* we're still here and still talking to it.'

'Your hypothesis, then,' A.J. said, 'is that *Tevake* needs our input in some way.'

'It would be an explanation as to why we were invited in the first place,' Morgan said. 'And it's Sophie's hypothesis. It's a developmental thing; the analogy she came up with is the developing human brain. Human infants need sensory stimulation to grow. And they need touch to live.'

'Human infants,' Victoria said. 'This . . . entity, if it is an entity and not a machine . . . is not human.'

'Look,' Morgan said intensely, 'we have done our best to understand it, but we cannot interpret what we see in anything other than human terms. Historically, great leaps of understanding have only been achieved when some analogy has already been achieved – the development of computation gave models and metaphors to the study of human cognition –'

'Misdirected it at times, too,' Sophie could not help but say. He cast her a look redolent with, '*et tu, Brute*'. She smiled apology at him.

He continued, 'What we have is all we've got, analogies, metaphors, knowledge – they're determined by what we are and what we know. We can only hope that the aliens have allowed for this. That they have given us a fair chance of finding a solution, with what we have, being what we are, that if our lives are not precious to them, then *Tevake is*, and they want *it* to have a fair chance of survival, too.'

'Assuming,' A.J. said, 'that what is happening will affect the ship's viability. All the die off seems to be in the fixtures and fittings. I see no breakdown of the underlying structure. We could be starved and frozen to death, and then reabsorbed as the system rebuilds itself.' He shrugged slightly. 'Who knows how many times that has already happened?'

'Right or wrong,' Morgan said, 'this is my best interpretation of what I have seen. We'll keep working. But we may just not have *time*.' His raw tone made them all look at him. 'I'm sorry,' he said. 'But what I've seen next door – it scared me.'

'Uncle Stan,' said Hathaway from the doorway, 'I gotta talk to you.'

54 Morgan

'I want you to read this,' she said, holding out two sheets of paper. She stood draped in a blanket, with a fold covering her head and a hem trailing down the back of her knees, her face set.

'Hath,' he glanced over his shoulder at the opening to the Crescent, 'I need to get back there. We might have found a pattern to the die off –'

'I heard,' she said. 'You did good. But you're right. It may not be enough. So just read that. It'll explain a bunch of stuff. It's OK,' she said, answering another glance Crescent-ward. 'Arpád'll get them all organised.'

He looked at her face once more, and then took the papers. She turned away as he started to read, not turning her back, but gazing across the cavern and not watching him read. He scanned them quickly, gauging their importance, and then reread them, every word. 'Oh, Hath,' he said, quietly.

She nudged against him, a brusque plea to be held. He put his arms around her and did so, feeling her baby move between them. 'I'm sorry I asked you, Hath. Sorry I put the onus all on you.' She didn't answer. When he eased back to look at her he found her still staring across to the blighted end of the cavern. 'I still gotta do it, Uncle Stan,' she said, in a low voice.

'No you don't. You heard – we think the die off is connected with human activity. All we may need to do is –'

She pulled back suddenly, looking at him with her old stubborn expression. 'You don't *get* it. OK, so maybe I didn't write the rest of it down, but I got thinking about – well, about being me. And I thought I gotta do this. Because otherwise I wouldn't be me. I mean, I carried my mom and the kids all these years. I was proud of doing it. I wouldn't let anyone take it away from me. It made me *me*.' She swallowed. 'I'm going to have a baby soon. I'm going to be her one and only. I'm going to have that kind of responsibility all over again. So I guess – I guess I can't just toss it aside. If I'm the one, I'm the one. Does that make sense? If you really think I could do it – and be totally honest with me, because you're the smartest guy I know – then I got to do it.'

'You know,' he said, absurdly, 'it's such a shame we're related.'

She grinned at him, quite evilly. 'How much'll you give me not to tell Sophie you said that?' But almost at once the grin quenched itself and she took a grip of his sleeves and held on, hard, saying nothing, leaving him searching for words.

'Hathaway,' he said, at last. 'I think you should try.' She nodded, her eyes evading his. 'I think that the direct link could put us in touch in a way that the shaping and the painting won't. But I want,' he laid his hands on her arms, 'I want you to know that I'm – well, I'll have to admit I am hoping for a miracle – but I'm not expecting one. We really have no way of knowing if nothing comes of this whether you did not succeed or it was the wrong thing to do. And knowing you, knowing how tough and valiant and . . . pig headed you are, I *know* that if you don't manage to make contact or stop what's happening from happening, then it's not because you didn't try. I suppose what I'm trying to say is you may not succeed. But you won't have let us down.'

She said, blinking, 'I'd say the same thing to you if you hadn't said it to me better first.' She slid her arms around him, hugged him hard. 'OK, let's go.'

'Go where?'

'Down to the spire, of course.' She shrugged as though it was too obvious for words. 'Where Stephen was.'

The warmth in the spire was both comforting and disturbing after the barren cold of the caverns. Comforting because this was a place they had not lost. Disturbing because it was a place they might yet lose. Hath did not look at the blasted ash landscape of the mural. She took and shook out Stephen's sleeping bag liner from the mound of equipment pushed back against the wall and spread it out over the least uneven portion of the ramp. 'Here?' she said. Morgan nodded. She lowered herself down on to it and sat on one hip, leaning on one hand. 'Jeez, I dunno how I'm going to take a nap here,' she complained, looking up at him. 'Is it ever lumpy.'

He crouched beside her. 'Stephen's notes say that eventually he was able to contact the ship while conscious.'

'OK.' A short pause, then resolutely, 'So what do I say to it?'

He had been thinking about this all the way from Kastély to the base of the ramp. 'Stephen said he turned on the light by wishing –'

She scoffed. 'You got to be kidding. "Make a wish"?'

He took her cold hand. 'You are strongly visual, Hath,' he said. 'Visualise the ship as it used to be. Visualise the light, the matting all green again, the water running clear, the gingerbread – lots of gingerbread, all clear. Visualise the people, too. Not as they are at the moment but as they were say seven days ago – contented, productive.'

She shook her head. 'All kinds of stuff was about to go down seven days ago. *Not* a good idea.'

'Then visualise what you would like. "Make a wish." Think of the cavern the way we're going to shape it. Put Sophie and me in our lab. Put Marian there. Yourself, if you want. Add the aliens if you want to, as friends. I don't know what the message needs to be, I just don't know, but start out by just telling *Tevake* we're willing to try again, as often as we have to. Tell *Tevake* that we won't fight among ourselves any more.' She looked sceptical to the point of scorn. He said, 'Hath, if getting wrapped up in our own affairs and excluding *Tevake* was the cause of this, people *will* be motivated to resolve conflict in other ways. And if you get any intimation this happened on some other account, well, I for one would spread the word about the other account but I sure as hell will not tell anyone we're free to conduct our little wars. I don't want to go through anything like the past five days ever again.'

'You'n me both, Unc.' Impulsively, she shuffled up on her knees and slid her arms around him, holding hard. 'And if this doesn't work –' she said in a high whisper. 'I don't want to die.'

He let himself be held, but did not return the hug, looking past her at the blasted desolation of Stephen's landscape. 'If this does not work,' he said, simply, 'then we'll have to come up with something else.'

She let him go, cuffed him gently across the jaw the way she used to when she was just ten or eleven. He cuffed her back. 'OK, Uncle Stan,' she said, letting herself down on her side. He listened to her hair rasp against claystone as she tried to twist her head into a comfortable position on the flat ridge she had chosen to use as a pillow. 'Tell me a bedtime story,' she suggested. 'You never know, someone might be listening. Tell me my favourite.'

How apt, he thought. He moved his tongue to moisten his mouth. 'Once upon a time,' he began, 'on a small planet maybe far, far away, there lived a man called Galileo Galilei. But really this story does not begin with him – it began possibly a million years before that, when the first man, or woman, looked up at the stars – or it maybe began even earlier when the first particles of dust accreted to become the seed of the planet Earth. But if I try and tell all their stories we'll be here all night. So we'll begin with Galileo, who an astronomer, a man who studied the stars . . .' And so he told the story he had told the young girl who carried earthly responsibility whose weight he had not grasped until now. The story of the astronomers, Galileo, Kepler, Brahe, of the rocket builder Werner von Braun and how war bestowed its ambivalent gifts upon outward gazing humanity. He told her of Sputnik and Russia, Mercury and Shepherd, Apollo and the Moon, Challenger, Pathfinder and Mars. He offered up – for the woman the child had become – the whole pungent brew of human and national ambition, scientific curiosity, corporate greed, individual and collective vision, imagination, and yes, story, that had taken humanity off its own world, out into space. He told the story as the best stories are told, when the teller discovers for himself new textures and resonances. He would never tell it quite as well again. Near the end he went to shift her hand on his and found that a film between them tore a little. His pulse doubled; he breathed shallowly for a moment, inspecting the inside of his mind and finding nothing out of place. If *Tevake* was listening, it was not speaking to him. He said, 'Hath.'

She breathed. 'The pictures. The pictures, Uncle Stan.'

He could feel her pulse beating against his. 'That hurts,' she whispered, and twitched her hand in his. He eased off his grip so that their pulses separated. 'Hath –'

'Don't stop,' she said. 'Tell the rest of the story.'

'There isn't –' he said, and stopped.

'Just keep going.'

And so he did, into unfamiliar terrain. He told the story of a poor boy in the land of dreams and opportunity, a bright and not particularly brave boy who could see for himself neither dreams nor opportunity but who nevertheless took the only course he could see, step by step to the stars. He told the story, as he knew it, of a girl growing up in comfort and privilege and the knowledge that she might not live to greet her fiftieth birthday. He told the story of another girl from a poor background, a courageous girl who had supported her family through its worst years, and who could not find comfort among peace and plenty but who had to find other challenges and bear other burdens. And he found himself telling the story of their voyage, an apologia for this flying splinter of the human race, which in microcosm carried all the strengths and ills of the whole. He faltered again on the boundary of past and future, afraid, he knew now, of what his words might conjure.

She opened her eyes, like chips of obsidian. 'It's OK, Uncle Stan. I guess I can finish the story.' She pulled her hand from his, a softly stinging sensation, and used it to push herself up. ' "And they all lived happily ever after, and went many interesting places and did all kinds of wonderful things." ' She paused, her gaze inward looking. She shrugged and added, 'Like we can hope.'

'Hath?' he said in a voice barely above a whisper.

'Pictures,' she said, her eyes unfocused. 'Lots and lots and lots of pictures like it was downloading them into me. Do you see brain oozing out my ears – I really don't think there's enough room in my head.' Looked at him without a smile, 'I guess that's what you get when you study real hard. Like I should know.' That should have been a joke, but her delivery was flat.

She started to get up, lost her balance, said, with the first glimmering of Hath. 'Hey, gimme a hand here, Uncle Stan.' He helped her carefully to her feet and she steadied herself by holding on to his sleeves. 'I think,' she said, as though at an effort of translation, 'you're right. *Tevake needs* to be touched. Not just with fingers but with heads. It's been wiring us up. It's ready for us. We gotta go talk to it, Uncle Stan. Talk to it all the time. OK.'

'OK, Hath.'

'It'll change us too,' she said, brow drawn as though with pain. 'Prob'ly we can't go back to Earth, in the end. Prob'ly we won't even want to. The crew makes a ship. The ship makes a crew.' She blinked again, a rapid fluttering of eyelids as though images were passing before her eyes so swiftly that they were a mere blur, or an irritating flicker. 'I'll draw it for you. But we gotta get downstairs now. Stephen'll be coming out and I don't want anyone freaking out and shooting him again. *Tevake* doesn't either. I think it's gotten kind of fond of him. He was the first person it really got to talk to.' She stopped, staring down at the empty space beyond their arms. 'Jeez, Uncle Stan, that was some trip.' Looked up and grinned, an expression that made his heart turn over with relief. 'We could put all the pushers on Earth out of business with this, I tell ya.'

'I'm sure,' he said, 'we could.' He could hear rising voices from below them, and started to turn her, sliding one hand behind her back. And then stopped, utterly, seeing for the first time what was behind her.

The picture had changed. No longer the stark, ash and char strewn landscape. The wall was black as char, and pointed with stars. For a moment, his mind still on Earth, he had the bizarre impression that this was an empty beach scape at night, sky merging with the invisible sea, low cast moonlight or starlight painting the curves of round stones strewn into the distance. His gaze flickered to Hath, the question on his lips. And he saw her eyes were wide and brilliant, gazing at the image. Through her eyes he saw that the stones were ships, thousands and tens of thousands of ships, each one limned to an arc by the dim light of the distant sun.

EPILOGUE

Hathaway

Dear Mom & Peta & Dave & Johnny & Joy. & Allen, too, I guess.

I know I haven't written for so long. Everything got so crazy and hopeless there for a while that there didn't seem any point since there'd be nobody to send my letters off. And you didn't want to read about me dying all over again. And after I got in touch with *Tevake* there was just so much to do. I was talking and drawing and talking and drawing for days until I never wanted to pick up a stupid pencil ever again. But it settled down when other people started to figure out how to listen and I'm real glad. Emilie thinks I could have my baby any time now and *I* say it couldn't happen soon enough. I'm exhausted with moving my great big stomach around and not sleeping with leg cramps and needing to pee every five minutes. The baby keeps trying to prise me apart like I'm two halves of an eggshell and she's a chick trying to get hatched. I know she's squished – my stomach and liver and *guts* are squished *too*, baby – but if she wants to stretch she should come *out* and stretch.

And I'm *dying* to see her and know she's normal. I've been having these horrible dreams where she comes out all twisted or with scalefeathers like the owls or with eyes of different sizes and colours. Sophie says that all pregnant women have dreams about deformed babies but I've got a reason. This hasn't exactly been the kind of pregnancy the books approve of with the 'flu and Uncle Stan's assemblers and my brain getting hooked into *Tevake*. I don't know what I'd do if she was a mutant – try to love her, I guess. Melisande's kittens were OK. She had five and everyone has to shuffle around carefully so they don't get stepped on. Whatever tom did the dirty deed was long haired and yellow. All of them have little creaky voices like Mel's. Right now I wish I was a cat because by now *my* kitten would be almost grown.

Stephen's alive. When Uncle Stan and I got down on to the floor of the spire he'd just started to move inside his shroud and the army guys had their guns out and Sophie had her scalpel like she didn't know whether to cut him out or stab him. I was so pissed off at them all that I just marched over and started grabbing hunks of the grey fuzz and pulling them away. The stuff just fell apart in my hands and there was Stephen. Stark naked and totally confused. He doesn't remember who he used to be. In fact he practically had to learn to walk and talk all over again. His personality is totally changed, much softer and more patient. I find it a little creepy after knowing him before but most people seem to like him better this way. I've heard Sophie and the other docs going on about synaptic connections and neuronal plasticity and all kinds of technicalese but what it comes down to is they think *Tevake* couldn't stop parts of Stephen's brain dying off, and what those parts knew being lost, so it did what it could to make sure he could relearn everything. Sophie thinks his brain is like a baby's brain and able to pick things up real easy. Obviously he remembers *something* of who he was because he's real timid around the army guys and their guns. He makes pictures of the forests back on Earth with oftentimes a woman in a red jacket walking away into the distance. He watches her and his eyes get lost and shiny. Some people would rather he didn't make the pictures because he gets other people thinking that maybe he's still the same man and ought to be punished for what he did to Rosamond. But that's an argument that never really gets started, *because* of Rosamond. She's one of the people who takes care of him. It started out weird and twisted like she couldn't stay away and she had to keep checking that he *didn't* remember her, and wouldn't, ever. But you could tell he remembered something because he looked at her sort of the same way she looked at him. Like he wanted to be sure that she could never hurt him again and so had to keep watching her all the time. Sometimes at first she'd do mean little stuff like putting something bad-tasting in his water and then have a big angst attack about what a bad person she was – without saying what she'd done – and have everybody telling her no no she wasn't. Until Marian caught her and scolded her in that *surgical* English way for tormenting a handicapped man. Marian's like a strict but decent nanny determined to bring him up right. Lately Rosamond's been real gentle with him and he talks to her more than to anyone else. I know Dove's a little worried that he'll start acting like a man towards her and she'll freak. But she doesn't wear that horrible sack dress any more and she's growing her hair longer and I've even seen her flirt with some of the guys in a skittish sort of way. So with her acting like she can forgive Stephen it keeps the crime-and-punishment gang off him. There's some talk about giving him a formal pardon since he did die and *then* making it into the law that this is a one-off. But, like Marian says, it will be hard if people come back innocent as babes.

'Course, we're not sure that anyone else is going to come back or whether Stephen actually was a one-off. All the people who were killed in the raid didn't. Their mounds are all flattened out now. Uncle Stan thinks it could have been because our cavern was suffering from die off and didn't have the energy to rebuild them. I actually think it's because of where Stephen died but more about that later. Sometimes Uncle Stan talks like we all have to *really believe* in fairies so Tinkerbell will live. He has all kinds of fancy scientific explanations for it while Sophie comes up with what she calls biological analogies – but what it comes down to is that *Tevake* is like a baby and it needs stimulation to develop and touching and attention just to stay alive. He thinks that's what the die off was about – we were neglecting it because we were so busy fighting each other. He doesn't know whether it did the die off just to get our attention or whether it was really dying off. But nobody's taking any chances. They're all painting and shaping like mad – even the ones who practically wrap their heads in plastic when they lie down because they're paranoid about *Tevake* getting into their brains. Sophie says you can practically hear *Tevake* purring. Marian said how wonderfully whimsical it was to think that the molecules of this ship were being held together by art. *Tevake* has kind of left me alone – the weird dreams I have are my own weird dreams – because I don't wake up stuck to the ground. I guess *Tevake* knows I need my sleep. And anyway it has lots of people to talk to now. Even Uncle Stan is sort of getting the hang of figuring out what it has put in his mind though he still can't translate. Sophie and Uncle Stan have these long intense *groping* conversations with lots of handwaving and picture drawing when they run out of words for what they're trying to say. The physicist from Erehwon who made the candles says *Tevake* talks to her in equations like she's never seen and she puts them up on the walls and sits staring at them. She'd sit like that for days if Sergeant Bhakta didn't haul her away and feed her. She'll get the picture – the whole picture – some time in the next seventy years. *Sophie's* getting the picture a lot quicker than that. I saw her and Uncle Stan sneaking out of one of the side caves looking a whole lot more flushed than ever they get talking science. Obviously Uncle Stan's hand is *way* better though he still has nightmares he only talks to Marian about. Sophie said that she thinks once everyone sees that my baby's normal a whole bunch of the women will turn up pregnant. She said it all scientific-like as though it has nothing to do with her. What *I* say is that birth control pills and condoms can't last for ever though I know some of the women are trying to get *Tevake* to make a contraceptive. *Marian* says there is no reason why *Tevake* should not be able to control our fertility since the mechanism is quite straightforward and it probably has its own ideas as to how many people it wants to keep around. A whole bunch of people got very indignant about that. I bet *Tevake* has fun talking to the other ships about its fruitcake crew. I can just hear them saying: Don't worry, give them time to adjust. This is Just a Stage.

The real surprising person in all this is A.J. He spends ages sitting leaning against the wall in the spire and then spends more ages talking to Sophie or Morgan or Victoria. His guys are a little jealous of it for getting his attention rather than him for getting its attention. Sometimes they're just like big kids. They tease him a lot and just now are calling him Buddha. Sophie thinks the ability to talk to *Tevake* comes with mental make-up and she has this theory that too much education gets in the way because it shapes the mind a certain way. But that doesn't really explain why Arpád can't really talk to *Tevake* much since he's not loaded down with advanced degrees. Still he goes around bossing all the various projects and arguing with Victoria and the other people working on the Montreal Accord Mark II and generally being a total grouch – so he must be pretty happy. Victoria and the others have been looking over articles of confederation of places like Switzerland and working out how every cavern can be independent and still get along. Which makes Astarte and the rest of the original women's group happy since they decided to come back once Erehwon began to grow again and try to do what they originally came to do way before all the trouble started. They're even using Hannah's plans to build a village.

It's not all sweetness and light and sugar candy of course. There were *major* arguments about what to do with the people who'd been involved in the attack. Some of them have gone to other caves and there's been all kinds of talk about trials and extraditions but everybody's still being real cautious because the die off scared them and they don't know what the ship'll let them off with. I think the green beret guys and the scouts have their own ideas about what'll happen if some of those people ever show their faces around here again. There are still people who think they're going to turn *Tevake* around and drive it back to Earth – Sophie's still sort of that way but she's prepared to be patient about it. But they're a long way from learning how to steer and *Tevake* isn't real cooperative about talking to them. It may be alien and it may be a young intelligence like Uncle Stan and Sophie think – but it ain't stoopid. And it does take a suggestion. The most fun I've had lately has been watching people find out their knives and guns and spears and things were falling apart. Just about everyone thinks it's me who did it and I'm totally happy to take the blame. A whole lot of people have even come to thank me. Way more than they would ever thank – say – Stephen. I'm not saying he did it of course. I don't know who did it. But to everybody I'm just a little mommy making peace because that's what little mommies do. They're not worried about *me* taking *control*. Hooh, yeah!

What I haven't told anyone – and why nobody's getting to read this letter just yet – is what we're supposed to do once we get ourselves sorted out and what the 'control room' really is. There's a whole series of pictures *Tevake* showed me which I drew but haven't let anyone else see. I'm just not ready to tell people about it, not while some of them still want to take *Tevake* back. Even if it might help them understand it's just too risky if they don't. See, everyone thinks the spire is some sort of superbrain and sooner or later we'll be able to drive *Tevake*. But I don't think we can drive *Tevake* any more than we could drive a whale swimming in the sea. *Tevake*'s going where it's going with all the others and we're going along for the ride like we were promised. I'm not real sure about whether *Tevake* is alive or some kind of machinery but I don't think it really matters because *Tevake* acts as though it is alive. I got to admit I'm looking forward to the moment when all those macho guys (and macha women) find out that the part of *Tevake* they thought was most important i.e., its *brain* is actually *her uterus*. Like my drawings show I saw a ship – which I'll bet is *Tevake* – growing inside the spire of another ship which I bet is the owls' ship. I sort of get the idea the arrangement is that each new crew is supposed to grow a new ship for the next bunch of people they pick up. And then because they want each ship to grow into its own person they just have to leave the new ship and the new crew to work it out. It must be real hard because they're like its parents and *Tevake* showed me what happened when crews don't make it the way we nearly didn't make it. The die off was for real. I know they interfered at least twice with us. Once to get the army guys out of the spire when they went in there way before we'd figured out the first thing about *Tevake* and what not to do and what not to hurt – and the other time to save me when I was dying, I guess either because I could talk to *Tevake* or because I was having a baby myself. Or both. I hope they didn't get into too much trouble for that. One of these days I hope to meet them and get to say thanks. I think we will – one of the pictures that's real popular (they're doing a big version of it for the wall) is of some kind of get together for all the crews. It looks like quite a party, if a little bizarre. Make that totally bizarre. Some of those aliens are *strange*. I'll draw you some pictures, promise.

There's one other thing I'm not going to tell everyone for a long time. Maybe never. It's about that guy Seth who tortured Uncle Stan. I think when I was inside *Tevake* I killed him. It was like one of those dreams you have when you're inside someone else's skin. I was inside his and he was in a little cave which kept getting smaller and smaller until there was only a bubble around his face. It was horrible. At least I know it was horrible now but then I was glad. I thought now he'll never hurt anyone again. It was because I thought that that I think I did it or *Tevake* did it for me. I'm not sure. But he hasn't been found even though people have looked all over. I just try not to think about it a whole lot.

Going to stop now for a while. Writing that upset me even though it's true and every time the baby shoves I'm getting this really bad cramp. I'm going to walk around a bit so she'll stop shoving even though having everyone ask me how I feel will make me crazy.

(Later) I started my walk and just kept feeling worse and worse with these big cramps coming along every so often. They weren't even real painful but they made me feel like I was being squished between rocks. And then I was standing talking to Astarte when suddenly I had this horrible long squeezing *pain* and I doubled over and grabbed my stomach just like on a soap opera. I'll leave out the rest of the gory details because I went straight from being sort of OK to not being OK at all. *Sophie* says it was a very quick and easy labor and I hope she has one just as *quick* and *easy* sometime. I didn't even notice them fussing over me except for Uncle Stan who did the whole panicking-father routine – begging me to breathe and hyperventilating himself until he just about passed out and Dove had to shove his head down between his knees. I would have laughed but I was *so* grateful to him for just *being* there. And besides I was too busy *dying*.

But the baby is *perfect*. I hope you don't mind that I'm calling her Hannah. I missed her very first moment because it was like I'd reached the top of an enormous mountain – I just got lost in the feeling of being *over* the top instead of pushing and climbing and pushing and climbing. It took me a minute or so to remember yeah this is all about a baby. She didn't breathe at first so Emilie had to clear out her mouth and rub her. I didn't know that until later because by the time I looked to see her she'd started crying and moving around and going all pink underneath the guck. Sophie was there checking over every inch of her like she was a rare painting and she was looking for the signature. I guess she was thinking the same things I was about her maybe not being normal. But just as I was ready to clamber out of the puddle of placenta and blood and pee and sweat and yuk and *grab* for her Sophie gave me a big smirk like *she'd* done it all and handed her over. Her skin was wrinkled and red with all the veins showing through like tiny little threads. She had a scruff of dark hair on her head – they told me about that when I was trying to push her out – and squinty incredibly dark blue eyes. Whoever got the idea baby blue was pale anyway? Her hands are so small, little barnacle hands with white stuff in the creases. She kept tucking and untucking them while her eyes bumped around in her head at all the people who kept pushing their faces at her and making goopy noises. We were all bleating like the bunch of sheep Arpád says we are when he's being particularly insulting. I could hear people cheering outside like I'd given birth to a crown princess or something. But it just felt so right. I wish I could phone you all and tell you all about her and send pictures and all that. Maybe some day you'll get these letters. There's a painting of her just born going up on the walls and it'll be beautiful. There's also one of me with my knees out and my stomach sticking up and hanging on to Uncle Stan and yelling. It's kind of explicit – not rude – I mean all the bits are hidden, but it makes my stomach cramp to see it. But still somehow I like it. Or I don't *like* it – I mean I'd have liked to have been smiling blissfully through it all and not screaming my head off. Though at the time screaming my head off was definitely the right thing to do. But I think it fits there. It's what being human is like. I was sitting nursing her and looking at the pictures when I suddenly had this weirdest feeling like I'd come unstuck in time and I could see her grown up with babies of her own, and them grown up and so on and so on for years and years ahead. Like I was the start of a long, long line which went on and on further than I could imagine. I could see her great-great-great ever so many great grandchildren looking at that picture and the picture of her and the pictures of the war and all the other pictures. I wonder who these people will be. I wonder where they'll have been and what they'll have seen and done. I wonder what they'll say about us, who were right here at the very beginning.